Wonder of the Worlds

Sesh Heri

Lost Continent Library
Publishing Company
California

Wonder of the Worlds
Copyright © 2005 By Sesh Heri

All rights reserved.

No part of this book may be reproduced or utilized in any form or by any means, electronic or mechanical, including photocopying, recording, or by any information storage and retrieval system, without permission in writing from the publisher.
Inquiries should be addressed to

The Lost Continent Library Publishing Co.
7231 Boulder Avenue #505
Highland, CA 92346-33133
www.lostcontinentlibrary.com
lostcontinentlib@yahoo.com

FIRST PRINTING SEPTEMBER 2005

ISBN: 0-9727472-8-1

Cover Art: BOB AUL

Printed in the United States of America
at Morgan Printing in Austin, Texas

Introduction

It is with great excitement and pride that I present to you the first edition of a novel that is bound to become a favorite among adventure fantasy readers. I cannot begin to list the synchronicities between the vision of this company and the author's experience in the writing of this book. What I cannot say enough is how talented Mr. Heri is as writer and illustrator. It is rare upon first read of a submission to find a work so polished technically as this novel was on the day I received it. Rarer still is a vision so well realized and crafted through the story. I believed from that first reading that here is a future classic in the genre.

I would like to acknowledge two very important people whose contribution to this book make it all the more the best offering this company has produced so far: Bob Aul, our extraordinary cover artist; and Sierra Guggolz, our fine editor who diligently journeyed through this wonderful story when it was just a wonderful manuscript.

There is much in this novel that history buffs will recognize and enjoy, as the author's research has been exhaustive, specifically relating to Nikola Tesla and Mark Twain. Students of alternative history will rejoice.

Young readers take note: though some of these people may not be within your personal frame of reference, the heroes of this tale really lived and knew each other, in most cases. So did the technology. So, too, could have a world envisioned by Mr. Tesla.

Maybe it does . . . .

Walter Bosley
Publisher
Rancho Mirage, 2005

Foreword

Wonder of the Worlds is a work of fiction written in the style of *fantastic realism*—*realism*, because the story's setting and characters are based upon historical places and persons—*fantastic*, because some of the facts upon which the story is based are not a part of our conventional model of reality.

The most fantastic reality in *Wonder of the Worlds* is the main character, Nikola Tesla, a person who once really lived and whose real accomplishments were every bit as fantastic as the legends that swirl around his name.

Another fantastic reality in *Wonder of the Worlds* is the group of anomalous formations on the planet Mars in the region of Cydonia. Whether these formations are artificial, as Richard C. Hoagland has claimed for over twenty years, or are natural as NASA has insisted for just as long, these oddly shaped masses on the Martian surface *are* fantastic, for even as natural formations they are an enigma; their geo-morphological processes are unknown and fractal analysis shows a discontinuity between the formations and the surrounding surface of the planet.

The claim that there is a connection between ancient Egypt and the anomalies of Cydonia is certainly fantastic, but the reality of the claim has not yet been established with conclusive proof. There are, however, several bits of evidence to suggest that knowledge of Mars has been secretly passed down for thousands of years through various groups and individuals. Perhaps there *is* a golden chain which reaches back to ancient Egypt, Atlantis, and ultimately to the planet Mars. That is the premise of *Wonder of the Worlds*. It may be fiction. It may be fantastic fact.

You decide.

Sesh Heri

Prologue

> Do you reckon Tom Sawyer was satisfied after all them adventures?
>
> — Huck, *Tom Sawyer Abroad*

New York City, January 3rd, 1943

"Impossible! Mark Twain is *not* dead!"

The words exploded from the lips of Nikola Tesla, addressing his messenger boy, Kerrigan, who stood on the threshold of Tesla's apartment. A sealed envelope was held outward in the messenger's right hand.

"This is not like you, Kerrigan," Tesla said. "Step inside."

Kerrigan obeyed and closed the door. He watched Tesla, who was dressed in a dark blue bathrobe, move across the room. Tesla stopped in front of his cage of pigeons and looked in through the bars at the gray and white birds.

"Did you feed them?" Tesla asked.

"Yes, sir."

Tesla studied his pigeons, then turned back around. Kerrigan noticed that Tesla's face was paler than usual, and that the old man's luminous blue eyes were strangely out of focus.

"Now let's have it. Why haven't you delivered the envelope?"

"I did exactly as you said, sir."

"Are you sure you went to the correct address?"

"Yes, sir. 35 South Fifth Avenue. Only it's not South Fifth Avenue anymore. They changed it to West Broadway. And the people there told me that Mr. Samuel Clemens was Mark Twain, the man who wrote *Tom Sawyer*."

"That is correct."

"And they said he was dead."

"Nonsense. They always say he is dead. Haven't you ever heard the famous Mark Twain saying, 'The reports of my death are greatly exaggerated'?"

Manhattan had reached its electrical capacity.

Kerrigan shook his head.

"Go back," Tesla said. "Go back and deliver the envelope. Mark Twain is alive. He was here last night and sat in that chair for an hour. He is in financial difficulties and it is imperative that he receives my envelope."

Tesla opened the door and waved Kerrigan out. Kerrigan went through the door, but stopped in the outer hall and looked back, confused and helpless.

"Go back, Kerrigan. Mark Twain has never let me down. And I shall never let him down."

With that, Tesla slammed the door.

Kerrigan stood in the hallway a moment longer, trying to decide what to do. He knew it was pointless to try to deliver the envelope again. But how would he deal with Tesla? Then it occurred to Kerrigan that his supervisor would know what to do.

Back at his Western Union office, Kerrigan stood watching as his supervisor opened Tesla's envelope, unwrapped a blank sheet of paper, and took out twenty-five one-dollar bills.

The supervisor said, "This wouldn't help Mark Twain pay for his cigars, even if he were alive. Tesla's lost his marbles."

New York City, January 8th, 1943

It had been five days since Tesla had hallucinated Mark Twain. Since then, he had moved through a mental haze, broken at intervals by a lucidity which left him panicked. Sharp pains would stab his chest. He would sit down until the pain ceased and the mental haze descended once again.

On the morning of January 4th, Tesla found himself
looking into the window of Macy's on 34th Street. He did not know how he got there, what he was doing, or where he was going. Then he felt in his pocket a bag of birdseed and remembered he was on his way to feed the pigeons on the steps of the library before going to see his assistant, George Scherff.

Tesla strode toward Fifth Avenue. When he reached it, he stopped, gasping for breath, a pain shooting through his heart. He leaned against the wall and looked up at the Empire State Building. A thought flashed through his mind: I shall meet my end here. But then Tesla caught his breath. The pain was gone. He turned, and proceeded up Fifth Avenue.

Among the crowd, Tesla was only a tall, gaunt old man, dressed in a dark gray suit, the best fashion of an earlier generation. The crowd on the sidewalk flowed past Tesla in both directions, an alternating current of human energy. The people in the crowd passed with no awareness that the source of the energy upon which they depended for their daily existence now moved among them like an unlighted beacon.

Tesla reached the library and stopped in front of its steps. Pigeons clustered about his feet. He brought out the bag of birdseed and began scattering it. Gray and white wings fluttered.

"No need to crowd, my friends," Tesla said. "Enough for all."

Tesla's view of the birds sharpened his focus. Suddenly, his lucidity returned. No! The birdseed was meant for this afternoon! He was scheduled to meet with George Scherff at ten o'clock. It was now ten minutes to ten.

Tesla threw out the remainder of the seed and hurried to see Scherff, who was waiting across 40th Street in Tesla's office twenty stories overhead.

When Tesla entered his office, Scherff was already at work, adjusting a bank of vacuum tubes, which comprised a large and complex electrical switching system.

Scherff said, "The Navy liaison officer called. He wants to know when we'll have the switching system available."

Tesla said, "I will not be held to a deadline when men's lives are at stake. The system must operate safely, and—"

Tesla could not close his mouth. A knife of jagged pain ripped from his throat to his chest to his right armpit to the tip of his right finger. A chill shot up his spine. Tesla's knees gave out, and he collapsed into a chair. Scherff lunged forward. Tesla held up his hand, holding Scherff back.

"Not a word!" Tesla gasped.

"I must call you a doctor—an ambulance!"

"No. No doctor. No ambulance. That is final."

Scherff stood looking at Tesla, saying nothing. Tesla sat, marshalling his strength. After a long moment, Tesla stood up and said, "I am going home."

He walked to the door and opened it.

Scherff said, "I'll finish up here."

"You *are* finished here, Mr. Scherff," Tesla said. "Both of us are. Close the office for me."

"But what about the Navy?" Scherff asked.

"They are no longer my concern."

"Mr. Tesla. . . ?"

"Conflict, Mr. Scherff, conflict. Without it nothing can stand, nothing can manifest. And what comes of the manifestation? More conflict, Mr. Scherff, more conflict.

More conflict on and on and on. For so long I did not understand. For so long I engaged myself in the conflict.

But now I understand. Only now. And now I am free."

Tesla swayed slightly in the doorway. Scherff stood with his hand over his mouth, his eyes wide.

Then Tesla said quietly, "Close the office and take that vacation of which you have long dreamed. For myself, I am going home. Goodbye, Mr. Scherff," and he turned and went out through the door, closing it behind him.

On the morning of January 5th, Alice Monaghan knocked at Tesla's door, and said, "Mr. Tesla! It's maid service."

Tesla called weakly from inside, "Come in."

Alice inserted her key and opened the door. Tesla was sprawled in an arm chair. He was wearing only his pajamas, with a blanket thrown over his knees.

"Mr. Tesla!" Alice said. "Are you all right?"

"I have a slight cold; that is all. You do not need to clean today."

"Shall I call for the doctor?"

"No. I have no need of doctors. Only quiet and rest. Put the 'Do Not Disturb' sign on the door as you go out."

Tesla gave Alice the 'Do Not Disturb' sign that he had been clutching in his hand.

"But are you sure—"

"My dear lady, let us not argue. Now go."

Alice turned reluctantly and went out, closing the door of Tesla's apartment behind her. She hung the 'Do Not Disturb' sign on the doorknob, and then pushed her cleaning cart on down the hallway.

The 'Do Not Disturb' sign hung on Tesla's door for the next two days.

On January 6th, Tesla heard a faint knock at his door. He rose from bed slowly, made his way unsteadily to the other room, fumbled with the doorknob, and opened the door. No one was there. He looked up and down the outside hall. It was empty. He was about to close the door when he saw something lying on the floor in front of his doorway. It was a book bound in red leather. He bent over slowly, picked it up, looked up and down the hall again, and finally closed the door.

Tesla slumped into a chair and opened the book. It was a thin volume, only thirteen pages long. He began to read. On page four his eyes became heavy, but he made a great effort to focus on the page of the book and stay awake. He kept reading, and finally finished page thirteen.

"The spirit comes forth from the day, and the letter passes away," Tesla said, and drifted off to sleep.

Tesla awoke in the chair. The red book was gone. He looked about the room. The book was nowhere in sight. His door was still locked from the inside.

Tesla nodded. He understood. He had no questions.

On the evening of January 7th, a massive electrical storm formed over New Jersey. It pushed eastward and, by nine o'clock, approached Manhattan.

Before the path of the oncoming storm, the island of Manhattan lay sprawled, an eight-mile long granite mass, a natural electrical body charged within a few volts of its full capacity. As the electrical storm passed over the Hudson at 10:25 pm, those last few deficit volts were flowing into the island's granite bed-rock: they were flowing from the shuffling feet of pedestrians and from the sparks of subway wheels; they were flowing from the relentless pressure of continental drift and from the tide-friction of Manhattan's two rivers; they were flowing from the ground wires of electrical machines and from the bedposts of the city's sleepers. The electricity flowed into the island's granite bedrock volt by volt—the electricity of life—and death.

At that moment, Nikola Tesla, laying in a coma, awoke, his eyelids fluttering.

He looked at the ceiling, and whispered, "Draw back the bolt, Ba-bi! Open the door!" Then his eyelids fluttered again, and closed.

Nikola Tesla stopped breathing. A faint electrical impulse shot out from his heart as it contracted for the last time. The electrical impulse traveled through his bed to the floor of his apartment, then downward 33 stories through the steel skeleton of the Hotel New Yorker and into the granite bedrock of Manhattan. From 7th Avenue it sped eastward under 34th Street to the Empire State Building where it joined millions of other electrical impulses that were gathering in a crowd to rush up the steel skeleton of the great building. Tesla's electrical impulse rushed forward, twisting its way up through steel beams and pipes, then broke through to the outside granite walls, rushed over the observatory deck and to the building's pinnacle—the radio tower.

The storm clouds were directly overhead. Manhattan had reached its electrical capacity.

The electrical impulse of Nikola Tesla exploded with a bone-shuddering crack and boom from the tip of the Empire State Building's radio tower. In an instant, the millions of other electrical impulses below were drawn along with Tesla's, forging themselves into a blazing white sword of lightning poised upward at the gray-black clouds. Tesla's impulse was the point of the sword. The point pierced the veil of clouds and thrust home to eternity.

Now, on the morning of January 8th, the electrical storm of the preceding night had nearly dissipated. Off to the east, out over the Atlantic, white bolts of lightning would flash at long intervals, followed many seconds later by a low rumbling. The rain had turned to snow, sprinkling the rooftops and streets of the city with a thin, white slush.

Inside the Hotel New Yorker Alice Monaghan realized that the 'Do Not Disturb' sign on Tesla's door had been hanging out for the last three days. She knocked at Tesla's door. When she received no response, she used her key and entered the apartment. The smell of bird guano filled the air. Alice entered Tesla's bedroom and found him lying in bed on his back. She approached the bed. Tesla's gaunt, unmoving face told her he was dead. He was 86 years old.

Within fifteen minutes Tesla's apartment was filled with men in dark suits. They sent Alice Monaghan away and began searching the apartment from ceiling to floor. One of these men—a man with a face that bore no expression whatsoever—this man made a series of calls from Tesla's telephone. First he called President Franklin Delano Roosevelt. Next he called Kenneth Swezey, then Tesla's nephew, Sava Kosanovich.

After informing Kosanovich of Tesla's death, the blank-faced man asked, "Do you know the combination to Tesla's safe?"

"No," Kosanovich said, "Maybe one of his assistants knows it—George Scherff or Kolman Czito, but I doubt it."

The blank-faced man called Scherff, but received no answer. He next called Kolman Czito.

The receiver lifted on the other end, and the shaky, high-pitched voice of an old man answered.

"Hello?"

"Kolman Czito?"

"Who is this?"

"My name's not important. I'm with the Majestic Seven Oversight Committee. Does that mean anything to you?"

"Yes. Yes, it does."

"I'm here at Tesla's apartment. I have bad News. He's dead."

"No."

"Yes. He's dead."

"How?"

"Heart attack, we think."

"No."

"We don't have any time to waste. Do you know the combination to his bedroom safe?"

"I used to know it. Long ago. He probably changed it since then."

"Can you come over here and give it to me?"

"It'll take a few minutes."

"Make it quick."

Czito hung up. He sat for a moment without moving, then slowly slid out of his bed and stood up alone in the half-darkness.

Ten minutes later, a little old man stepped out of a Checker cab in front of the Hotel New Yorker. It was Kolman Czito wearing a heavy coat over a pair of pajamas. He slammed the door of the cab and stepped up on to the sidewalk. He stood for a moment to catch his breath and looked up at low clouds, dragging along with them veils of rain and snow. Czito glanced directly overhead in time to see a lightning bolt flash within the recesses of a cloud. At that same instant a drop of rain struck the right lens of Czito's spectacles. The cloud blurred and rumbled.

Czito removed his spectacles and wiped them with his handkerchief as he slowly shuffled toward the entrance of the Hotel New Yorker. He reached the entrance, put on his spectacles, and pushed his way through the heavy glass revolving door.

Inside the lobby, Czito stopped to catch his breath. In the middle of the lobby, two uniformed New York police officers stood as if at attention. Czito looked to his right and noticed a naval officer speaking on the telephone at the hotel's reception desk. Czito looked up to the ornate chandelier hanging above the mezzanine.

"Are you Kolman Czito?" one of the policemen asked.

"Yes," Czito replied.

"They're expecting you up there," the policeman said.

"I know," Czito said, walking forward.

"Need any help?" the other policeman asked.

"No," Czito replied, picking up his feet a little more. "I'll manage."

Czito made it across the lobby and stepped into the open door of an elevator. "Thirty-third floor," he said to the elevator operator. The operator closed the door and started the car up into the hotel.

Tesla dead, Czito thought, and the thought struck him as abstract and unreal. Only several months earlier Tesla had been in Philadelphia working harder than he ever had before, and since Tesla's return to New York he had been working intensively with George Scherff on a complex switching system. Although Czito no longer worked for Tesla, he knew that switching system well, for he had assisted Tesla with building earlier models for the last fifty years, and, only several weeks ago, Tesla had confided to Czito that the latest and final model was nearly perfected. It only needed some work done on its astronomical gravimeter. Tesla had said, "Soon we shall place the fixed stars on the pans of the balance scale." Czito now thought of Tesla saying this. These words were the last that Tesla had spoken to Czito. At the time Tesla had spoken them, Czito had thought that Tesla looked more vibrant and alive than he had in years. Tesla dead, Czito thought again as he approached the 33rd floor of the Hotel New Yorker. But the thought was only words, and the words sank down and away into nothingness, for Czito could not make the words attach to anything his mind could imagine or conceive.

The elevator door opened. Czito stepped out into the hallway. Three men in dark suits stood before him.

"Kolman Czito?" one of them asked.

"Yes."

The man flashed an F.B.I. credential in front of Czito's face and said, "Come with me."

Czito followed the man down the hall and they entered the door of Tesla's apartment. The odor of guano and decay hit Czito with a jolt. He turned his head involuntarily and his glance fell upon a dead pigeon lying on its back inside its cage. Czito's stomach contracted into a knot, and that knot was Czito's certain knowledge that Tesla was dead, for Tesla in life would never have allowed a pigeon to be neglected in this way.

The blank-faced man approached Czito, and said, "I'm the one who spoke to you on the phone."

Czito recognized the blank-faced man's voice, an emotionless monotone.

"Yes," Czito said, "can you identify yourself as a proper representative of the committee?"

The blank-faced man reached into his jacket and brought out a card, the king of diamonds from a poker deck, and handed it to Czito. Czito turned the card over. On the back of the card, enclosed within a white border, was a photograph of a colorful tapestry design, an intricate, abstract woven pattern of lines and dashes. To the uninitiated, Czito held what appeared to be only an ordinary playing card.

Czito held the back of the card up a few inches away from his face. He looked over the top edge of the card to the apartment wall several feet away. He concentrated on the wall while simultaneously trying to notice the back of the playing card in the lower periphery of his field of vision. In a moment, the back of the card began to glow. Czito began slowly lowering his gaze toward the top of the card, keeping his eyes focused in the middle distance all the while, until the white border of the card began to take on the look of a window frame. Beyond the window frame, Czito could see into a glowing blue field several inches in depth. Czito looked into the glowing depth of the field. Czito's visual cortex subconsciously recognized the subliminal cues embedded and encoded into the design on the surface of the card, and this recognition automatically locked Czito's eye muscles into an exact focus, allowing him to instantly see a stereoscopic image, the white border of the card taking on the appearance of a window frame surrounding a three-dimensional scene beyond. The scene was the image of a three-dimensional color photograph of the blank-faced man's face floating in front of a field of glowing blue. Next to the blank-faced man's face blazed the symbol of Majestic Seven: an eye emitting seven gold rays to form the shape of a pyramid. Below the blank-faced man's face floated the numbers: 27811323981732. Below this series of numbers floated the words "Assignment: Gold Pigeon."

Czito blinked. The back of the playing card instantly changed back to an abstract two-dimensional tapestry pattern. Czito nodded to the blank-faced man and handed the playing card back to him.

"Come on," the blank-faced man said.

The blank-faced man turned and went into Tesla's bedroom. Czito followed. In the bedroom Czito saw the unmoving silhouette of Tesla's profile against the gray glow of the window. Czito turned his head away, his glance falling upon the opposite wall. A painting had been removed from the wall, revealing a safe with a key lock. The safe door had been opened, and, inside, a ring of keys lay on one of the shelves next to some papers and stock certificates.

The blank-faced man said, "This is the only safe we can locate in the apartment. But we know he had a combination safe in here before."

"Yes," Czito said, "he had that one moved and put back here." Czito nodded toward the back of the safe as he removed a small metal box from his pocket. He pushed a button on the box and it emitted a rapid series of high-pitched beeps. Czito then reached under one of the shelves, pressed, and the whole back wall and shelves detached in a single piece. Czito handed the false panel and its contents to the blank-faced man who sat the panel down on the floor and leaned it against the wall.

Now Czito faced the real safe door that had been hidden behind the false panel and shelves. This real safe door had a combination-wheel lock.

"We have to be careful," Czito said. "Sometimes Mr. Tesla set booby-traps."

"That's why we called you," the blank-faced man said, "to keep things simple."

Czito reached in and spun the wheel seven times, then tried to pull the handle, but it was locked fast.

"Maybe you have the numbers mixed up," the blank-faced man said.

Czito turned and looked up at the blank-faced man. "No," Czito said, "I never get numbers mixed up. He changed the combination."

"We'll take it from here," the blank-faced man said.

Czito stepped back.

A man with a medical bag entered the bedroom.

"You the doc?" the blank-faced man asked.

The doctor nodded. The blank-faced man waved the doctor toward Tesla's bed.

One of the other men in dark suits came into the room.

"We'll have to crack it," the blank-faced man said to his associate. "Do you have the stethoscope?"

The other man brought out a stethoscope from a steel suitcase.

At that moment the doctor opened his medical bag and took out his own stethoscope.

The doctor pulled back the bedcovers from Tesla's body, unbuttoned Tesla's pajamas, and put the bell of the stethoscope on Tesla's chest.

The man at Tesla's safe put the bell of his stethoscope on the door of the safe and spun its combination-wheel.

The doctor listened for Tesla's heart beat.

The man at the safe listened for the click of the tumbler.

Lightning flashed across Tesla's unmoving face, followed by the crack and boom of thunder.

The doctor removed his stethoscope and shook his head.

"Goodbye, Mr. Tesla," Czito whispered, a single tear traced down his cheek.

The doctor pulled the sheet over Tesla's head.

"Jackpot!" the man at the safe said.

Czito and the doctor turned around. The man with the stethoscope was reaching into the safe. The blank-faced man stood ready with his hands extended to take the safe's contents. The steel suitcase stood open on a table next to the blank-faced man.

The doctor glanced at Czito, then turned quickly and walked out of the room.

The man with the stethoscope removed from the safe a thick manuscript bound in twine and a stack of notebooks.

The blank-faced man put the manuscript in the suitcase and then took the notebooks and opened the one that was on the top of the stack. On the first page was a schematic diagram of an electrical circuit. It was captioned "Complete Method of Utilizing Radiant Energy." He turned the page and came upon the drawing of a cigar-shaped airship. He turned the page again, and came upon the outline drawing of an oval-shaped crystal. Next to the drawing was a list of elements and minerals. He closed the notebook and slid the whole stack into the suitcase.

The man with the stethoscope reached all the way to the back of the safe, sliding his hand side-to-side, feeling for further false panels. Suddenly a flash of gold tumbled from the safe to the floor.

Czito looked down and saw that it was a gold medal. He suddenly recognized it.

"That!" Czito cried. "That is Mr. Tesla's medal! The Edison Medal!"

"So what?" the blank-faced man asked, stooping to pick up the medal.

"It is the *Edison Medal*!" Czito said. "The greatest honor that can—"

"Keep it, Pops," the blank-faced man said, tossing the medal to Czito. "It's just junk to us."

Czito caught the medal in his trembling hands.

The blank-faced man closed the suitcase with a snap and spun its combination-wheel. Czito saw another flash of metal—this time from a pair of handcuffs. The blank-faced man snapped one bracelet of the handcuffs to the handle of the suitcase and the other to his left wrist. He then nodded to the man with the stethoscope, and the two men started toward the door.

"Is that it?" Czito asked. "Is that all?"

The blank-faced man stopped and turned back to look at Czito.

"That's it," the blank-faced man said evenly with no interest. "That's all. That's all it ever was." The blank-faced man nodded toward Tesla's shrouded body. He said, "*He* understood. *He* knew. He always belonged to us. And everything he did."

"You know nothing!" Czito shouted. "He belonged to no one—but *himself*!"

"If you say so, Pops," the blank-faced man said with genuine indifference. Then he turned and went out the door.

Czito took out his handkerchief and wiped the Edison Medal. He then went over to the safe, stooped and lifted the false panel which the other men had emptied except for the ring of keys. He snapped the panel back into place inside the safe, and then looked at the Edison Medal which he held in his hand. He placed the Edison Medal on the shelf next to the keys.

Czito stood looking at the keys and the medal a moment longer. He then took a step back, turned, and walked out of the room.

A University Somewhere in the United States, January 15, 1943

The blank-faced man and his associate (the man who had used the stethoscope) sat in front of the professor's desk, their hats in hand. The professor sat behind his desk studying one of the manuscripts taken from Tesla's safe.

The professor was an expert on the life and works of Mark Twain. He first read Twain as a boy, but later, when he was a young man attending Columbia University, he went to hear Mark Twain speak at Carnegie Hall.

The professor still remembered Twain's peculiar gait as he made his way up to the lectern, something like a waddling duck or a metronome missing a beat. When Twain spoke, his tenor voice crackled and drawled, forming long, pulled-out words, his hands tracing slow figure eights in the air as if the words he had spoken now floated in front of him, now become invisible taffy ready for further pulling.

Mark Twain's hand would pause in mid-air, his face would freeze, and then, barely perceptible beneath shaggy eyebrows, his eyes would shift to one side and stare at some point somewhere, some spot in the hall that had absolutely riveted his attention. Not a sound in the hall. Then Mark Twain would whisper one syllable, and the entire assemblage would explode in uncontrollable laughter. The laughter would roll across the house from left to right, then toward the stage, then to the back of the house, then forward again. A backwash of laughter—nervous titters and iconoclastic cackling—would splash and trickle from the balconies, then the chaos would subside. Mark Twain's eyes would shift again. Another silence. Then another whispered syllable would rustle and whistle with incredible procrastination from beneath Twain's bushy mustache. Now true chaos reigned. The young, would-be professor saw the men who were sitting in front of him bend double and roll in their seats; he heard a man behind him gasp between fits of laughter, "Make him stop! Make him stop! I'm in pain!"

Suddenly the young, would-be professor realized he had no idea what Mark Twain had been saying. He had been entirely focused on Twain's *manner* of speaking and moving. Yet it did not matter. Twain could have been speaking Latin; it would have made no difference. The young, would-be professor realized that here was an actor, an actor as much as any Booth or Forrest or Irving.

As the young, would-be professor thought about this, Mark Twain shifted his position on stage. There was a rustle of air in the hall; the crowd settled down. It felt as if something had passed over the house; the mood had changed. Twain was looking down at the lectern. When Twain looked up again, the young, would-be professor realized he was seeing an entirely different man. This Mark Twain spoke a little faster, did not drawl much, and did not saw the air with his hands. He stood straight and talked straight and seemed to be making sense. The young, would-be professor began trying to focus on what Mark Twain was saying.

Twain was speaking about American Imperialism. His remarks were surprising, his attacks bitter. He spoke with even, measured tones. No one laughed. Twain was not waiting for anyone to laugh. He was talking fast now, pouring out invective; it sounded like profanity, but only because there was no music in his voice, unless a drumbeat could be considered music.

Mark Twain was asking the audience, "Are we qualified to enlighten and purify the rest of the world while our own hands are unclean? Will not our attempts to help our foreign brothers who sit in darkness only lead inevitably to their enslavement? How can beneficence enslave, you ask? *Conditional* beneficence is no beneficence, but a cold contract promoted by a party looking out for its own interests. *Conditional* beneficence gives with one hand and takes back twice as much with the other. The *conditional* beneficence which we now so nobly hold out to our foreign brothers who sit in darkness will bind them in a more loathsome enslavement than the world has ever known, because it will be slavery hidden under a new and unrecognized name. Shall we go on conferring our civilization upon our foreign brothers who sit in darkness, or shall we give those poor things a rest? Shall we bang right ahead in our old-time, loud, pious way, and commit this new century to the old game; or shall we sober up and sit down and think it over first?"

Mark Twain stood for a moment, his eyes moving from person to person in the audience. Then he turned and sat down.

The silence of uncertainty hung heavy in Carnegie Hall. The other speakers sitting on the stage next to Mark Twain looked at each other; they knew Twain had departed from his prepared text. Down in the hall there were furtive whispers. Then one lone pair of hands in the balcony began a slow clapping; that pair was joined by another, and another—and another. A tumult of applause broke in the air of Carnegie Hall. When it died down, Booker T. Washington was introduced.

The young, would-be professor kept his eye on Mark Twain who sat ramrod straight, looking ahead. Twain did not seem to be listening to Washington, or to be even thinking his own thoughts. He was absent, elsewhere, thought the young, would-be professor. Where was he? Where had he gone? Back to the Mississippi River? Or some foreign, exotic land? India? Egypt?

Mark Twain scratched his cheek and pulled at the corner of his mustache. He was back for a moment—then gone again—somewhere off into space. Or was he gone? Was this distant, solemn man the real Mark Twain and the funny little man on the platform the imposter? Or were both men real? Or neither?

This was the beginning for the professor. He never saw Mark Twain again—and he never stopped looking for him.

"So what can you tell me, Professor?" the blank-faced man asked.

The professor looked up.

"Excuse me?"

"What can you tell me? Is it the real McCoy?"

The professor came to himself. He picked up his magnifying glass and scrutinized the manuscript.

"Well. . . The paper looks right. The typewriter characters seem to resemble some I recall on some of Mark Twain's manuscripts written around 1906. He was dictating them to a stenographer who later would do the typing. Usually there are a few corrections or additions on the typewritten page done in Mark Twain's own handwriting. This manuscript seems to have none."

"I can tell you. It doesn't," the blank-faced man said.

"Yes," the professor said, "it's a finished manuscript, retyped from another draft. Very difficult to determine authenticity with such a thing. Even if we matched typewriter characters and paper stock, we couldn't be absolutely sure that Mark Twain was the author, although the evidence might suggest it. In such a case, provenance becomes very important. Where did you find this?"

"Can't say," the blank-faced man replied. "We just need you to tell us if this was written by Mark Twain."

The professor frowned at the blank-faced man; he was not accustomed to dealing with individuals such as this.

"Well," the professor said, his voice taking on an edge, "if you want a definitive opinion—"

"We do."

"That will take some time."

"How much time?"

The professor looked over at the blank-faced man's associate, who had not said a word. Suddenly the professor felt uneasy.

The professor said, "Well. My schedule is very full, and—"

"We'd like you to take care of this first," the blank-faced man said, and his eyes finally took on a hint of an expression: his eyelids drooped, casting a ruthless shadow over his narrowing pupils.

"I see, "the professor said, "I see. You have a reason for the urgency."

"There's a reason. It's none of your business."

The professor felt a sting from the words.

"Well. . ." The professor's mind raced. He did not want to deal with these men. He wanted a way out. But the dean had insisted that he see them. The dean would not tell the professor who these men were, only that they were with the federal government, and that it was of utmost importance that the professor give them full cooperation.

"Well. . . can you give me until tomorrow?"

"Tomorrow?"

"I need to study the whole manuscript. Analyze the style of writing. The vocabulary. Subject matter. I can only draw a conclusion from that. But I'll tell you now: there's no way to determine with absolute certainty who wrote this without its provenance."

"I told you. We can't give you that."

"Of course you did."

The professor flipped through the manuscript. It was too long to read in a single evening, but he figured if he read fast, he could, if he spent the whole day and evening, skim the manuscript and get some sense of it.

"Tomorrow," the professor said. "Say—nine am?"

"If that's what *you* say."

"*That* is what I say."

"All right."

The blank-faced man rose along with his associate.

"We'll be here at nine tomorrow," the blank-faced man said.

The two men went to the door. The blank-faced man stopped and turned around.

"Oh," the blank-faced man said, "and Professor. Don't discuss this with anyone. And I mean anyone. You understand?"

The professor looked up.

"I understand, young man."

The blank-faced man studied the professor's face a moment, and then turned back to the door.

"Oh—and young man," the professor said.

The blank-faced man stopped and looked back.

"Don't ever question my patriotism," the professor said. "About anything. And I mean anything. Do *you* understand?"

"Just read the words, Professor," the blank-faced man said, and then he turned along with his associate and the two men went out.

The professor felt as if a pressure had been released in the room. He exhaled and took another breath. Then he looked down at the manuscript and thought: What the hell is this all about? He picked up his magnifying glass and studied the paper again, noting its yellow-brown edges. Other than that, it was in pristine condition.

The professor lay his magnifying glass aside, rose from his desk, and went to the window. He saw the two men who had been in his office walking away across the campus. They walked stiffly, with a military precision.

The professor shook his head and sank into an armchair near the window. He took out his reading glasses, perched them on his nose, and looked down at the manuscript in his lap.

The professor began to read, and, as he read, he could not help hearing the sound of the words in his head. It was a voice talking easy and slow, the long, pulled-out sounds of sweet taffy. . . .

Chapter One

The Typesetter

> As near as I can make out, geniuses think they know it all, and so won't take people's advice, but always go their own way, which makes everybody forsake and despise them, and that is perfectly natural. If they was humbler, and listened and tried to learn, it would be better for them.
>
> — Huck, *Tom Sawyer Abroad*

Everybody was coming to Chicago for the fair that spring of 1893. In fact, it seemed like the whole world was coming, which was only natural, I suppose, considering that it was called "The World's Fair."

It was to commemorate the 400th year since the discovery of America by Columbus. The fair was a year late. But what is the difference of a year or two after you have waited four hundred? Even Methusalah would not have quibbled over that.

They said the fair was a wonder, and I suppose it was, too. But they also said it was a wonder that Columbus had discovered America. I would argue that. Considering the size of America, it seems to me that it would have been a wonder had he come this way and missed it.

The fair did not only seem to contain all the people in the world, but every *thing* that was in the world as well. So it was a world unto itself. Its parts shifted and turned, clattered and clamored, up, down, in, out, over, under, round and round. And all those parts were driven by—the Machine—the usurper god of our age. But this was not the machine forged by our fathers' hands; its blood was not water and its breath was not steam. The Machine of the Columbian Quaternary had veins of copper, and along them flowed a mysterious, new blood—electricity.

He dropped feet first into the Chicago River.

Of course, electricity had always been known to a select few throughout the generations of the human race. The ancient Egyptians at Edfu built lightning rods long before Franklin ever flew his kite. But the world's golden sages knew how to keep a secret. So when—four hundred years ago—Columbus observed ball lightning on the mast of his ship, he could only call it "St. Elmo's Fire," which only shows that just because someone can be right about one thing there is no reason he cannot be ignorant of just about everything else. Columbus was right about the round world, but he mistook America for India and electricity for a miracle. The discrepancies shouted from the treetops, but Columbus had his one truth and to all others he was deaf.

It was easy for our generation to scoff and feel superior, but we were no different from Columbus; he knew how to make a circuit of the world, we knew how to make a circuit of electricity. The fair, in showing us the truth or two we knew, shouted at us the world of truths we still had not seen or heard. But, of course, as usual, most of us were not listening.

The fair was spread out over a mile, north to south, along the shore of Lake Michigan, and it reached inland about a mile to the west along a narrow stretch of ground that was called the "Midway Plaisance," a giant carnival unlike any the world had ever seen up until then. Along its magic avenue sprawled what seemed to be every country on the face of the globe, and if one country did not suit you, you need not bother with a steamship passage or a railroad trip—another country was only a step away. There was an Eskimo village and a South Sea village; there were the castles of Germany and the pagodas of Japan; there were the streets of Cairo where you could wind your way around on the back of a camel; there was an Algerian village with a "cultural exhibition" of the *danse du ventre*—the belly dance, otherwise known as the Dance of the Seven Veils, or, as the vulgar referred to it, the "Hoochie-Koochie" (roughly translated: "By George, would you look at that?") It seemed like every gentleman who stepped into the Algerian village suddenly got a strong hankering for some cultural exposure. Some got several exposures until their wives pronounced them "overexposed" and put an end to their cultural development with a parasol tap to the back of the head, a tap which would send the gentleman's bowler down over his eyes—a sort of Dance of the Eighth Veil.

The major portions of the grounds lay parallel to the shore of the lake. It was here that sumptuous marble palaces rose up splendidly to the sky—only they were not really marble; they were really only frameworks of timber covered over with sheets of "staff"—plasterboard. Outside them, you might think you had wandered into Athens or Rome or Venice or some other place that had never existed before, except in a dream. Inside them—well, inside them, they looked something like a barn.

But, then, nobody seemed to notice.

Maybe the reason nobody noticed the inside of the fair's buildings was because of what those building walls contained—a collection of the world's superlatives: the oldest, the newest, the biggest, the smallest, the fastest, the slowest. If the relics of George Washington, the Tombs of the Bastille, or the dungeons of the Inquisition did not make you want to crane your neck, a 3,000 year-old 312 foot high Mammoth Redwood carted all the way from California would make you wish you were a giraffe. Over in the Hall of Agriculture there was an eleven ton block of cheese, enough to feed a World Congress of Rats and most of their relatives. When the rats finished feasting on the cheese, they could top off on a 1,500 pound chocolate Venus de Milo, and it would be good that it *was* a Venus de Milo because that rat congress would have no room left for the arms.

Everybody clustered and crowded, squeezed and poked, stepped on and stepped up to see—to see—what they had never seen before in their lives! People had not come to see the elephant—but to see a dynamo the size of *two* elephants—a locomotive the size of *twenty* elephants—a battleship of steel that could transport a *hundred* elephants and still have room for an inaugural ball and a baseball game. People had come to have the wind knocked out of them by the gigantic power of the electrical machine. In the Midway Plaisance, people would plunge on the incline of the scenic railway, gasping for breath. Everyone began calling it "the rollercoaster," and they were riding it to beat all hell into the Twentieth Century.

To balance this raucous atmosphere, the organizers of the fair sought a weight. Someone decided that the one thing that could slow down all that breathless dipping and plunging could be expressed by one weighty word—religion. "Yes," someone said, "let's have some—religion!" And, of course, it being a world's fair, they could not be satisfied with just one religion, or even a handful. A handful of Presbyterians, Catholics, and Mormons could no more quell that world tide of human passion than a fan could cool Hades. No, the only solution—from an engineering standpoint—was to bring in *all* the world's religions, yes, a "World Congress of Religions!" And so they did. Three years later, when I visited India, I found people there who had heard about the World Congress of Religions and thought that Chicago was a Holy City. I did not have the heart to expurgate their theology.

The fair had brought forth a congress of another kind as well—not of holy men—but of harlots, whoremongers, and hell-raisers. Every pickpocket, card-sharp, and confidence man in the country was converging on the fair. The police commissioner and the mayor, studying that Hell-Congress, concluded that while vice could not be eradicated, it could be regulated and put on a sound financial footing. All members of the Hell-Congress were warned off the fairgrounds and admonished to conduct all their business downtown—at least all that was of a publicly perceivable nature. The admonishment had its effect. The fair had the placid air of a Sunday-school picnic, even if, around the corner, behind the board fence, the devil was still working his old stand with both of his left hands.

The people of Chicago would not want this News distributed about, because they believe they are the best people, so much so that every time a citizen of Chicago goes to hell, Satan has to explain that the Chicago people are not the best down there, merely the most numerous.

But whether with sinners, saints, or Sunday-only sanctifiers, Chicago was filling up fast that spring with people from all four corners of the globe, and from two or three other corners no one even knew existed. They were coming in sarongs and in turbans, in wooden shoes and in sandals, wrapped in fur and wrapped in— maybe something resembling a diaper. It was hard on the eyes to gaze on all that variety at once, occasionally hard on the nose to smell it. Yes, you could see the whole world there, and smell it, too. When you did, you knew the world was real, that you were a part of it, and, because of that, the world was you.

The best place to take in your view of the world was atop the monster-sized pleasure wheel designed by George Ferris. Situated at the center of the Midway, its sky-cabins rose 250 feet in the air along the rim of the giant wheel. Each sky-cabin could carry 60 passengers. You could stand in one of those sky-cabins as it rose in the air, and look out its windows, and watch the world drop away at your feet. The people below would become midgets—then mites, while the trees and buildings and telegraph poles would shrink down and become a toy-land made for the habitation of dolls. From the top you could see: to the north, the steeples, smokestacks, and skyscraping towers of downtown Chicago; to the west and south, the open plains of Illinois; to the east, the fairyland of white domes and towers which were the fair's exhibition buildings— and among the glimmering white buildings you could see blue lagoons and canals dotted green with wooded islands—and—if you looked close enough— you could see boats plying their way along those canals as if lost in some 400 year-old Venetian dream. Further away, perhaps half a mile, you could glimpse another kind of movement: little black specks sliding along the lakeside pier. These would be the passengers on the electric moving sidewalk. Beyond the pier, you would see only the blue waters of Lake Michigan, twinkling white sparks of sunlight, twinkling and stretching off to the horizon so that—if you didn't know better—it would seem you were gazing off to an infinite sea at the edge of the world.

Notice that I say, "*You* could see such-and-such," because—*I* never did. I had hoped to ride the big wheel to the top and be delighted with the view like everybody else. But all I know about that view is second-hand information. I never got up there. It is the purpose of this narrative to tell you why.

The story I have told to the world, to my friends, and to my family about my stay in Chicago in 1893 is a lie. It was not my first lie. I do not recall my first lie, it was too far back. But this was probably the best lie I ever told for size and construction and detail of duplicity. It was a lie told with great art, craftsmanship, and mature skill. It was a lie that reached neither too high nor too low, but kept its claims modest and temperate and went off on no tangents of boasting. And thus it was a lie destined to be believed as iron-clad Truth, and thus so sturdy and strong it could have served as the basis of a new religion, if it needed to serve in that capacity, which it didn't.

I will also note that it was a necessary lie, the kind of lie that keeps the world's wheels greased and turning and keeps us all happy and satisfied. It was a masterful lie, but, as lies go, not a very big lie, for it was not about general principles, or geometry, or metaphysics. I was not up to manufacturing those kinds of quality lies. No, this lie was only about something I did, or did not do, I should say.

My lie had one main theme, and it was this: that while I was in Chicago I had a cold and lay in bed and nursed it nearly the whole time. This main theme was so simple that it took care of a lot of loose ends that usually dangle around the edges of common, ordinary lies. If it had not been for that main theme, I would have had to come up with a lot more little lies to hide all those dangling loose ends. But as it was, to any inquiry about my stay in Chicago all I had to do was reply, "Oh, how I was sick! Sick, sick, sick, the whole blamed time!" And that ended it right there. That lopped off all those loose ends right at their base; for who wants to hear about somebody being sick? I am sure you can see the simple genius in this lie, but I'll confess here that I cannot take full credit for it. Another person was the author of the main theme of my lie. I don't mind admitting that, for the author of my lie's main theme could out-lie me any day of the week. Amateur liars such as I am have no chance of competing against professional liars such as the author of my main theme. But I am getting ahead of myself.

To tell a lie is easy; to tell the truth is hard. That is probably why the truth is so seldom told. The truth is a precious commodity; let us economize it. I will try to tell the truth here. I *will* tell the truth here, to the best of my ability, but the truth with a small t. I know it will be the truth with a small t, because while most of what I have to tell I experienced first-hand, the rest is hear-say provided by people whom I trust implicitly—as you shall see. When I tell their part of the story I am relying on their testimony and filling in what I did not witness or experience with what I imagine was the most likely course of events. But is this not exactly what our historians do in *their* books? Only they do not admit that the knowledge-gaps in their books are patched up with their own inventions. No, that is when they put in a footnote. You see, those footnotes are there to throw you off, to distract you from the patchwork.

Actually, I do not believe *any* story has ever been told with a capitol T kind of truth. The theologians tell us the Bible is true—and it is, but only in a small t kind of way. The gospel had to be told four times and even then the authors could not get all their facts straight—not one gospel completely agrees with another. Now, if that thought offends you, you should not be reading this anyway. You should be reading your Bible, because it is clear to me you have not been reading your Bible. Start with the genealogies and compare them generation by generation. You will see they do not match up. For those of you who have no religion, I ask you to read the Congressional Record, your Newspaper, or a letter sent to you by anyone. Read it slow, stay awake—and *think*. You will realize a truth about Truth: You are reading small t literature.

So—if you want to know what "really" happened to me back there in Chicago in 1893, that is, my own small t version of events—then read on. I figure you will read on, because if you have managed to lay your hands on *this* manuscript, you probably are the kind of person who has some small t truths of your own, truths that nobody else knows about, truths that nobody else would believe. In fact, if you are reading this, I most likely have been dead a century or two, and it does not matter to me if you like, dislike, believe or disbelieve any of my small t truths. I speak from the grave, and from the grave I am sublimely indifferent to your opinion, or the opinion of anyone else. So read on and contemplate, and after you have read this, you can scratch your head and wonder, "Could it be? Is it true?" To which I would reply, "Of course it's true—in a small t kind of way."

But I do not think I have strayed very far from the facts. We were all interviewed by President Grover Cleveland in 1893, and again by a secret government commission in 1902 in the aftermath of the assassination of President McKinley. I have heard that a few of the facts of "The Chicago Incident of 93" (as it is called by certain parties in Washington) have been withheld from some of our highest elected officials, including President Roosevelt. I find it hard to believe that President Roosevelt does not have all the facts in hand, although I have never spoken to him about these matters, so I cannot say for certain. When we enter the Mirror House of State Secrets, it is almost impossible to tell who knows what and how much. It is also impossible to tell which small t version of events is *the* Truth. But are we not back around the barn at where we started?

During the 1902 governmental inquiry it was requested by the commission that I write a secret history of 1893 for safe-keeping in their archives, but I declined due to financial and personal concerns. I have now settled most of those concerns for good or ill and now feel an urge to set down the events of 1893 in my own small t way. Whether I will submit this account to the government, keep it for my heirs and assigns, or burn it—I have not yet decided.

While riding the big pleasure wheel had been on my mind that spring of 1893, it was not my reason for being in Chicago. I had left my family behind in

Florence, Italy to come back to America to take the helm of my sinking financial ship. This was during the awful bank panic of '93 and about a year before the humiliating bankruptcy of all my business concerns.

It is best we do not know the future, for we often could not bear the present. At the moment, however, in my blessed ignorance of the future, my spirits were high, although, from time to time, I felt a foreboding, like a pressure on my head trying to push me down. But I was not going to let it.

After spending a short time back east in New York, my business associate Fred Hall and I boarded a train for Chicago. It seemed to me that our train was the slowest and oldest in the United States. I asked the conductor if it had been in the War. He said he did not think so. That was before his time, he said, for he was only a boy back in the 60's. I said, no, I did not mean the Civil War, I meant the Revolutionary. He did not seem to think that was so funny, and went on his way.

When we pulled into Chicago's Polk Street Station, Hall and I stepped out of the car and on to the station platform, and Hall stretched his arms out in front of him and took a deep breath.

"Smell that," Hall said.

"I'm afraid to," I replied.

"Go ahead. Take a deep breath," he insisted.

I chanced it and took a draw of air.

"What do you smell?" Hall asked.

"Coal dust, metal, oil. . . dirt. . . horse manure. . . and hog fat." I said.

"You smell hog fat," Hall said smiling, "I smell the future."

Well, that was fine with me if hog fat smelled like the future to Hall. It seemed he was always uttering banalities like that and uttering them with such an earnest and sincere and enthusiastic air that he made you feel that what he was saying had some real meaning. It made you want to laugh, cry, and ponder the Eternal Mysteries all at the same time. I should say that, from time to time, Hall had good perceptions, and sometimes they were good business perceptions. I say, sometimes. Both of us were sharp businessmen—sometimes. Trouble was, in business, "sometimes" was not good enough.

We got all our trunks together and had a porter cart them out to the front of the station to put on an omnibus to take to the hotel. When we got out to the sidewalk in front of the station, I spied a sign above a building across the street that read "MOOS CIGARS" and in much smaller letters "sold here."

I said to Hall, pointing up to the sign, "Say, I forgot to get cigars when we were inside, and that's my brand up there."

"You smoke those?" Hall asked.

"I have since I got back to America. I'm experimenting."

"What's the experiment?"

"How long it will take before they kill me. They're the worst cigars I've ever smoked."

"Then why smoke them?"

"I can see you don't know anything about cigars. You stay here and handle our baggage. I'm going over there and get provisioned."

I went on over to the store, got a box of cigars, some matches, and some pipe tobacco.

After I paid for everything, the store clerk said, "I know who you are. I recognized you as soon as you came in. No foolin'—ain't you Buffalo Bill?"

"You've recognized me," I said with a proper air of modesty.

"I saw your show over at the arena," the clerk went on. "Bully show. But, say, what do you want to buy those cheap cigars for? Here, let me get you our very best from Havana."

"Oh, no," I said, "these will do fine."

"Oh," the clerk said, "I know. You're getting those for your Injuns. That's it, ain't it?"

"Yes," I said, "they like this kind. Can't get them to smoke any other. And lord knows I've tried."

"Say," the clerk said, "no offense, but you looked to be a bigger man in the show. More robust."

"I know," I said, "It's your Chicago water. It's swiveling me up something awful. If you could see my spine, well, it's folded up just like an accordion. Chicago water always does that to me. As soon as I get back out west, and get to drinking clear spring water, I straighten back up and fill out again to my normal height and dimensions. At first the doctors thought it was Bright's disease, but now they've discovered that it's Ebner's Sponge Syndrome."

"No fooling," the store clerk said with concerned gravity.

"Yes," I said, "well, I have to get these cigars back to the Injuns before they get agitated and start scalping people."

I started out, and as I was going through the door I heard the store clerk say, "Guess what? That's Buffalo Bill! He's buying cigars for his Injuns!"

When I got back to the front of the station, Hall was supervising the porter who was shoving all our cases and valises on to an omnibus. I believe I counted twelve trunks that belonged to Hall.

"All that heavy work makes me tired," I said.

"But you're not doing any of it," Hall said.

"Looking at it being done is wearing itself," I said.

I took a cigar out of the box and lit it up, took a puff, and said, "Yep, this is a Moos. You know what they say."

"No, what do they say?" Hall asked.

"When you light up a Moos, all hell breaks loose."

"Yes," Hall replied, "that cigar smells like hell. Smells like a killer."

"Yes, it kills. It moderates all this Chicago air. Sterilizes all the hog-fat and sin microbes floating around."

When the porter finished his work, Hall tipped him, and Hall and I went over to a row of hansom cabs waiting across the street. We got into one, and Hall said to the driver, "Great Northern."

The omnibus with our baggage started away from the station, and our cab followed behind it.

I asked, "What do you have in all those trunks, Hall?"

"Clothes," he replied.

"All those trunks of yours are full of clothes?"

"Not full. I'd say less than a third full."

"Hall, you've got to learn to pack with more efficiency."

"What are you talking about? I know how to pack. I need that extra space. My wife has given me a shopping list and the purchases will go in all those spaces."

"Your wife trusts you to do her shopping for her?"

"Doesn't yours?"

"Ha! Livy doesn't trust me to buy my own neck ties."

"Now that's funny. Here you are with all these big deals brewing, and your wife won't let you buy your own neck ties."

"It's all a question of proportion, Hall. Livy is afraid I'll come home with some kind of polka-dotted, rainbow-hued, circus clown absurdity. And she knows that once I bought it, I'd insist on wearing it."

"You wouldn't wear anything like that."

"I would if Livy'd let me. At least at home."

"You're serious."

"Of course I'm serious. You want to know what I think is ridiculous? Grown men walking around in undertaker costumes three hundred sixty-five days out of the year. Like out there on the street. Could you please tell me what everybody's mourning?"

"I don't know. Maybe the bank panic."

"The people of the Orient know how to dress—long flowing silk robes in all the colors of creation."

"Chicago's too cold for silk robes."

"Well—that's a problem, too. Chicago's a fine city, just too far north. It needs to be moved south—to about the latitude of St. Louis."

"Why not New Orleans?"

"Oh no. Too hot down there. And anyway—all the solid land down there has already been bought up. All that's left is swamp. No, Chicago will just have to make do. But then, that's what Chicago has always been good at."

We reached the Great Northern Hotel on the northeast corner of Jackson and Dearborn Streets, a 14 story tower of brick walls and bay windows. We got out of the cab and went inside to the desk. Because of the fair, the lobby was full of people, and the hotel desk clerk told us that, despite its 500 rooms, the hotel was booked to capacity. If Hall had not wired ahead, we would have been out of luck in getting rooms and would have had to seek lodging elsewhere, if we could have found it anywhere.

Hall signed the register, and then I set down my name.

"Here for the fair, Mr. Clemens?" the desk clerk asked.

"Yes. I want to see that big wheel you've got down there."

"I'm sorry to say they don't have it up yet."

"Don't have it up yet?"

"Just some scaffolding last time I was down there."

"When was that?"

"Day before yesterday. But just you wait. When it's up, it'll be more thrilling than the Eiffel Tower."

"Well, it'll take some doing to beat the Eiffel Tower. I'll have to see it for myself. That is, if they finish it before I leave town."

"I hope you can. I know you'll be amazed."

"Yes, well, that's what I'm after. Amazement."

Hall and I went to our rooms, which were right next to each other. An inside door connected his room with mine; I closed it, and collapsed into a chair and just sat. I was dog-tired, but did not want Hall to know it. I was feeling that pressure on the top of my head again.

The next day was a big, long day, one I will never forget as long as I live. It was followed by another, even longer day that I could not forget in ten lifetimes. These two days comprised a turning-point, you might say. I have been asked what the turning-point of my life was and have replied that there have been many. These two days were the turning-point I could never reveal. After this, I would never look at the world in quite the same way again. Looking back, I also realize that this was the turning-point of the financial disaster that would hit me not long into the future. On these two days the Paige typesetter's fate was sealed. The fortune I had invested in it was destined to be lost in its entirety. After this, we would struggle valiantly with the promotion of the machine for some time to come, and my delusion of its imminent success would grow deeper and more intense. But the death blow had already been struck here in Chicago on this next day—and the one following it. I will tell you how it happened.

That next morning I met Hall down in the lobby of the hotel. He was sitting there, reading the morning paper.

"There you are," Hall said. "I was about to go up and knock on your door."

"I was a little slow getting up this morning. I didn't feel very well last night," I said.

"I thought you looked a little tired yesterday. Do you want to stay here while I go see Paige by myself?"

"No, no," I said. "I'm fine. Let's have some breakfast. I'll feel better then."

We strolled across the lobby to the hotel's restaurant. A young waiter seated us, and soon I was enjoying steak, eggs, and coffee, and beginning to feel like a member of the human race again.

Hall said, "I see in the paper that Cleveland's coming to the fair on May first to preside over the grand opening."

"That so?" I replied. "Too bad he's not here now. There's a thing or two I'd like to discuss with him."

"Yes. The bank panic."

"Somebody's got to do something. Somebody's got to pull in the reins on you-know-who."

"J.P.?"

"All that man knows how to do is grab. An expert grabber. I'd like somebody to tell me—what has he built?"

"He's built an empire."

"Do you have that right! And if somebody doesn't do something, it'll be the Empire of the United States, not the Republic—and J.P. will be the emperor."

"J.P. already *is* the emperor."

"I know that, you know that, and J.P. knows that.

But when the waiter knows that—when the doorman knows that—when the bootblack down the street knows that—we're all in for a world of hurt."

Hall and I finished breakfast and hailed a cab outside the hotel. Hall gave the driver an address scrawled on the back of one of his calling cards. The driver shook the reins and took us out on to the street and around the side of the hotel, and then left up State Street. We moved past crowds and shops and streetcars and on north toward a bridge spanning the Chicago River. We passed over the narrow river canal which was lined on either side with docked sailing vessels. Up ahead were some villainous looking warehouses. We reached the warehouses, and our driver turned the horses on to an alley with muddy gaps in its paving stones, and then drew the horses to a halt.

"This is it?" I asked Hall.

"I think so," he said.

We got out of the cab and looked up at the warehouse. It was a bleak, gray place.

I said to the driver, "Wait for us. I'm not sure how long we'll be."

Hall opened the grimy door of the warehouse and we went in. We stepped inside a big, empty room. The typesetting machine stood in the far corner with James W. Paige bending over it. Paige was his usual self: a bright-eyed, sharply dressed little man whose hands moved incessantly over the workings of the machine, polishing, adjusting, stroking, petting, just as I have seen a racehorse jockey do when handling a thoroughbred. James Paige was the inventor of the machine—nominally. Several other people had done the actual inventing: Farnham had conceived the basic typesetting mechanism, Thompson had designed the distributor, North had the created the automatic justifier, and Von Schriver had arranged the letters on the keyboard. Paige had combined and coordinated all these inventions. But I think he had convinced himself that he had created the machine in its entirety. I know he had convinced himself that he was a genius.

I was about to speak to Paige when my eyes fell upon the floor of the warehouse. There I saw sheets of brown wrapping paper laid out in rows, and upon them lay nearly all the internal parts of the typesetter, row upon row of little cog-wheels, levers, screws, and other parts to which I could not put a name. An old man and two boys of about ten years of age sat on the floor, and they were going over every one of those parts with oily rags.

"What the hell is *this* all about?" I snapped at Paige who turned, startled. When he recognized Hall and me, he smiled.

"Mr. Clemens. Mr. Hall," Paige said evenly.

"Mr. Paige, just what is the meaning of this?" Hall asked, saying the same thing I did, but in a slightly politer tone.

"Oiling and inspection, Mr. Hall, oiling and inspection," Paige said, smiling blandly.

"Wh—What's wrong?" I stammered. "Something happen to the machine?"

"Nothing's happened. Everything's fine. Just a little inspection, that's all," Paige said.

"That's what you always say when the machine breaks down. A little inspection. Next thing I know, a week's been lost! A week long inspection! Is that any way to run a business?"

"Mr. Clemens," Paige said, holding his hands out like a supplicant at a prayer meeting, "I'm just trying to get the machine ready for its big demonstration tomorrow. You want the machine ready, don't you?"

"Of course I want the machine ready! What a question! What I want to know is: How in the living hell is it going to *be* ready by tomorrow with all its parts strewed out here on the ground?"

"Mr. Clemens, Mr. Clemens," Paige said, "you are perfectly justified to feel frustrated. I feel frustrated.

Mr. Hall feels frustrated. Don't you feel frustrated, Mr. Hall?"

"Very," Hall said.

"We are all frustrated, Mr. Clemens. But we must keep a level head."

"*My* head's level. It's *your* dome I'm worried about."

"Mr. Clemens, please. I've been working all night. Please, I need your patience. I know you are a patient man, a patient and wise man who—"

"Don't grease me with any of your oil! I ain't one of your machine parts!"

"Mr. Clemens! I am going to have the machine ready in time! And it will run to perfection."

"Perfection's fine, if you can get it. If you can't—let it run to *imperfection*. All I want for it to do is *run*! Can you understand that part?"

"I understand that part—to perfection! I mean—I *understand* that part."

"Paige, you've got to learn you can't get every detail right. It can't be done. It's never been done. It never will be done. The entire world is nothing but a compound fracture of mistakes! Why do you think the Good Lord rested at the end of six days? He was worn out over getting all the details right!"

"Mr. Clemens, I just want the machine to live up to its potential. You can understand that. You know the machine's potential."

"If I didn't, I wouldn't have invested in it."

"The machine—the machine is like. . . like. . . a living creature. Yes—a *thinking*, living creature. A sentient creature. This is not merely a printing machine—oh no! *That* has already been invented long ago by Gutenberg. This—this is a *thinking* machine!"

"I know that!" I snapped.

"Then you must know that a living thing must be nurtured. Yes! Let others smirk! But it is true! The machine must be nurtured. It is in its infancy. But it will grow. And when it grows up, it will grow into a giant, a giant looming over the nineteenth and twentieth centuries—no, over the next five centuries—*ten* centuries. It shall define the millennium! The age of the printing press has passed. We are leaving the age of print and entering the age of *information*—yes, information itself as a thing unto itself! And who shall stand upon the threshold of that age? Who stood upon the threshold of the Renaissance? Fust and Gutenberg! Gutenberg and Fust! Who shall stand upon the threshold of the coming age? Clemens and Paige! Paige and Clemens! The great Mark Twain charting the course of the age of information through the dark night of doubt and ignorance! Now—would you *really* have me cut corners *now*?—Now, when triumph is at the tips of our very fingers? When the very age itself sparkles before us in all its golden glory, beckoning—beckoning for us to reach, grasp—yea, to pluck, hold, and taste the fruit of our time? I ask you, Mr. Clemens, you, a man of vision, while the rest of the world gropes in the stygian night!"

Paige had talked himself red-faced. I just stood there looking at him. It seemed that whenever I was with Paige, he could talk me into anything. But the moment I got away from him and reflected, I always perceived some flaw in his assertions. This time I was determined not to be led by the nose.

I said, "You must think I'm the biggest fool in the world! You wrote me that you were preparing a factory here in Chicago capable of manufacturing ten thousand machines. And I come here to a ram-shackled cow barn to find *one* machine with its guts strewed out on the ground. You're doing to me the same damn thing you did two years ago when that humbug Jones came to Hartford. We had some potential investors *then*—and what did you have to show *then*? Parts and promises! Parts and promises! All strewed out on the floor! That's not going to happen this time! I want you to get this machine put together and *operating. To-day*—not tomorrow—*today*. Do you understand?"

"I understand," Paige said.

"And who are those people over there?"

"An old man and his grandsons."

"Why don't you have regular mechanics doing that?"

"You told me you wanted to economize."

"I didn't mean for you to engage slave labor. Pay them regular mechanics wages. At least the old man. You can pay the boys at the apprentice rate."

"Whatever you say."

"And you keep your eye on them. Don't let 'em lose any of the parts, for God sakes."

"Certainly not. I have them well in hand."

"Now you get the machine together and stop by my hotel this afternoon and let me know you've done it. I'm staying at the Great Northern, room 204."

I wrote my hotel address and room number in a little memorandum book, tore out the sheet, and handed it to Paige.

Paige took the sheet of paper and said, "It will be ready. I assure you."

"Don't assure. Just do it."

"I will. I will. Now there is one matter I need to discuss with you. There are a few expenses I've incurred while I've been in Chicago, and—"

"What? *More* money?"

I looked over at Hall. I could see he knew nothing about this.

"Only a small amount," Paige said with a nervous smile.

"How small? Wait. Don't tell me. Hold off on that. I don't even *want* to think about putting out more money right now. You get this machine together and get it *running*. *Then*—we'll talk about more money."

"But—"

"At the hotel," I said, walking away. "Five o'clock—no—four. And don't be late."

I went out the door and Hall followed me. Yes, I was mad as hell, and disgusted, too.

Hall and I got in the cab and we rattled our way down the alley and back out on to the main thoroughfare.

"Head back to the hotel," I said to the driver.

"What are you going to do?" Hall asked.

"About what?"

"I mean, right now. Back at the hotel."

"I have some letters to write. One to Livy and several to the New York investors."

"What are you going to tell them?"

"What do you think? That everything is just dandy."

"If only we could get people to understand the machine's potential."

"Yes."

"Paige can go on, but, you know, he was speaking the truth back there."

"I know. Why do you think I put up with him? He's got something there in that machine, all right, if I could just get him to quit tinkering with it."

"The talk now among all the big money in New York is for the Linotype."

"Shoot! The Linotype is nothing but a jittering cotton gin. The Paige typesetter is a locomotive."

"You've seen a Linotype operate?"

"Well, no. I can't say I have. But I know what it can do. And compared to Paige's machine, it can't do much."

"*The Chicago Daily* News is using Linotypes in their composing room now."

"Let 'em use 'em. They won't be using 'em for long when the things become obsolete."

"Maybe we ought to run over there and take a look at one of them."

"What for?"

"I don't know. Sometimes you just have to go and look before you know what you're looking for."

"Hall, you are usually a very logical fellow, but your logic escapes me on that one."

Just at that moment I heard somebody yell, "Hold it up there!"

I turned my gaze toward the street. We had reached the bridge over the Chicago River and a policeman was shouting for our driver to stop. A crowd was beginning to form on the bridge, and it was growing thicker by the second.

"What's wrong, officer?" I asked.

"An exhibition on the bridge," the policeman said.

"Exhibition? What sort of exhibition?"

"A preview of something that's going to be at the fair. Some kind of circus boy. He's going to make a jump."

"Jump? What do you mean 'jump'?"

"Off the bridge."

"What for?"

"Damned if I know, but he has a permit, and you'll have to wait."

"We can't wait. We have business to attend to. We'll turn around and take another bridge."

"You can't turn around," the policeman said, pointing behind us.

I leaned out of the cab and looked back. There was a line of carriages and wagons behind us stretching all the way back to Wisconsin.

"Well, damn!" I said. "We're trapped. This is a fine state of affairs."

Then I caught sight of the figure of a boy moving up on the bridge's railing. He was a wiry, muscular little fellow with a curly mop of blackish-brown hair framing a pale, olive complexioned face. He was dressed in a gray bathing suit trimmed in red piping. He moved up on the railing the way a snake would, that is, undulating and twisting, not climbing; he did not seem to have any bones in his body, just muscle.

"Come on, Hall," I said. "We're stuck here. We might as well see the circus boy, too."

Hall and I got out of the cab and edged our way into the crowd, trying to see. The circus boy stood up on the bridge railing perfectly balanced like a tightrope walker. He stood still, looking straight ahead. I studied the boy's face. It was set on a large, wide head. His nose was sharp and aquiline; his lips were thin and shut tight. His eyes were a pale, intense blue that showed up even from where I was standing, about forty feet away. His thin eyebrows arched upward, casting an oriental mystery over his face. I kept being drawn back to his eyes; they were not the eyes of a boy. They were the eyes of a mesmerist.

"Lay-dees and gen-tle-men," the circus boy said, not shouting, but in a high-pitched voice that seemed to come from some far-away world. "Allow me to introduce my-self. I am none other than Hou-deen-ee! I am the one you have heard about—the one you have talked about—the one you have wondered about!"

"I've never heard of him in my life," Hall said.

I shrugged. "He's heard of himself, that's for sure."

Houdini held up a pair of handcuffs, and said, "A regulation pair of handcuffs from the Chicago Police Department. I have here one of Chicago's finest to vouch for their impregnable strength!"

A Chicago policeman came forward, took the handcuffs and locked them on the boy's wrists. Houdini held his arms above his head, to show the crowd that his wrists really were shackled together.

"Doubters, behold! Witness for yourselves the mystery of Houdini!"

Houdini drew his hands to his chest. His lips and jaw tightened. He continued to stand absolutely still. He seemed to be waiting for something, a sign, or a call to move. I could tell he was feeling for the moment, the same way I would feel for the moment to utter the "snapper" word of a joke when I would speak before an audience. I watched the boy's face. His eyes shifted to the side. He had heard his call. I did not see him jump. One instant he was standing on the bridge railing, the next he was spinning in mid-air in a blurred somersault, once, twice, three times—and then dropped feet first into the Chicago River.

A shout went up, and the crowd rushed forward to the railing, and Hall and I were pushed forward, too. We looked down upon the surface of the gray waters. A full, well-rounded stench let us know that this body of water did double duty as both a river and a sewage canal. All conversation ceased, and an odd kind of city quietude fell upon the place as each of us meditated upon the predicament of the shackled boy. A silent minute passed—then two; no

Houdini. My mind went back to my boyhood days and the boys I had known who had drowned: there was Lem Hackett who fell from a flat-boat, and, being loaded with sin, went to the bottom of the Mississippi like an anvil; there was "Dutchy," a German lad who was exasperatingly good, but did not know enough to come in out of the rain. He dove down in a muddy creek where we were all swimming and 'seeing who could stay under the longest' and got helplessly caught in a pile of green hickory hoop poles sunk there by coopers to soak. After a minute or two of waiting, all talking among us boys ceased, hearts began to beat fast, faces to turn pale, and our horrified eyes wandered back and forth from each others' countenances to the water. Now here on the Chicago River it was the drowning of "Dutchy" all over again. That time with "Dutchy" it fell my lot to go down in the murky water and feel for the boy's lifeless hand where it had been entwined in the hoop poles. This time, someone else would do that deed, but the vividness of what would be found down there in the murk of the Chicago River was real enough for me.

Three minutes had now passed since Houdini had plunged into the river. Now people began fidgeting and whispering. The nervous cough that masks the manly desire to scream began to sound. Then somebody said it out loud: "Houdini must be dead." Voices rose in response and above them somebody said it again: "He is dead."

Then we heard somebody shout: "There he is!"

We all turned around and there stood Houdini on the railing on the other side of the bridge. He was dripping water, his hair flattened against his head. He held aloft in his left hand the opened handcuffs. The crowd broke into applause.

Houdini held up his right hand and said, "Come one! Come all! To Kohl and Middleton's New State Street Globe Dime Museum, and, on May 1st, Kohl and Middleton's Globe Dime Museum Annex at the World's Fair Midway Plaisance! Come see the Impossible Made Possible!"

Houdini waved to the crowd again with a sort of salute over his head as the crowd applauded again and shook their hats in the air. Two men came forward out of the crowd and carried Houdini away on their shoulders.

"Quite a show!" Hall said.

"Yep," I said, "mighty strange circus boy there. Let's get back to the hotel."

Hall and I got back in our cab and in a moment we were on our way across the bridge. We passed Houdini, who was being carried along the sidewalk with several boys and dogs scampering along behind. Houdini waved at the carriages and wagons going by, and, when we got even with him, he waved at us. I waved back, and Houdini gave me a grin and threw his chin up in the air.

"Phew!" Hall said. "Somebody should give that boy a hosing down."

"Yes," I said, "the mystery of that trick was how he managed to stand the stench of the river."

"But really," Hall asked, "How do you think he did that?"

"Mesmerism, no doubt," I replied.

"Mesmerized the whole crowd?"

"And why not? Kings and emperors have been doing it for thousands of years."

These days, Houdini is fairly well known in the States as a star in that gaudy firmament known as "vaudeville." But back there in Chicago he was just a boy, and nobody knew who he was, even though he insisted that they did.

We got back to the hotel and I went to work on my letters. I tore up the one I was writing to Livy twice. Then I gave up completely, and decided that I would write nothing to Livy until I had some positive News. I decided on the same policy with the New York investors. Instead of letters, I took out my manuscript of *Adam's Diary* and sat down at the desk in my room and began working on it. After some time, there was a slow rapping at my door. I got up and answered it. It was Eugene Field. He had run into Hall down in the hotel lobby, found out from him that I was in the hotel, and had then rushed home to fetch a book he wanted to give me. We sat there and had a pleasant chat about old books, which Field loved to collect. He looked like an old book himself—a thin, old volume with a lot of worn pages. As soon as he left I returned to my writing, only to be interrupted about five minutes later by another knock—this knock fast and impudent. I rose again and swung the door open. This time it was my brother, Orion.

"What are you doing here?" I asked.

"Good to see you, too, Sam," Orion said.

"When I wrote you I was coming to Chicago, I didn't mean for you to come up here. How did you find out where I was staying?"

"Oh, you're an open book. I know you like to economize, so the Palmer House was out. I also know you don't like to economize too much. So it was just a matter of checking a few hotels."

"You've been traipsing all over the city asking for me at hotels?"

"Just up the street at the Grand Pacific. Guess what? You weren't there."

"Ha, ha."

"How's the machine coming?"

"Hall and I were just over there this morning. Paige is getting it ready to be seen by some investors. Just a minute. I want you to meet Hall."

I knocked on Hall's door, which opened on to my room. In a moment, Hall came out.

"Hall," I said, "I want you to meet my brother, Orion. Orion—this is Fred Hall, my manager for Webster and Company."

"Or-ee-yun?" Hall asked.

"That's right," Orion said, shaking Hall's hand.

"I thought your name was pronounced like the constellation," Hall said.

"No," Orion said, scratching his gray beard, "it's pronounced the way my mother pronounced it. And who's to say she was wrong?"

"Well," Hall said, "I've wanted to meet you."

"Why is that?" Orion asked.

"Well," Hall said, "I've just imagined you must be a remarkable person."

Orion laughed. "There have been those who have remarked *on* my person, like this youngster here." Orion nodded toward me. "But he never seems to mention the good turns I've done him. Lots of good turns. Like supplying him with the notes."

"Notes?" Hall asked.

I said, "He's talking about the journal he kept during our Overland Stage trip out west."

Orion said, "You know you could've never written *Roughing It* without the notes."

I said, "Whenever you mention the 'notes' I know you're up to something. So what is it this time?"

"What's what?"

"Your latest scheme."

"Now what makes you think I have a scheme? Can't I just visit you without you asking that?"

"All right. So you just came all this way up to Chicago to visit with me."

"Well. . . ."

"So you *are* up to something. You *did* receive my last check, didn't you?"

"Oh, certainly! Is that what you think? That I came here for money? You break my heart in two, you surely do."

"Time heals all."

"You're a hard man, Sam."

"And I wished to God you were the same. Maybe you'd finish what you start once in a while."

"You just can't understand anybody who acts upon Principle instead of personal interest. The road is broad for the man looking out for number one all the time. But for the man who stands on Principle, he has a fight on his hands. Sometimes, for conscience sake, he has to fight himself."

"I'd say you're an expert on that."

"Yes, I'm going to write a book on that very subject when I get on my feet."

"And when will that be? You've been working on getting on your feet for the last twenty years, I reckon."

"Say what you want, but my day is coming. Yes, my day is coming. I'm not through yet. No sir!"

"You're up to something. Spill it."

"Shoot!"

"Spill it."

"I'm going to land me a berth. A writing job."

"How? Where?"

"It's a mystery to you. It's a mystery to you that other people could see my quality. Well, the mystery is about to be revealed!"

"What are you blabbering about?"

"I've got prospects. As an author. And not as the brother of Mark Twain, don't you worry about that. I'm going to land a berth on a Newspaper all by myself."

"What Newspaper?"

"There's two I have in mind."

"One would be sufficient."

"There's two. Keokuk's *Gate City* and the St. Louis *Republican*."

"What would they want to hire you for?"

"Correspondent—to the World's Fair."

"Don't you think they have people lined up for those jobs already?"

"Fair hasn't started yet. Doesn't open full-blast 'til May 1st. That gives me time to make my pitch. I am not going to be just another reporter. Oh, no. I am going to have a view-point. Commentary. Commentary is what I'll have to sell. Orion Clemens' Commentary on the Decline and Destruction of Western Civilization as Illustrated by the Chicago's World's Fair!"

"The decline of—! That is the most idiotic, asinine, ignorant pile of swill I have ever heard! The fair illustrates no decline whatsoever! What are you thinking?"

"You can't see it, Sam. You're too engrossed. You're so engrossed you don't even know you touched on the whole text in *Connecticut Yankee*. You know it and you don't know it. Your moral cogitation is so muddy you don't even know why you're doing what you're doing. But looked at from the perspective of Principle, the signs are clear. As it says in the Good Book, *Revelations*, chapter—"

"Hold on! You start quoting *Revelations* to Newspaper editors and they'll throw you out on your ear! By God, I'll help 'em!"

"Well... Maybe I could tone it down a mite."

"Yes. Tone it down. Tone it *way* down."

"But I won't compromise Principle, no sir!"

"Not until you find another principle, which won't be long, I know."

Orion bowed his head. I put my hand on Orion's shoulder, and said, "Orion, you old fool."

Orion looked up at me, grinned, and said, "Sam, you young fool."

"I wish I was young. When I see you, I feel older by the second."

"Well, I don't want to age you any more than you already are, so I'll go now."

"Yes, well, Hall and I *do* have a lot of work to do."

"Work? Why, Sam, you know you've never done a day's work in your life. All you know how to do is play."

"Yes, well, by some miracle of God my play has paid all your bills for years."

"Yes, that's what it is. A miracle of God. And I do give the praise, thanks, and glory to *Him*."

Orion punctuated his utterance with his forefinger thrusting heavenward.

I looked over to Hall who was studying me out of the corner of his eyes. I turned back to Orion.

"Yes," I said, "let's all give thanks for the glad blessings of the Lord."

Orion went to the door, and I opened it.

"How long do you expect to be in Chicago?" I asked.

"A few days," Orion said. "My mission will take at least a few days."

"Well, stop by to see me when you complete your mission. I'll probably be here another couple days myself."

Orion nodded.

"Good to meet you, Mr. Clemens," Hall said.

"Mr. Hall," Orion said with a nod, and then he went out, and I closed the door behind him.

"So that's your brother," Hall said.

"That's my brother."

"I thought when you knocked, you had Paige in here."

I glanced at my pocket watch. It was ten minutes to four.

"No," I said, "and how much do you want to bet he's not coming?"

"Oh, I think he's coming. Paige likes to play the fool, cipher about while you're talking, and pretend he's not listening, but it's all part of his salesman's pitch. He thinks if he pretends he didn't hear 'no,' he can keep his prospect from believing he just said it."

"Now do you have *him* pegged! That's *exactly* what he does!"

"But he heard you today loud and clear. And—do you know? I think you frightened him."

"You do?"

"Yes."

"Well—good. Maybe a little fear will motivate him."

"I think he thought you were going to fire him."

"Really? You think so? I mean, I don't see how I *could*... *ever* fire him. After all, he's the designer of the machine."

"Yes. And so was Gutenberg."

"Eh?"

"Don't you know that Gutenberg was fired by his financial backer, Fust?"

"No. I never heard that one."

"Well, he was. Fust fired Gutenberg, and then brought in Schoeffer, the calligrapher from the University of Paris. And it was Schoeffer who completed the first printed book that in subsequent years was attributed to the hand of Gutenberg."

"Well, I never knew that, but it's a good thing to know. And I'll tell you something that's just occurred to me. If Paige doesn't come through that door within five minutes and tell me he's got the machine put back together, I'm going to serve him his walking papers and sue him in court for every penny I've invested."

"Really."

"Re—actually, no. But if I could—and if I won the court's judgment—and if Paige had the money to pay up—don't you know it would be heaven?"

There was another knock at the door. This time it was Paige. I let him in and I could tell by the look on his face that he had been eavesdropping on Hall and me from the other side of the door.

Paige asked, "Have I interrupted something important?"

I said, "Mr. Hall here was just giving me a lesson on the history of printing. Did you know that Fust fired Gutenberg?"

"Yes," Paige said, "I thought everyone knew that."

"I didn't. But that should come as no shock. There's a lot I don't know. I quit school at the age of twelve. But it hasn't stopped me from paddling my own canoe and knowing what's what and who's who when it comes to handling my own business. Did you get her put back together?"

"Yes."

"Every part?"

"Every part."

"Did you discharge Grandpa and the boys?"

"Yes."

"And give them their pay?"

"Yes. And fed them as well."

"Good. So the machine is working."

"It's working."

"Good. Say no more. That's all I want. It's working. I am satisfied. How about you, Hall? You satisfied?"

"I'm satisfied," Hall said.

"Good. Then we're all set for tomorrow."

"All set," Hall said. And then he turned to Paige, and said, "Here's something I suggested to Mr. Clemens earlier today, and it occurs to me now that maybe it's something we should do."

"What's that?" Paige asked.

Hall said, "I think we ought to take a look at a Linotype machine. Just to see how our competition is being used."

"I don't think that's necessary," Paige said.

"Ah!" I cried, "for once Paige and I agree on something! Wait a minute. That doesn't seem right. Why don't you want to see a Linotype?"

Paige said, "It's an unquestionably inferior machine. We have nothing to learn from it."

"I beg to differ," Hall said. "We can always learn something from a competitor, even an inferior competitor."

"The lesson of a bad example," I said.

"Something like that," Hall replied.

"You've done this sort of thing before, haven't you, Hall?" I asked.

"I always spy out my competitors. You'd be surprised what you can learn from people who do the same things you do."

Paige said, "I'm sorry, but I have never learned anything new from another mechanic."

I shot a glance over at Hall. I was thinking about the other designers of the typesetter: Farnham, Thompson, North, and Von Schriver.

Hall said, "We might not necessarily learn anything mechanical. I'm thinking more along the lines of sales, advertising, and marketing."

I said, "I'm beginning to see your point."

Paige said, "Well, if you want to inspect a Linotype, I suppose I could go along with you. To explain things."

"Now that's fine," I said. "Didn't you say something about a Newspaper, Hall?"

"The Chicago *Daily News* has a roomful of Linotypes, and I know their publisher, Victor Lawson."

"Well," I said, "let's go down there right now."

"Very well," Paige said, "only there is still the matter of my expense money. You said you'd have it for me."

"I said nothing of the kind! I said if you had the machine ready we'd *talk* about the money. How much do you need?"

"Seven thousand dollars."

"Seven thou—Good God! Seven thou—! I can't even say it! You've spent seven thousand dollars without my authorization?"

Paige dropped his hands to his sides. He looked over at Hall, then back to me, and said:

"Seven thousand dollars is not that much."

"Not that much? It *is* that much when you haven't got it!"

"But surely you have it."

"I have it and I don't have it."

"What does that mean?"

"It means I've already economized my family all the way to Europe and now you want seven thousand more of my dollars? Where do you want me to send my wife and children next? China?"

"I don't want you to send them anywhere. I just want to finish the machine."

"The machine *is* finished as far as I am concerned, and the prospective investors will see it tomorrow."

"Mr. Clemens!"

"How in God's name could you spend another seven thousand dollars?"

"Some of the machine's parts broke."

"Broke?"

"Yes, broke! They had to be recast. The recast parts did not fit in certain places. The tolerances of the die-forms were inaccurate. I was able to adjust some parts, other parts had to be recast again."

"Again?"

"It was all the unavoidable result of trying to combine the old, original machine with the new model. What we now have is a composite machine the flaws of which can only be discovered through repeated test runs. The only real solution for sound construction is to build an entirely new machine."

"An entirely new—! You listen to me! It's your job to *make* the machine we *now* have operate correctly! We're playing the hand we've been dealt! You understand that? Do you?"

"Yes."

I turned away from Paige, and said, "I want to see all the receipts and bills for the re-castings and for any other work and expenses which you have incurred. I cannot believe all your goddamned tinkering has amounted to seven thousand dollars. A few years ago I was paying out seven thousand dollars for your *yearly* salary."

"It was not just for the re-castings and adjustments. There were other expenses."

"What other expenses? I've already agreed in New York to pay you five thousand for your monthly stipend."

"Mr. Clemens, you ask for bills and receipts—you worry about a few dollars and cents—"

"A *few* dollars and cents!"

"—when the greatest invention in the history of the world—"

"Don't start that again!"

"—sits across the river in a warehouse for want of—"

"More money?"

"Mr. Clemens! We must not lose courage now. Not now! Only a little more work and I will be able to pronounce the machine finished!"

"God damn you!"

I spun about and stepped up to Paige, and looked at him. He looked back at me with absolute calm and confidence.

I said, "Eight years ago you pronounced the machine finished! Eight years ago! We could've marketed the machine then! But no! You said we must wait and wait and wait while you tried to figure out how to install the automatic justifier. And how much did you estimate that extra work would cost? Nine thousand dollars? Then adjusted upward to thirty thousand? And what's my investment now? One-hundred fifty thousand dollars—and climbing! We should've started manufacturing and selling the machine eight years ago *without* the justifier. Then—when we made some money—we could've added the justifier to later models! But no! Hell no! We had to submit to your chuckle-headed idea of perfection—and submit to it for *eight years*! I've lived through eight years of your tinkering and ciphering and fidgeting, waiting, and hoping, and praying, while the prime years of my life ran through my fingers! I was in the prime of my life when we partnered up! Now I'm a worn out old man, a worn out old man who's given you thousands upon thousands of my dollars and my wife's dollars to finish the machine! And *still* there's no end in sight! Where is the end, Paige? Where is the end? *Is* there an end?"

"Mr. Clemens!" Paige shouted above my voice, "I have incurred expenses! Legitimate expenses out of my own pocket! I am not a wealthy man like you."

"Oh *that's* it. I see it now. Oh, ho! I see it all. *That's* what you're after. Milk Clemens for all he's worth. Is that your game?"

"I have no 'game,' as you put it, sir, and I do not care to be spoken to in this manner."

"Well, why don't you hit the road, then?"

Paige's eyes narrowed. He had no intention of going anywhere until he got what he wanted.

"Mr. Clemens," Hall said, coming up beside me. "Maybe you could advance him a little money. He *has* been working hard."

I walked across the room and looked out the window. The traffic down on the street was getting mighty thick.

I said, "I did not agree to begin the five thousand dollar monthly stipend until next month. I'll write him a check for three thousand dollars. He has that coming for his monthly stipend under our old agreement."

"Three thousand is not enough," Paige said with ice in his voice.

"Make it enough!" I shouted, spinning back around to him. "Chicago's the city of making do! So you *make* do! And if you want more money, then you'd better make the demonstration of your life to the prospective investors tomorrow. Now. I'm writing you your check."

I reached inside my coat and took out my check book and sat down at the desk. I took out my fountain pen, and said, "I'm making it out for three thousand dollars."

I began writing the check, almost gouging the paper with the pen.

"Three thousand dollars," I said. "Three thousand dollars and no cents. That's what I've got. No sense! For giving you one more damn penny! I'm going to sign this check, but I want the bills and receipts for every penny of the seven thousand dollars you've spent, and I want them tomorrow."

I signed my name to the check, tore it from the book, and held it aloft between my thumb and forefinger.

I said, "Now take it and get out."

Paige looked at me, then at the check, then at me again.

I said, "I mean it. Take it."

Paige took the check.

I said, "Now get the hell out of here."

Paige started out.

Hall said, "We'll see you in the morning."

Paige stopped, looked at Hall, nodded, and then went out the door, closing it loudly behind him.

"I think you hurt him," Hall said.

"And he's hurt me. Down deep. He's gouging me, Hall, gouging me for every penny I've got! Every penny!"

"It takes money to make money."

"Money, money, money. That's all my troubles. I've gone money crazy!"

I collapsed into a chair, and held my head between my hands. "Damn it!" I said. "Damn it all to hell!"

I sat there for a minute or two, and Hall stood looking out the window.

After a while, Hall said, "Things are not so bad. Not so bad at all. The machine is ready to be seen. We have some promising investors coming to see it tomorrow. I think we should just relax now and let events take their natural course."

"You relax all you want," I said. "I'm planning on having a running fit, myself."

"We really should take a look at the Linotypes," Hall said.

"You ought to learn a new tune, Hall. The one you're singing is getting mighty old."

"All right," Hall said. "Just sit there."

I stood up, and said, "All right, all right. We will go see those goddamned Linotypes. Go get your hat and coat. Go on. I'll wait. Anything to get you to quit singing that tune."

Hall went into his room. I added, "You know you can't sing, Hall. People who can't sing should talk, not sing."

Hall came back in wearing his coat and hat, and said, "I'm talking now. Let's go."

I said, "Your talking sounds an awful lot like singing. It sounds like Wagner—just when you think it's going to stop, and your faith in God and heaven is restored, it starts up again and stumbles and tumbles you straight to hell."

We went out, and took the elevator down to the lobby.

Hall said, "We'll walk over there."

"Walk? Hall, I've walked half my life. Why can't we take a cab?"

"The walk will do us good."

"You mean it'll do *me* good. All right, let's get it over with."

We came out of the elevator, and, as we started across the lobby, the desk clerk said, "Mr. Clemens, I have a message for you."

I thanked the clerk and took the envelope he was handing me. It was a sealed envelope of printed stationery. On it, in a beautifully flowing hand, was written "Mark Twain." The printed return address on the envelope's corner had been crossed out and obliterated with several strokes of the pen, but I could still barely make out the address beneath the pen strokes. It was a place in New York City, somewhere on South Fifth Avenue. The name above the address was completely inked over and indecipherable. At that moment I could not figure out who sent the envelope, for I knew a lot of people in New York. I opened the envelope with my thumb nail and slid out a thin sheet of paper. It was a note written in that same beautifully flowing hand. It read:

"Dear friend Mark, if you will be in tonight, I would like to see you. Please leave word with the desk clerk to give me your room number. N.T."

N.T.? Who was N.T.? I wondered.

"Something wrong?" Hall asked.

"Just a strange message," I said.

"How so?"

"Somebody's sent me a note, but whoever it was just signed the initials N.T.; I have no idea who it is."

I turned to the desk clerk and said, "There's no postage on this envelope. How did it come in?"

"By messenger," the desk clerk said. "Not more than five minutes ago."

I pondered the situation a moment. Was it some kind of practical joke? Hall was peering over my shoulder now with curiosity, so I handed him the note.

"N.T." Hall said. "May I see the envelope?"

I handed the envelope to him. Hall studied it a second, his eyes narrowed. Then suddenly, his eyes widened.

"I know this address," Hall said. "So do you."

"I do?"

"35 South Fifth Avenue. That's the address of Nikola Tesla's laboratory. N.T."

"Of course! What a thick head I am! It's Tesla!"

"Yes, Tesla's here in Chicago. He's at the fair. In fact, some say he *is* the fair. Did you see the morning paper?"

"I haven't seen any paper all day."

Hall reached over the clerk's desk, snatched up the morning's paper, and slid it across the counter to me.

Nikola Tesla's picture shone out on the right side of the front page, while on the left side of the page was a drawing of the giant pleasure wheel designed by George Ferris. In thick, black type, the headline read: "WONDER OF THE WORLD!"

I ran my eyes over the text of the article. It was all about Tesla and the fair. It was telling how the fair would be using the alternating current system of electricity invented by Tesla. His system would be lighting all the incandescent light bulbs in the exhibition buildings and running all the electrical machinery on the grounds. It would be powering gigantic electrical lights that would shine up in great beams to the night sky, while other lights would illuminate and bejewel the outside walls of the fair's exhibition buildings in a dazzling array of colors. For the first time in history, a city at night would come alive with a noon-day glow by the power of electricity.

The fair had not opened yet, but, across the street from the main entrance, Buffalo Bill was presenting his "Wild West Show." In order to take advantage of the thousands of people coming to Buffalo Bill's arena with money in their pockets, the fair's organizers were selling passes to the unfinished fairgrounds. People were referring to these passes as "inspection tickets," for, with one of those tickets, anyone could set himself up as an "inspector" of the unfinished fairgrounds. People could study scaffolding and lumber piles and mud puddles and criticize or praise according to their temperament and politics. And they could note, perhaps, that, if the building of the fair was behind schedule, it was not because the workmen were laying down on the job. Building the fair was straining the capacity of every industry in the world. The things being done there had never been done before, and it was becoming obvious that the unprecedented would keep to no schedule. Although the interior of the Electrical Exhibition Building was still unfinished, on this day, the paper announced, special groups with their "inspection tickets" would attend lectures and demonstrations there by Nikola Tesla who was in the process of installing his electrical system throughout the fairgrounds.

"Well," I said, "if people didn't know who Tesla was before, they will now. He's going to be more famous than Edison."

Hall said, "I never thought any inventor would be more famous than Edison, not in my lifetime. But, you know, I think you're right. Tesla's a man who will change the world. Yes—now there's a man who will define the next millennium."

"But how did he know I was in Chicago? And—why did he sign his note N.T.?"

"Who knows? Tesla's a very strange bird. Who can guess why or how he does the things he does? I've heard some of the most peculiar things about him."

"Peculiar is all a matter of proportion. Perspective and proportion. One man's peculiar is another man's P's and Q's. And I always try to mind my own P's and Q's."

I turned back to the desk clerk, and said, "Mr. Nikola Tesla will be here tonight at—at—"

I turned to Hall, then back to the desk clerk.

"Well," I said, "Mr. Tesla didn't say *what time* he will be here to see me. But he will be here some time tonight. You'll be sure to let him know how to get up to my room when he comes, now, won't you?"

"Why, certainly, Mr. Clemens," the desk clerk said.

"And there's no need for him to send up a card. Just give him my room number."

"Yes, sir," the desk clerk said.

I turned to Hall, and said, "All right, let's go see those Linotypes."

"And we'll walk," Hall said.

"All right. We'll walk. I just hope I don't throw out my left knee. You know I've got rheumatism in that joint now."

"No, I didn't know."

"Well, I do."

"The walk will do you good. That's *why* you've got the rheumatism. You sit around too much. You've got to get up and move around. Keep limber."

Hall and I stepped out of the hotel and headed down the sidewalk. It was thick with office workers going home. We reached a wagon-tangled intersection and crossed it, barely avoiding getting trampled by a horse and flattened by a streetcar and crushed to pulp by a dray overburdened with barrels. We got across that street whole and intact and nearly sane, and continued on foot through the streets of always-changing, always-moving Chicago.

A dry, dusty wind whistled past us, scattering loose rubbish and sailing shreds of old Newspapers into the blue of the afternoon sky. The wind had moved all the coal dust out of the air, moved it off to wherever coal dust goes when it is no longer needed or enjoyed. This made breathing somewhat possible. I say "somewhat" because breathing is only somewhat possible inside a cyclone.

We shuffled along the crowded sidewalk, every few seconds being jostled and bumped by one of the herd. Ahead, a flotsam of black derbies bobbed like driftwood on the surface of a river, and, here and there, a lady's hat decorated the flow with a splash of color. The air boomed and cracked with the sound of steam hammers, and beneath all that booming and cracking was a dull roar of streetcars sliding along on their cables and horse hoofs and carriage wheels clattering and rattling over paving stones and Newsboys shouting at street corners. All that roaring and booming and cracking and banging and shouting vibrated in my head in a most disagreeable way until it felt like my skull was ready to split apart. Then my knee began bothering me; it was a dull ache in the left knee-cap. I began questioning my sanity for giving in to Hall's urgings, but it was too late to turn back; I could see the office building for the *Daily News* up ahead at the corner of Wells and Madison. We made it to the *Daily News* and went past a freight door and a long line of delivery wagons that several men were loading with bags of Newspapers, and on up to the building's main entrance.

"Feel that," Hall said, pointing down to the sidewalk.

He was talking about the vibrations coming from the steam printing presses inside. "That's gold," he said.

"Yes, their gold, not ours," I said.

"For the time being," he said.

We went inside and took the elevator up to the publisher's office. Victor Lawson had already gone home for the day, but his secretary was still there. He said he would be glad to show us their Linotype set-up.

The three of us went back down the elevator to the composing room. When we entered their shop, forty or fifty Linotypes were working away, making a clattering racket that would wear out a rabbit's ear drums. I thought of the elegant, cat-like purr of Paige's machine, and a warm, cozy feeling came over me, the sort of feeling a spinster has, I suppose, when she hears the caterwauling of her sister's nine children.

Hall and I approached one of the Linotypes. An operator was working at its keyboard, his fingers flying with great expertise. At the end of each word he would hit a little space bar lever on the left side of the keyboard. With every stroke he made on a key, a brass matrix would slide out of the distributor and down through the inside of the magazine with a loud whish and plunk. The wheels and their belts whizzed and whirled, clicked and clattered. Mechanical arms would lift, drop with a snap, and lift again. A line of brass matrix slugs—negative molds of letters—slid along a little track like prisoners lining up for a firing squad. When a line of brass slugs would be completed, a little mechanical finger would push forward and squeeze the slugs together, giving the line a crude and inartistic justification. A pause. Then the line of brass matrix slugs would suddenly be fired upon with a sizzling spray of molten lead. Another pause. The solid but not-cooled lead slug would then be moved away by another mechanical finger.

I looked down through the tangle of mechanical arms and pulleys and studied the molten lead sizzling and bubbling in its pot.

I said, "That little crucible pot in the machine there for melting the lead—seems like a dangerous device. You ever have any problems with it?"

"Well, not really," the publisher's secretary said.

"No?"

"Well. . . once in a while, if the operator doesn't put enough brass matrices in a line, the molten lead will be ejected through the gaps and out of the machine. When that happens it scalds and burns the operator. We call it 'the squirt.'"

"'The squirt?'"

The publisher's secretary nodded, and said, "The operator has to watch out for that."

"Yes," I said, "I suppose he would want to avoid that."

I walked around to the back of the machine, then came around to the front and looked at Hall. He was smiling.

"Makes a lot of noise," I said.

"Yes," said the secretary, "but you get used to it. It's very reliable. A real workhorse."

"How often do you have to shut her down for repairs?" I asked like a fool.

"Repairs?" the secretary asked.

"I mean, when it breaks down," I said.

The secretary sort of smirked, but he was trying not to show it, for he knew all about our work with the Paige typesetter.

The secretary said, "The Linotype doesn't break down, not so far, at least. The operator checks it out after each run, and the mechanic shuts it down and opens it up for oiling once a month. But repairs? We figure by the time it breaks down, we will have profited from its use a thousand times over. It probably won't be repaired when it breaks down, just discarded and replaced with another machine."

I felt like the secretary was making an idle boast. How little did I know that what he was speaking was about as close to the truth as a body could get.

I said, "Well, that's good. That's all fine. I'm glad to see you're happy."

I had seen enough and told Hall so. We said goodbye to the publisher's secretary and left.

When we got to the lobby, I said, "We've got 'em beat, Hall. That Linotype ain't worth a damn. It's got the squirts. And did you hear all the noise it made?"

"Yes," Hall said, "and I saw all the type that it was setting up."

"Ah, that's nothing. When Paige gets his machine up and running, it's going to out-typeset the Linotype the same way the tortoise out-ran the hare. We've been slow getting started, but we've been running steady, and the finish line is in sight! I tell you, we're going to run the Linotype people out of business!"

"Maybe," Hall said. "Let's just take one thing at a time."

"That's what I like about you, Hall. You don't get excited and you don't get sidetracked—even when the facts are telling you everything's a go. You just stay calm and cool even though you know you're holding four aces! I tell you one thing—I'd never play poker with *you*!"

We went on up to the lobby entrance. I opened the door and saw a young lady approaching from outside. She had blond hair and penetrating blue eyes. I pulled the door back and held it open for her to pass through.

"Miss," I said, tipping my derby.

The young lady nodded to me, looked away, and then jerked her head back suddenly to look at me again. I knew the look on her face, for I had seen it many times before. She had recognized me as "Mark Twain." Usually this recognition was followed by some kind of praise, or request for advice, or my signature on their card, or—sometimes—a request for a loan, an investment in a business scheme, or an outright gift to them of a sum of money. I braced myself for just such a response from the young lady, but none came. She only looked at me, her eyes wide. She was thinking something—but what, I had no idea. It was only for a moment, but it seemed like a long time.

Finally she said, "Thank you." And she turned and went past me into the lobby.

Hall and I went on out to the sidewalk. I looked over at Hall and he raised his eyebrows twice and grinned.

"Now, Hall," I said, "you're a married man."

"So are you," Hall said.

"Ha! I'm so married, I'm petrified."

We went on our way down the sidewalk. It seemed a trivial incident, but it was not trivial. That young lady had recognized me—and her recognition would change everything for both her and me—very, very soon.

Chapter Two

Bolt from the Blue

> Idiots! They said it wouldn't go; and they wanted
> to examine it, and spy around and get the secret out
> of me. But I beat them. Nobody knows what makes it
> move but me; and it's a new power—a new power, and
> a thousand times the strongest in the earth!
>
> — The Professor, *Tom Sawyer Abroad*

I was first introduced to Tesla at a dinner hosted by George Westinghouse about 1890, I believe, but I first heard of Tesla some few years earlier—around 1888—when I first saw his alternating current patents. I immediately recognized that these patents were the most important invention since the telephone. I would have invested in Tesla's company then and there, but my finances were already heavily extended with the Paige typesetter.

Soon after I saw Tesla's patents they were purchased by Westinghouse and Tesla's fame began to soar meteorically. To this day, I am not sure exactly how much Tesla made on the deal, but whatever amount the initial payment made to Tesla was, it was a mere bagatelle compared to the royalties that were promised to him. At the rate of $2.50 per horsepower of electricity sold, Tesla was on his way to becoming the richest man on earth—literally. And, of course, that fact brought him to the attention of the few other richest men on earth. Do you think they wanted to welcome him to their club? Does a wildcat share its meat?

I had read about Tesla and had heard about Tesla, but these preliminaries did not prepare me in the least for meeting Tesla himself. I have met just about every famous person in my time with the exceptions of Billy the Kid and Jessie James. On reflection, perhaps I did meet Jessie once; at least I know I was robbed. Most of the famous people I have met have been a disappointment. I have no doubt that I have been a disappointment to all of them, too. Famous people hardly ever live up to their advertising; they are nearly always a little less of everything that they are supposed to be. But Tesla was something more than his advertising made out, something more, perhaps, than advertising was able to express, something that there is no word for in the English language, nor in any other language in the world, I suppose. For this reason, as well as another, I have never attempted to write about Tesla for publication. I have literarily exploited the characters of a number of friends and relations who I have deemed unique and interesting, but not Tesla. You see, no one would believe Tesla; he is too much—too much of that something for which there is no name. The truth about Tesla was stranger than any fiction I could ever invent. Fiction deals in probabilities—while Tesla dealt—and deals—with improbabilities so far from ordinary experience that—well—you would just get lost while you're on your way trying to measure the distance.

As for the other reason I have never written about Tesla: he is *verboten*. As of 1903, Tesla has ceased to exist as a public person by decree of J.P. Morgan. Actually and precisely, Morgan did not decree that Tesla had ceased to exist; Morgan decreed that Tesla *never had existed*. More than once over the years my friend Henry Rogers has advised me that it would be unwise for me to mention Tesla in any of my published writings. For these reasons, I have made no reference whatsoever to Tesla in any work of mine meant for publication, not even in my autobiography. Yet, I probably know Tesla as well as anyone.

Tesla himself is only amused by all of this. Fame and fortune have never been Tesla's guiding stars; they have only been means to further ends; he has always aimed at Something Else. Knowledge? Yes, but knowledge applied to humanity, given to humanity, developed in humanity in order to transform humanity. Into what? Something more than it is—something more than it is now advertised to be—something more than a cow on its way to the slaughterhouse. Tesla's aim has been something along these lines. But when man is free, what will man do *then*? I think Tesla has something in mind here, too, or he is in contact with someone or something that has something more in mind for man—the next step for our species. Then there are those others who want to keep us cows trotting down the chute to their own particular slaughterhouse. . . .

That night at the Westinghouse dinner I had just come through the door when Westinghouse took hold of my arm and said, "Clemens, he is here."

I turned in the direction that Westinghouse was pulling me and saw an extremely tall man surrounded by a group of women. I immediately knew it was Tesla. There was something about him that I would call "unearthly," also something about him that I would call "earthly". Those two qualities orbited

"Watch! Watch me reverse it!"

about him invisibly, charging his whole being with a kind of physical energy and high consciousness I have never encountered in another human (assuming for the sake of argument that Tesla is human).

"It's him," I said.

"Yes," Westinghouse said, "let's see if I can pry him away from the ladies."

Westinghouse went up to the group and said, "Sorry, ladies, but I need Mr. Tesla. Can you get along without him for a moment?"

A strikingly beautiful woman said, "Only for a moment. Then you must release him. There is more to life than business."

"Only for a moment. Come along, Tesla," Westinghouse said, dragging Tesla by his arm.

Then Tesla saw me. He had recognized me as "Mark Twain," and I felt disappointed that he did not see me as I really was. But as he approached, the expression on Tesla's face evolved from recognition, to awe, to a kind of smiling, boyish joy. He didn't seem to be looking at "Mark Twain" anymore, but at Santa Claus. I had not expected this. I had expected a grave, intense thinking machine. But the Tesla I saw was a fantastically tall boy, and it was Christmas morning.

"What happened to the frog?" Tesla asked, beaming.

"The frog?" I asked, completely lost.

"Yes. The frog! What ever became of him?"

I looked over at Westinghouse, hoping he could give me a clue. Westinghouse was giving me a grin that was all dollars and cents. Then it dawned on me. The frog.

The damned frog. The dirty, damned frog of Calaveras County! The frog from that villainous backwoods sketch I had penned twenty-five years earlier when I was a callow youth destitute of wit and learning. I had vacillated on my estimation of the literary value of that frog story for years, and had finally settled on the public policy of acknowledging that, for its particular line, it was a good folk-tale. Privately and secretly, though, I knew the truth; it was only a fragment of something that might have been worthwhile, if effort had been applied to it. But when I wrote it, I applied no effort of any kind to it. It was only a fleeting thought, a fleeting after-thought, but a fleeting after-thought that had introduced me to the world as "Mark Twain" and that had, through the years, achieved a world-girdling fame. I could do only one thing with such a fortunate child of my imagination—pretend that I was proud of it.

"The frog," I said.

"Yes, yes, the frog," Tesla said.

"Dan'l Webster?" I asked.

Tesla bent double with laughter. He straightened, and said, "Dan'l Webster! What a name for a frog!"

Tesla broke into laughter again. I looked back to Westinghouse. The dollars and cents were ringing up his bicuspids faster than ever. I looked back to

Tesla. He was trying to compose himself. He was preparing himself. For a story. From me.

I thought: If Nikola Tesla wants to hear about that damned frog, I'll tell him about that damned frog.

"The frog," I said.

"Yes. The frog," Tesla said, like a child waiting for a bedtime story.

"Well," I started, "you know, Dan'l Webster belched out all that shot. And when he did, he looked around and looked around and he saw nobody was watching, except maybe one fellow in the corner, and he was drunk. So Dan'l Webster took a jump—and another, and that second jump put him out the door. And he just kept jumping all the way back to the swamp. When Jim Smiley came back and saw Dan'l gone, he lit out for the swamp, and Smiley slopped around down there for an hour or two trying to catch him, but Dan'l would always slip through his fingers. Finally Smiley gave up, and said, 'Just look at him settin' there all wise and satisfied and full of flies. It's clear—Dan'l Webster is educated now and won't work for nobody exceptin' hisself!'"

Tesla bent double again, letting out a high-pitched laugh. Westinghouse's smile had rung up all the profits and was just beaming with the pay-off. I thought my little impromptu tale as devoid of wit as its predecessor, but I stood there, pretending to be satisfied.

Tesla straightened out and wiped a tear of laughter from his eye, then said, "When I was a boy, I was very sick. They said I was dying. I said to my father, 'If you will let me be an engineer, perhaps I will get better.' He said, 'I will let you. You must get better.' Then he set down a book he had brought me from the library. I picked it up. It had a picture of a frog on the cover. The picture made me smile. I opened the book. It was written in English. I liked to read English. I read about Jim Smiley and his jumping frog, Dan'l Webster, way out in the Wild West of America. I laughed. I didn't feel so bad anymore. I got better."

"I–I never imagined. I never imagined that story could do. . . that."

Tesla said, "You have sent joy throughout the world. May that joy, in its long journey, find its way home again to you."

Nikola Tesla was born during a gigantic electrical storm on the stroke of midnight between July 9th and 10th in the year 1856 in the village of Smiljan, which was in the province of Lika, which was held by the Austro-Hungarian Empire as part of Croatia and Slovenia. The village of Smiljan was probably not much different than my boyhood home of Hannibal. Tesla's father was a parish priest in the Serbian Orthodox Church and wanted his son to follow him in that profession. But Nikola had other ideas.

At the age of five Tesla invented a bladeless waterwheel. At the age of nine he invented a motor powered by sixteen June bugs. By contrast and comparison, at the age of nine, I was squashing June bugs with my big toe. If I use myself as a measuring rod to get at the size of Tesla, you can see that if I am two fathoms, then Tesla is twenty thousand leagues.

Both Nikola and his brother, Dane, seem to have been born with extraordinary powers of the mind. It was not just that they were inventive or unusually quick thinkers; it was that their very *way* of perceiving the world was entirely different from everybody else. Whenever Nikola or Dane would get excited by anything, their normal field of vision was obstructed by flashes of light and the appearance of images. These images would be three-dimensional and fully colored. If someone spoke a word it would produce the corresponding image in the boys' field of vision; the word "dog," for example, would produce a fully colored, three-dimensional image of a dog. And it would not be a vague approximation, either. It would be a *particular* dog which they had seen somewhere at sometime in the past, and thus it would be an exact *memory* dredged up from the bottom of their minds, a memory complete down to every last detail of form and color.

I once asked Tesla if these images were like a colored stereoscopic photograph, and he replied in the negative. He said, "I can walk around them on all sides. I can even put my hand through them. They float there, existing in real space. I can even set them in motion, and stand back and watch them as they move, work, and live."

Sometimes the boys could not tell if what they were seeing was real or an image. But usually they could tell the difference. The image would usually be something out of place, or a thing that suddenly came into being where there had been nothing before. Tesla insists that the images they saw were not hallucinations, but a kind of memory, a memory so exact in every detail that it was consciously perceived as it was originally experienced. The images, then, were a projection of some kind from the deepest part of their minds.

Dane's great promise ended abruptly at the age of 12, when he died after a fall from a horse. If he had lived there is no telling what the two brothers could have accomplished together.

As the years passed, Tesla made prodigious progress. He learned several languages, memorized long passages of poetry, built mechanical models of full-sized machines, and began his first efforts to design a flying machine. He read about Niagara Falls and imagined a big wheel operated by the majestic, flowing waters, a big wheel that would run all the machinery of the world. He told his uncle that someday he would go to America and carry out his vision.

During his boyhood Tesla was struck with a series of mysterious illnesses. Finally he was struck with a recognizable malady—cholera, and everyone thought he was going to die. I believe that was when he was given my Jumping Frog book.

Tesla gradually managed to get control of his memory-images. He did this by imagining worlds of his own. Every night, he would set forth on imaginary journeys. His imaginary worlds were filled with things and people every bit as real to him as the people and things of our "real" world. Then, at seventeen, he found he could imagine into existence images of three-dimensional fully colored machines. This led to Tesla's unique method of invention, which has nothing in common with Edison's trial-and-error method. Tesla was able to visualize his inventions in fully colored three dimensions. He could see every part of the machine, every detail, the kind of metal out of which the machine was made and the minute scratches on its surface, if it had any. Tesla's visions of his imaginary machines were so exact that he could tell exactly what part of a machine would break down and how long it would take for it to break; for he would do *imaginary test runs* on his machines. These test runs could go on for hours, weeks, or months at a time. Tesla could look in on these test runs at intervals, to see how they were progressing. When actual, physical models of the machines were constructed and tested, Tesla's engineers would find that the real machine behaved exactly as Tesla's imaginary test-runs had predicted!

Such a power as Tesla's could not be had without a cost. Tesla became beset with a number of unexplainable fears. I can state what I know of Tesla's fears from direct observation. He is terrified of germs and takes extreme measures to avoid them. As a general rule, he does not shake hands with people. He never wears a shirt collar more than once. When he eats (which is usually alone) he always uses exactly 18 napkins, which he tosses to the floor in sequence through the course of his meal. He cannot stand the sight of pearls; they literally turn his stomach. He cannot bear to touch the hair of other people. When Tesla pours a drink, or lifts a spoon of food, he has to calculate its cubic volume before consuming it. He counts his steps when he walks and memorizes the number of steps between places he frequents. Then he always has to take exactly that same number of steps every time he goes from one of those places to the other.

These and other fears and obsessions separate Tesla from the rest of his fellow human beings. He is a living paradox: a highly sociable, unsociable man. Understand that Tesla has always been a generous and affectionate person—up to a point. Beyond that point, a line is drawn and no one dare cross it.

In 1875 Tesla enrolled at the Austrian Polytechnic School in Graz, his tuition being paid by the Military Frontier Authority.

At the Polytechnic School, Tesla encountered a Gramme Machine, a direct-current electrical device which could be used as either a motor or dynamo. Tesla noticed that the machine sparked a great deal as it operated. He suggested to his professor that if the wire-wound armature and commutator were removed, and the machine switched to alternating current, the sparking could be eliminated. The professor dismissed Tesla's suggestion as an impossible idea.

Tesla's fellowship evaporated and he was faced with the possibility that he might have to drop out of school. He tried to borrow money, but failed. Then he tried to gamble to raise money. He became an expert billiard player—too expert. The city police of Graz shut Tesla down and the Polytechnic School expelled him.

Now Tesla turned to gambling full-tilt. His luck in cards went bad—and from bad to worse. Finally his mother came to him one day, held out a roll of bills, and said, "Go to the card tables and enjoy yourself. The quicker you lose everything we have, the better it will be for all of us."

That was the end of Tesla's gambling.

In 1879 Tesla's father died. After that, Tesla went to Prague and sat in the university library reading books. Sometimes, when he could, he would sneak into a classroom and listen to one of the professors lecture. He could not afford tuition. This went on for nearly two years, when Tesla decided he had learned all he could from the university. He left without a degree; he was essentially self-taught.

In 1881, Tesla got a job as a draftsman at the Central Telegraph Office in Budapest. At night he worked on his ideas about dynamos using alternating current electricity.

He worked day and night without sleep, and almost without food. The pressure built in his mind and body. But Tesla went on, working day and night. And then—of course something had to give. Tesla collapsed. He was carried home in a delirium.

Tesla lay in his bed in complete agony. He could not stand to be touched. He was awakened from a confused sleep by the sound of a giant gong being struck rapidly by some madman. He pleaded for the noise to stop. Those who were attending him finally discovered that the gong Tesla was hearing was *the ticking of a watch three rooms away.*

It was discovered that Tesla had become super-sensitive to all vibrations: mechanical, sound, and light. He could hear a fly land on a nearby table with a thud. A carriage passing by outside on the street shook his body down to his bones. The voices of people in the room sounded like thunder. When he heard the sound of a train whistle twenty miles away, the shrill noise seemed to be splitting his head in two.

His doctors prescribed large doses of potassium, and, with the unassailable pseudo-logic of know-nothing experts, pronounced Tesla's mysterious ailment incurable.

Tesla's pulse was highly erratic, dropping below normal some of the time, while at other times speeding up to as many as 260 beats per minute. It was when this was brought to Tesla's attention that he began to affect his own recovery. He began concentrating on his pulse, and found that he could control it at will. He kept up the concentration until his pulse leveled out.

Tesla's friend, Anital Szigety, a master mechanic, came for a visit. Tesla told Szigety about his progress with his pulse. Szigety was an amateur athlete and convinced Tesla that exercise was the key to his recovery.

Szigety began an exercise program with Tesla lying in bed, then sitting in a chair, and finally outside in the garden.

Szigety took Tesla out in a carriage on a sunny day. As they passed under a bridge and into its shade, Tesla felt a blow on the back of his head. Tesla found any abrupt interruption of strong sunlight would cause a crushing pressure on his skull.

In the dark, Tesla could sense the position of an object at a distance of twelve feet by a tingling sensation on his forehead. Tesla told me, "It was a creepy sensation. I felt like I had the powers of a bat."

With exercise, all of these strange sensations began to leave Tesla.

I asked Tesla what he thought was the cause and nature of his illness. This is what he said:

"I have never talked about this before with anyone, Mark. But I will tell you. It was not really an illness, but a *transformation*, a preparation for the work of my life. What induced it? I do not know. Some outside force was at work, some intelligence, or, perhaps, some aspect of nature, the unfolding of the flower of humanity signified by the transit of Venus across the face of the sun. The time had come for a new development in the human race. And it came this way. A revelation. A revelation as the ancient prophets had their revelations. Mine was a revelation of the nature of the physical energies of the universe. The Great Flow of the Great Circuit—and I was the valve."

Tesla began to gradually mend; not physically, there was nothing physically wrong with him. But the thing that had snapped in his mind and had let in a flood of perceptions began to mend.

In February of 1882, Tesla was well enough to walk in a park in Budapest. One evening, while walking in the park with Szigety, Tesla's glimpse of the setting sun triggered one of his visions. Suddenly, before him floated an alternating current motor operating at full speed. He walked over to it and studied it in detail. It looked like the one he had been working on in his mental workshop before his illness struck. But this motor was different in a few details. Those few differing details solved the problems which had brought Tesla to a deadlock.

"Look at it," Tesla said, transfixed. "It's beautiful."

"Look at what?" Szigety asked.

Tesla circled around the motor to study its other side.

"What are you doing?" Szigety asked.

"Watching it work," Tesla said. He came back in front of his visionary motor, reached out and thrust his hand into the machine's rotating magnetic field.

"Watch me," Tesla said, "watch me reverse it."

"Reverse what?" Szigety asked with growing concern.

"My motor here!" Tesla said.

Tesla saw the direction of the rotating magnetic field reverse. The red ball of the sun began setting against Tesla's vision. The motor became translucent, suffused with the sun's red glow. Tesla could see into the internal parts of the motor as if it were made of glass. An alternating current of electricity would charge a coil which would attract a magnet. The charge would fade and be replaced by an overlapping current nearby. This would pull the magnet around. A succession of charges and fades of current in the coil pulled the magnet in a circle. Tesla saw that the magnet was always facing the electrical charge and moving along with it, just as the daylight of the Earth always faced the sun and moved along with the sun's apparent motion in the sky. Tesla was seeing on a grand, cosmic scale a model of his principle of energy in the action of the sun setting over the horizon—while the sun filled the glowing spaces of his visionary motor.

"As above, so below," Tesla whispered.

Tesla felt light, powerful, and free. Like the visionary magnet in his visionary machine, he wanted to take flight and follow the sun in its retreat, follow it, like the magnet followed the electric charge, follow it across mountains, lakes, valleys, oceans, continents—follow it around the very circumference of the world.

Then Tesla remembered a passage from Goethe's *Faust* and finally understood its meaning, a meaning deeper than he could have ever imagined before. He began to recite the passage as Szigety looked on, fearing for the sanity of his friend.

"The glow retreats, done is the day of toil;
It yonder hastes, new fields of life exploring;
Ah, that no wing can lift me from the soil,
Upon its track to follow, follow soaring!"

Szigety made Tesla sit down on a park bench. But Tesla could not be silent. He picked up a tree limb, broke it in half, and used the sharp end to scratch a line in the dust at their feet. There in the dust Tesla drew a diagram of the first alternating current motor in the known history of the world. Szigety began to understand. Tesla stood up, teetering on his feet as he bent over to complete his sketch. The infant electrical age had just taken its first upright step.

In Tesla's mind he was already fabulously rich, even though his meager pay indicated otherwise. He described his position at that time in this way: "The last 29 days of every month were my only periods of financial deprivation."

Then through family friends he was recommended for a job with Continental Edison in Paris. His position was that of troubleshooter, someone who could work the kinks out of the electrical systems of Europe. In Alsace, he built his first crude alternating current motor.

When a promised bonus failed to materialize, and none of his supervisors could be induced to pay him, Tesla resigned from the Edison Company. But

Charles Batchelor, the manager of the Edison electrical plant in Paris, recognized Tesla's abilities and urged him to go to America, and went so far as to write Tesla a letter of introduction to Edison. Well, this was Tesla's meat. Here was his chance to finally go to America, the land of his dreams!

Tesla sold all his possessions and junked his alternating current motor. He put everything he had in one valise, including his letter of introduction to Edison, and headed for the railroad station. When he got to the station, he discovered his money and ship ticket were gone. He proceeded on his train journey, talked his way on board the ship, and arrived in America with only a few pennies in his pocket. At least that is the story he has told to the magazines and Newspapers.

What he told me one night about how he came to America had a little more detail. It went like this:

The day after Batchelor told Tesla he would recommend him to Edison, Tesla began selling all his books and furniture. Tesla was out on the Boulevard St. Marcel in front of his hotel helping a man load a bookcase into a wagon, when he noticed two men watching him from across the street. He called to them, asking them what they wanted. Instead of answering, they turned and walked away, not saying a word.

That night Tesla was walking back to his hotel after selling a rare book. He walked along the Seine. It was a moonlit night, and as he walked, the moon slipped behind a cloud. It got dark very quickly. Tesla heard a sound like pebbles falling upon the pavement. It seemed to be coming from behind him. He stopped and looked back, but saw nothing but darkness and a few winking, reflecting lights bouncing off the surface of the Seine. He turned back around.

A man stood directly in front of him. The man held a knife. Tesla stepped back, but the man lunged forward, slashing at Tesla, the knife blade making a brilliant, white arc in the velvety darkness. Tesla grabbed the arm that held the knife and tried to hold the flashing blade away. The blade came close to Tesla's face. He could tell it was razor sharp. The blade hovered near Tesla's throat. Tesla could feel the man's breath on his face.

Then there was a crack in the air—a gun shot!

The man with the knife dropped into the darkness. Tesla heard a splash, looked down, and saw the man floating face-first down the Seine.

Then Tesla heard quick steps approaching. Out of the darkness appeared a well-dressed man in a long coat and a tall silk hat. He spoke to Tesla in English.

"Go away from here. Now!" the man in the silk hat said.

"But—"

"No buts, Mr. Tesla. Go. Meet me tomorrow at noon on the steps of Notre Dame Cathedral."

"You shot him—"

"Get out of here!" the man in the silk hat said, and he shoved Tesla with great force.

Tesla began walking away quickly, counting his steps as he went. Then he stopped. He knew he should call for the police. He turned around and retraced his steps to the place of the bizarre incident. No one was there; no man with a silk hat, no body floating in the river.

Tesla turned, took a few steps, and then began running. Tesla reached his hotel, ran up the stairs to his room, went inside, and locked his door.

The next day, at noon, Tesla stood on the steps of Notre Dame.

The man in the silk hat came up to Tesla. Although Tesla had been looking for him, he did not see the man in the silk hat approach; he seemed to appear from behind Tesla suddenly.

The man in the silk hat said, "You must be more careful, Mr. Tesla. We cannot have you being killed. It just would not do."

"Who are you?" Tesla asked.

"You might think of me as your protector."

"Protector? Why do I need protecting?"

"You ask that after what happened last night?"

"Who was that man? Why did he try to kill me? Why did you kill him?"

"What makes you think I killed him? What makes you think he is dead?"

"He is not?"

"We only kill when it is necessary. We prefer other methods of conflict. Killing, whether wholesale in war or retail in the dispatch of an individual, is only the last movement in the great ritual of conflict. Magnificent building, isn't it, Mr. Tesla?"

The man in the silk hat was looking up at the cathedral.

"Conflict," the man in the silk hat said, "conflict. Without conflict nothing can exist, nothing can manifest, nothing can stand. This building is nothing but conflict. It is a great idea of conflict made real. For every stress in it, there is a counter-stress, for every weight, a levity. It is said that from conflicting ideas, light bursts forth. Would you agree with that, Mr. Tesla?"

"Who are you? And who do you represent?"

"Come. Let us sit over there on the bench. Here."

The man in the silk hat held a bag out to Tesla. Tesla took it and opened it up. Inside the bag was bird seed.

"For the pigeons," the man said, "I knew you'd want to feed the pigeons."

The man in the silk hat held his gloved hand out gesturing for Tesla to go with him to the bench. Tesla studied the man for a moment; then walked with him to the bench, and there they sat down.

Tesla began throwing out the seed to the pigeons.

"How do you know I like to feed the pigeons?" Tesla asked.

"We know. We know many things. For example: your grandfather. He had very long teeth in front, I mean, his two front upper teeth. They were very long, weren't they?"

"Yes. And I suppose you will not tell me how you know that either."

"You see, that's what your name 'Tesla' means in your native tongue: *tesla*, 'spade' or 'adz.' It is in reference to the upper teeth. Those long upper teeth cut like an adz, something like the teeth of a beaver, the word *beaver* itself evolving from the ancient Egyptian *bava* 'to cut with an axe.' Your ancestors had good teeth for biting ropes, for cutting through seals. That's what your forefathers did. Long ago. They were breakers of seals, solvers of secrets. We are very interested in your lineage, Mr. Tesla. And you, Mr. Tesla, you are the culmination of that lineage. Would you believe me if I told you we have your complete genealogy tracing back to the year 13,500 B.C.?"

"No. No, I would not. I would believe you are a mad man."

"You believe I am mad?"

Tesla nodded.

"You are an unconvincing liar, Mr. Tesla. If you believed I was mad, you would not say so."

"And why not? You are mad, but you have given me bird seed, and for that I will listen to your ramblings."

"A little better. You try to help your lie with a truth. I know you appreciate the bird seed, and you are quite welcome. But as for my madness, let us both concede that I am quite sane. You just do not know who I am or how I know the things I do. I cannot answer all your questions. But I have something which will answer those questions for which you now need answers."

The man in the silk hat held out a book. It had an old green faded cloth cover.

"Go on," the man in the silk hat said, "take it."

Tesla took the book and opened it to the title page, which read, "Order of the Flaming Sword."

Tesla flipped the pages and read, "Chapter One: The Secret History of the World."

Tesla looked up at the man in the silk hat.

"What is this?" Tesla asked. "Some kind of Masonic tract?"

"Hardly. Read the book and you will see what it is. You will understand. The Order of the Flaming Sword is a secret society which has existed in all countries and in all times."

"Then it is Masonic."

"In some cases it has existed within Masonry. It has also existed within the Church. But it is not Masonry and it is not the Church. And as I have said, it has existed in every country, but it does not represent any one country."

"I am not a joiner," Tesla said. "I belong to no secret societies, and never will."

"Oh, Mr. Tesla! Mr. Tesla! You already *are* a member of a secret society! You have been born to the Order of the Flaming Sword only you do not know it yet!"

"You *are* mad."

"Read the book, Mr. Tesla, and you shall see if I am mad. And after you have settled that, I want you to ask yourself these questions: Why were the cherubim ordered by Yahweh to stand guard over the Tree of Knowledge and the Tree of Life? What did the Elohim fear? And, finally, Mr. Tesla, what will *you* do when you grasp the Flaming Sword yourself and set the world ablaze with its power?"

The man in the silk hat stood up and looked at Notre Dame Cathedral, and said, "The spirit comes forth from the day, and the letter passes away."

The man in the silk hat looked at Tesla and said, "When you understand that, Mr. Tesla, you will understand everything you need to know."

The man in the silk hat turned and began walking away.

Tesla asked, "How do I contact you again?"

The man turned back and said, "If we need to meet again, I will contact you." With that, the man in the silk hat turned and walked away. A closed carriage pulled up. The man in the silk hat opened its door, got in, and closed the door. Tesla noticed that the door of the carriage bore a brass plate with the number "44" engraved upon it. The carriage drove away, disappearing into the streets and crowds of Paris.

Tesla went home and began reading the book. It was a strange book, even for Tesla who had, in his time, read several strange books. The green book bore no author's name, but a preface stated that some of the maps and drawings in the book were close reproductions of the originals held in the Atlantean archives of the Vatican. These originals had, in turn, been acquired from the library at Alexandria. These Alexandrian originals were themselves copies of even more ancient manuscripts from Poseid. There was a chapter on the history of the world going back 500,000 years. It told about god-like beings that came here from other worlds and dimensions and created "Adamic mankind" by a breeding program with themselves and primates already existing on Earth. It told about the rise of Atlantis, described its society, its religion, and its science. It told about the planet Mars and a civilization there, and about beings who lived underground on the Moon. Another chapter was on language, symbols, numerology, and the science of karmic frequency. This science holds that one's time of birth and death is predetermined and interrelated to the times of the births and deaths of all other beings in the universe. Another chapter was on geology, chemistry, alchemy and archemy. That chapter described how continents moved over the surface of the globe during long geological epochs, how volcanoes formed, and how gold "grows" in volcanoes. There were chapters on electricity, magnetism, atoms, sub-atoms, ether, and gravity. There was a chapter on dreams, how to see the past and future, and how to will your mind to leave your body and go to distant places. There was a chapter on the Great Pyramid at Giza explaining why and how it had been built and how it was used before it was damaged.

There were other chapters to this book that Tesla told me about, but this is all that I can remember. As Tesla described it, it was a fantastic book. The more Tesla read of it, the more sense it made to him.

When Tesla told me about reading this book, I stopped him in his tale to tell a tale of my own.

I said, "What you said about Mars. It rang a bell. Reminded me. . . 1861, summertime. The war had just begun. I had left the river. I didn't want to get shot at while trying to keep my boat off a sand bar. I went up to St. Louis, trying to figure out what to do next. During that time, I was initiated into Freemasonry. One night, I was in the lodge. They had a room in the back where all of us could just sit and talk, or read. While I was sitting there by myself reading a book, a man who I had never seen before came in and sat down across from me. We struck up a conversation. The fellow told me his name was Percival Penrod. We talked about the war and what we thought might happen next, how long it would last, that sort of thing. Somewhere along the way Penrod said that people could not understand present events because they were entirely ignorant of the past. People believed, he said, that man had only been on Earth six thousand years, when, in fact, some kind of human has been here for millions of years. He claimed that many of the inventions made since the Renaissance were the result of individuals being helped by secret scrolls preserved from the time of Atlantis. He also said that a long time ago people had flying machines and could fly to the Moon and to other planets. And he said that Mars once had a civilization but it was destroyed in a war against Earth. The last survivors on Mars sealed themselves inside a giant volcano and were never heard from again. But to this day, he claimed, the ruins of cities still exist up there on Mars."

"Did you believe him?" Tesla asked me.

"No," I said. "I thought he was a damned ignorant fool and lunatic. Of course, I didn't tell him so. I just smiled like an idiot myself and nodded to him. But then, a few years later, when I was out west, a fellow I knew from the St. Louis lodge told me that Percival Penrod was working for Lincoln as a special agent, that he was, in fact, the person who made the secret arrangements for Grant and Lee to meet at Appomattox. Years later, Grant confirmed to me that he knew Penrod as a secret messenger working for Lincoln, although he said that Percival Penrod was not the man's real name, but only an alias he sometimes used. Then, just a couple of years ago, another man who knew Penrod told me that it was really Penrod who died in that barn where they claimed to have killed John Wilkes Booth. Thing is, Penrod looked a lot like Booth."

After Tesla finished reading the faded green book, he packed it in his valise, then went to say goodbye to some friends. When he returned to his hotel room, he looked in his valise. His train ticket, his steamship ticket, and his pocketbook with most of his money were all gone. Gone also was the faded green book. His letter of introduction to Edison had been left in his valise.

Tesla knew there was but one thing to do. He picked up his lightened valise and went straight to the train station. He had just enough money to buy another train ticket for the coast of France. He got on the train, rode it to port, and boarded the steamship for America. He explained to the purser he had lost his ticket and the purser allowed him to wait until the last moment before departure. No one claimed Tesla's stateroom. So the purser allowed Tesla to take it and go to America.

On board ship, Tesla would lay awake nights, bringing the image of the green book back to his mind. The book would form as a glowing three-dimensional image floating in front of him in the darkness. He could will the cover of the book to open, and will each of its pages to turn in succession. Each night of the ocean voyage to America, Tesla would study the green book. By the time he had reached America, he had memorized the green book, not only unconsciously in the deep recesses of his mind where he formed those memory-images, but consciously on that bright mental surface where we all reason and measure.

Tesla now believed the Order of the Flaming Sword to be a real organization. According to the green book, the function of the Order was to monitor and control the development of civilization on Earth—here seeding certain kinds of knowledge into the course of human events, there withholding certain other kinds of knowledge and suppressing its discovery by anyone else. The Order held that human history was an alchemical process and that it should correspond to the cyclical movements of the universe, the astrological ages. The green book said that the present human race was approaching the "blackening" stage of the alchemical process, a stage marked by total war, civil strife, deterioration of the individual's mind, body, and spirit, and a complete reliance on machines. The Order held that this was a necessary stage in the development of the human race, one through which we must pass before we could fulfill our destiny.

Tesla saw the future of man in different terms. To him, the machine would liberate man from the tyranny of his fellow men. It was the machine's only function and reason for existence. The thought that the machine could be used as a tool of tyranny was repugnant to Tesla. He was determined to oppose any attempt to make it so, and if this meant opposing the Order of the Flaming Sword, then so be it, he told himself.

Tesla thought about the man in the silk hat and the man that was shot and fell into the Seine. It now occurred to Tesla that the man might not have been shot at all; that the whole incident might have been a theatrical play staged for Tesla as sole audience. But for what purpose? The possibility that the incident was a ritual initiation, with the man in the silk hat and the man with the knife taking the parts of Castor and Pollux, did not occur to Tesla at this time.

Tesla wondered why his supervisors at Edison Continental repeatedly refused his request for payment of his bonus, yet Batchelor was willing to recommend him to Edison in America. Was it only a coincidence, Tesla asked himself, that the man with the knife attacked him the day after Batchelor wrote the letter of introduction to Edison?

It seemed to Tesla as if someone wanted him out of Europe and over in America, and that almost everyone he knew was either prodding him with a stick to stay in Europe or enticing him with a carrot to go to America. And what was the result of all this? The theft of his ship ticket and money had only fired his enthusiasm to go to America! Could this have been its intended effect? Tesla had a vague sense of a web being stretched out over him, and those helping to weave the web being as ignorant of the web's purpose as Tesla was himself.

Tesla had always wanted to go to America, but to go on his own terms. He felt now that he was being manipulated by unidentified forces. He decided he would buy a gun, keep it on his person, and become expert in its use. When he arrived in America, he did do this, and later also required his assistant Kolman Czito to become an expert marksman.

On June 6, 1884, Tesla arrived in lower Manhattan. After checking through Castle Garden, he strolled through Battery Park, and on up along Broadway. As he continued on up Broadway, he passed a shop where a man was cursing a machine. Tesla stopped and volunteered to help the man repair it. The man accepted Tesla's offer, and, when Tesla got the machine running again, the man gave Tesla twenty dollars.

Bolstered with this quick, small fortune, and his letter of introduction, Tesla met with Edison the next day.

"What can I do for you, mister," Edison snapped when he saw Tesla's tall figure looming above him.

"My name is Nikola Tesla. I have come from Paris to see you."

"What for?"

"I have a letter of introduction from Mr. Batchelor, sir."

"Batchelor, eh?"

Edison took the letter.

"I worked for Continental Edison in Paris."

"Um hum. Sit down."

Tesla sat down. Edison read the letter. Part way through, Edison started chuckling to himself. He looked up at Tesla, grinning.

Edison quoted Batchelor's letter, "'I know of two great men and you are one of them; the other is this young man!' Ha! That's some recommendation. Some big talk. But talk doesn't get the job done, does it? What can you do?"

"I was a problem solver for Continental Edison. I worked all over Europe. I can fix any kind of machine, electrical or mechanical, that you might have. Also, I have made some discoveries which will interest you. I have designed an induction motor for alternating current which utilizes a rotating magnetic field and which—"

"Hold up there! Did you say *alternating* current?"

"I did."

"That's pure nonsense."

"But—"

"Alternating current is dangerous. A damned boob-trap!"

"The machine I have designed is quite safe—"

"*I'm* telling you it's a boob-trap! That junk'll fry ya dead! You're in America now, my Parisian friend! In America we're only interested in what works—and what works is *direct* current. It's what we're set up for, people like it, and it's all I'll ever fool with. Have you got that?"

"Yes, sir."

"All right, then. That's more like it. You're young and a foreigner. You've got a lot to learn. But if Batchelor vouches for you, maybe you have possibilities. But if you're going to work for *me*, you're going to do things *my* way. Is that understood?"

"Yes, sir."

"All right, then. I might have a job for you. Think you can fix a ship's lighting plant?"

Of course, by now you know that Tesla could fix a ship's lighting plant all to hell and back, so I shall not linger here except to say that Tesla toiled all night on board the S.S. Oregon and by dawn the job was finished.

Edison was mightily impressed with Tesla and put him to work full time.

Although Edison refused to discuss alternating current, when Tesla criticized Edison's direct current dynamos, Edison said, "Think you can make a better one? There's fifty thousand dollars in it—if you can do it."

Tesla took Edison at his word and set to work. After months of toil, Tesla successfully demonstrated his improvement. Edison brought several of his other employees into the room along with Tesla to look at the redesigned dynamo.

Edison said to his employees, "Now, do you see that? All you fellows need to take a lesson from Tesla. He doesn't tell me what he's going to do; he shows me what he has already done. Results! That's what it's all about, fellas!"

Tesla said, "Thank you, Mr. Edison, you are very kind."

"Not at all," Edison said, "Just stating facts."

"But I do thank you. And I was wondering when I should expect my check."

"Check? What check?"

"My check for fifty thousand dollars. The one you promised me if I improved the dynamo."

"The one *I* promised?"

"That is correct. Several months ago."

"Did anybody hear me promise?"

None of the other men moved.

"Nevertheless," Tesla said, "you promised."

"Did I?"

Edison laughed, and then stopped like the laughter was turned off with one of his electrical switches.

"Well, maybe I did. Maybe I did say something like that."

"You did. I recall it clearly."

"Yes. Well. I was joking."

Tesla stared at Edison.

"I was joking, Tesla! Don't you get it? It was a joke. And *what* a joke! Right, fellas?"

Edison's men gave a hearty laugh.

"You said—"

"Did you really think I'd pay you fifty thousand dollars to do a little tinkering?"

"It was not a little tinkering. It was a fundamental design change."

"Now look here. You're a foreigner. And a young fella. So I'm going to give you a little lee-way. You're a foreigner and you don't understand some of our ways here in America. Why, here in America we're always pulling jokes. Isn't that right, boys?"

Edison's men nodded, and piped in, "That's right, boss."

Edison turned back to Tesla, grinning, but he let his smile fade until his face was grim, then he said, "Tesla, you just don't understand our American humor."

"Then you're not going to pay me."

"No. I'm not going to pay you. Do you understand now?"

"If I do not receive the bonus, I will resign."

"Tell you what. I'll give you a raise. Eight dollars a week. How's that?"

Tesla did not answer, but picked up his hat and walked out.

Edison said quietly to his men, "Get back to work."

Tesla next formed the Tesla Electric Light Company. His financial backers were only interested in his arc light inventions. After a short time, Tesla was eased out of the company, receiving only an engraved stock certificate of little value.

It was 1886 and Tesla was reduced to digging ditches.

At noon, Tesla would sit and watch with rising nausea as his fellow workers ate sandwiches held in their muddy, filth-grimed hands. On one such day, Tesla's foreman on the work crew arrived after being gone all morning and approached him.

"What are you doing here?" the foreman asked.

"Trying to eat. But I cannot."

"I mean, what are you doing here digging ditches?"

"Trying to earn enough money to live."

"You shouldn't be here."

"I have no choice."

"I happen to know A.K. Brown, manager of Western Union. I spoke to him about you this morning. He's heard of you and knows about the work you did with Edison. He wants to talk to you."

Tesla looked up at the foreman, and said, "Really?"

"He's very interested in alternating current."

"I would like to talk to him."

"Go home. Wash up. Then meet me back here. We'll go see him."

"Right now?"

"Right now. As of right now you're fired here. Now go on."

With the help of A.K. Brown the Tesla Electric Company was formed and finally Tesla's system of alternating current began to be developed and patented. George Westinghouse went to see Tesla at his new laboratory and there they struck their famous deal.

Now Tesla came into his own. Soon his childhood dream of taming the energy of Niagara Falls seemed within his reach when Westinghouse bid for the contract to build an electrical generating station atop the falls. And soon New York society discovered Tesla and the most exciting event of the season was a soiree at Tesla's laboratory where the mysterious inventor would juggle balls of fire, hurl lightning bolts, and carry about from room to room glowing incandescent light bulbs attached to no wires whatsoever.

And so I also came into Tesla's orbit. From the Westinghouse dinner, I invited Tesla to the Players Club, where he became a member. There, Tesla, Joseph Jefferson, the actor famed for portraying Rip Van Winkle, and I began what was a little informal club of our own. We would meet at the Players or at Tesla's laboratory and spend a night engaged in fantastic conversation.

Once, late at night in his laboratory, Tesla looked out the window, gazing upon the dark buildings of lower Manhattan, and said:

"Mark, someday soon the world shall be transformed. Today men toil by the sweat of their brows. They live short lives of suffering and ignorance. But tomorrow—ah, tomorrow. Things will be different."

"How?" I asked.

"I cannot say just yet. But I will tell you this. I have discovered something—something that goes beyond all my previous inventions by orders of magnitude. Its conception came to me all in an instant—as a bolt from the blue. It is a new power—a new power—and a thousand times the strongest in the earth."

One night Joe Jefferson sent a note down to Tesla trying to coax him out of his laboratory and up to the Players Club, but Tesla sent back a note asking us to meet him at his laboratory at midnight. Joe and I took a cab to Tesla's laboratory down near the tip of Manhattan.

We got out of the cab and banged on the door. We could see a light on inside. After a minute, Tesla opened the door.

"We're here for the show you promised us!" I said.

"Yes," Joe chimed in, "We want a show!"

Tesla said, "You've come just in time. We have another member to add to our audience. Mr. Chauncey McGovern of *Pearson's Magazine*."

"An Englishman!" I said. "I know McGovern. He'll make a good audience. You're sure to fetch him. Just be sure to throw in plenty of thunder. *That's* what will impress him."

Tesla said, "Thunder's good. Thunder's impressive. But always remember, Mark, it is lightning that does the work."

"Tesla!" I cried. "I wish I'd have said that! Can I steal it and put it in one of my books?"

"It's all yours, Mark," Tesla said.

Tesla put on a show for us to beat anything I ever saw—juggling mysterious balls of fire that appeared out of nowhere in mid-air—bathing himself in a sheet of electricity and lightning bolts.

Then Tesla set me up in one corner of his laboratory. He created one of those strange balls of fire and tossed it to me. I caught it in my hand and felt a tickling sensation, like a thousand ants crawling on my palm.

"Throw it to Joe!" Tesla shouted.

I threw the ball and Joe caught it in his hands and let out a whoop. Then Joe threw the ball to McGovern who missed the catch. The ball of fire drifted to the floor, bounced, flew up in a corkscrew spiral—and disappeared in mid-air.

"Yee-how!" I shouted. "Make another one!"

Tesla snapped his fingers and another ball of fire appeared in his hand.

McGovern said, "I'd like to see Kellar do that!"

Tesla threw McGovern the ball. McGovern caught it, and said, "It tickles! What is this?"

"Ball lightning," Tesla said.

"You mean—it's really lightning?" McGovern asked. "How do you make it?"

Tesla said, "It comes from the generator over there. Waves of electricity permeate the space around us. It only takes the proper trigger to condense the energy into a spinning ball."

"And what is the trigger?" McGovern asked.

"The snap of my fingers. The friction creates static electricity. This creates an asymmetry in the field which can then be shaped with the proper resonance."

"Resonance?"

"Everything in the physical universe is a manifestation of vibration and its frequency. If you know the correct frequency, you can attach your machines to the very wheelwork of nature and accomplish anything you can imagine."

"Anything?"

"Anything."

"What's this, Tesla?" I asked, looking at a strange platform.

"An experimental therapeutic device designed for use in hospitals. It still needs work."

"What does it do exactly?" McGovern asked.

"It promotes the healthy growth of muscle and bone tissue and aids the digestive and circulatory systems by slightly increasing the speed of blood flow without an increase in blood pressure."

"How does it do that?" McGovern asked.

"Through vibration," Tesla said.

"Vibration again," McGovern said.

"Yes," Tesla said, "vibration and frequency."

Tesla flipped a switch on the machine and the platform began to hum and vibrate over a rubber pad.

"So you think this really works?" I asked.

"Oh, it works," Tesla said.

"Would it work on rheumatism and lumbago?" I asked.

"Most definitely," Tesla said.

"Let me try it," I said.

"I don't think so," Tesla said. "It is only in the experimental stages of development."

"I don't care," I said. "You said it works. It either works or it doesn't. Which is it?"

"All right, Mark. You can try it—but only for a few moments. When I give the word for you to get off, you must get off."

"I'll get off, just let me get on first!"

I stepped on the platform and suddenly every molecule in my body was vibrating. It was the most delightful sensation. It felt like every kink and tangle in my anatomy was being relaxed. After a few seconds, I almost felt like I was floating. The pain in my left knee was gone, also the pain in my right elbow, which up until that moment I did not know I had, because I had become so used to it. With the pain gone, I felt free and alive. I felt like a boy again. I started whooping and waving my arms.

"All right, Mark," Tesla said. "You've had enough now."

"Yee how!" I shouted. "I'm just getting started!"

"You'd better believe me," Tesla said, "it's best that you come down now for your own good."

I said, "You couldn't entice me off of here with a jug full of whiskey—or pry me off with the lever of Archimedes!"

The moment after I said that, I felt a sharp, grabbing pain in my abdomen. Something had backed up down there in my bowels and had locked up and was not going any further, even though it kept trying. I could hardly lift my foot up to step down off the platform.

As soon as my feet hit solid ground, I knew I was in trouble. From my stomach down I was all urgency.

"Quick, Tesla!" I groaned. "Where is it?"

Tesla took hold of my arm and guided me toward a door in the corner of the room. I shuffled across the floor, stooped over and pigeon-toed. As we approached, Tesla's assistant, Kolman Czito, rushed forward and opened the door. I realized by the concerned look on Czito's face that this thing had happened before—probably to Czito, or to Tesla, or to both of them.

I went through the door and Czito closed it. There before me gleamed mercifully the white porcelain seat of the toilet.

A few minutes later, I returned to the laboratory with a look of peace and repose on my face.

I said to Tesla, "When you said it worked, you didn't say *what* it worked!"

"I warned you," Tesla said.

"That you did. That you did. And next time I shall observe your warnings. I am one of those fools who always believe that experience is the best way to find out about anything. But anyway, at least I am thoroughly purged."

"Purged?" Joe Jefferson asked.

"Yes," I said, "purged of everything that was in me, including all my sins."

"Oh, no! Not you!" Joe said.

"Yes," I said, "I now know how those saints in the olden days felt when they swallowed the host and achieved sanctification as it passed down through their digestive tract. They were stercoranated. That's what I am—stercoranated!"

"I can't believe that," Joe said. "An old sinner like you can only release the sulphuric vapors of Hades! And what was that awful noise I heard in there? Vesuvius?"

"Watch your mouth, Joe Jefferson, or I'll learn you!"

"Oh, you will?"

"I'll strap you on that vibrating torture rack of Tesla's and let it shake you where the sun don't shine! *Then* we'll see who's the Vesuvius!"

Now everyone was laughing, Tesla, Joe Jefferson, McGovern, and even Czito. I stood there looking at them all. Then I started laughing, too.

Tesla said, "It is a lesson for us all. Too much of anything is bad. Moderation is the key."

Tesla brought out a bottle of whiskey and began pouring drinks. We sat down and began moderating that bottle.

"Mr. Tesla," McGovern said, "I still don't understand. The artificial ball lightning and that sheet of flame and electric bolts that engulfed you—that was a million volts or more of electricity going through that platform. Why did it have no effect on you?"

"It is a skin effect," Tesla said. "The electricity never passed through me at all, but rather *over* me. As long as the frequency of the electricity is high and the amperage is low, large voltages can move over the surface of the skin with no injury. However, it is not a stunt for amateurs. It is very easy for something to go wrong. And then the effect is fatal."

It was nearly dawn when Tesla closed up his laboratory and said goodnight to us. Joe and McGovern went downstairs to wait for the cab. I stayed and watched Tesla as he stored away some of his machinery in cabinets.

I asked, "How's that new force of yours coming?"

"Interesting you should ask," Tesla said. "Czito and I have been working on something, assembling it over in New Jersey. It's a very big project."

"Just you and Czito working on it?"

"Over a hundred men have been involved in its construction directly or indirectly. But none have seen the separate parts assembled. No one knows what they have been working on. Only Kolman Czito knows what it is."

"Can I see it?"

Tesla stood up from the cabinet and turned around. He smiled at me, and seemed to be thinking something about me. Then he nodded slowly.

"Someday," Tesla said. "Someday soon I will show it to you. And you will not believe it."

I could not imagine what it was of Tesla's that I would not believe, because he had already shown me things that seemed impossible. But I did not ask him anything further. I knew that if Tesla said he would show me his mysterious invention, he would show me—when he was ready.

Chapter Three

Your Work and My Play

> He made Tom steer the ship all about and every which way, and learnt him the whole thing in nearly no time; and Tom said it was perfectly easy. He made him fetch the ship down 'most to the earth, and had him spin her along so close to the Illinois prairies that a body could talk to farmers, and hear everything they said perfectly plain; and he flung out printed bills to them that told about the balloon, and said it was going to Europe.
>
> — Huck, *Tom Sawyer Abroad*

The day after I arrived in Chicago, Tesla made his first public demonstration in the Electrical Exhibition Building on the grounds of the World's Fair.

May 1st was still the scheduled Grand Opening, but on this day, Friday, April 14th, 1893, small groups of sightseers with their "inspection tickets" spread out over the grounds. Most of the fair remained fenced off, locked up, or unfinished. A handful of people strolled along the pathways beside the lagoon, stepping over sand piles and loose boards. A number of others, just fresh from the excitement of Buffalo Bill's "Wild West Show," made their way to the Electrical Exhibition Building. The outside of this exhibit hall had just been completed the day before with a final coat of white paint to convey the impression of white marble. The paint had been applied to the walls rapidly using a new invention made especially for the fair's construction: the paint was put into a compressing device and sprayed out in a fine mist through the end of a gas pipe. Temporary railroad tracks ran alongside the exhibit hall's south side through the Court of Honor, and here and there packing crates lay stacked alongside the tracks.

Among the visitors approaching the Electrical Exhibition Building were three men who, if you looked at once, seemed like everybody else, but who, if you looked at twice, seemed a little different from anyone else. If you looked at them a third time—these three individuals would seem so strange to you that they would send shivers along your skin. But you probably would not look at these people three times; you would be looking at the fair.

So these three individuals, these three strange people, passed by everybody unnoticed; or if noticed, only seen as some strange foreigners from some far-away country.

These three individuals probably thought they looked a lot more like everyone around them than they actually did. When we try to imitate the manners and dress of foreign people, we usually are blind to the small things that the foreigner considers important or significant. As a rule, our imitations are superficial and clumsy. Thus it was with these three individuals who were attempting to look like Americans on holiday.

The three individuals all wore black, and looked like undertakers. But something was wrong with the cut of their clothes. The cut of their lapels were like nothing to be seen in Europe or America at that time, or any earlier time, for that matter. Each wore a black derby, but the brims of those derbies were rather wide and flat, and the crowns were a bit tall. So their hats were not really derbies at all, or any other kind of hat. It was as if the maker of their hats had never seen a derby before but only had it described to him. Each wore spectacles with dark-colored glass, like the glass of a patent medicine bottle, the sort of spectacles worn by the blind; but these three individuals were not blind, not at all. All three of them wore heavy beards and their hair covered their ears. So the only part of their faces you could see was their noses, and a hint of their foreheads and cheeks. If you looked at them once—or twice—you might notice they had unusual papery-looking skin. If you tried for that third look—maybe through the dark glass of those spectacles—you would see something you would not want to see. In fact, you would tell yourself you did *not* see it, after you *had* seen it. You would want to believe you had not seen it, and you would go back to looking at the fair, and even forget about trying to look at those three strangers, until you woke up later that night in a cold sweat remembering what you *had* seen. Yes, these three individuals were different from the rest of us, all right, but they were trying to be the same, and they were succeeding—as long as nobody looked too closely.

Nikola Tesla was too busy to be looking at people. For the last several days he had been supervising the installation of twelve seventy-five ton electrical generators and a 2,000 horsepower Allis-Chambers steam engine, all in the

"Shoot, Tesla, flyin' this airship's child's play."

south nave of Machinery Hall. The work was not finished, but enough had been completed to power Tesla's show in the Electrical Exhibition Building.

But Tesla was not thinking about electricity or machines this morning. He stood on the shore of the lagoon feeding pigeons and ducks. Birds fluttered in the trees across the lagoon sensing the feeding going on at Tesla's feet. Some of these other birds swooped over the lagoon, the blue sky shining above them, and landed near the pigeons and ducks, hoping for a morsel of their own.

When Tesla saw the first fair visitors strolling along the edge of the lagoon, he threw out all his bird seed, turned around, and walked over the bridge to the exhibition buildings. He walked past the Transportation Exhibition Building, walked past the Mining Exhibition Building, and on toward the Electrical Exhibition Building.

Tesla passed by a colossal statue of Benjamin Franklin holding his famous kite, through the mammoth arched entrance of the Electrical Exhibition Building, and on into its interior.

Inside, the building was finished, but none of the electrical exhibits had yet been installed in the second-story mezzanine. As Tesla entered the building, he looked up at the lacework of steel and glass arches enclosing the interior space. Directly in front of him was an ornate arch topped by a sign which read:

"WESTINGHOUSE
ELECTRIC
&
MANUFACTURING
TESLA
POLYPHASE
SYSTEM"

Beyond the arch lay General Electric's elaborate exhibit. At its center stood an eighty-foot Columbian Column topped by an eight-foot tall incandescent light bulb, the largest in the world. Far beyond the Columbian Column on the back wall of the exhibit building was a large portrait of Columbus done in profile. Above Columbus were the words "WESTINGHOUSE ELECTRIC & MANUFACTURING."

Tesla's exhibit stood below this sign. He was still working for Westinghouse, now as a consultant on a $5,000 a month retainer.

Tesla walked under the Westinghouse arch and passed in front of and around General Electric's exhibit. He stopped, looked up at the Columbian Column and the giant light bulb perched on its top, and smiled. He then proceeded toward his exhibit, mounted the steps to the stage and looked at his machinery. He went to a control board and closed a knife-switch. A hum sounded and indicator needles on gauges swung forward to their proper places.

A moment later Tesla heard voices echoing above the hum of his electrical machines. He turned and looked back across the exhibit hall. The first people were wandering into the exhibits. Stopping near the entrance, they were stupefied, looking up and around and over at everything, trying to take in all the sights in one, big glance. In a moment, the people realized that one, big glance just would not do, and so they moved forward to take in each part of the exhibits in smaller glances, glances that grew into intensified gazes of amazement.

Tesla watched from his stage as the people slowly moved toward him. They were bending over the iron railings of the General Electric exhibit and pointing at this and that. Some of them laughed. The people gazed at a display of flickering incandescent light bulbs, each light bulb blazing out in the brightness of 100 watts of electricity. More people came into the hall, gentlemen in derbies and a few in straw hats, and ladies in spring bonnets and wide-brimmed, flower-trimmed hats. Then Tesla heard the cry of a baby echo through the building and saw two children, a boy and a girl dressed in sailor outfits, darting through the crowd. The boy held aloft a red and white stick of hard candy. The girl reached and grabbed it, and disappeared back into the crowd with the boy following after her.

For Tesla, the fair had begun, and he was ready for it. He stood alone upon his stage observing the crowd's reaction to the exhibits. He had prepared for this moment and now went into action. He turned back to his control board and began closing more knife-switches in rapid succession. Each switch closure would produce a slight spark, and the rapid production of sparks made some in the crowd turn their heads away from the Columbian Column and toward Tesla's stage. Some of the crowd began nudging their neighbors, and so more people began looking toward Tesla.

The electrical devices on Tesla's stage had come to life. They were spinning, rolling, undulating, shifting—here, there, everywhere. Tesla stood amidst a mechanical maze that looked as if it might take flight any second—or explode.

The crowd began moving toward Tesla's stage. Tesla stepped forward and held his arms out wide. More people came forward, filling the open space in front of the stage. And then those further back, and those near the entrance, began hurrying forward too, because that is the way we are, we human beings.

Tesla must have been a sight for all those people to behold. He stood six feet and some inches tall, and on this day he was wearing cork-bottomed shoes, which brought his height closer to the neighborhood of seven feet. To most of the people in the crowd, Tesla must have seemed a giant, but a smiling giant dressed in formal white tie and tails. Tesla had his black hair parted down the center of his head and combed to a brilliantine sheen. His forehead was high, his nose hawk-like, and beneath it, a neatly trimmed mustache edging perfectly white teeth. The proportions of his legs and arms were long and stretched out, but his limbs were powerful and sinewy.

Tesla snapped his fingers and a ball of lightning appeared at his fingertips. He tossed the ball into the air and it disappeared. The crowd gasped involuntarily; they had not expected magic. Tesla snapped his fingers again, producing another glowing ball. He tossed it in the air, snapped his fingers again, and tossed a second ball after the first. Now the audience saw Tesla juggling three balls of light—then—four! The balls sped in a high arc over Tesla's head, around and around. Suddenly, Tesla clapped his hands together. The balls vanished!

The onlooking crowd broke into astonished applause. They were not sure of what they had just witnessed. Was it a magic trick, a demonstration of science, or some kind of supernatural power? The applause faded and was replaced with murmuring voices. Tesla held up his hands and said:

"Ladies and gentlemen, you have just witnessed the effects of one of my latest inventions, the transmission of electrical power through etheric space without the use of wires of any kind. And please allow me to introduce myself. My name is Nikola Tesla. I am an inventor of electrical machines, generators, motors, transmission systems, and many other devices. Please allow me to welcome you to this special preview of the Columbian Exhibition of 1893, our World's Fair!"

Tesla bowed slightly and the crowd broke into applause again. Tesla held up his hand, and said:

"This fair is the first of its kind. There have been attempts at world's fairs before, beginning with the London fair of 1851. But those predecessors were only attempts; they only held out a vision of what might be. Here, today, we show the reality of what is. Four hundred years ago, Christopher Columbus made a voyage. It was not a pilgrimage of faith, but a quest informed by knowledge. Since that time, the world has moved forward, continuing the quest of Columbus, a quest informed by—and in search of—knowledge. Here in this land discovered by Columbus we have built the beginnings of an industrial civilization. It is now for us to complete the task and embrace all that it means. And what does our industrial civilization mean? What is the goal at which we have been aiming? It can be summed up with one word: freedom— freedom from the tyranny of our fellow man, freedom from the tyranny of limited time and space, freedom to be all that we can be, all that we were meant to be, all that we should be. To that end, I present for your inspection today my latest inventions available for your immediate use, the greatest of which is my polyphase or alternating current system of electricity."

Tesla spoke in his high-pitched voice which carried out over the heads of the crowd and resonated and echoed far into the exhibit building. The crowd stood transfixed.

Tesla said, "Allow me to direct your attention to the left of the stage."

The crowd turned to look. Tesla closed a switch on stage and down below in a row of exhibits something began to move. It was an egg rolling around in circles on what appeared to be a metal drum. A closer look would reveal that the egg had been copper-plated. The copper-plated egg rolled faster and faster, circling the edge of the drum head. Then it lifted up on its pointed end and began spinning on its long axis and whirling about in circles like a toy top. The crowd gathered about the exhibit of the spinning copper egg, trying to catch a glimpse of it over the shoulders of other people.

Tesla said, "This is my answer to the challenge of Columbus to balance an egg on its end. I do it with electricity and magnetism to create a veritable whirlwind!"

Tesla continued to speak, describing to the crowd several other electrical devices in the display below, most of them meant for use in the home. The crowd's interest intensified with every passing moment. It was beginning to sink in on them. Electricity was no flight of fancy, no mere scientific fiction to be marveled over at a fair; very soon it was going to begin lifting the burdens of their daily lives, re-shaping the form and pattern of their hours and days, liberating them from carrying and fetching, waiting and wanting. Electrical machinery was real, and it was here to stay. What could be better?

Tesla finished his lecture to strong applause. He bowed and swept his arms out to either side of the stage, gesturing at all of his strange machines, as if they were fellow cast members in a play.

As the applause of the crowd began to die down, Tesla heard a voice shout. Then he heard it again, and he made out what it was saying: "Fraud!"

Tesla dropped his hands to his sides and stepped forward, peering down into the crowd.

"Fraud!" the voice shouted a third time. The crowd grew quiet.

The man to whom the voice belonged stepped forward, and the crowd stepped aside to let him by.

The man who had shouted was one of those three strangers dressed in black and wearing those spectacles that looked like they had been made out of glass from a patent medicine bottle. This man, who I will call "Bottleglass," was tall, about the same height as Tesla. Bottleglass brought a gloved hand up to his long beard and stroked it as he looked around at the people in the crowd. The people around him stepped back further, and children moved away and clutched at their mother's dresses.

Bottleglass took a stance with his legs spread apart, looked up, stretched out his right arm, pointed his finger directly at Tesla, and said:

"You're a fraud, Tesla! Thomas Edison says your new-fangled contraptions are going to electrocute the whole country!"

Tesla's eyebrows went up in amazement. Bottleglass did not look like an Arkansas farmer, but that is exactly what he sounded like. Tesla's amazed expression lasted only for an instant. He suspected this was some kind of absurd stunt concocted by the directors of General Electric. He decided to play along with it.

"Does he now?" Tesla replied coolly to Bottleglass.

"Yessiree, Bob!" Bottleglass said. "That junk will fry you dead!"

Tesla said, "Allow me to prove otherwise," and he reached out and closed a switch.

A rectangular metal platform on the floor of the stage began to hum and glow with a blue halo of electricity.

Tesla said, "One million volts of electrical power are coursing through the plate at this very moment."

Bottleglass said, "It's a trick! Ain't no electricity going through that."

"You don't believe me?" Tesla asked.

Bottleglass stood in silence.

Tesla said, "Then come up here and stand upon the plate!"

"No!" Bottleglass shouted.

"Why not?" Tesla asked.

Bottleglass looked around the crowd. Then he said, "I see it now. It's shootin' sparks. I ain't about to get up there."

"Why?" Tesla asked. "Afraid of a little shock? Must you force me? Must I always do everything—myself?"

Tesla stepped toward the plate and lifted his foot up over its surface. Gasps were expelled from the crowd, followed by a flurry of whispers.

A man in the back of the crowd shouted, "In the name of God, man, don't do it!"

Tesla stepped upon the electrified platform in a single, swift motion, and in that instant was enveloped in a literal sheet of fire and lightning. The sheet expanded outward in a horrific spiked nimbus, orange-red at its points, yellow and white around the surface of Tesla's body. Tesla stood immobile inside the nimbus while bolts of electricity crawled and undulated over him like writhing white snakes.

A woman screamed, triggering a wave of panic which swept over the crowd. Several men pushed their way to the front of the now shouting, surging crowd, then stopped one by one as they each realized in their desperate helplessness that they could go no further. The air surrounding the nimbus was as hot as a furnace. Everyone was certain that Tesla was being roasted alive before their eyes.

One of the men at the edge of the stage shouted, "We've gotta do something! It's cooking him!"

Another man shouted, "It's killing him! Somebody turn that damn thing off! Smash it to hell!"

At that Tesla raised his hand and shouted, "Ladies and gentlemen! Ladies and gentlemen! Calm yourselves! Calm yourselves! I am in no danger! No danger! I am safe! Do you hear? Safe!"

The crowd began to settle down, their jaws going slack in amazement. Tesla waved his arms up and down inside the electrical inferno.

"One million volts of alternating current," Tesla shouted, "one million volts passing—not through me—but *over* me—like a gentle flow of warm water—nothing more!"

Now the crowd was very quiet, for now they were observing something even stranger yet: Tesla was spinning his hands about rapidly, pivoting them at his wrists. In a moment, a glowing ball of fire, much brighter than the ones Tesla had created earlier, seemed to condense and form upon the palm of his hand.

Tesla said, "My alternating current system of electricity has lit every pit and pinnacle of this great fair. And tomorrow, ladies and gentlemen, tomorrow, it shall light your homes!"

Tesla threw the ball of fire. The brilliantly glowing ball flew across the exhibit hall and crashed against a bank of knife-switches on the wall. The crash jarred one of the knife-switches from its open position; the blade dropped, closing an electrical circuit which lit the model of a house on the side of the stage. The crowd exclaimed a collective "Ah!"

Tesla spun his hands again, forming another ball of fire, and said, "It shall light your farms!"

Tesla threw the second ball of fire. It sped through the air and crashed against another knife-switch on the far wall, closing it—this time lighting the model of a farmhouse and barn.

Tesla spun both his hands now, forming two more balls of fire. He said, "It shall light your cities!"

Tesla threw the third ball. Its crash closed a switch that lit the model of a city.

Tesla said, "It shall light the whole, inhabited world!" and he threw the last ball. The brilliantly glowing ball of fire sped above the heads of the crowd, up into the open space of the exhibition building, clearing Edison's giant light bulb atop the Columbian Column, and rocketing on upward toward a knife-switch attached to one of the building's steel arches. The ball of fire crashed against the knife-switch in a shower of sparks.

A gigantic globe of the world hanging from one of the steel arches blinked on, glowing with blue electric light. Around its equator, Tesla's name flashed on, spelled out by the glowing line of electric light-tubes. The glowing globe began to rotate above the heads of the crowd.

The people below burst into wild applause, whistling and cheering and throwing their hats into the air. Tesla waved and bowed inside his electrical nimbus.

Then Tesla looked down among the people and saw that Bottleglass was gone.

That afternoon, after leaving the offices of the *Daily News*, Hall and I made our way along State Street and looked in the store windows. The idea was to allow Hall to figure out where to go to shop for his wife's wish list. Instead, our talk was all about the typesetting machine, what it could do, what it was going to do. I was feeling low before I saw those Linotypes. But now I felt a new vigor that ran through me from head to toe; I could not stop talking, and, as for walking, I was ready to go anywhere afoot.

We worked our way back to the hotel to freshen up. Hall wanted to go to Rector's for dinner, but I was undecided. We finally wandered across the street to the Monadnock Building and ended up having dinner in a restaurant off the main lobby. We got a seat by a big window with a view of the street so we could watch people go by in the twilight. The world took on a kindlier aspect, even a beauty. The people passing by were smiling and laughing, and I recalled with a faint surprise that "my calling" was that of "humorist." I had felt very little humor lately. But this day had been a good day. I had met and dealt with Paige without scalping him or strangling him. Here was an accomplishment. I had worked on *Adam's Diary* until I had got it to suit me. Here was an accomplishment of some substance. And I had seen a Linotype and been thoroughly unimpressed. Here was sublime triumph!

After dinner, Hall and I returned to our hotel. At the desk in the lobby, I requested that a decanter of hot scotch be sent up to us. In short order it arrived, rolled in on a serving table. I gave the bellman two bits, and began pouring Hall and myself drinks.

I had turned on only one electric light over the writing desk when we came in, and now I decided to leave the room in half darkness so that I could see out over the city beyond the windows. We put two armchairs by the bay window and sat down in them. I lit up one of my cigars, and all seemed right with the world. I watched the carriage lamps move along on the street below, coming and going, all so orderly, and quiet, and complete. Hall did not complain about my cigar, he was enjoying his scotch so well, I suppose, or maybe he was just getting used to my smoke.

Each of us took turns piloting the conversation along the shoals and eddies of the past. Hall spoke about the idiosyncrasies of the publishing industry, maybe spoke a little too much; for he revealed his ignorance about several aspects of publishing with which I was well acquainted. I could see that even at this late date Hall did not have a firm grasp on the idea of subscription publishing. We both rehashed Webster's many blunders. We trailed off from that subject and on to some other trivial matter which I don't remember now until somehow I veered on to talking about the German language. Hall veered away larboard from that and on to the subject of his mother-in-law. I could see the conversation was rapidly deteriorating in quality, so I steered us starboard away from the dreary subject of Hall's mother-in-law and on to something brighter and more cheerful—the bank panic.

I said, "I couldn't get anybody to sign a note in New York to advance me two cents. And now here is Paige blithely holding his hand out for seven thousand dollars."

"I'm sure every penny of that seven thousand was spent legitimately," Hall said.

"That's what scares me," I said. "I'm going to have to make good on it. I'm bound by that damned contract to support the machine, and I have no idea how I'm going to come up with that extra money without making some personal sacrifices."

"You could stop smoking cigars," Hall said.

"I said *sacrifices*, not crucifixions."

"You'll think of something," Hall said.

"I hope so, for at this moment Webster and Company is sitting on the Mount Morris Bank volcano—and it could blow us sky high any second."

"I don't want to think about the debt right now," Hall said.

I looked over at Hall. There was a look in his eyes I had never seen before, something close to despair. I suddenly realized that I was very wearing on him. I said nothing more, but just watched the scene on the street below.

Finally Hall said, "Looks like Tesla's not coming. I think I'll call it a night."

"All right," I said.

Hall got up and went to the door leading to his adjoining room. He started to close the door, but then stopped and said, "You'll think of something. I know you will." Then Hall went out and closed the door.

Hall's last words were optimistic, but his tone was quiet and subdued, like he was trying to believe what he was saying. I felt guilty. Hall was usually so optimistic and happy. But after several days of close association with me, it seemed that I was draining him of his hope and joy. Yet now *I* was the one feeling optimistic and sure. Perhaps a transfer of faith and hope had occurred between Hall and me. Hall had given and I had received. But had I taken too much?

I sat there thinking about this for a long time. Then I lit up another cigar, and looked down on the street, not really thinking about anything, but just seeing and smelling and tasting and hearing and feeling. There were only my immediate feelings, no past, no future. I almost *was* my feelings, my feelings alone, without family, friends, or enemies. I felt like a fragment of a feeling floating down a dark void, drifting, and lost to the world.

Then there was a knock at the door.

I staggered to my feet, went to the incandescent light knob, and turned it on. The room blazed with white electric light. I blinked and squinted, got my bearings, went to the door, and opened it.

It was Tesla. He was wearing a derby and overcoat.

"Mark, how are you?" Tesla asked, smiling.

"Drunk, damned, and decimated," I replied. "Come on in, Tesla. I'm having a hot scotch. Want one?"

"Why, yes. I think I do," Tesla said.

I went over to the table and began pouring drinks. Tesla took off his coat and threw it over the arm of a chair. He carefully sat his derby down on the writing desk.

Tesla said, "I'm feeling in need of a little stimulation. Been speaking all day at the exhibit hall.

Two morning lectures, and two in the afternoon."

"Putting on your electric show," I said. "That's some show."

"It has Edison's attention."

"Hell, it has everyone's attention. Have you seen the papers? You are *the* thing at the fair. You and that big wheel Ferris is putting up. But you don't mind parading yourself out as the freak of the century, now do you?"

"Not if it makes my work known and accepted. My work. That is all that matters."

"A noble sentiment. Let us drink to it."

I gave Tesla a glass of scotch and then raised my glass to his, and said, "To your work—and my play—and may never the twain meet."

Tesla nodded and grinned. We clicked glasses and drank. As Tesla swallowed, he looked at the golden liquid in his glass. I knew he was calculating how many ounces of his drink remained.

Tesla said, "Ah, Mark. There is more to you than mere play. How is that typesetting machine of yours coming?"

"Not so good. I had the machine's designer in here today. You know—Paige?"

"Oh, yes."

"I was prepared to give him his walking papers, but the only paper he walked away with was a check with my name on it. I tell you—that man could entice a fish to get up out of the water and walk. But do you think you could make Paige himself take a walk? You couldn't. You see, Paige has got a monopoly on convincing."

"So work on the typesetter isn't going well?"

"Depends on who you talk to. If you talk to Paige, it's going wonderful. And he will tell you of its success in such beautiful gilt-edge words and phrasings, for Paige is a poet. He is a poet of the cog-wheel, lever, screw, and inclined plane. He can make a machine sing—for a while. It sings—then it croaks. When it croaks, he has to go back and work up on his poetry again."

"Nothing wrong with poetry. I consider myself a poet."

"Yes, but your stuff rhymes and scans. Paige's epics don't have any meter and they never end. And they're running me to the poorhouse."

I drank the rest of my scotch, then picked up my cigar, and blew a couple of smoke rings for Tesla's entertainment.

"I knew a poet once in San Francisco," I said, "good friend of mine. He said his life was not worth living and all that. He was always saying that.

Every day. Finally he put a gun to his head. I said, 'Go ahead. Pull the trigger!' And... and... he did. And do you know...? That was the best decision he ever made! You see, while the bullet cleared out all the grey matter in his brain, it also carried away with it the *poetic faculty*—and now that fellow is a useful member of society again. Why, last I heard, he had a seat in Congress."

I took another puff of my cigar. Out of the corner of my eye I could see Tesla smiling and nodding to himself. I realized he appreciated my attempt at humor, but he was in no mood at the moment to laugh. Something was weighing on his mind.

"You wanted to see me, Tesla?"

"I have something I want to show you."

"By jings! I knew it! I knew it!"

I crushed out my cigar in an ashtray.

"You've finished it, haven't you?"

Tesla smiled and inclined his head.

"That mysterious new invention you've been hinting about."

"Yes, and I want to take you to see it. But first we must wait here for someone."

"And who would that be?"

"You'll find out any moment. He's on his way up here."

"By jings! I knew it! I knew you had something up that long sleeve of yours. Why—last time I was in your laboratory in New York with Joe Jefferson, I told him—"

A knock at the door interrupted me. I looked to the door, and then to Tesla who gave a quick nod.

"Ah," I said, "our someone else has arrived!"

I went to the door and opened it. Standing in the threshold, looking down on me with the calm of the tornado's eye, was Stephen Grover Cleveland, twenty-second, and now twenty-fourth, President of the United States of America. I was knocked for a loop and a half by his rotund presence.

"You boys ready?" Cleveland asked.

"Yes, Mr. President," Tesla said.

I found my tongue and blurted out, "President Cleveland! Your Excellency!"

Cleveland put his forefinger to his lips to "shush" me, like I was a child; then said very quietly, "We'll sneak out down the back way—Tom Sawyer style."

"By all means, Mr. President," I said, grabbing my hat and coat, "lead the way."

I followed Cleveland out the door, and then Tesla came along, closing the door behind us.

While all this was transpiring, down in the lobby of the hotel someone was pacing back and forth. That someone was the young lady I had encountered at the door of the Chicago *Daily News*—Miss Lillie West, known to the readers of the *Daily News* by her pen name "Amy Leslie." Lillie, as all her friends called her, was the drama critic for the *Daily News*, and quite competent in that line. But lately, she had wanted something more. She wanted to be a "real" reporter—God help her!

If only I could have taken her aside right then and there and explained things to her. You see, first God made invertebrates—then He made Newspaper reporters; He was practicing, you see. A Newspaper reporter will write as conscience dictates—the conscience of his editor. The Newspaper reporter hasn't got any conscience to speak of. Well, neither has an editor, but he has something that has a vague resemblance to a conscience. It is called Newspaper Policy. This comes from the publisher. And where does the publisher get his Policy? Why, from his pocketbook, of course. So there is the reporter, boldly sallying forth to tell the whole unvarnished tr—I mean, to tell the partially unvarnished tr—well, to tell the slightly whitewashed, partially papered-over, somewhat corrugated, intermittingly dissimulated tr. . . Come to think of it, perhaps it was best that I didn't take Lillie aside to explain things to her. Perhaps some things are best learned for oneself. And anyway, it is a sad thing to shatter the illusions of youth.

So, as I said, there she was, Miss Lillie West, pacing back and forth in the hotel lobby.

Just then someone else entered the lobby. That someone else was a young man wearing a fedora and gray suit. He was a striking figure, coming into the place with an easy, confident stroll. He had a noble-looking face somewhat modified by a smile that went past Aloof, but that stopped at the city limits of Sarcastic. His smile was a mask to keep the rest of the world from knowing what he was thinking and feeling. He could have been a leading man on the stage, but he was not. He was a Newspaper reporter. Yes, he was one of those later-model invertebrates I just spoke of; I know all about that species because I once belonged to it myself. That's not to say that this young man had no conscience or backbone; he did. He just was not a fanatic about making use of them. He was not reluctant to tell a lie when he believed it necessary, but neither did he run from the truth just because he was afraid of it. Truth and falsehood were something he put in the balance scale of business, and he was always looking to make a profit.

This young man was none other than George Ade, and at that time he was a reporter for the Chicago *Record*, the morning edition of the Chicago *Daily News*.

As Ade entered the hotel lobby, he immediately noticed Lillie pacing back and forth over by the elevators. He drew his stride up short and came to a dead stop. It seemed to Ade that wherever he went lately, Lillie West was already there ahead of him. In a way, he wasn't surprised to see her there. But in another way, he felt almost a little electric shock; for he had been expecting to encounter something unusual before entering the lobby, only he did not know exactly what it might be.

Ade had been drawn to the Great Northern by an incident that had happened to him only a few minutes earlier. He had been down the street at the Grand Pacific Hotel with his partner and roommate John T. McCutcheon, the illustrator. They had just stepped out of the hotel, when two other gentlemen passed them going inside.

One gentleman said to the other, "You couldn't have seen him. He's not scheduled to arrive until May first."

The other man replied, "Well, if it wasn't him, it was his twin brother. I saw him go into the Great Northern."

That was all Ade heard. He had hardly been paying attention, but suddenly it seemed that his mind was following those two gentlemen back into the hotel.

"What do you say?" McCutcheon asked Ade.

"What?" Ade asked.

"I asked if you're ready to head back."

"Oh," Ade said, "uh. . . no. I don't think so. I think I'm going to walk about a while."

"Walk about?"

Ade nodded, and said, "Uh-huh. Just to get some air. Say, Mac, how about filing the story for me?"

"Suit yourself," McCutcheon said, taking Ade's notebook. "See you back at the mansion."

McCutcheon threw up his hand and walked away.

Ade stood there for a moment, then slowly turned his head to the left to look east along Jackson Street to the Great Northern a block and a half away. He felt a tingling on the back of his neck. He thought of this as his "reporter's instinct." From that same instinctual prompting, he had sent McCutcheon on his way. Reason would have had him speak his mind to McCutcheon. He would have said, "Let's go down to the Great Northern. I suspect something doing down there." But because of some urge that even Ade did not understand he wanted to be left alone to go down there to the Great Northern all by himself.

Ade began to walk toward the Great Northern slowly, then gradually faster with that easy, confident stroll I have just described. He thought about what the man back at the Grand Pacific had just said. There was only one person that Ade could think of who was not scheduled to be in Chicago until May 1st, and that was President Cleveland.

When Ade saw Lillie pacing there in the lobby of the Great Northern and felt that little shock, he knew that there was a connection to what that man at the Grand Pacific had said and what Lillie was now doing, for Ade was a man who did not believe in coincidences. He did not know what Lillie was up to, but he was going to find out.

When Ade had come through the hotel entrance, Lillie was pacing with her back to him. He took advantage of this to alter his demeanor and pretend innocent surprise.

"Well, hello, Lillie," Ade said. "Fancy meeting you here."

"Hello, George," Lillie said, turning around.

"What brings you out to this dreary hotel this time of night?"

"None of your business."

"Some players you've come to interview? No, I don't think so. You must be here after some real News. Unless your editor—"

"My editor is none of your business, either."

Lillie turned away from Ade, but he circled around and came up in front of her.

"I tell you, Lillie," Ade said, "you may think you're Helen of Troy, Betsy Ross, and Susan B. Anthony all rolled into one, but I know what you are."

Lillie just looked at Ade, although she might have raised one eyebrow a little.

"You're not going to ask me what I know you are?" Ade asked.

"No," Lillie said, and then fought herself not to smile.

"There!" Ade said, "that's just like a—"

Ade stopped. He was staring over Lillie's head. He had just missed seeing Cleveland and Tesla, but he had looked up just in time to see me step out of the elevator behind them and slip down the hallway toward the back of the hotel.

Lillie's glance darted over Ade's face.

"What?" Lillie asked.

"I just thought I saw someone," Ade said.

"Who?" Lillie asked, "Who?"

Lillie turned her head around to see who Ade was looking at, but no one was there. She looked back at Ade.

"Well," Ade said, still looking toward the hallway, "it looked like...."

Ade looked down at Lillie, and said, "It looked like...."

Ade could see that Lillie was too eager.

"Wait a minute," Ade said, "wait *a* minute! You know something."

"Nonsense," Lillie said, and she started walking toward the hallway leading past the elevators to the back of the hotel.

"You—" Ade started to say, but stopped. He rushed to catch up with Lillie, came up along side of her, and kept right on going, leaving her behind.

"Oh, no you don't!" Lillie said. "I'm coming, too!"

Ade spun about, and said, "Well, come on if you're coming!"

And the two of them rushed down the hallway leading toward the back of the hotel.

Cleveland led the way through the hotel. He took us through an empty kitchen, then into a room filled with crates of vegetables, then through another room and out through a door which opened on to a side street. Waiting at the curb was a landau with its top up. Cleveland got in it, then Tesla, and then I piled in behind them. Before I could close the door, the driver shook the reins and sent the horses into a gallop. We turned right on State Street, left on Jackson, then right again going south down Michigan Avenue.

Lillie and Ade had reached the street just as our landau was pulling away from the curb with our horses in a gallop. Ade had hailed a passing cab. It stopped, and as Lilly and Ade climbed inside, Ade said to the driver, "Follow the landau—but not too close!"

The cab carrying Lillie and Ade started forward slowly. When our landau turned on to State Street, Lillie and Ade's driver shook the reins of his horses and they broke into a little trot.

"Now just who are we following?" Ade asked.

"Now just what makes you think I'm going to tell you?" Lillie replied.

"Professional courtesy?"

"I let you in the cab, that's professional courtesy."

"I hailed the cab."

"And I got in it."

"That was Mark Twain I saw getting out of the elevator."

"Really? You think so?"

"All right. I can wait."

"Yes. You can wait all you want."

Ade looked ahead, and spoke up to the driver of the hansom, "They're turning on to Michigan Avenue! Don't lose them!"

I sat in the landau facing Cleveland. Tesla sat on Cleveland's right side. Both of them looked ahead blankly. I was sitting with my back to the direction in which we were going, a position I never liked to take in stagecoaches and carriages. But at the moment I didn't mind, and, anyway, I was sure we were out for a short drive. I looked to my right and saw a gray billow of steam from the rail yards along the lake front. I looked back at Cleveland. He was still staring blankly ahead.

We rode along in silence through the streets of Chicago. I kept waiting for Cleveland to say something, but in a moment realized that he intended to sit there in silence the whole way.

Finally I said, "Where are we bound for, Your Excellency?"

"You'll know when we get there," he said.

"So this is going to be a surprise party—with me being the party who'll be surprised."

"If you want to look at it that way."

"I take it no one knows you're here in the city."

"No one knows—officially. Unofficially, only my wife; Dan Lamont, Secretary of War; Robert O'Brien, my private secretary; and two other people know I am here."

"Won't you be missed by everyone in Washington?"

"Joseph Jefferson has secured for me a discreet actor whom Jefferson says is my exact double. I say he is too fat. But I suppose he will fool people at a distance."

"So, only Mrs. Cleveland, Lamont, O'Brien, Joe Jefferson, and this double of yours know you are here."

"That's right."

"And now Tesla and I."

Cleveland nodded.

"Why don't you want anyone else to know?"

"These are delicate times. Very delicate times. And they call for extreme discretion. That is all I'll say for now."

We rode along in silence quite a while longer. Cleveland kept looking at me with his blank poker face which was always impossible for me to read. Tesla was unusually quiet and kept his head bowed down slightly, studying his coat buttons.

Finally, after a number of minutes had passed, Cleveland said, "Cold as hell."

"Yes," I said, "Yes, yes, it is."

"Chicago's always cold as hell," Cleveland continued.

"Cold and the wind blows. Damn cold weather is giving me a sore throat."

Cleveland studied me a moment longer, then added, "You don't look very well yourself, Clemens."

"I'm a sick old man, Your Excellency. Worn out before my time with money worries."

"Money worries? Ha! You?"

"Yes, and this bank panic has exacerbated my troubles."

"*Exacerbated*? That's a ten dollar word."

"If I could've found a higher priced one, I would've used it. Ten dollars don't begin to meet the bill on my money troubles."

"You are truly a humorist. There are bread lines in this country stretching from one coast to the other, and you have the temerity to talk about *your* money troubles."

"I've seen those bread lines. *That's* what's worrying me—that me and mine will be standing in one of them before too long."

"I consider that a remote possibility."

"Well, you are an optimist, Your Excellency."

"Optimism has nothing to do with it. I just happen to know that men like you are always taken care of. Men like you always land on their feet. I ask you:

Will Mark Twain be allowed to stand in a bread line, Mark Twain, the symbol of America?"

"Mark Twain is the symbol of America?"

"Don't play coy. You have said yourself that you aren't just *an* American, you are *the* American."

"Mark Twain is *the* American. Sam Clemens is just another son-of-a-bitch everybody will enjoy kicking when he gets down."

"Well, maybe being down a little won't hurt you a bit. Maybe you need to get a little down. I remember when I was Sheriff of Buffalo and you were the high and mighty publisher of the *Buffalo Express*. You wouldn't give me the time of day."

"Now, Your Excellency, I thought I explained all that to you."

"Yes, you explained. You explained you were a snob."

"I was in society. I couldn't very well associate with the town sheriff. You can understand that. You're President now. Do you associate with just anybody? No, sir, you're particular, as well you should be. You know what Anson Burlingame told me over twenty-three years ago? He said: 'Climb! Climb! Always associate with your superiors, never your inferiors.'"

"And you've taken his advice. Admirably. You married well. You positioned yourself well."

"And so did you, Your Excellency. I'd say you did everything I did."

"I don't have your money."

"I don't have your power."

"I have power?"

"Yes. And the time has come for you to use it. You've got to do something, Your Excellency."

"About what?"

"You know what. The bank panic."

"And what would you suggest I do about that?"

"Let's talk plain. We both know that J.P. Morgan is behind this whole mess."

"Do we?"

"Morgan's behind the collapse of the Philadelphia & Reading Railroad. Him and Vanderbilt. They backed Archibald McLeod into a corner and forced him to unload his stock in a falling market."

"*Forced* him?"

"I'd say when a person can merely *whisper* an unfounded claim of financial instability and have everybody believe him—*that* is *force*. And that is what Morgan has done. Morgan collapsed the P & R and then picked up the pieces when it went into receivership. But Morgan's not just interested in grabbing a railroad. He wants to collapse the entire economy."

"Why would he want to do that?"

"You know why. The same reason he collapsed the P & R Railroad. So he can come in afterwards and pick up the pieces. So he can own everything and everybody. Now what I want to know is: What are you going to do about it?"

"It is not the function of government to interfere with the normal process of business activity."

"*Normal* process? I'd say the normal process of business is one of digestion. And there is a world of difference between digestion and stomach cancer."

Cleveland flinched when I said that, his poker face breaking. I did not understand why—then. But later, I was to learn that a cancer was eating away the roof of his mouth at the very moment I was speaking to him. By the summer of that year, he would undergo a secret operation that would save his life. But at that moment while I was talking to him, he must have known what was wrong with him, or at least suspected. The very word "cancer" was hard for him to hear.

Cleveland said, "I'm going to pretend I didn't hear that—for your sake. I always make allowances for a gentleman in his cups. The problem this country faces now is one of imbalance between gold and silver reserves. We must repeal the Sherman Act of 1890. If we can accomplish this, then what is happening now in the banking centers will correct itself as part of the normal course of business. But we cannot set this country's house in order until we protect our gold reserves."

"And how are we going to protect them? No—don't tell me. I'll tell you: with government bonds bought by Morgan, right? And just how much will he make on that deal?"

Cleveland's eye flinched again.

"Your Excellency, let me make my position clear. I have no objection to people making money. I have no objection to people *having* money. What I object to is when somebody reaches into *my* pocket to get *my* money. And that's what's happening now. I'm being robbed—and so is every citizen of the United States. Morgan's playing a poker bluff with the bank reserves. He knows their Achilles heel—their inflexibility. The day after you were sworn in, Morgan hit the reserves hard. Seems he's expecting something from your administration. Question is: will he get it?"

Cleveland looked out the window. He didn't seem to be listening to me. But I went on:

"I know Morgan's powerful. Damn powerful. One of the most powerful men in the world. But you've got power, too, the power freely given to you through your lawful election by the people. You have the power to tell Morgan a few things. You can tell him that he can go ahead and pick up what he's already shook from the tree. But tell him the time has come for him to *stop shaking the tree. Tell* him to stop—or you will tie him up with so much legislation that he won't be able to put his hands in his *own* pockets."

Cleveland looked back at me. I asked him:

"Now, are you going to sit there and tell me you're going to do nothing to rein in Morgan?"

"Rein in Morgan?" Cleveland asked. "Ha!" he said, his face set like unresponsive stone. "Hilarious. A knee slapper. Everyone says Morgan is pulling *my* strings."

"I know better."

"What do you know?"

"I know *you*. I know you are going to do what is right for this country, just as you swore in your oath of office: preserve, protect, and defend."

"Preserve, protect, and defend—the Clemens' family fortune? Ha! You *are* a genius of the absurd. Don't you worry about the Clemens' fortune. I happen to know that Morgan, Vanderbilt, Rockefeller, and Rogers just adore you, and, at the right time, if it becomes necessary, they'll throw you out a safety net."

"I wish I had your optimism."

"I'll say it again. Optimism has nothing to do with it."

I did not say another word to Cleveland while we were in the carriage. It occurred to me that he was telling me in his own guarded way that he was doing all he could to get the country back on track. Yes, I knew that Cleveland was "Morganized." I knew Morgan was the driving power behind Cleveland's campaign for the Presidency. I knew Cleveland worked for the law firm representing Morgan before assuming office for his second term. Yes, I knew Cleveland was "Morganized," but it must be remembered that Morgan was a master poker player who never blinked or flinched, and who had, ultimately, the only game in town. It was a lesson many of us would learn. Before the century came to a close, all of us in that landau—Cleveland, Tesla, and I—would receive tutelage from Morgan. Yet, Cleveland was a subtle man and underestimated by almost everyone. To my mind, at that time, he was everything a President of the United States ought to be. And I still hold to that estimate; for Cleveland always saw the big picture, and many of his finest deeds were carried out in secret, and remain to this day unheralded in the history books.

Tesla had kept his head bowed down throughout my conversation with Cleveland, but now he looked up, and said, "We're approaching the fair."

Tesla stuck his head out of the carriage and waved. A voice outside said, "Good evening, Mr. Tesla." It was a sentry guarding a gate.

We passed through the gate and into the fairgrounds.

About a block away, the driver of Lillie and Ade's hansom shouted, "They're going into the fairgrounds! I can't get in there! See? They've turned in. There's a sentry up there at that gate—to keep the union men away from the workers. I don't think he'll let me in."

Ade said, "That's the Midway Plaisance they've gone into. There's only one way out of the fairgrounds from here—the south gate. Turn right up here and go around to it. We'll see if they come out there. If they don't come out of the south gate soon, we'll come back here and wait until they come back this way."

Inside our cab, we looked out on the half-finished fair. Here and there, at intervals, incandescent lights illuminated the surrounding murky darkness and threw strange shadows on exotic temples and mysterious castles built of plaster and wood. We passed a big heap of wooden scaffolding—all that yet existed of Ferris' giant wheel, Tesla told us. We passed under a railroad bridge. Beyond us lay a black nothingness.

Tesla took a little metal box from his coat pocket and pulled out a telescoping steel rod which was on the box's top.

"Mr. President," Tesla said, "I know you will push the button to start the electricity for the fair on Opening Day, but I thought I'd give you a little preview tonight. I've arranged things for your special viewing."

Tesla handed Cleveland the metal box, and said, "Just push the button. It is a wireless electrical control switch."

Cleveland waved the telescoping metal rod around in the air, and asked, "Do I need to point this in a particular direction?"

"No, Mr. President" Tesla said. "Just push the button."

Cleveland pushed the button. Suddenly shining out before us in the distance was a white city of dreams, a city suddenly brought into instant existence out of what had been a black void. Great domes and towers were lit up bright as noon against a stark, black night sky. Gigantic beams of light in red, blue, green, and yellow swept the black expanse with a carnival of colors, glowing magic wands of light, waving, crossing, and uncrossing. The edges of all the buildings glowed with jeweled necklaces of incandescent light bulbs. Everything was glory, glitter, and heaven-glimpsed.

"Tesla," I said, involuntarily.

"I know," Tesla said, "I know."

We gazed in silence while the panorama of domes and towers kept moving past us. Then, just as we reached the most spectacular vista yet, Tesla took the metal box from Cleveland's hand and pushed the button again. The white city ceased to exist. There was only the black void, and complete silence.

"Hey!" It was the driver of the landau. "Hey, did you fellows just see that?"

Tesla leaned his head out, and asked the driver, "See what?"

"The fair!" the driver said. "It just—just lit up! Just lit up! The whole world just lit up! Didn't you see it just now?"

"Are you all right?" Tesla asked the driver.

"You didn't see it?" the driver asked.

"Drive on," Tesla said.

"Well, I saw it!" the driver said, more to himself than anyone else. "I don't care what anybody says! I saw it! Queerest thing!"

We reached another sentry and passed through another gate and out of the fairgrounds. In a moment we turned left and went east a number of blocks. After turning right and going south for a few blocks, the driver turned left at a corner. At the next corner he turned left again. The driver had turned us back in the general direction in which we had come. He proceeded up the street two blocks then drew our landau to the curb. Cleveland got out, then Tesla, and then I stepped down.

"Now really," the driver asked, "didn't you see everything light up out there?"

Tesla did not reply, but gave the driver his pay.

Then Tesla said, "Now, I suggest you go and have some strong coffee."

"What?" the driver said, "You think I've been drinking? Ah, never mind!" And he slapped the reins of his horses and the landau started away with a jerk.

I looked about. We were in front of a windowless warehouse about five stories tall. It had been painted white to match the buildings of the fair. The front of the building had been given a classical façade, but the rest of the warehouse looked like a big, featureless box.

"What's this?" I asked.

"A warehouse built specially for the fair," Tesla said. "It was used this last winter to store some of the colossal statuary and some building materials. They're letting me use it right now."

Tesla put a key in the door of the warehouse and opened the door, and we all went in.

Two blocks back up the street, the hansom cab carrying Lillie and Ade stopped in the inky darkness. They had circled about the fairgrounds to the south gate and had waited until our landau came rolling out. Then they had followed us here to the warehouse, keeping well back the whole time.

Lillie got out of the cab and said to the driver, "Pull up to the curb and wait." She handed the driver a roll of bank notes. "Wait," she said. "There will be more when I get back."

"Don't you worry, Miss," the driver said. "For this much, I'll wait all night for you."

Ade got out of the cab and held the crook of his elbow out to Lillie. She ignored it, and started down the street, walking fast. Ade caught up with her, and the two of them made their way up the street toward the big, white warehouse.

They reached the door of the warehouse. Ade tried the knob and found it locked.

"So much for that," Ade said. He looked at Lillie, and asked, "Now what?"

Lillie peered around the corner of the warehouse, and then slipped around it into the shadows. Ade looked up, down, and across the street, and then followed her.

Tesla, Cleveland, and I had stepped through a hall and into a work room filled with electrical machines the like of which I had never seen before, even in Tesla's New York laboratory. Kolman Czito, Tesla's assistant, sat at a workbench, wiring together some kind of electrical device. Czito was a small man of about 35 years of age at that time, I believe. He had small, squinting eyes which flashed from behind a pair of spectacles, and he combed his light brown hair the same way Tesla did, parted down the middle and shining with brilliantine. Like Tesla, he wore a small, neatly trimmed mustache. This night, he wore a shop apron over his shirt and tie. Czito looked up as we entered, pushed his work aside and stood up.

Tesla said, "You both know my assistant, Mr. Czito."

"Mr. Clemens, Mr. President," Czito said, bowing slightly.

"Hello, Czito," Cleveland said. "You're looking well." Cleveland handed Czito his coat and hat.

"Kind of you to say so, Mr. President," Czito said.

"How are you doing, Czito?" I asked.

"Very well, thank you," Czito replied.

I took off my coat, looking Czito up and down the whole time, and said, "You look taller than you were the last time I saw you. Have you grown?"

"Elevator shoes," Czito said, looking at me with his solemn squint.

I gave Czito a knowing nod, took off my hat, and started to give him my coat and hat, but then saw that he held Tesla's hat in his right hand and Cleveland's in his left. I studied Czito a moment; then lay my coat over Tesla's where it lay across Czito's right arm. Then I dropped my derby on Czito's head. It went down over his eyes.

Czito pushed the brim of my derby back and peered up at me, a little irritated.

"Why, Czito!" I said. "If you ever decide to quit electrical engineering, you could make a fortune—renting yourself out as a coat rack!"

Czito said, "Only if I went through all the pockets."

I chuckled and looked over at Cleveland. The President was all ready for a hand of poker, as usual.

Tesla said, "Gentlemen." And he walked forward through a door. Cleveland and I followed.

Outside the warehouse, Lillie and Ade approached an iron grillwork which closed off access to a fire escape stairway which went up, landing upon landing, all the way to the top of the building. Ade shook the grillwork and looked down to see a lock.

"Very interesting," Ade said, "a locked fire escape. Why would anyone want to do that?"

Ade crouched down and studied the lock, which was dimly visible in the moonlight.

"Hairpin," he said, holding out his hand to Lillie while he continued to study the lock.

Lillie reached up to her hair and pulled out a pin. Her long tresses tumbled down around her shoulders. Lillie held the pin out to Ade between the tips of her fingers. Ade turned his head and looked up at Lillie.

"Much better," he said.

"The lock," Lillie said, holding the pin up into Ade's face.

Ade took the pin, bent it out almost straight, and inserted it into the lock. He felt for the wards, and then pushed. The lock sprang open. Ade stood up and swung the iron grillwork forward on its hinges.

"Ah," Ade said, "at least the lock is not unconquerable."

"The lock is only a lock," Lillie replied, and she rushed past Ade, and up the stairs. Ade shrugged, and followed behind her.

Inside the warehouse, Tesla led us down a dark hallway which came out upon a large open space some sixty or seventy feet high by one-hundred fifty feet wide by two hundred feet long. In the center of the space stood a ship made of metal. It was shaped like a cigar, one hundred fifty feet in length and two decks tall. I immediately thought of Jules Verne, and chuckled inwardly. Verne was dreaming about machines just like this, but here Tesla had built a real one and hidden it here under the nose of the whole world. I could not tell what kind of ship it was; it fit no category I could bring to mind. It seemed that it might be a submarine, and for the moment I settled on that.

I stepped forward to get a better look. The upper deck had a row of portholes running fore to aft along the length of the entire ship. To the fore of the upper deck was what looked to me to be a dome-shaped pilothouse with mullioned windows. On the roof of the pilothouse was a little round cupola which was actually a pill-box type gun tower capable of pivoting 360 degrees. The upper deck at the stern of the ship consisted of a curve of mullioned windows, covering what appeared to be some kind of observation deck. On top of the ship were two large metal rods that looked like flagpoles, each rising about fifteen feet from the top of the ship, and each of them was capped by a shiny copper ball. The ship stood on four, massive telescoping metal legs. On the lower deck were two doors; one of them stood open, and a set of steps led up to the door's threshold.

I began to slowly walk along the length of the ship. Tesla walked ahead of me, Cleveland behind. A thousand questions ran through my head; it was just too much to take in all at once.

"By jings!" I said, "By jings! It's the most. . . It's amazing. . . beautiful. . . spectacular. . . ! What is it?"

"It's an airship," Tesla said.

"Of course! An *airship*! But. . ."

I stepped up to the underbelly of the ship and rapped on its hull with my knuckles. There was a dull sound.

"Solid steel," Tesla said, "encased in a ceramic shell made from powdered uranium."

"Why, she must weigh tons!" I said. "No balloon could ever lift her."

"She doesn't use balloons," Tesla said.

"No balloons?" I asked. I looked up and down the length of the ship, then stepped back as far as I could to take in her whole view at once.

"A rocket!" I said. "Why, she's a rocket airship, by jings! But. . . still. . . can you make her go? Why, you'd have to pack her with so much gunpowder, it'd blow all her passengers to kingdom come!"

"She's not a rocket, Mark," Tesla said.

"Not a rocket. . . ?" I asked, half to Tesla, half to myself. "Not a balloon. . . She's a. . . she's a. . . Well, damn, Tesla! What the hell *is* she?"

Tesla said, "She is an electro-gravitic vessel."

"A. . . *what*?"

"A vessel which operates on electricity."

"Electricity! Of course! E-lectricity! But. . . how? What makes her go? What's her motive force?"

Tesla said, "I will explain all that in due course. Suffice it to say, her operation is electrical in nature. She's capable of flight through air, under the sea, and in the vacuum of interplanetary space."

"You say. . . space?" I asked.

Tesla said, "She's capable of flight to other worlds. To other stars, in fact."

"How fast can she go?" I asked.

"In Earth's atmosphere—ten thousand miles an hour. In the vacuum of space—her potential speed is without limit—infinite. You see, in flight, she has neither mass nor inertia. She can sustain constant acceleration indefinitely. Her practical limit is the life-span of her crystal converter, which does eventually burn out and must be replaced. She can travel faster than sound—faster than light—if pushed to her absolute limit—faster than thought."

I stopped and turned around. Tesla and Cleveland stopped too. I noticed Cleveland's face. He would have lost this hand; I could see the details being explained by Tesla were News to Cleveland as well as to me. Both Cleveland and I were staggered by the implications of a ship so powerful that it could fly to other worlds—to other stars!

Tesla walked forward now, ahead of Cleveland and me.

"Theoretically," he said, "she could fly to the farthest reaches of the known universe—and still continue without end."

Tesla stopped and turned around to face us, and said, "So far, however, she has only made it across country from New Jersey and out over Lake Michigan on our secret test runs which Mr. Czito and I carry out each night."

Lillie and Ade had reached the roof of Tesla's warehouse and had gone to the rooftop access door. Ade tried the door, but it was locked fast. He bent down and looked at the door's lock. He tried Lillie's pin, trying to probe the keyhole with it. This time the wards would not give. He removed the pin and bent it slightly on its end, then inserted it again. Still the wards refused to budge.

"This may take some time," Ade whispered to Lillie.

Inside the warehouse, I stood at the bow of the airship and looked up at the pilothouse.

I said to Tesla, "So this is what you've been doing with all your money."

Tesla said, "Yes, every penny I have has gone into this—and my laboratory in New York."

I said, "I bet J.P. Morgan doesn't like that."

"He has nothing to say about it," Tesla replied.

"That's what I mean."

"I've tried to interest the Navy in my airship, but, despite President Cleveland's urgings, they have been strangely unresponsive."

I laughed, and said, "They're waiting for Morgan to give them the go-ahead. And Morgan ain't going ahead until he *is* the head."

"It was *my* head that created this ship. *I* will decide its use."

"Morgan doesn't see things that way," I said. "Does he, Mr. President?"

"I'm afraid not," Cleveland said. "But even Mr. Morgan's view has its limits. For example, our friend J.P. Morgan doesn't know we are here tonight."

"I thought Morgan knew all about everything and a little more on top," I said.

"Not this," Cleveland said.

"That so? Now you *do* have my interest."

"In fact," Cleveland said, "there are precious few people in the world who know we are here tonight."

"So you've let me in on a big secret," I said. "Why?"

"In recent days," Tesla said, "the President and I have discreetly approached a handful of the greatest minds on the planet—scientists, philosophers, theologians—to seek out their council and advice on a very grave matter."

"Well," I said, "it has always been my ambition to be a preacher, if I could get some religion in me. But so far. . ." I shrugged, and said, "I don't understand. How can I help you?"

Cleveland said, "Drop the false modesty, Clemens. You've given a great deal of thought to the human condition, its origins and ultimate development."

"Yes, Your Excellency," I said, "I've put on my thinking cap from time to time over the years. But you know, I'm really nothing but an old Mugwump."

"Mugwump my ass," Cleveland said. "What do you think about the planet Mars?"

I looked over to Tesla. He was studying me closely.

"Your Excellency," I said, "I can honestly say I don't think *anything* about the planet Mars. I've never been there, nor have any of my relatives. What I think about is my rheumatism and my bank account—just like everybody else."

"You've never heard the secret legends?" Cleveland asked.

I looked over to Tesla again, and he gave me an almost imperceptible nod. I knew he had told Cleveland what I had said about Percival Penrod. I went up to the airship and studied a riveted seam on its hull.

"Well, now," I said, "I've heard some things in my time. . . . Tall tales told late at night in the back room of the lodge."

"Tall tales?" Cleveland asked.

"I've heard some things, yes."

"And you've heard about Mars. The cities up there."

"Hell, if you're asking—you *know* I have. But now—I don't like to discuss those things much."

"It's all right, Clemens. It's just you and me and Tesla here. I want to know: Do you think they are still there—the Martian people?"

"I can only give you my opinion. I'd say—yes, they *are*. After all, we are still here."

"True enough," Cleveland said. "For the last several years, our astronomers have seen through their telescopes what appears to be a vast network of canals stretching from the north pole of Mars to its equator."

"I've read about those," I said. "Isn't there some disagreement over whether or not they really exist?"

"Yes," Cleveland said. "There is a controversy. But it is only a small part of the picture. Starting in 1877, and continuing at intervals of two years thereafter, our astronomers have sighted artificial objects orbiting some fifty miles above the Earth. The authorities of Europe and America have been able to keep the existence of these objects a secret from the general public, and thus have avoided wide-scale panic. The appearance of these objects roughly coincides with the close approach of Mars to our world."

"I had no idea," I said. "I've heard nothing of this."

"Neither you nor anyone else were supposed to hear a particle of it," Cleveland said. "In 1889, our astronomers sighted a spindle-shaped object a tenth of a mile in length hovering above the United States at a height of one hundred miles. At that time I approached Mr. Tesla here through George Westinghouse, and asked him if he knew of any way to build a ship which could travel beyond the atmosphere of Earth. He informed me that he had been designing just such a thing. We decided it best for him to finance and build his own prototype airship with the understanding that the cost of the prototype would be reimbursed should our military find use for his ship. This plan gave us the greatest latitude of secrecy—and Mr. Tesla the greatest latitude for the creative development of his ideas. Now, recently, one of our battleships out in the Atlantic sighted a foreign airship. It came up out of the ocean and flew away into the sky until it was lost to sight. It is of utmost importance that we find the origin of this foreign airship. We think this airship has come from either the Moon or Mars."

"More likely Mars," Tesla said.

I said, "Moon—Mars—it has to be coming from some place off the planet, for I am certain that you are the only person in this world who could design and build a flying machine."

"Come this way, gentlemen," Tesla said, "I'll show you something *really* interesting."

Tesla turned and walked back toward the front of the warehouse. Cleveland and I looked at each other; then followed Tesla back down the hallway. Halfway down the hall, Tesla turned and went through a door and Cleveland and I went through it after him.

We entered a room that was bare save for a couple of workbenches and a locked cabinet. Tesla went behind one of the workbenches and touched something and a panel on one of the walls slid back to reveal a large combination-lock wall safe. Tesla went to the safe, spun its wheel back and forth and opened the safe door.

The moment he cracked the door open, light flooded out from inside the safe. The light was prismatic, a rainbow of colors, and it brightened and dimmed rhythmically at regular intervals in a way which reminded me of the beating of a heart.

"Gentlemen," Tesla said, and he motioned us to step forward and look into the safe.

Cleveland and I approached the open safe and looked in. Mounted on a ceramic pedestal was an oval-shaped crystal about two and a half inches in diameter by about six inches in length. The pulsing, prismatic light came from the interior of the crystal, seeming to originate from several twinkling points. As I watched, I could see other little sparkles of light circulating through the crystal's interior, moving like flowing blood. The sparkles would move in sinuous arcs from the inside surface of the crystal to its center, and then back toward the surface again. The more I looked at the crystal, the less I thought of it as an inanimate object, and the more I thought of it as a living being. I would learn that Tesla himself thought of the crystal as just such a being—a living mineral.

"Jumpin' Jehosophat!" I said. "What South African glory hole did that come out of?"

"None," Tesla said. "The crystal is entirely artificial, grown by a special electrical process over a three year period in my New York laboratory. It is a special kind of quartz, its lattices layered with minute veins of a new kind of metallic element made from gold and other metals of the platinum group. It is the new element and its geometric distribution within the lattices which is the key to the crystal's function."

"What does it do?" I asked.

"In essence—it converts cosmic rays and electrical charges imbedded randomly in the ether into useable electricity. Those colorful flashes of light are the visible companions of invisible electrical waves of energy."

"So this powers the airship?" I asked.

"No," Tesla replied, "the cosmic rays of the universe and the electricity embedded in the ether are the power. And that power is infinite in extent and of absolutely no cost. From this single crystal can flow all the electrical power needed by everyone in the world."

I began to understand that this crystal was not a fuel, but a living machine that converted one form of energy into another—a form of energy that had lain like a sleeping lion within the hidden recesses of space itself—a form of energy infinite in extent, cheaper than air, impossible to price, impossible to parcel, impossible to sell. It began to dawn on me that this crystal was not just another invention to do things a little faster and a little better, but was the obsolescence of scarcity itself. And without scarcity, how could there be any commercial value in the material realm? Here I perceived the dim outline of a "New World" that was much greater than the one sighted by Columbus. In this world, no coal need be dug, no oil need be pumped. In this world, people would go to and fro without cost or care. In this world, the poor would become as the rich, the weak as the strong. In this world, all labor would be rested, all sickness cured, all ignorance informed, all wrong righted, all sorrow ceased, earth raised to heaven, all hopes fulfilled, all barriers broken down, all boundaries of time and space and life and death—obliterated. In this world, men would no longer exist—for they would have become gods.

These thoughts did not come to me at the time as words, but as vague, uneasy feelings. I could hardly sort them at the time. After a moment, I struggled to orient my thoughts, to find some compass to point my way in a familiar direction. My thoughts sailed in circles, and then landed ashore on the mechanism of the crystal's workings.

I said, "If your airship was a steamboat. . . then this crystal would be the boiler. . . and the cosmic rays would be. . . the firewood?"

"Very good, Mark," Tesla said, "This crystal is a converter of energy, like your steamboat boiler. Only the energy being converted here is unimaginably greater than any derived from the boiling of water. A small piece of this 'Master Crystal,' as I call it, can serve the conversion needs of the airship for some time before its molecular lattice collapses."

"Eh?"

"Before it 'burns out.'"

"Oh. So you have a piece of this crystal in your airship already?"

"That's right."

"Can I see it?"

"By all means."

Up on the roof of the warehouse, Ade was making no progress on the lock. Suddenly, the end of Lillie's hairpin broke off inside the keyhole. Ade stood up, pushed back his hat, and said, "That lock is more than a mere lock. Whoever made it knew what they were doing."

Lillie looked around the rooftop, which was mostly flat. But traversing the long axis of the building was a gabled skylight. In order to look through its windows, one had to climb up a slanting rooftop.

"What about that?" Lillie said, nodding up to the skylight.

"Maybe," Ade said.

Ade gingerly climbed up the slanting roof and grabbed hold of the edge of the skylight. Then he lay against the roof, and peered down over the edge of the windows.

"Can you see anything?" Lillie asked from below in a loud whisper.

Ade rubbed the dew off the window in front of him with his coat sleeve, and looked down through the clear glass.

"It's some kind of big machine," Ade said, "a battleship maybe."

"Help me up there," Lillie said, and she tossed off her shoes and began to climb up the roof in her stocking feet. Ade reached out, grabbed Lillie's hand, and pulled her up next to him.

Lillie looked down through the glass.

"So it's true," she said.

"What?" Ade asked.

"Tesla's airship. It really does exist."

Then Lillie and Ade caught sight of Tesla leading Cleveland and me back to the airship.

Down below in the warehouse, Tesla went up the steps leading into the airship. I followed up the steps behind him.

"Toot! Toot!" I piped. "All aboard! All aboard that's coming aboard!"

I entered the airship through her door and planted my foot on her lower deck. Cleveland came in behind me. We stopped, looking at a new curiosity. It was another strange vehicle, maybe a boat, maybe a flying machine. It was domed over with a bubble of glass.

Tesla said, "This is a smaller version of the airship. It can carry up to six people in an emergency."

"A lifeboat," I said.

Then I looked over to the bulkhead and saw some kind of canvas garments hanging on hooks. Above each garment hung a helmet, a clear bubble of glass to somehow be fitted over the head, apparently.

I pointed to the garments, and asked, "What are those?"

"Air pressure suits," Tesla said. "For movement through a vacuum."

Tesla ascended a vertical steel ladder leading to the upper deck. I followed him on up, and Cleveland came up behind me, barely squeezing his stomach through the hatchway. Tesla grabbed Cleveland's hand and helped him pull himself up out of the hatchway and on to the upper deck.

Then Tesla went to a large cabinet which extended from the floor to the ceiling, a little over seven feet high. He slid back the door of the cabinet and revealed a maze of electrical machinery. There was a large spiral coil of wire mounted on a big spool and a number of metal boxes, each with a little glass tube attached at the top. There was a maze of other electrical equipment. Amidst all this was a little metal rod, and, mounted upon its tip, a tiny crystal flashing with a rainbow of light.

"There is the child of the Master Crystal," Tesla said. "It is the drive crystal for the airship."

"What about those two fancy flagpoles on the top of the ship?" I asked. "What are they?"

"They are the aerial conductors," Tesla said.

"Lightning rods," I offered.

"Of a sort," Tesla said. "One conductor absorbs electrical charges from the strikes of cosmic rays. The electricity is conducted down into the ship here. Originally, the electricity flowed into a bank of special glass vacuum tubes. The tubes, when given a slight charge, would draw random electrical charges directly from the surrounding ether. Unfortunately, the tubes burned out relatively quickly, and were very expensive to manufacture. On an extended interstellar voyage, the ship would need to carry a large supply of the tubes. However, last night I replaced the tubes with the drive crystal."

Tesla pointed into the electrical circuits. Cleveland and I stepped forward to get a better look.

Tesla said, "The generated electricity passes into these banks of condensers and is then discharged in pulses through the circuit controller and into this magnifying coil. From the coil an intense pulse of electricity passes through space to the secondary coil."

Tesla went to a second cabinet and slid open its door, revealing a second coil.

Tesla went on, "The electricity from the secondary coil passes back up to the other aerial conductor where it is pulsed out over the surface of the ship as a skin wave.

So there it is: a self-generating dielectric vehicle."

"Do you understand any of that, Your Excellency?" I asked.

"The ship runs on electricity," Cleveland said.

"Yes," I said, "that's what I gathered."

"It is really simpler than it sounds," Tesla said.

"It usually is," I replied, "but let's pretend we understand you. The ship draws electricity from the surrounding space."

"Essentially—yes."

"And this electricity is everywhere in abundance."

"Yes. It is everywhere. And it can never be used up."

"Well, that's. . . that's remarkable in and of itself."

"Yes, it is."

"But I still don't understand how that makes the ship move—much less fly through the air."

"It is really very, very simple. As I told you some time ago—this whole invention came to me suddenly in such beautiful simplicity. It was a sudden realization, just like my realization of the system of alternating current. This time, I was also in a park—this time, Central Park in New York. A group of children were picnicking under a tree. A boy had tied a rope swing to a branch of the tree and a girl got on the swing. The boy pushed her. Every time the girl would return on the swing, the boy would push her again. Each little push added to the last and in a short while the girl was swinging high into the air, almost achieving a 90 degree arc. This is the principle of resonance. I then wondered what would happen if some giant could come along and bend that branch upon which hung that rope swing. And I wondered what would happen if the giant only bent the branch at the exact moment the boy made his push, and bent the branch in such a way as to make the girl's path of motion bypass the spot on the ground where the boy stood. The answer to what would happen is obvious: The boy would not be able to reach the girl. He would not be able to push her anymore. The girl would slow down and stop! Amazing! So from that it is quite obvious how my airship operates."

"It is?" I asked. "I must've missed something. Did you miss something, Your Excellency?"

"Girl on swing. Boy pushed her. Giant bends branch. No more pushing," Cleveland said.

"Yes," I said, "I gathered all that. But how does that make the airship move?"

This here illustrates Tesla's genius. What was absolutely opaque to everyone else was clear and bright and obvious to Tesla. A million men in each generation could see the same thing for a million years and not recognize one iota of what they were seeing. But a man like Tesla comes along and—at a glance—sees in a mote of dust the spinning truths of the cosmos.

Tesla said, "The boy is the gravitational field, the girl is the substratum of matter, its atomic structure. The gravitational field is the ether vibrating in waves of a certain frequency with a certain intensity of force. The atomic structure of matter is vibrating in a certain resonance with the vibrating ether, the gravitational force. Matter is affected by gravity because it is in resonance with it. I call this my 'Dynamic Theory of Gravity.'"

"I begin to see your point," I said. "But—the giant? Who—or—I should say—*what*—what is the *giant*?"

"Electricity," Tesla said. "Electricity is the giant."

Tesla slid the door of the cabinet back and snapped it shut.

"You see," Tesla said, "what I have discovered is that electricity has a direct influence on atomic and molecular arrangements within macroscopic bodies. An electrical charge passing through a dielectric body will change its length. Moreover, a current of sufficient charge passing through a dielectric will cause it to move in the direction of its positive pole. This is because the electrical charge partially changes the frequency of oscillations and the orientation of the spin of the atoms in the dielectric. What I subsequently found was that *any* material body can be made 'gravitationally transparent' or 'gravitationally reversed' if the voltage was great enough and the frequency of electrical pulsation high enough to match the frequency of the waves in the local gravitational field. The rest was only a matter of details, engineering, and construction."

I asked, "Did you get all that, Your Excellency?"

Cleveland said, "Electricity. Girl on swing pushed by boy. Giant bends branch. Swing misses boy. Giant stops swing. Cosmos runs giant."

"That's it," Tesla said.

I added, "Your electric field. . . your electric field grabs your atomic field by its shirt collar—and yanks."

"You have it," Tesla said.

"Where's the pilothouse?" I asked.

"Follow me," Tesla said.

Up on the rooftop of the warehouse, Lillie began carefully climbing along the edge of the skylight, scampering sidewise like a crab.

"Where are you going?" Ade whispered.

"To get a better look," Lillie whispered back.

Lillie kept crawling along until she reached a window pane that gave a direct view down into the pilothouse windows of the airship. She reached out with her hand and wiped the dew off the pane and looked down. When she did, she saw Tesla enter the pilothouse, then me, and then Cleveland.

I peered around the pilothouse. It looked vaguely familiar. I had a faint recollection of a recurring dream. I was back on the Mississippi River piloting a steamboat toward Hat Island. It was pitch dark with a thick fog, no star to steer by, no land, either. I had to feel my way by memory just as a blind man would; for without light of any kind I *was* blind. I could not tell by looking whether I was headed into the island, down the channel, or on to a sand bar—or the river bank. In the dream, I was always standing in a strange pilothouse—a domed-shaped pilothouse with mullioned windows—the pilothouse I stood in now.

"Not much different than the pilothouse of a steamboat," I said.

"Some difference," Tesla said. "The ship is controlled with this wheel."

"Starboard and larboard," I said, "just like a steamboat."

"The wheel is on a universal joint," Tesla said.

"*Not* like a steamboat," I said, tilting the wheel back slightly.

Tesla said, "Tilt the wheel back you go up, tilt it forward—you go down. Press this pedal with your foot—and the ship accelerates forward. Press this pedal—the ship slows, or stops. Press this one—the ship backs up."

I looked at the levers and pedals and realized that however complicated the airship's engine was, the pilot's controls were so simply made that any fool could operate them, and I figured that qualified me to be an airship pilot. This was not like piloting a steamboat, where you had to call down in a speaking-tube to the engineer every two minutes for him to slow down, give her a head of steam, back up, or stop. It seemed that here in this airship you did all that yourself, and did it instantly with the push of a pedal. And in an airship you did not have to worry with sandbars, snags, or floating timber—or with boiler explosions, or any other kind of explosions. I could not imagine what could worry the head of an airship pilot, and it seemed to me that a berth on this airship held all the delights of piloting and none of the worry and strain.

"Ain't it a charm!" I said. "How do you start her up?"

"Close this switch," Tesla said, "and you connect the aerial conductors to the ship's circuits—electrical conduction begins—and you're ready for flight."

"Can I. . . can I try her out?" I asked.

Tesla glanced over at Cleveland. Cleveland looked at me, then back to Tesla, and nodded.

"The wheel is yours, Mark," Tesla said.

Tesla went to the steps leading down to the airship's top deck and called down into the ship:

"Mr. Czito—come up here and prepare us for flight."

Czito immediately came up the steps and flipped a switch next to the pilot's wheel. Beyond the windows of the pilothouse I saw the walls of the warehouse open up and slide apart—two giant doors opening up a space some sixty feet tall and fifty feet wide to allow the airship passage.

Beyond the widening opening, the nighttime waters of Lake Michigan lay shimmering in the moonlight.

Tesla said to Czito, "Just engage the main capacitors; we won't need the auxiliaries."

Czito nodded and went to a desk at the back of the pilothouse. This desk was long, running the entire width of the pilothouse, and had a great number of electrical switches and rows of little incandescent light bulbs. He closed some of the switches and left the rest open. Then he went back down the steps leading out of the pilothouse.

In a moment, I heard a clang below and an incandescent light on the board next to the pilot's wheel flashed on. I realized that this light indicated whether the door to the airship was opened or closed.

Tesla said, "You may proceed anytime, Mark."

I nodded, took a deep breath, exhaled, and grabbed hold of the pilot's wheel.

"Take her out low on the water—like a boat," Tesla said.

"Like a boat—I know," I replied.

I closed the starter switch, and I immediately heard a low, undulating hum.

"Listen to that!" I said, "Reminds me of the sound of a steamboat engine! Gentlemen, we're going out!"

I pressed the accelerator pedal ever so slightly with my foot and at the same time carefully tilted the wheel a fraction of an inch. I felt no movement, but I could see that we had instantly—and I mean *instantly*—lifted up, and were slowly and steadily moving forward through the open doors and out of the warehouse!

I steered the ship between the edges of the open doors, calling on every bit of finesse that I could from my piloting days on the river so as not to crash the airship into the edge of one door or the other, or lift the airship too high and crash into the ceiling. I got the airship aimed at the center of the open space in front of us, and I gave the accelerator a feather-weight tap with my foot. We sailed out of the warehouse in a straight line. I brought the airship down on to the surface of the lake; we touched down with a gentle splash, and plowed along the lake surface like a ship under a full head of steam.

Above on the rooftop of the warehouse, Lillie and Ade had watched the airship glide out of the doors. When she realized the airship was moving out, Lillie turned and climbed down the roof with Ade following behind her. They ran to the rooftop's parapet wall and looked down to see me pilot the airship on to the waters of Lake Michigan.

Lillie and Ade watched us depart, the ship's hull glowing with a blue electrical nimbus and bolts of electricity flashing between those two fancy lightning rods which Tesla called the "aerial conductors." They kept watching the airship move away until it appeared to be only a blue ball of light skimming the surface of the lake.

"It's a boat!" Ade said.

Suddenly the blue ball of light shot straight into the sky.

"It's an *airship!*" Lillie shouted, her long, blonde hair blowing wildly in the wind.

"Yee-how!" I shouted. "Yee-hooow! Damned if I ain't a white hot rocket from hell!"

I was piloting the airship straight up through the clouds—to the Moon!

We were standing stock still, and we were flying a thousand miles an hour— all in the same instant! White clouds approached us like angels barring the gates of heaven. They encircled us, beseeched us to go no further, but we broke past to the inky expanse beyond. Now there was nothing to bar our way, only eternity lay before us, waiting, waiting, as if it had always been waiting for this moment when we would break all bonds and ascend to the Moon and stars. All I could do was grip the wheel and follow the onward moving force— and I was astonished to realize that the force was nothing more than my own will to move!

"I'll be double-damned in hell if this ain't the most. . . !" My words failed. I took the airship larboard and then down in a great arc.

Chicago lay slumbering 10,000 feet below us. I could see the dim glow from the streets and buildings all ranged out along the shoreline of Lake Michigan. I spotted the tall buildings of downtown and aimed the airship toward them.

"Yee-how!" I shouted.

"Clemens! Clemens! Clemens!" I heard Cleveland shout from behind me and I thought he wanted me to speed up.

"Yes, sir, Your Excellency," I said, "I can make her go faster!"

"No—no—I—"

Before Cleveland could say another word, I pushed the wheel forward and the accelerator pedal down a mite. The airship rocketed down through the skies and we swooped over the tops of Chicago's highest towers.

"I'm going to loop her!" I said.

I pulled the wheel back and the airship nosed up to the sky. We were moving toward the Moon again, then the Moon passed *under* us, and, above us, through the pilothouse windows, we could see the streets of downtown Chicago. I brought the airship down this way, on its back, so to speak. It seemed that we were not moving, but that the city of Chicago was lowering down on us from above. I looked starboard out the pilothouse windows and caught sight of the tops of buildings hanging upside down—that is, they *looked* upside down. Either we were upside down, or the world was; it was moot. It did not seem to me that we were upside down. I felt a normal pull of gravity downward to the floor of the airship. It seemed I had turned the world on its back, or, I should say rightly, Tesla had.

Here was a moment sublime, not to be hurried over unnoticed and unfelt, but savored and appreciated for the full measure. I took out a cigar, struck a match on the pilot's wheel, and lit up.

"Shoot, Tesla!" I said, "flying this airship's child's play. And that's my meat and 'taters—child's play!"

Tesla grinned back at me. I clinched the cigar between my teeth, grabbed the pilot's wheel, and pressed the accelerator pedal.

"Yee-how!" And I took the airship around in another loop which brought us upright again.

Now I turned the airship about and sped north over the city of Chicago, rising higher and higher through the clouds—faster—and faster—

"Clemens! Clemens!"

Cleveland was shouting, I suddenly realized. He shouted:

"I order you to bring this ship to a halt! Now!"

"Yes, sir, Your Excellency!" I said, and slammed my foot on the brake pedal.

We came to an instant stop among the clouds. A flock of birds passed our window and seemed to peer in on us and wonder who we were and where we had come from. I heard Cleveland let out of sigh of relief.

"Ah, Tesla," I said, "you *are* a genius! And your ship's a beauty!"

"Thank you, Mark," Tesla said, "You are the only person besides Mr. Czito and me who has ever piloted my ship."

"Well," I said, "I'm honored."

I held out my hand for Tesla to shake, and, although Tesla did not care much for shaking hands, he reached out and gave my hand a hearty grip with his.

"Mr. Clemens!" Cleveland said, "do you think you can get us back to port without getting us killed?"

"Why, certainly, Your Excellency, right away, sir," I replied.

"And slowly, man, slowly!" Cleveland added.

I nodded and turned the airship starboard away from the Big Dipper and swung her around south toward the Moon and downtown Chicago. Then I sent her forward and up, climbing above a bank of clouds that lay before us. I kept taking us up. We entered the cloud bank and everything went deep black. Then, in a moment, we came out upon the tops of the clouds. I steered the airship along the tops of those clouds, as if I was following a great, fog-bound river in the light of the Moon. Finally the clouds began thinning out, and I began bringing us down in a slow descent toward Lake Michigan.

I'm not sure exactly where we were, but I don't think I would be far wrong to say we were probably somewhere over lower Wisconsin and about 30,000 feet up in the sky. I kept on bringing the airship down. We passed through another layer of clouds glowing in the light of the Moon. In a little while, glimmering through the thin, cottony layer of clouds, I saw the lights of Chicago again, and at that moment I began to feel like an old hand at the airship piloting business. I got very easy and comfortable at the wheel, and would take a draw on my cigar and puff out a smoke ring or two. Soon we came abreast of downtown Chicago and I brought the airship down to about 1,500 feet above the lake front. I moved the airship along slowly and we looked out upon the city, fairly certain that we would not be noticed at this altitude in the air—for who would be looking up at the sky this time of night?

Just as we were most comfortable and serene, a large, dark object suddenly sped up beside us and hovered there, not fifty feet away. Our airship was rocked by a wake of displaced air.

"Whoa!" I cried. "What the hell is *that*?"

As soon as I said that, the dark object sped off into the sky like it was shot from a cannon and disappeared from sight in less than five seconds!

"That's it!" Cleveland shouted. "The foreign airship!"

"They could'a killed us!" I said.

"What do you say now, Clemens?" Cleveland asked. "What do you think we should do?"

"Wait—watch—and watch out," I said.

Cleveland turned to Tesla, and asked, "How long would it take you to produce a fleet of these airships?"

"Roughly—two years," Tesla said, "possibly one—if I had the money and man power."

"And money means Morgan," I said.

"I can swing a loan to the government from Morgan," Cleveland said.

"Really?" Tesla asked.

Cleveland nodded.

Tesla said, "You should know that Morgan has spied out my laboratory operations and views my advanced ideas with great suspicion."

"Yes," Cleveland said, "I realize the conflicting interest. But I also realize we are faced with a formidable, unknown foreign threat—a threat to all of us, including Morgan. I believe I can convince Mr. Morgan of the necessity of financing these new inventions of yours as a secret military project. Such a secretly contained industrial development need not affect our public economy. Let me deal with Morgan. *You* think about building airships."

Tesla nodded, but I could tell that his agreement was cargoed with extreme wariness.

I piloted the airship on in silence. None of us felt like talking, so we did not.

Lillie and Ade had watched us fly away in the airship until we plunged into a cloud about 10,000 feet above Lake Michigan.

Lillie turned abruptly, retrieved her shoes from where she had tossed them, and started for the rooftop fire escape.

"Where are you going?" Ade asked, following behind Lillie.

"To file my story."

"What story? You don't have a story."

"I have the story of the century."

Lillie sat down on the fire escape landing and began putting on her shoes.

"How do you figure that?"

"You need it spelled out? All right. Mark Twain is piloting an airship. That's a story. President Grover Cleveland is a passenger on the airship. That's a big story. Nikola Tesla has invented an airship. That—is the story of the century."

Lillie had on one shoe and was putting on the other.

"Lillie, you don't know what you're getting into. We need to sit on this until we really know what's going on."

"I know what's going on."

"Lillie—"

"No. I know what you're after. You want to slow me down just enough so you can file the story yourself. Well, it won't work. Not this time."

Lillie had both shoes on. She stood up, and shot down the stairs.

"Lillie!"

But Lillie was gone. She had disappeared down into the darkness.

Ade descended the fire escape. When he got to ground level, he caught sight of Lillie's silhouette moving toward the street. He followed after her, but not too quickly, for he was all the while thinking to himself: Let her fume; when she calms down I can reason with her.

Ade stepped out on the street in front of the warehouse. He saw Lillie marching quickly back to the cab which now stood only a half block away. Lillie reached the cab, got inside, and the cab lurched forward. Ade stood on the side of the street, waiting for the cab to come abreast of him; but when it did, it did not slow down.

"Hey!" Ade shouted. "Hold up there!"

For an instant Ade saw a flash of Lillie's face as the cab rushed by in front of him. He saw her face in profile, and it looked indifferent as a statue.

Ade ran out into the street as the cab rolled away, leaving him behind.

"Hey! Hey!" he shouted.

But the cab kept going, rattling and jingling and clip-clopping away into the night.

"Damn!" Ade said, kicking a stone across the street.

Ade stood there a moment, contemplating. Then he slowly looked up at Tesla's warehouse and beyond it to a sky of stars and thin clouds shining with moon-glow, and, above those shining clouds, a little blue point of light.

That little blue point of light was Tesla, Cleveland, Czito and me sailing along at an altitude of about 10,000 feet.

Inside the cab, Lillie tried hard to think about everything she had to do, while at the same time forcing the image of George Ade from her mind—the laughing, mocking face of George Ade who always seemed to be one step ahead of her in every story she had tried to cover.

Lillie's cab circled the fairgrounds, turned up in the vicinity of Washington Park, and then got on to Michigan Avenue and headed north toward downtown. As the cab neared the lake front, the driver suddenly drew the horses up and they came to a stop. The street ahead was blocked by a tangle of carriages stopped dead-still. A crowd was gathered all around, looking up into the night sky. Lillie looked up and saw a glowing blue cigar—Tesla's airship.

A man asked, "Did you see the other one go by?"

"That was a meteor," another man said.

"No," said the first man. "It was another airship."

The crowd stood there watching until the glowing blue cigar that was our airship drifted into a cloud and winked out of sight.

Lillie pushed her way through the people until she reached the place where the two men stood who had been speaking. She told them she was with the *Daily News* and asked if they would state what they had just witnessed for publication. They assented and recounted what they had seen. As they talked, Lillie made notes in a little memorandum book. Others approached and began telling what they saw. Lillie wrote rapidly, taking down their statements and the witnesses' names and addresses.

A policeman approached the crowd on horse back.

"You will have to move these carriages," he said.

The crowd dispersed. Lillie got back in her cab and proceeded toward downtown.

As she approached the *Daily News* building, Lillie began to think about what George Ade had said, and suddenly, now that her anger had cooled, she perceived the wisdom of his words. Perhaps, she thought, a certain degree of caution was called for. If the President denied Lillie's story, it would completely discredit her. However, if her story were to run in two parts, with the first part consisting of eyewitness accounts of the airship from the citizens of Chicago—it would make it much more difficult for Cleveland to deny the second part: that he, himself, was a passenger on the airship.

Lillie decided that she would show the city editor only the first part of the story, and only after it ran on the front page would she spring on him the second part. It was a pretty good plan, or, at least, she thought so at the time.

Lillie ordered the cab driver to stop. She had to get out and walk. She was too excited. She paid the driver, and he went on his way.

Then Lillie was struck with a final link in her plan. Instead of giving her story to the *Daily News,* she would take it to the *Record.* This would kill two birds with one stone; Ade was one of the birds, and her editor on the *Daily News* who had resisted Lillie's efforts to write "straight" News—was the other.

When Lillie entered the office of Harry Yount, city editor for the *Chicago Record,* Yount was bent over his desk looking at the proofs for the next day's front page. He looked up.

Yount said, "Well, Well, Miss Lillie West, or should I say 'Amy Leslie?' To what do I owe this visit?"

Lillie said, "I want to see Charles Dennis."

"He's not here," Yount said.

"And where is he?" Lillie asked.

"He's gone home for the night." Yount replied. "Anything I can do for you?"

"Yes. Not print that," she said, taking the proof sheet out of Yount's hand.

"The hell I can't," Yount replied.

"Read this," Lillie said, handing Yount her memorandum book.

Yount began reading Lillie's notes. After a minute, he said, "This stuff's crazy. What's the matter with you, coming in here bothering me with this?"

Lillie said, "Read the names of the witnesses."

Yount ran his eye down the column of witness names, which included addresses. Yount noticed the name of a doctor whom he knew. He picked up his telephone and called the doctor—and the doctor had arrived home just in time to answer his telephone.

"Hello, Doc. This is Harry Yount. . . . I'm doing fine. . . . The wife's fine. . . . Yes, all the children are fine, too. Listen, Doc, I've got Amy Leslie here in my office. She just told me a funny story, a crazy story really, and. . . well, I hate to bother you with it this time of night, but she says you told her you saw an airship tonight. . . . You did. . . ? You did. . . ? You *did*. . . ? You didn't! . . . You *did*. . . . Well, if you did, I'll be damned. . . I already am? Well, if you say you saw it, Doc, I believe you. . . Yes, I believe you saw *something*. . . Yes. . . yes, sir. . . yes, sir. . . yes, I know. So you don't mind us printing your name in the paper and that you say you saw this thing? . . . You don't. . . ? You don't. . . ? You *don't*? You do! . . . You *don't*. . . ? In a court of law. . . ? Well, all right. You're sure you want to do this. . . ? Uh-huh. . . uh-huh. . . well, all right. If that's what you want. . . . All right, thanks, Doc."

Yount hung up. He sat a moment looking at Lillie's notes.

"And you say you saw this thing, too," Yount said.

"Me and half of Chicago," Lillie said.

"Well," Yount said, rubbing his chin. He stood up and went to the window and looked up into the sky.

"All right," Yount said, "we'll print your notes. Just as they are. Especially the names of the witnesses. Give me back that proof sheet."

"But if you're going to print my story, you won't be needing this," Lillie said, holding up the front-page proof.

"Oh, I'm printing your story," Yount said, snatching the proof sheet out of her hand. "As an extra. For downtown distribution *only*."

"But—"

"We'll gauge the public's reaction. If it goes over, we'll run the story again in the next day's edition. If it doesn't, we'll bury it."

"But—"

"Take your notebook down to the Linotype operator and give him this to let him know I give approval."

Yount scribbled a note and handed it to Lillie, then went to the door.

"Hey, McCutcheon!" Yount shouted.

John T. McCutcheon looked up from his drawing board where he was working on a pen and ink sketch.

"Take a look at this story Miss West brought in," Yount said, holding up Lillie's notebook.

McCutcheon came over, nodded to Lillie, and took her notebook from Yount's hand.

"How have you been?" McCutcheon asked Lillie.

"Just fine, Mac," Lillie said.

He began reading Lillie's account.

"Is this supposed to be a Jules Verne satire?" McCutcheon asked.

"No!" Yount said. "The people on that list are real! I know the doctor, and he just confirmed the story to me over the telephone. I want you to drop what you're doing and work up a sketch of the airship. Make it a big cigar flying through clouds. But don't get too fancy. This is no joke. It's News."

McCutcheon scratched the back of his head.

"What's the matter?" Yost asked.

McCutcheon shrugged, "It just seems far-fetched."

"Miss Leslie says she saw it," Yost said.

"George saw it, too," Lillie said to McCutcheon.

"Ade?" Yost asked.

Lillie nodded. "He was there."

Yost laughed, "Oh, boy! You hear that McCutcheon? Your buddy Ade saw it, too. Still think it's far-fetched?"

McCutcheon shrugged again.

"Get to work on the sketch. And make it snappy," Yost said.

"Do I get a by-line?" Lillie asked.

"Amy Leslie Chases Airships?" Yount asked. "Doesn't sound right. Maybe we should use your real name. I don't know. Never mind about that now."

Yount took the notebook away from McCutcheon, gave it back to Lillie, and said, "Just get this notebook down to the compositors. I'll be down there in a few minutes myself."

Lillie started off.

Yount called after her, "If your story goes over with the public, then we'll see about a by-line."

Chapter Four

Pesterin' and Persistin'

> Well, then he got on his troubles again, and
> mourned and grumbled about the way he was treated,
> and couldn't seem to git over it, and especially
> people's saying the ship was flimsy. He scoffed
> at that, and at their saying she warn't simple and
> would always be getting out of order. Get out of
> order! That graveled him; he said that she couldn't
> no more get out of order than the solar sister.
>
> — Huck, *Tom Sawyer Abroad*

George Ade's earliest memory was of sitting on a fence in Kentland, Indiana, and looking up at a blur of illumination in the night sky. He was watching the city of Chicago, eighty miles to the north, burning up in a most efficient and business-like way. It was 1871, and Ade was five years old.

Perhaps George Ade watching Chicago go up in flames like that forged the first link in a chain of destiny that would pull him to the city by the great lake, and make him forever a part of that place, no matter where he would go, no matter what he would do.

George Ade was born February 9th, 1866 in the town of Kentland. His father was the cashier for the town's bank. Upon graduating high school, Ade lit out for Purdue University. There he excelled at watching football games and pulling practical jokes with his fraternity brothers of Sigma Chi. Somehow, by some unknown process, he learned enough by 1887 to become commencement speaker for his graduating class. His speech was "The Future of Letters in the West."

After graduating, Ade went to work for Newspapers in Lafayette. These paid mostly in meal tickets to a cheap restaurant which was a heavy advertiser.

Then Ade began working for a patent medicine company in Purdue. His job was writing Newspaper and catalogue advertising. Ade's literature was stirring and persuasive, and it was more—it was on a high moral plain. It set the lofty goal for itself of reforming the whole world. Its primary doctrine was that the whole world is born diseased, and because of this we are all desperately in need of patent medicines of various sorts. Some of us need certain kinds, some of us need others. But all of us need some kind, and most of us need all kinds, and need them not just everyday but several times a day—and in quantity.

Here in Ade's advertisements were not only the usual castor oils and liver pills, but exotic purgatives, guaranteed muscle builders, and the very latest blood purifiers. The pinnacle of this literature was Ade's advertisement for a nicotine addiction cure he named with poetic aptness "No-Tobac." This product, Ade wrote, was guaranteed to "slay the smoking habit." To vivify and drive home this claim, Ade had his college friend, John T. McCutcheon, draw an illustration of a Roman soldier putting his sword to a dragon labeled "Smoking Habit." The advertisement guaranteed results only if the customer followed the directions, the first of which was "discontinue use of tobacco."

Despite the moral elevation of Ade's patent medicine literature, it did not completely fulfill his literary aspirations. So in 1890, Ade joined his fraternity brother, McCutcheon, in the city of Chicago.

Ade and McCutcheon located in a delightfully situated "hall-bedroom" on Peck Court. It was on the third floor up from the ground, in the back, and was a spacious twelve by ten feet, and those dimensions made it very convenient. If you needed anything, you didn't have to get up and go get it, you just had to reach for it; usually you didn't even have to straighten out your arm. And it was the perfect abode for the aspiring artist and man of letters: there was nothing in that room to distract the mind from the contemplation of artistic and literary aspirations. In fact, there was nothing in that room at all—except two beds, two chairs, and an ancient desk decorated with a jack-knife. However, from his window, Ade had a most picturesque view to the west. Just outside his window sill stood a neatly stacked heap of empty beer and whiskey bottles. Beyond the bottles lay an artistically arranged pile of discarded boxes and crates covered with a delicate patina of mold and slime. Beyond this verdant landscape, rose a small hill of colorful bric-a-brac, donated shoes and corsets, slightly damaged dishware, and generous portions of meals from tables around the neighborhood. This hill was a particular favorite of stray dogs and pigs. Further away, beyond the hill, and beyond dainty walls of soot covered brick, Ade could see a row of chimneys with their black smoke blotting out all view of the sky. And far away, in the ruddy half-light of the setting sun, Ade could, on a very clear day, barely glimpse the smoky silhouette of the Polk Street Station tower. It was an inspiring view; that is, it inspired Ade to find another view.

"You still don't have a byline."

Ade applied to what was then the *Chicago Morning News*, which later became the *Chicago Record*.

The city editor said, "If you can prove you're not a college man, you might be able to get into the advertising department and make forty dollars a week."

But Ade said he wanted to "keep tabs on the human race." So he took a cub reporter's position for twelve dollars a week. His first assignment was the daily weather report. Ade told me, "I tackled that assignment with the same enthusiasm I would have had if I had been covering the elopement of an archbishop with a chorus girl." Ade's enthusiasm was rewarded. The managing editor of the *Chicago Record*, Charles Dennis, began giving Ade a variety of assignments: reporting on baseball games, horse races, and politics. Then Ade's stories started hitting the front page—the Homestead Strike, the Democratic Convention of 1892, and "the fight of the century" in New Orleans between "Gentleman Jim" Corbett and "the Boston Strongboy" John L. Sullivan.

Ade did so well with these assignments that he was given the run of the city. He was to report on anything and everything as he saw fit. He and McCutcheon would scour the city of Chicago from north to south, east to west, Ade writing, McCutcheon illustrating what was written. They would find News in the hotels, in the slums, in the finest mansions, in the police station houses, in the freak shows of the dime museums, in the factories, and in the slaughterhouses.

In 1892 Charles Dennis gave Ade a special assignment covering the World's Fair. He was to have his own column on the same page as Eugene Field's "Sharps and Flats." It was to be entitled "All Roads Lead to the Fair." John T. McCutcheon was to illustrate it.

It was some time along here that Ade made the acquaintance of Miss Lillie West. The particulars of their first meeting I do not know, but I imagine that their paths crossed somewhere in the offices of the *Record* where Ade was employed, or the *Daily News* where Miss West was employed. The *Record* was the morning edition of the *Daily News*, so the connection between Mr. Ade and Miss West probably began in one office or the other. Although there were nine or so daily Newspapers in Chicago at that time, most of the reporters for those nine all knew each other. So it was inevitable then that Miss Lillie West, the only woman reporter in Chicago, would come to the attention of Mr. George Ade, probably the only reporter of the male species who could truly appreciate a woman reporter.

I seem to have the impression from what I have been told that the friendship of George Ade and Lillie West grew by a gradual and natural series of steps, that neither took a great, sudden passion for the other, but that both gradually and unconsciously began taking a growing liking for the other. These two had a great deal in common. Both had talent with the pen; both loved the theatre and its bold effects; both had an eye for detail and the ability to discover the remarkable in the unremarkable.

I do not know exactly when Lillie West was born. She has never been anxious to divulge that information. It has always been my impression that she was born some time after the War Between the States, making her about the same age as George Ade. But others have told me that she was born *before* the War. George Ade has told me that he believes she was born about 1860, though even he does not know that for a fact. All I can say is that when I knew her, she seemed young, exceedingly young—younger than I ever was, and I was once *very* young. Lillie West was also beautiful: a petite blond-haired, blue-eyed enchantress. She was one of those women who would turn the heads of all the gentlemen who passed by her on the street. This kind of beauty is never entirely physical, but relates more to a projection of personality, energy, and intelligence, a projection always felt as an over-all impression, never a mere awareness of some detail of face or form.

I do know that Lillie—and I will call her that from here on out, for that's the name she preferred when I knew her—I do know that Lillie was born in West Burlington, Iowa. Her father was a merchant, and, for a brief while, I understand, a Newspaper publisher. During her girlhood she attended private schools in Missouri and Indiana. Her main course of study was vocal music. After graduation, she went to Europe for private tutoring and then came back to America to attend the Chicago Conservatory of Music.

Some time in the mid-1880s her history becomes a bit more definite. It was then that she achieved some fame among lovers of operettas. She played the role of Fiamatta in Edmond Andran's operetta *La Mascotte*. Sometime along then she married one Harry Brown, a fellow player and the comedian of the company. She and her husband toured America for the next several years and had one son, Francis Albert.

In 1889 young Francis, aged four, died of diphtheria while Lillie was performing in Gustave A. Kerker's *Castle's in the Air* and Harry Brown was out on a drinking spree. Such a double tragedy of death and betrayal would have destroyed many another woman—or man. But it seems that Lillie, grief-stricken though she was at the time, drew from some wellspring of strength deep within herself. She quit the stage and went back to Chicago, and, with the help of her mother, obtained a divorce.

Also with her mother's encouragement, Lillie sought out work as a writer. She submitted a piece of writing to a reader's contribution column in the *Chicago Daily News* entitled "What One Woman Thinks," and signed it "Amy Leslie." H. Ten Eyck White, who was then managing editor of the *Daily News*, found her article so striking that he engaged her to write dramatic criticisms.

Lillie found a rebirth of body and soul as "Amy Leslie." She was not merely a capable drama critic, but an exceptional one. She knew what she was writing about, because she had once done it herself, and done it better than many of the performers she was reviewing. This is rare with a drama critic. Most of them have never set foot on a stage and only know how things are "from the front of the house." I was once that kind of drama critic in San Francisco. I would review plays by the wholesale method, seeing a little of this one, a little of that, so that by evening's end I would have "reviewed" four or five plays. I would never see the end of any one of them. What I didn't see, I would make up in my review. I never had to worry about discrepancies, because no one ever read any of my reviews.

For a year or two Lillie was satisfied with her work and her life. But about 1892 she began wanting to do something more than write drama reviews. As a concession to her constant requests to cover "real" news, her editor made her "Woman's Correspondent" for the World's Fair.

Lillie decided she would create a book out of her articles about the World's Fair in the hope that this would show the editors that she could write something besides drama reviews. She also started going about the city taking notes of everything she saw and experienced. Often she would encounter Ade and McCutcheon who were out looking for a story of their own. Somewhere along the way, Ade started taking Lillie along when McCutcheon and he were out covering a story. This gradually turned into just Ade and Lillie taking buggy rides alone out to Lincoln Park on Sundays. Something was happening between Lillie and Ade, but neither would name it to the other. It grew as an unspoken understanding.

Then in the fall of 1892 a grand "Exposition Ball" was held in Chicago's Auditorium Building. It was the beginning of celebrations for the World's Fair. All of Chicago society turned out, led by Mrs. Bertha Palmer and General Nelson Miles. In the great hall, John Phillip Sousa played the "Coronation March."

Of course Ade, McCutcheon, and "Amy Leslie" were there to observe as reporters. But perhaps it was these three among all the rest who seemed the most at home in "society." Ade, especially, carried himself through the crowd with a grace so light and easy that one might have easily supposed that he was the son of old money and certainly not a sixty dollars a week Newspaper reporter whose father was a small town bank clerk.

One person was particularly taken with Ade: a debutante whose father Ade had long been attempting to interview. Ade saw his chance and asked the young lady if he might have the honor of a waltz. She accepted and the two of them floated across the floor. Afterwards, Ade took the young lady to a secluded corner of the ballroom in the hope that he might obtain through her an interview with her father. The young lady was fresh from an eastern finishing school where she had been sent by her parents to reform her wild ways, and she mistook Ade's intentions. Somewhere in the conversation she glanced about, believed she saw no one looking, stood upon tip-toes, grabbed Ade's lapels, and fire-branded Ade's lips with her own. It was at that exact moment that Lillie came upon them. The young lady, sensing something, spun about, and came face to face with Lillie. The two locked eyes, then the young lady made a swift retreat.

Ade stood looking at Lillie, not knowing what to say. Finally, he managed, "Lillie—"

That was all he was allowed. Lillie turned away from Ade and left the ballroom.

Ade did not see Lillie again for a long time after that. When he did see her, she did not seem particularly interested in conversation. From then on Lillie somehow always seemed to find out where George Ade was bound for in search of a story, and she would always arrive on the scene before he did. She would then write up the story and submit it to her editor, and, of course, the editor would always reject Lillie's story. "Oh, now, Lillie," he would say, "just stick to the drama. That's what you're good at."

On April 3rd, 1893, Buffalo Bill Cody opened his "Wild West Show and Congress of Rough Riders of the World" across from the main entrance of the World's Fair. Two days earlier, "Amy Leslie" came to interview Buffalo Bill for her book on the fair. In the course of the interview, "Amy Leslie" revealed that she herself had once been a performer, that she was, in fact, Lillie West. This jogged Colonel Cody's memory; he remembered seeing Lillie on the stage. Now Colonel Cody began interviewing Lillie West, and found out that she considered herself a good marksman; she revealed that she had taken up target shooting as a girl and that she still liked to go bird hunting in the dunes at the southern tip of Lake Michigan. This so delighted the Colonel that he called for Annie Oakley, and when Miss Oakley arrived, he proposed a shooting match between Miss Lillie West and Miss Annie Oakley. The two ladies were game, but agreed to the match only if it were kept a private matter between the three of them. Colonel Cody looked about the arena where they stood and eyed a number of workers and Indians loitering about. He asked if these people's presence would be allowed. The ladies agreed.

And so the match between Annie Oakley and Lillie West commenced. An Indian was recruited to throw the clay targets. Miss Oakley shot first—and hit, of course. Then Miss West shot—and hit. The two ladies continued in this fashion a number of times in quick succession, stopping only to reload their rifles.

Somewhere during this match, George Ade walked into the arena. He had come to interview Buffalo Bill as well. When he saw Lillie shooting a rifle alongside Annie Oakley, he stopped in his tracks and watched. And as he watched, he reflected that Lillie West had beat him to a story once again—and that this day must be in honor of him, for it was April 1st.

Ade kept watching. Then—after reloading for yet another time—Lillie missed a shot; Lillie's rifle sounded, but the clay target continued in an arc across the sky and dropped to the ground with a thud. A hurrah went up from the few onlookers scattered around the arena.

Lillie turned around and saw Ade standing there. She gave her rifle to Annie, and said, "Thanks for the match, Miss Oakley,"

"No," Annie replied, "thank you, Miss West. It's not often I can find someone who can work me up to a lather."

Lillie inclined her head and started out of the arena. She passed Ade who was still standing there.

Lillie said, "If you're looking for Colonel Cody, he's over there." Then she continued on her way.

Ade said, "That's some straight shooting—for a woman."

Lillie stopped, turned around slowly, and said, "Most of the men I've known rarely manage to get a shot off, and when they do, it's usually in the foot."

Ade stood there speechless as Lillie walked away. Who can say what he felt? I do not know. But, surely, a wall had grown up between Lillie and Ade, and I don't think either of them really wanted that wall between them.

Such was how things stood between George Ade and Lillie West the night they followed Tesla, Cleveland and me to Tesla's warehouse south of the World's Fair.

That night after Lillie left Ade standing alone in the street in front of Tesla's warehouse, he walked the perimeter of the fairgrounds and finally came upon a hansom cab rattling down a dark street. Ade took the cab back to his lodgings where John T. McCutcheon lay in a deep sleep. When Ade came in, McCutcheon came to a groggy wakefulness.

"Hey," McCutcheon asked, "what's going on with you and Lillie?"

"What are you talking about, Mac?" Ade asked, tossing his hat on the desk.

"She said you and she saw an airship tonight."

"Did she tell that to anyone else?"

"Yes, indeed. She told Yost. Not only that, she had a whole story written up with names and addresses of witnesses down on Michigan Avenue who saw the thing flying over the lake."

Ade took off his coat and hung it on the back of a chair. He then sat down on his bed, leaned his elbows on his knees and put his head in his hands.

McCutcheon went on, "Yost is running the story and he had me do a drawing of the airship."

Ade said nothing, but just kept holding his head in his hands, looking down into the dark.

McCutcheon said, "It's all coming out tomorrow morning as an extra. What do you say to that? Say, George! What do you say? Did the two of you really see an airship?"

"Did Lilly say anything about Grover Cleveland?"

"President Cleveland? No. Why?"

"Or Mark Twain?"

"Mark Twain? No!"

"How about Nikola Tesla?"

"Tesla? Tesla? Wait a minute. What are you getting at?"

"Never mind. It's nothing."

"Nothing? Nothing! Sure."

"Look—it's better you don't know. Just forget I said anything."

"You and Lilly! What a pair!"

"All right, Mac. You want to know? We saw it. We saw the airship. Just like she said. It's an invention of Nikola Tesla's. We saw Tesla and Cleveland in the ship's pilothouse. And Mark Twain was at the pilot's wheel."

"George, have you been drinking?"

"I'm telling you what we saw. Believe it, or don't. But that's what we saw."

"You're not drunk, and you're not laughing."

"I'm not laughing."

McCutcheon let out a long, low whistle in the dark.

"What a story!" McCutcheon said, "And we got it!"

"We?"

"You and Lillie and me."

"Lillie does not work with us."

"I think she will after this."

"Lillie is a very headstrong woman. There is a lot she doesn't understand—you know what I mean—about the way the world works. If she doesn't watch out, she's going to get herself into a lot of trouble. She's going to get us all in a lot of trouble."

"Oh. She's going to get *us* in trouble. For a minute I thought you were just worried about Lillie."

"I'm beat," Ade said, loosening his tie. He took off his collar, slipped off his shoes, and lay back on his bed. In a moment or two, his snoring was keeping McCutcheon awake.

The next morning, Ade left his rooming house and took a streetcar headed north up State Street for downtown. He intended to go to the offices of the *Record* and test the waters there with Yost and Dennis. Ade did not know what the reaction to Lillie's story would be, but he knew that, whatever it would be, it would be in the form of some kind of trouble.

Ade had only traveled a couple of blocks when he caught sight of a Newsboy at a corner selling the *Record*. Ade jumped off the streetcar.

The Newsboy was shouting, "Extra! Extra! Read all about it: Mystery Airships Over Lake Michigan! Extra! Extra! Read it in the *Record*!"

"I'll take one of those," Ade said, dropping two pennies in the Newsboy's hand.

"Thanks, mister," the boy said, handing over the paper.

Ade looked at the front page. He saw that Lillie had not been given a by-line—no "Amy Leslie," no "Lillie West." Ade ran his eye over the story. There was McCutcheon's drawing of the airship: a black cigar silhouetted against a moon half-shrouded in clouds. There was nothing in the article about Tesla, or President Cleveland, or me, or a warehouse. Instead, it was only an account describing a crowd blocking traffic on Michigan Avenue while they stared up at two airships flying through the sky. Perhaps Lillie had listened to him after all, Ade thought.

Ade folded the Newspaper and decided to forget about going to the *Record*. He had to see Lillie. He felt he had to find her before she did something else to make matters even worse.

Ade started walking north up State Street toward the Great Northern Hotel. If he knew Lillie, he told himself, that is where she would be this morning.

Ade made his way up State Street until he reached the intersection of Van Buren. As he walked along State Street in that vicinity, he passed a storefront hung with banners and displaying a garishly painted sign that read "Globe Dime Museum." Ade glanced at the sign, but did not break his pace; he kept marching toward Jackson Street. There he crossed the intersection over to the north side of Jackson, and turned left to cross State Street, heading for the Great Northern Hotel a block away.

In a moment, Ade caught sight of Lillie up ahead in the crowd. He quickened his pace and caught up with her. When he came up beside Lillie, he opened the Newspaper and held it out in front of her.

"You still don't have a by-line," Ade said.

"Keep watching," Lillie said. "I will."

Lillie kept walking, not breaking her pace for an instant. Ade kept walking beside her.

"There's no mention of Tesla," Ade said.

"Nor of Cleveland. Nor of Mark Twain."

"Why not?"

"That's for tomorrow's edition. Part Two of the story. Front page. Where my by-line *will* be. Now, if you'll excuse me."

Lillie quickened her pace and turned the corner at Dearborn, heading for the Great Northern's main entrance.

Ade caught up with Lillie.

Ade asked, "Going to see Mark Twain, eh?"

Lillie shot a glance at Ade and kept going. Ade caught up with her again as she entered the lobby of the hotel.

"You look lovely this morning, Lillie," Ade said.

"Oh, please."

"You have my full attention—just as you did last night."

"I didn't seem to have your full attention at the Exposition Ball."

"That heiress? She meant nothing to me but a story."

Lillie stopped in the middle of the lobby.

"Well," she said, "You had your 'story.' So now why don't you let me have mine?"

"I'd like to. But I worry about you."

"What on earth for?"

"I'm afraid you're going to get into something you can't get out of."

"And you've decided you're going to be the one to get me out of it."

"Maybe."

Lillie started off across the lobby again, toward the hotel's main restaurant, with Ade at her elbow.

"Maybe you're the one who is in need of rescuing," Lillie said.

"*Moi?*"

"Maybe you're going to get into something you can't get out of. And when you do—you better hope *I'm* around."

Lillie and Ade stopped on the threshold of the restaurant. They saw me sitting at one of the tables with Fred Hall.

"There he is," Ade said. "Let me handle this."

"Why you?"

"Mark Twain is an old newspaperman from way back. And I know old newspapermen."

"My father was an old newspaperman," Lillie said, "and he always told me to watch out for young newspapermen. We'll both handle it."

Lillie and Ade approached our table. Ade stepped forward and took off his hat, holding it against the folded Newspaper in his left hand.

"Excuse me, sir," Ade said smoothly, "but. . . aren't you Mark Twain?"

"Yes, sir," I replied to Ade in the hale and hearty tones of Mark Twain. "I've been sittin' here the last half hour hopin' somebody'd notice, haven't I, Hall?"

I looked back up to Ade, and added, "I'm as vain as a cat and almost as smart."

"George Ade," the young reporter said, holding out his right hand. I shook hands with him.

"I'm a big admirer of your works," Ade said. Lillie nudged Ade with her elbow.

"Oh," Ade said, "and please allow me to introduce my friend, Miss Lillie West."

I rose to my feet, and said, "Charmed. We have met before, have we not? At the *Daily News*?"

Lillie seemed to catch her breath for a moment, and then said, "At the door."

"At the door," I said.

"I'm surprised you'd remember," she said.

"I'm surprised you'd think I'd forget," I replied. "Are you folks staying at the hotel?"

"No," Ade said. "Actually—we're reporters."

"Oh."

Ade said, "I'm with the *Chicago* Record, and Miss West is with the *Chicago Daily News.*"

"What can I do for you?" I asked.

"Well," Ade said," you see, I. . . that is, we. . . were wondering if you'd consent to an interview?"

"This time of morning? I make it a rule never to give interviews in the morning."

I looked over to Hall, and added, "Nor in the evening, come to think of it."

Ade took a half step toward me. I turned to him and said, "Interviews are unwise—day or night."

"But—" Ade started.

"Young man!" I said, dropping the Mark Twain mask. "I am very busy! We were just finishing breakfast. Perhaps you could see Mr. Hall later this afternoon. Mr. Hall is my business associate and is handling all the details of my schedule for this trip."

Lillie said, "Can't we just have five minutes of your time?"

"Well—"

"Three minutes," she offered.

"You're persistent," I said. "I like that—"

"Thank you—"

"—in a man. Hate it in a woman."

Lillie held my gaze. She did not blink, flinch, or fidget. I kept looking at her, and she kept looking back at me.

"Have a seat, Miss," I said. "I'll give you *two* minutes."

I looked at Ade as I sat down, and said, "You too."

Lillie and Ade sat across from me. I took out a cigar.

"Now just what did you want to interview me about?"

"The fair," Ade said.

"And your friend. Mr. Tesla," Lillie added.

Ade shot a glance at Lillie, and then looked back to me.

"Oh," I said, "Mr. Tesla."

I lit the cigar.

"What about him?" I asked.

"He's a wonder," Ade said. "Isn't he?"

"I'd say so. Wonder of the world."

"May I quote you on that?" Lillie asked.

"If you'd like. But I'm only quoting what you Newspaper people have already said about him."

"You're a great admirer of his theories, aren't you?" Lillie asked.

"Well, I. . . now—do you want to interview me or Tesla? He can tell you more about his theories than I ever could."

Lillie said, "I want to know what *you* think about Mr. Tesla's ideas. From your point of view. You've been to his laboratory in New York many times, have you not?"

"I have, along with a lot of other people. New York society, mostly. I usually go there with Joseph Jefferson. You know—the actor?"

"Rip Van Winkle," Ade said.

I nodded. "Ol' 'Pool-Cue' Jefferson, Tesla and I call him; he's always ready for a game of billiards. Ol' 'Pool' and I go to Tesla's and have a hootin', howlin' time juggling electric lightnin' bolts at each other."

Ade asked, "But all these fireworks of Tesla's—aren't they just some kind of sideshow?"

"Now, if I thought for one second that you really believed that, young man, I'd say you were a complete idiot. You asked me about the fair. Tesla's electrical system is going to light that fair and run every machine in it for over a square mile. You call that a sideshow? It's a reality. Tesla isn't just promising us the future—he's built it—and he is setting it running on the shores of Lake Michigan—lock, stock, and barrel."

"What about Thomas Edison?" Lillie asked. "He has a system of electricity."

"Direct current, yes, D.C. Tesla's system is alternating current, A.C. Direct current electricity can only be transported about a mile before it loses power. Every mile you've got to build another electrical power generating plant. Do you have any idea of the cost of wiring the whole country for electricity when you've got to build an electrical generating plant *every square mile*? Well, I'll tell you, the cost has been figured—and it's prohibitive."

"But Mr. Edison—" Lillie started to say.

"Mr. Edison," I said, "knows how to keep his mouth shut and milk the cow 'til she runs dry."

Ade asked, "Well, doesn't Mr. Tesla's system have the same problem? Doesn't it lose power over distance?"

"No, sir," I said, "it doesn't. Alternating current can be transported through wires for hundreds of miles without losing any significant power. In fact, it's probably possible to transport it *thousands* of miles."

Ade said, "It sounds like you think Tesla could do anything."

"I don't know," I said, "maybe he could."

"Could he build an airship?" Ade asked.

"You're referring to that Newspaper article," I said.

"So you've seen my article," Lillie said.

"Now was that *your* article? Good Newspaper hoax! Wrote a few myself in my younger days."

"Are you accusing me of fabricating a hoax?"

"Not at all, my dear, not at all. I'm just saying you didn't get your facts straight. Get your facts straight first, then you can distort 'em any way you like."

Lillie said, "The facts are that last night several dozen people witnessed an airship flying over Lake Michigan."

"Those aren't the facts, my dear, those are the *claims*."

"And," Lillie asked, "what do you *claim* are the facts?"

"Most likely. . . that, uh. . . somebody got hold of some bad whiskey, and. . . had a case of the *delirium tremens*."

"*Many* people say they saw the airship."

"I have found that many people will say just about anything."

"But several witnesses were respected citizens of Chicago," Ade said. "I don't think they would make up a story like that. Now. What do *you* think?"

"I think that your two minutes are long gone. Come on, Hall."

Hall and I stood up.

"But Mr. Twain—" Lillie started, she and Ade standing up.

"Clemens. Call me Clemens. Mark Twain's just my *nom de plume*."

"Haven't I heard that Mr. Tesla calls you Mark?" Lillie asked.

"Well, now. Maybe you have. And maybe he does. Mr. Tesla can do whatever he likes. Geniuses usually do. Now. If you'll excuse me."

"But—"

"Young lady, persistence is one thing—pesterin'—quite another."

Hall and I strolled away toward the entrance of the restaurant. There we retrieved our hats and coats. I turned back and gave Lillie and Ade a little grin and wave. Ade grinned and gave a short wave back.

"Cagey old rascal," Ade said in a low tone between the teeth of his grin.

"Don't say anything," Lillie said.

Ade said, "I'd just like to know what's going on. Are you going to tell me? Or are you going to give me the brush-off again like you did last night?"

"Not here. Come on."

As Hall and I got into a cab out on the street, I saw Lillie and Ade coming out of the hotel's entrance. I looked at them around the edge of the cab and they stared back at me.

We drove off, and I said, "I've just figured out how I'll pay Paige's seven thousand dollar bill."

"How?" Hall asked.

"Remember that story I wrote last summer about Huck Finn and Tom Sawyer going to Africa in a balloon?"

"I do. *Tom Sawyer Abroad*. Sort of an imitation Jules Verne."

"I should say not! *Burlesque* Verne, always! Imitate Verne, *never!*"

"All right. What are you going to do with it?"

"I'm going to polish it up a mite and we're going to publish it as a book."

"And you think that will bring seven thousand?"

"Or more. People are interested in airships now. They've got airships on their brains. They're seeing airships every time they look at a bird or the Moon. And they'll buy my airship story."

"All right. I'll see if we can fit it into our publishing schedule."

"If? We *will* fit it in. I'll give you a finished manuscript shortly. But first I want to work on a character in the story—the inventor of the airship."

"Yes. What was his name?"

"He doesn't have a name. I just call him the 'Professor.' He's just a lunatic inventor. I've modeled him after Paige."

"Oh, ho! After Paige? I thought you were going to say Tesla."

"There might be a little of Tesla there, around the edges. But the main height and bulk is all Paige."

"But do you think the public will accept Tom and Huck traveling around the world in a balloon?"

"Hall, haven't you learned by now that 'the public' will accept whatever they are given? Besides, Tom and Huck are my property and I can do whatsoever I desire with them: put them in an airship balloon, or starve them on a desert island, or elect them Presidents of the United States, or drive them crazy and shut them up in a lunatic asylum, or hang them as horse thieves—just as I see fit."

"Are you saying there is no literary logic to the characters of Tom and Huck?"

"Literary logic? That's a contradiction itself. There is no logic to literature, only the illusion of logic. Very little of what happens in literature has any real logic to it, only contrivance."

"What about life?"

"Life has neither logic nor contrivance. It is just one damned thing after another and then it ends as senselessly, as meaninglessly, as illogically as it began."

"And what about the afterlife?"

"I cannot speak on that, for I have no experience there. But from what I have been told there seems to be no logic in heaven; we are all forgiven for our sins for no good reason at all, a completely undeserved forgiveness. Can you find any logic in that? As for Hell—there may be some logic in Hell. And that's the thing about logic: we always want it applied exclusively to the other fellow."

Lillie and Ade walked east along Jackson Street. Every once in a while, Lillie would glance quickly over her shoulder then look forward again just as quickly. The third time she did this, Ade asked, "What?"

"I think I'm being followed by a Pinkerton agent," Lillie said.

"Well," Ade said, "looking behind won't help. If you were being shadowed by an ordinary 'fly man,' he'd be easy enough to spot, but if a Pinkerton man is after you, you'll never know it."

"Let's just keep walking," Lillie said. "I don't want to talk here."

They kept walking along Jackson Street several blocks until they reached Michigan Avenue. There they crossed the avenue and proceeded along a wide cement walkway that led out to a pier terminating on the shore of Lake Michigan; it was one of the new piers that were just being completed for the lake steamers going down to the fair. Under the pier, the trains of the Illinois Central ran along their tracks belching steam and coal dust.

At the end of the pier Lillie and Ade stopped and looked out over the lake. For a moment they watched a cargo ship steaming along out on the distant horizon. Then Ade turned with his back to the lake and leaned on the pier's railing.

"Nobody's behind us," Ade said. "I don't think anyone can know what we're saying."

Lillie turned around and looked back at the buildings along Michigan Avenue.

"No one could hear us," Lillie said. "But a man with a spyglass could read our lips from the window of one of those buildings."

"I don't think a man with a spyglass is in any of those windows," Ade said with a smile. "If Pinkerton's men wanted you, you wouldn't be walking around here. You'd be in their custody."

"Don't be so sure," Lillie said. "What makes you think Pinkerton's men would want to put me in their custody? They want to find out what I know and what I'm going to do next. They can't find that out by putting me in their custody. Do you think I am a fool?"

"No, Lilly." Ade said, "I do not think you are a fool. Far from it."

Lillie kept looking back at the city.

"All right," Ade said, turning back around. "No one is out on the lake. Are you going to tell me what's going on or not?"

Lillie turned back around to the lake.

"Two weeks ago I had lunch with a former classmate of mine. Her father is an astronomer. She told me that her father and his associates have observed through their telescopes a ship flying over the United States."

"You mean they've seen Tesla's airship?"

"Not Tesla's. This ship was a tenth of a mile in length and floating one hundred miles above the surface of the earth."

Ade turned and looked at Lillie for a long moment, then looked back at the blue horizon before them.

Lillie went on, "These astronomers have met with President Cleveland and Nikola Tesla and know about Tesla's airship. Tesla has built his airship to use it to find the origin of the giant ship. At the moment they all suspect that the giant ship comes from Mars."

"So last night. . . "

"Yesterday afternoon I covered the Wagner concert at the Auditorium. Afterwards, I went down to the *Daily News* to file my review and there was Mark Twain coming out of the building. I knew that he's friends with both Cleveland and Tesla, and I already knew that Tesla is in the city for the fair. It was a coincidence, and I don't believe in coincidences."

"Neither do I."

"So after seeing Mark Twain, I decided to follow Tesla just to see what would happen. I went down to the grounds of the World's Fair and found Tesla leaving the Electricity Building. I followed him back to his hotel and then to Grand Central Station. There he met three men with broad brimmed hats pulled down over their faces. One of the men was quite large."

"Cleveland."

"Cleveland. They went out of a service entrance at the station and got into that landau. I followed them to the Great Northern. Then you showed up."

Ade had listened to Lillie with great attention, weighing her every word. Although Lillie's reasoning was a little faulty, she impressed Ade. But actually, my presence in Chicago had nothing to do with Cleveland or Tesla. Cleveland had come to Chicago to see the airship, and when Tesla found out I was in town, he decided to bring me along to see it, too.

"So what do you intend to do now?" Ade asked.

"I'm going back to that warehouse and get photographs of the airship and anything else that can prove my story."

"I take it back."

"Take what back?"

"That you're not a fool. If you go back to that warehouse, you won't just be a fool, you will be a fool in bigger trouble than you could ever imagine!"

"George!"

"Lillie! You have to be crazy to think of going back there!"

"George, I'm going back there, and no one, neither you nor anyone else, is going to stop me!"

Ade looked away from Lillie and shook his head.

"George, don't you understand any of this?"

"Yes! Do you?"

"Can't you see what they're doing—Cleveland and Tesla? They're deciding for us—for *us*, George, what reality will be."

"Lillie, the rulers of the world have always decided what reality will be."

"Yes, I know. But here in the United States there has been a glimmer, a mere ray of hope, shining out from beyond the empty, ignorant centuries, that for once—just once—people would be able to see the world as it truly *is*, not as they are ordered to believe it to be! Do you intend to walk away from that, George? Do you? Because if you intend to do that, if you intend to betray this—this—this precious opportunity to *know* things as they really *are*—and to tell people what you know—then you might as well walk away from your own life—your own self—your own soul! You might as well crawl in a hole and die the death of a dog and a slave! Go on, George! Go crawl! Go crawl and run and cower! But get the hell out of my way!"

Lillie turned, but Ade grabbed her by the arms.

"Let go of me!" Lillie shouted.

"No!" Ade shouted back. "Not until you listen to me! And you are going to listen! Do you think for one second that Yost and Dennis and Lawson are going to print anything you write about Cleveland? Hell, no! They'll turn you over to Pinkerton's men and let them throw away the key! Or even worse—they'll laugh at you to your face and then show you the door where you will then make a permanent exit from the Newspaper business!"

"If the *Record* won't print my story, I'll go elsewhere!"

"*No* Newspaper in this country will print your story!"

George tried hard reasoning, "Do you know what the 'Freedom of the Press' means? It means we are free to print exactly what we are told to print, no more and no less! The moment we step off the beam—we plummet—and, honey, it's sixteen stories down and no net!"

"I've always flown without a net 'honey'!" Lillie shot back, "And I'm not going to start doing otherwise now. I don't give a damn if every paper in this country slams its door in my face. I'm coming out with this story—and I'm coming out shooting with both barrels—and I'm aiming between the eyes! Let anybody else take their best shot. I do not give a royal damn. If I have to print my own story—if I have to shout from the street corners and the rooftops—I'm going to get the truth out, because the people have a right to know—the people have a right to know because they are not dogs and slaves and cattle. Do you understand *now*? Do you know who I *am*? I'm out to get the truth to the people, no matter what. Now let go of me."

"I'll let go of you! I'll let go of you if you'll just answer me one question! One question only!"

"What?"

Ade looked deep into Lillie's eyes, searching there for the answer to the question he was about to ask.

"Are the 'people' worth it? I'd really like to know. Because, in all honesty, I've never felt the 'people' were worth a good goddamn."

Lillie looked deep into Ade's eyes, searching for the answer to why Ade would ask such a question. Finally she said:

"The 'people' will never be worth a good goddamn until they start *being* the 'people'. And the 'people' starts with you and me. You and me, George.

We are the 'people.' I don't know about you, George, but I want to be a human being, not a cow. And I want it so much I won't settle for anything else. What about you, George? Are you willing to settle for anything less?"

George Ade stood looking into Lillie West's eyes. He let go of her shoulders and looked down. Lillie shook her head slowly, looking at Ade all the while, her eyes narrowed in bitterness and contempt. She turned, and began to walk away.

"Wait," Ade said.

Lillie stopped and looked back. Ade was looking at her, his hands hanging helplessly at his sides.

"I can't let you go there. . . by yourself."

"You can't stop me."

"Lillie. . . I know I can't stop you. I wouldn't want to stop you if I could. I just wish I could stop the world from doing to you what it is going to do."

"You can stay here and wish all you want," Lillie said, and she turned away.

"Lillie!"

Lillie stopped.

"I'm going with you."

She turned back to Ade.

"Why? You just said I was a fool."

"I know. And you are. And so am I, goddamn it."

Lillie stood looking at Ade who stood there with his fists clenched at his sides. After a moment, a faint smile came over Lillie's face. Ade's hands unclenched, and his mouth opened in wonder. He was seeing himself for the first time in his life.

"Well," Lillie said with a shrug, "come on if you're coming."

Ade stepped up to Lillie and held out the crook of his elbow. Lillie grasped it with her hand. The two of them looked at each other a moment and then turned and rushed off toward Michigan Avenue.

Hall and I reached the warehouse where Paige was holed up. The shabby alley that ran along the side of the building was filled with a line of private carriages. The coachmen stood together talking, and they all turned to look at us as we drove up. Our driver stopped the horses near the door of the warehouse.

"Wait here," I said to our driver, and Hall and I got out of the cab.

I approached the door of the warehouse, and had started up the cement steps, when I heard and felt a sickening crunch beneath the sole of my right shoe. I lifted my foot and looked down. I had stepped on a snail and had crushed its shell into a hundred fragments.

"Well, polish it on the shine box and damn it to hell!" I said, scraping the remnants of the snail from the sole of my shoe and on to the edge of the cement step. I looked up at Hall who was suppressing a laugh.

I said, "Can't Paige at least keep the front step clean?"

I opened the door and went in. A group of men stood around the machine looking it over. Paige was saying something. He looked up when Hall and I came in, and said:

"Here they are, gentlemen, Mr. Fredrick Hall and Mr. Samuel Clemens — known to the world as Mark Twain."

Everybody turned to look, and I felt like I was the elephant at the circus, or one half of the Siamese Twins—maybe Hall was the other half.

I said, "You fellows go right ahead there and don't let Hall and me interrupt. Paige, go right ahead with what you were saying."

Paige nodded to me, and gave me a tight little hateful smile. He said:

"I was just giving a little informal introduction until you and Mr. Hall saw fit to arrive."

I said, "We were detained by some very insistent reporters. I apologize for being late. Now please proceed."

"Well," Paige said, "I was just about to explain the differences between my typesetting machine and the Linotype. The Paige compositor is a true typesetting machine, while the Linotype is a typecasting machine. My machine takes dead matter from the compositor's forme and distributes it for re-setting. The Linotype uses a complex and unwieldy foundry to heat lead to a molten state and then inject the molten lead into brass matrices in order to produce a lead slug line. It is a dangerous and unnecessary process. Furthermore, the Paige typesetter justifies lines of type with mathematical precision, spacing the words and letters with a degree of artistry that can only be found elsewhere with the finest of hand-set type. The Linotype uses a crude mechanism to squeeze its brass matrices into justification. It does not space letters according to mathematical law as does the Paige typesetter, but rather produces a random spacing, sometimes pushing the letters too close together, sometimes spreading them too far apart. The Linotype, in short, is a primitive attempt at automating the typesetting process. Whereas, my machine is a true typesetter—and it is, in fact, more. It is—with no exaggeration of statement—a *thinking* machine. It counts the number of letters and words in a line of text, and then calculates the exact proper spacing of the letters in that line. The Paige typesetter is nothing less than a revolution in printing and a harbinger of a coming age when machines will store information in their mechanical brains and use that information to *think for themselves.*"

A tall man stepped forward, and said, "You have made some extraordinary claims, Mr. Paige. All quite general and unproved. Can you give us some specifics?"

"I would be happy to do so," Paige said. "I direct your attention to the machine shaft. Its speed is 220 revolutions per minute. With this speed, the machine can distribute some 7,500 EMS of solid matter per hour. An expert operator can set up and justify over 9,000 EMS per hour and 12,000 EMS on rush matter."

"Impressive," the tall man said.

Paige said, "Here you see the distributor of the type from the dead matter. It is possible to distribute type into the magazine and set the same type out of the magazine all during the same revolution of the cam-shaft. The distributor is capable of being filled with 200 characters. After the operator sets the type at the keyboard, the automatic justification of the type commences. The machine measures the words, adds the sum of these together, subtracts from the sum the length of the line, divides the number of the words—less one, and automatically selects a space—or combination of spaces—for insertion in the line which would justify the line within the limit of 0.005 inch. When the justification process is completed, a mechanism moves the completed line forward, ready for insertion into the live-matter galley."

"Can we see this accomplished?" the tall man asked.

"You certainly can," Paige said. He nodded to the operator, and the young man began expertly typewriting at the letter keyboard.

Everybody gathered around and watched the machine go into action. At each stage of the process, there were murmurs of "I say!" and "Here, here," and "Remarkable!"

After a couple of paragraphs had been justified, I stepped forward, and said, "We need only one more thing, Paige—a phonograph on the distributor to yell, 'Where in the hell is the printer's devil, I want more type!'"

Everybody laughed and nodded. I could begin to see the money shine in all their eyes.

The tall man said, "Mr. Clemens, this is most remarkable—*the* most remarkable thing I have ever seen."

"My sentiments exactly," I replied.

The words were barely out of my mouth before a squealing sound split the air—a sound like a pig down at the Chicago Stockyards getting its throat slit.

"Shut it down!" Paige shouted to the operator. "Shut it down!"

The operator pulled a switch down and the machine shaft disengaged and the machine came to a dead stop.

"What's wrong?" I asked.

"A jam," Paige said. "The machine's jammed. Probably from a speck of dust. I believe I can locate the problem in just a moment."

We all stepped back, as if giving the machine air.

"Will. . . will it be all right?" I asked.

"Just a moment!" Paige snapped. He was unscrewing the plate on the distributor.

"How often does the machine break down?" the tall man asked.

Paige said, "We have done several test runs. The machine is quite reliable. There are, however, a few minor adjustments yet to be made."

"Are the patents secured?" the tall man asked.

I said, "We are going through that process right now. The patents are pending."

Another man in the group said, "Do you know what they call this machine at the patent office in Washington? The Whale."

"That's right," I said, "and it's going to be a whale of a success, a whale of a money maker for anyone who invests in it."

"Well," said yet another man, "that is an interesting assertion. I, for one, however, would like to see some specific facts and figures on its test runs."

I said, "We are in the process of setting up another full test run for the machine right now."

"Well," the man went on, "until it has been properly tested, I think a man would be a fool to invest in it." And with that the man walked out, closing the door behind him.

I said, "That man doesn't know it, but because of his short-sightedness he has just lost a fortune! A fortune! I tell all of you there are millions to be made in the Paige typesetter—millions!"

I stopped. Everybody was staring at me. I realized that I was sounding just like Colonel Sellers.

I said, "But, of course, I do not expect you to take my word for it. I ask you to look at the machine and judge for yourselves."

I looked over at Paige. He was reaching down into the machine. He removed his hand, and I could see he was holding a little piece of twisted metal between the jaws of a pair of pliers.

"This," Paige said, "is the culprit. I only need a few minutes to replace it."

Everybody mumbled between themselves. Pocket watches were brought out and looked at. One of the men said:

"Perhaps we can continue this on another day. We all have appointments and cannot wait any longer."

"But—" I stopped, at a loss for words.

Hall spoke up in a cheery tone:

"Certainly, gentlemen. There is no rush. We will be in contact with you again very soon."

Everybody started on their way. One man stopped, and approached me, and said:

"My son and daughter just love your books. Especially *Tom Sawyer* and *The Prince and the Pauper*. I was wondering. . ."

He brought out a volume of *The Prince and the Pauper*.

". . . if you would sign your name to the front of this book?"

"Certainly," I said. I took the book, opened it to the title page, and wrote:

"Dear children, Be good, and you will be lonely. Truly yours, Mark Twain." And then I handed the book back to the man. He took the book, opened it, read what I had just written, and then looked at me blankly.

"But. . . what does it mean?" he asked.

"What does it—? Why, it's a joke."

"A joke?"

"Yes. Either you get it or you do not. That is the way jokes operate."

"Yes, a joke. Very nice. Only—I was hoping you would write something appropriate for children. Perhaps you could strike this out and—"

"Look here. You asked me to sign your book. I have signed it. I will not strike out what I have signed. What you do with it is your business."

"Well. I see. I see," said the man. "So you are Mark Twain. You are not what I expected. No, not what I expected at all. And that machine of yours there—I think your machine has some problems."

"Oh you do?"

"Yes. You had better work them out."

"We will work them out. You can bet on that."

"I am not a betting man."

"I am sure you are not."

The man turned around and went out. I turned and came up to face the vest buttons of the tall man who had been asking all the questions. He said:

"Mr. Clemens, I represent the Mergenthaler-Linotype Company."

"Do tell."

"Would you be interested in discussing terms for the purchase of Mr. Paige's patents when they are issued?"

"Terms? We have no terms. We have no intention of selling anything. We are only looking for investors. When we find enough we shall commence manufacture of the machine—ten thousand to start. At that point, your Linotype Company will be a thing of the past."

"I see," the tall man said. "I will communicate your answer to my superiors. Thank you for a most interesting demonstration. I found it absolutely fascinating."

The tall man bowed and walked out.

I contained myself until he was gone, then looked over at Hall and said, "We got 'em!"

I went to a table, took out my checkbook and wrote Paige a check for seven thousand dollars. I tore the check out of the book, got up and went over to Paige where he was tinkering with the machine.

I said, "Paige."

He looked up. I held out the check I had made out to him, and said, "Here's your check."

Paige took it and looked at it. When he saw the figure on it, his eyes widened and he snapped his head back up to me. He was too shocked to smile.

"Forget about yesterday," I said. "Forget about today. All these fools here today are of no consequence whatsoever—save one—the representative from Mergenthaler. We've got 'em on the run, Paige, we've got 'em on the run, and they know we're going to beat 'em! So don't you worry about money. I'll get you all the money you need one way or another—just get this machine up and running and *finished*—for we are sitting on a pot of gold! A pot of gold!"

Chapter Five

The Electric Bloodhound

> We tried to make some plans, but we couldn't come to no agreement. Me and Jim was for turning around and going back home, but Tom allowed that by the time daylight come, so we could see our way, we would be so far toward England that we might as well go there, and come back in a ship, and have the glory of saying we done it.
>
> — Huck, *Tom Sawyer Abroad*

"You do realize it's going to be nearly impossible to get inside that warehouse?" George Ade asked Lillie West as the two of them walked back up along Jackson Street.

"I was thinking," Lillie said, "that there must be some kind of master key or... what do they call it...?"

"A skeleton key."

"That's it."

"It would take a locksmith to make something like that. And he'd want to know what we are going to do with it. Wait a minute."

George Ade stopped and looked up the street.

"What is it?" Lillie asked.

"I just thought of something," Ade said. "There just might be a chance we can get inside that warehouse. Just a chance. Maybe. Come on."

Ade and Lillie went on along Jackson Street. In a moment, Ade said, "This way," and he turned left on to State Street.

"What's your idea?" Lillie asked.

"I know someone who might be able to get us into that warehouse. Might. That is, if we can convince him to help us."

"Who is he?"

"A kid I met the other day. He works up here in a dime museum doing a magic act."

"How can he help us?"

"He's an expert lock picker."

Ade and Lillie continued walking south down State Street until they reached Kohl and Middleton's Globe Dime Museum.

Kohl and Middleton's was like so many other "cabinets of curiosity" going back to P.T. Barnum's American Museum on New York's lower Broadway. Red and white banners hung from the walls and flapped in the breeze. A long, narrow poster announced a list of artifacts on display under glass in the Hall of Curios: a shrunken head from the Fiji Islands; a mermaid; the world's smallest printed book; a potato shaped like the head of Abraham Lincoln; an Egyptian mummy. Another long poster announced the following performers in the Hall of Variety: "Houdini Brothers, wonderful wizards; Miss Cozart, the longhaired lady; Oklahoma Bill, the prairie scout and his wife; Fannie Burdett, the dancing midget; the great Prof. King." Another poster announced that in the museum's annex magician Horace Goldin was presenting an extravaganza for the price of an extra dime.

Ade and Lillie went through the open doors of the museum and up to the box office.

"I'm George Ade with the *Chicago Record*."

The ticket clerk removed the cigar from his mouth and asked, "So?"

"I want to see the manager."

The ticket clerk studied Ade for a moment. He motioned to the entrance.

"Tell the ticket taker."

Ade and Lillie passed on inside to the ticket taker who was dressed in a gray and red usher's uniform.

"I'm with the *Chicago Record*. I want to see the manager," Ade said.

"Go ahead," the ticket taker said, waving his hand toward the manager's office door.

Ade and Lillie went through the turnstile and crossed the hall. Ade knocked on the door.

"Come in!" an impatient voice said from inside.

Ade opened the door and looked in at a man sitting at a desk.

"I'm George Ade with the *Chicago* Record."

"The *Record* you say?"

"That's right."

"What can I do for you?"

"I'd like to see Houdini."

"Houdini?"

"Yes, that's right."

Tesla and the dark spectacled rider were thrown into the air.

"He has a show in just a few minutes. You want to interview him?"

"Maybe. If I think what he has to say is of interest to our readers."

"Just a minute, just a minute," the man said, as he put on his coat.

The man held out his hand to Ade and said, "Hedges is the name. I'm the manager. Haven't I seen you in here before?"

Ade shook Hedges hand.

"Yes," Ade said. "I believe I spoke with your assistant the last time. I've been here to interview some of your players."

"That's right," Hedges said, "I remember you now."

Ade said, "And this is my colleague, Miss Li—ah, you may know her from the *Daily News* as 'Amy Leslie'."

"Of course, the drama critic," Hedges said with a nod. "Delighted to make your acquaintance, Miss Leslie. Come on down this way."

Hedges went out into the lobby and past a row of strength testing machines and the glass booth of a fortune-telling automaton. Ahead, a hallway divided in two directions, the hall on the left had a sign reading "Curios," while the hall on the right read "Variety."

Hedges turned right and went down the "Variety" hall, and Lillie and Ade followed him. They came out into a larger hall, an open floor in front of a long elevated platform divided into small sections and curtained. The hall's lecturer who introduced the performers stood to the side of the platform while Fanny Burdett the midget danced an Irish clog on her little section of the boards, accompanied by a pianist on an upright at the foot of the stage. Several early morning thrill-seekers stood in the gas-lit gloom of the hall, watching the show with blank, impassive faces.

Hedges went to the side of the stage, pulled back the flap of a red and white striped canvas curtain, and held it up for Ade and Lillie to pass through to the back of the stage. Behind the stage a narrow hall led to a series of doors opening on to tiny dressing rooms. Ade and Lillie followed Hedges to one of the dressing room doors.

"Hey, Houdini!" Hedges said, knocking at the door.

The door swung open and Houdini appeared in the doorway. He was dressed in a black wrinkled sack suit.

"So you've heard," Houdini said.

"Heard what?" asked Hedges. "I haven't heard anything."

"Jacob left town this morning," Houdini said.

"Left?" Hedges asked, "Why? What's happened?"

"His mother got sick back in New York. He had to go home and take care of family business."

"Oh, he did, did he? And why didn't he tell *me*?"

"He thought you wouldn't like him leaving."

"Oh, is that so? Well, he thought right!"

Hedges let out a huff and scratched the back of his head.

"All right, all right," Hedges said. "You go on by yourself."

"I can't."

"And why not?"

"I need Jacob to do Metamorphosis."

"I'll get Billy to fill in."

"That loafer? No doing. The effect requires speed and skill."

"So what are you going to do? Leave a hole in my show?"

"And I should do otherwise, Mr. Hedges? Jacob had to go. It was his mother, Mr. Hedges! We both have to accept that."

"I don't have to accept anything. I ought to fire the both of you."

"I've wired Jacob's brother, Joe. He can stand in for Jacob. Only one problem. It'll be about a week, week and a half before he can get here from New York."

"Forget his brother. You do a single. Just cut the trunk stunt."

"The trunk stunt's the show. If I do a single, I'll need some time to build an act. That'll take a few weeks. I ain't going on stage unprepared. No, I think I'll wait until Joe Hyman gets here."

"Oh, fine, fine," Hedges said. "That's just fine. And what are you going to do in the meantime?"

"Me? Oh, I'm going on holiday!"

"Wonderful! Where to? Paree?"

"Oh, no," Houdini said, taking Hedge's question seriously. "I'm going on a visit back to the old home place up in Appleton, Wisconsin."

"Oh, for joy!" Hedges said with disgust.

"I was wondering. Can I keep my equipment here while I'm gone? It would help out a lot."

"Oh, by all means! That's what I'm here for! To help out a lot! I'm a regular charity ward! Just be sure your stuff's locked up tight. I'm not going to be responsible for any loss or theft. You understand?"

"Yes, sir. Don't you worry a bit. Nobody can get into a trunk of Houdini's."

"See that they don't. You've got a couple people out here who want to talk to you."

Hedges turned and stormed off, shaking his head and mumbling to himself.

Houdini put his head out the door and saw Ade standing in the hall.

"Mr. Ade!" Houdini said with a broad grin. "Please come in! And your lady friend, too! Come in! Come in! Please!"

Houdini waved Lillie and Ade into his little dressing room, bowing all the while to them and grinning. They went in, and Houdini came in behind them and closed the door.

Houdini dusted off a chair with his handkerchief and gestured for Lillie to sit.

"That's all right," Lillie said, "I'll stand."

"This is Amy Leslie," Ade said, "of the *Chicago Daily News*. But all her friends call her by her real name, Lillie West."

"It is a pleasure to make your acquaintance," Houdini said, taking Lillie's hand gently and bowing before her. "I have oft read your great daily," he said. "'Twas once my ambition to be a literary man myself, but the siren call of the stage beckoned me forth, and since that day I have been its obedient servant." Houdini bowed his head solemnly.

Lillie and Ade looked at each other and smiled and tried not to laugh.

"Well," Ade said, "perhaps you have found your true calling."

"Ah," Houdini said, "so it seems, so it seems. Yet there is that tugging of the heart toward ever higher aspirations. Yet time and tide allow a man only so much. We who would achieve much must walk a narrow line. Such is life."

Houdini looked expectantly back and forth between Lillie and Ade, but they just stared at him.

Finally Houdini asked, "How'm I doin'?"

"Excuse me?" Ade asked.

"How'm I talkin'? Am I talkin' good?"

"I'm not sure I know what you mean," Ade said.

"All right, I'll level with you. What I just said wasn't all off the cuff."

"No!"

"No. I know I must've sounded real natural, but that was a speech I've been workin' over to try out on the gentlemen of the press—oh, and the ladies, too! Only, so far, I ain't had a chance to try it out! You two are the first to hear it. How'd it sound? Real good, I bet!"

"Oh," Ade said, "it sounded fine, fine."

Houdini looked at Ade with uncertainty, and said, "But maybe you could give me some pointers to make it better?"

"Well—" Ade started to say.

"But if you say it's fine, we'll leave it at that. Should I be surprised? Houdini is the son of a scholar. It's only natural that he should talk good."

"Talk well," Ade corrected.

"Yes," Houdini said. "No reason he should not talk like a scholar and a gentleman."

"Yes," Ade said. "No reason."

"So! Did you make it out yesterday to see my jump?"

"Yes," Ade said. "I was there."

"So you saw the whole thing?"

"Yes."

"Then why did I see no write-up in your paper today?"

"Well, we've had a lot of things going on lately. Lots of news, you know."

"None of it could be as big as Houdini. Did you see the crowd I pulled?"

"Yes. But, really, my editor decides what will run and when it will run."

"And this editor of yours, he's got something against running great stories?"

"Oh, he's all for great stories."

"So what's the problem?"

"Sometimes stories need a little nudge, a little push, a little. . . something."

Houdini nodded, his brow knit in intense concentration, when suddenly his face broke into a broad grin.

"A little something," Houdini said. "I'm agreeable. How much of a little something?"

"You mean money?"

Houdini frowned. "Ain't that what you mean?"

"Money is one possibility, yes."

"And what's another?"

"A trade."

"A trade. A trade. I like that. A trade. Trade what?"

"I—we—need a little help with something—a sensitive matter. I believe you're the man who can give us that help. You say you can get out of anything."

"Houdini accepts any challenge. You want to advertise something? I'll set it up."

"No, not that."

"Then what?"

"You say you can get out of anything. Does that mean that you can also get *into* anything?"

Houdini looked back and forth between Ade and Lillie, then turned his head to the side and looked at them out of the corner of his eyes.

"What are you askin'? What are you tryin' to pull here? You tryin' to get me to steal somethin'? What do you take me for?"

"I don't want you to steal anything."

"No?"

"No."

"What then?"

Ade looked at Lillie, then around the little dressing room, and then said, "You present your act as magic, but don't you yourself admit that it is all done mechanically?"

"Not mechanically. No, not necessarily. I only say 'naturally.' It is all done by natural methods. Nothing supernatural."

"And that means you must use some kind of keys or lock picks."

Houdini's expression changed from suspicion to the wary blankness of the poker player.

"I never discuss my methods," Houdini said. "Those are my professional property and secret."

"I understand that," Ade said, "but let's say—let's say someone needed to get inside some place—get through—say—a door. There must be some kind of key—I think they call it a skeleton key—that could open that door no matter what."

"Maybe, maybe not. I don't know."

"You don't know?"

Houdini shrugged, then crossed his arms, and stood,

"Sounds like you're up to no good."

Lillie proposed, "Let me ask you a question, Mr. Houdini."

"No 'Mr.'—just 'Houdini.'"

"Houdini," Lillie said. "Do you believe in democracy?"

"Well, what do you think? I'm an American. Of course, I believe in democracy."

Lillie asked, "Wouldn't you agree that the free press is one of the foundation stones of democracy?"

"Well, sure."

"And wouldn't you agree that sometimes people withhold facts which the public has the right to know?"

"What people? What facts? Sometimes secrets are necessary."

"Sometimes," Lillie said. "And sometimes they become tools of tyranny. Sometimes secrets destroy the well-being of the people."

Houdini shifted the weight on his feet and shook his head. He said, "A lot of maybes and might-bes and sometimeses. It don't amount to a hill of beans unless you tell me exactly what this is all about."

"I can't," Ade said. "You see, what this is all about is *our* professional secret."

"Look. I don't know what you're talking about or what you want. But I'll tell you this: I ain't no locksmith. I don't know nothing about locks and keys and all that. That ain't my game. I'm an artiste. You need to talk to a locksmith."

"You know a locksmith won't help us."

"And you think I will?"

Lillie said, "Maybe Jimmy the Phonograph will help us."

"Jimmy the Phonograph!" Houdini cried. "That *mumzer*? You go to him and you *are* up to no good. The Phonograph is nothing but a cheap criminal!"

"So you know Jimmy?" Ade asked.

"Know *of* him. Everybody knows *of* him. Nobody I know would touch him with a ten foot pole and wearin' two pairs of kid gloves."

"We don't want to go to Jimmy," Ade said. "We would much rather help you."

"Help me? Help me? Whaddya mean?"

"Why, with your write-up, of course! I'd like to see you get your bridge jump written up in the papers."

"You'd *like* to see it? You *can* get it printed? How?"

"I could put in a word."

"A word?"

"I could let my editor know that I thought it was an important story."

"And that would get me in?"

"I think I could do it. We're promoting the fair. And you're part of the fair."

"The most important part."

"Now, how do you figure that?"

"Because Houdini is great. That's how Houdini figures that."

"Yes, well, if you want anyone else to figure it that way, you're going to have to consider a trade."

Houdini slowly turned his back to Ade in a gesture of utter contempt.

"For example," Ade went on, "maybe that trunk there has some keys in it. Maybe it has a skeleton key—a key that could open any lock. That key could open a lock for you, Houdini, a lock that has been almost impossible for you to open—until now—getting your name in the Newspaper. So far you haven't been able to do that, have you? Maybe this is your break. All you have to do is work your magic—use your key—and the lock will open. But you've got to take a risk—a risk that I'm telling you the truth. That's going to take a lot of courage, a lot of grit. The question is: Do you have it in you? Do you have the grit? Does Houdini have the guts to be Houdini?"

Houdini kept standing with his back to Ade. Finally he said, "Getting you in gets my name out."

"That's right."

Houdini did not move for several more seconds; then he turned around.

Houdini said quietly, "I'm sorry, Mr. Ade. Maybe you're on the level. Maybe both of yez are jake. But I can't help you. Unless you tell me what you're up to, there's no way I can know whether I'd be helping you to do right or showing you the right way to do wrong."

Ade looked over at Lillie and gave a little shrug. She shook her head, frowned, rolled her eyes up, sighed—and then nodded.

"All right," Ade said. "All right, Houdini. We're going to tell you *our* secret. Look at this."

Ade gave his copy of the *Chicago Record* to Houdini. Houdini took it in both of his hands, looked at the front page, and smiled.

"Hey," Houdini said, "I saw this thing last night!"

"You saw it?" Ade asked.

"That's right. Down on the lakeshore. I like to walk at night. Helps me think and plan. I was walking down there along the lake shore and all of a sudden KA-ZOOMA! There was this airship up there in the sky! And then—KA-ZOOMA! There was another one right beside it! Then—KA-ZOOMA! That other one shot off! Then—KA-ZOOMA! The first one took off and went into a cloud! I saw them—saw them both. Just like this picture here. Only—one of 'em had windows—portholes! I could see portholes in it! I wasn't going to tell nobody. They'd think I was crazy! But now. . . . Say, this is your secret, ain't it?"

"That's right," Ade said.

"Oy! That's a secret, all right! You know what this thing is?"

"Better than that. We know where it is."

"*Oy vay!*"

"We want you to get us into where it's at so we can get a photograph of it."

"Oh, Mr. Ade!" Houdini said, and he sat down in the chair in front of his dressing room table, all the while reading the Newspaper article.

"Oh, Mr. Ade!" Houdini said again. Finally he looked up. "Who does this airship belong to?"

"Nikola Tesla," Ade said.

A light came on in Houdini's eyes.

"No kiddin'!" Houdini said. "No kiddin'. Well, well, well. So he's invented two airships."

"Not two," Ade said. "Just the one. The one you saw with the portholes."

"And the other one? What about the other one? Whose is that?"

Ade and Lillie looked at each other.

"We're not sure," Ade said.

"No?"

"No one knows for sure," Ade said.

"Ya think maybe Edison has built it?"

"No," Ade said. "Not Edison."

Houdini frowned. "Somebody over in Europe, then?"

"Who in Europe do you think could build an airship?"

"Then. . . what are you saying?"

Lillie said, "Tesla and his associates suspect the other airship comes from another world."

Houdini grinned wide; then his face went blank suddenly. He looked at Ade this way for a moment or two, then his eyes widened.

"You ain't kiddin'—are ya?"

"We ain't kiddin'," Ade said.

Houdini looked back down at the paper, and shook his head.

"Another world. Another world. It boggles at the mind, Mr. Ade. It boggles at the mind! Does the President know about this?"

"President Cleveland was a passenger in Tesla's airship last night," Ade said.

"*Oy!*"

"And Mark Twain was piloting it."

"Yer kiddin' me! Mark Twain?"

Ade nodded.

"And you want me to get you in to photograph this? Oh, no! Nothin' doin'! No way, no how, no, sir! This here is what is called a State Secret! Poke around a State Secret and you'll end up *in* the pokey!"

"Come on," Lillie said, "let's go. He's all talk and no guts."

"Hey!" Houdini said, jumping to his feet. "This ain't about guts! A person would be crazy to stick his nose into this. The government knows what it's doing, so let it do what we put it up there to do."

"The people have a right to know about this," Lillie said. "If we are going to war with another world, we all have a right to know."

"Ya can't scare the old people," Houdini said. "You gotta think about the old people who are set in their ways."

"When the foreign airships start attacking us," Lillie said, "there will be a lot of old people who will be scared out of their wits—and a lot of other people, too. Have you thought about that?"

"Well. . . no, but—"

"You know what I think, Houdini?" Lillie asked.

Houdini shook his head.

"I think you just like to talk big. And that's all. You're just talk. You couldn't get into or out of a tin can without somebody holding your hand. Come on, George, let's go. This Houdini is useless."

"Wait a minute!" Houdini said. "Wait a minute! Who's useless? Who can't get out of a tin can?"

"So? Can you get us in to photograph the airship?" Lillie asked.

"Can I get you in? Can I get you in? Of course, I *can* get you in! But *will* I get you in? I ain't going against State Secrets! No way, no how! Those federal boys won't just lock us up, they'll bury us so deep the daisies won't bloom!"

"And Houdini couldn't dig his way out?" Ade asked.

"Even Houdini can't go up against the government and win."

"It looks like," Ade said, "that Houdini—if he *is* Houdini—could get us in to see the airship—and get us out again—without anyone being the wiser. Or maybe I'm just expecting too much from Houdini. Maybe I'm confusing gab for grit. Maybe Houdini is only a name and a claim. I think you're right, Lillie. We're wasting our time here. This kid is just a second-rate amateur magician. Let's go."

Ade opened the door.

"Wait a minute!" Houdini shouted. "Wait a minute! Who do you think you are coming in here and saying Houdini is second-rate? Who do you think you are coming in here blowin' around with your high and mighty airs? Houdini can get out of—and into—anything! Anything in this world! Anything! You don't believe me, yez wisenheimers? No? Then come on! Come on! I'll show yez two wisenheimers! Nobody does dirt to the name of Houdini! Nobody! I'll get you in—and out—like a shadow! Like a shadow of a shadow! Come on, yez gutless wisenheimers! Houdini is taking yez *in*!"

Houdini had donned his overcoat. He now put on a derby and pulled it down at an angle over his eyes and marched through the door. Lillie and Ade looked at each other, smiling, and followed him out.

They reached the lobby of the dime museum and Houdini stopped in front of the exit turnstile, doffed his hat, and made a little bow, gesturing for Lillie to pass through ahead of him. Lillie came forward and passed through the turnstile.

"See?" Houdini said, "Getting in will be as easy as that," and he waved Ade on through, and then went through the turnstile himself.

"We shall see," Lillie replied, moving forward toward the street, but then she stopped suddenly.

"What?" Ade asked.

"That man down the street," Lillie said. "I saw him behind us earlier."

"Is there a back way out of here?" Ade asked Houdini.

"Why?" Houdini asked. "Somebody tailin' ya?"

"Creditors," Ade said.

"Ain't it always?" Houdini said. "Come on. That joker ain't ever been given the kind of slip we're going to give him."

Houdini waved Lillie and Ade back inside the museum. Ten minutes later the man out on the sidewalk entered the museum, and after searching the whole establishment for another half hour—a search that took in all the dressing rooms and the manager's office—he was unable to find Lillie, Ade or Houdini. He exited through the back fire escape door where his partner stood waiting. In his later report to his superior at the Pinkerton Detective Agency he noted that Lillie West, George Ade, and Houdini had not gone out the back fire escape, had not come out the front entrance, and the three subjects seemed to have "just walked through the walls." How did Lillie, Ade, and Houdini get past the Pinkerton agents? When they went back inside the museum, they simply stood in the gas-lit gloom with the rest of the onlookers. The Pinkerton agent had, in fact, walked right past Houdini, and had looked at him, but had not recognized him. As soon as the Pinkerton agent had slipped behind the red and white curtain to the back of the stage, Houdini gave a silent hand signal to Lillie and Ade, and the three of them simply walked out the front entrance of the museum.

"Like that," Houdini said, snapping his fingers as they walked out.

That very same morning while Hall and I met with Paige and the prospective investors, and Lillie West and George Ade went to see Houdini, Kolman Czito was working in Tesla's warehouse south of the fairgrounds. I have no idea what Czito was working on; he never told me, and I never asked. It was not the airship, for that was already completed, at least as far as I could tell. But Czito was working hard, testing little incandescent bulbs, or what Tesla calls 'vacuum tubes.' I had seen some of these the night before on Czito's workbench.

Czito sat there working with his mind in a very worried state. That morning he had walked around the outside of the warehouse, as was his habit, and came upon the gate to the fire escape that had been left open by George Ade the night before. Czito had gone up the stairs to the rooftop and checked the door up there and found the broken fragment of Lillie's hairpin still stuck in the door's keyhole. He had come back down, gone inside the warehouse, and come out again with a new and more complicated lock to replace the one that hung open on the gate to the fire escape. He had closed the gate and snapped the new lock on it, looked at the old lock, found it still workable, and snapped the old lock on as well.

Throughout the morning Czito kept thinking about doing all this, and wondering who had opened the locked fire escape the night before. He knew that he had to tell Tesla about what he had found as soon as he possibly could.

At some point in his work Czito stopped what he was doing and looked up. He thought he had heard something. He waited a moment, listened, and then went back to his work. Then he stopped again. He was sure he had heard a sound—maybe the shuffle of a footstep.

Czito got up from his work table and reached inside his vest to where he carried a holstered Navy revolver. He pulled it out and held it up with the barrel pointing to the ceiling. He stood up and slowly walked toward the hallway leading out to where the airship stood. He tip-toed a step at a time, his eyes squinting and his jaw clinched tight. When he reached the hall, he stopped and looked out into the dark. He saw nothing. Everything was still and quiet. Then—

It was a dark shape slowly emerging from the room with the hidden safe that held Tesla's crystal. The dark shape seemed to be that of a man—and it—he—moved toward the large open space where the airship stood.

"Halt!" Czito shouted in a high-pitched voice, ringing with both fear and determination. "Halt or I'll fire!"

The dark shape spun about. Czito saw a flash of light, then immediately heard an explosion near his ear. The edge of the doorway where Czito stood had splintered from the passage of a bullet.

Czito jumped back involuntarily. Then, just as fast, Czito lunged forward and fired his Navy revolver at the dark shape which was retreating rapidly down the hall. The dark shape fired back, but Czito had already dodged back behind the edge of the door again.

Czito lunged forward once more, his revolver held out in front of him, his right hand gripping his revolver, his left steadying his right. The dark shape had rushed past the airship and around to the big sliding doors which stood open with just a crack of daylight shining from outside.

Czito stepped forward and saw that the dark shape was a man, dressed all in black with a black hat, and wearing a beard, and—yes—dark, bottle glass spectacles!

The man fired back at Czito, the bullet hitting a wall. Czito had jumped behind the airship; when he looked again, the man with the beard and dark spectacles was gone—he had slipped through the narrow crack between the big sliding doors.

Czito ran up to the open doors and pointed his gun ahead of him as he looked outside. Straight ahead lay the waters of Lake Michigan. To the left, Czito saw only the distant buildings of the World's Fair. To the right, he saw nothing—save the shoreline of the lake.

Czito looked up and down along the edges of the big sliding doors. He could see no scratches or damage. The doors had not been tampered with, not in any obvious, physical way. But Czito knew there was another way to open the doors—a way using wireless electricity.

Czito holstered his revolver and ran to the airship, up her stairs, and through her opened door. He clambered up the ladder to the top deck and went to the pilothouse. There he flipped the switch that closed the warehouse's big sliding doors. The big doors shuddered for a moment, then slid shut and locked with a loud metallic click which echoed through the building.

Czito ran down the pilothouse steps and started to go back down the ladder to the lower deck, but he stopped. He went over to the door of the airship's engine, slid it open, and looked inside. All the machinery seemed in order. The drive crystal flashed as it always did, flooding the surrounding machinery with a rainbow of light.

Czito slid the door shut and descended the ladder to the lower deck.

Czito ran down the steps of the airship and back toward the front of the warehouse, to the room with the vault containing Tesla's crystal. Czito rushed into that room and stopped on its threshold, paralyzed with a horror and dread that started in his stomach and worked its way outward until his whole being was poisoned.

What Czito saw was this: The hidden panel in the wall was slid back. The door of the vault stood open. And Tesla's crystal was—gone.

"No," Czito whispered, shaking his head slowly and trembling from head to foot. "No."

Czito stumbled backward, not believing his eyes. For a moment he feared his knees would give out, but then he gathered his strength, stepped forward, approached the vault, and looked inside.

The ceramic insulating pedestal upon which the crystal had been mounted remained in place. The vault door did not have a scratch on it; it was simply standing open.

Czito turned and ran out to the airship with his revolver held high. He circled about the airship, looking in all the corners of the warehouse, peering around all the machinery. He came back around, closed the door of the airship, and locked it. Then he checked the other door of the airship, and found that it was still locked as it should have been.

Having secured the airship, Czito rushed to the front of the warehouse, through the front laboratory, and out through the door leading to the street. He closed the door behind him, locked it, and checked the knob, twisting it back and forth. He stepped back from the door, looked the front of the warehouse up and down, removed his spectacles, wiped his face with his handkerchief, and then slipped his spectacles back on.

Now Czito looked north up toward the fairgrounds. He had to find Tesla. Czito knew where Tesla was: the wooded island at the center of the fairgrounds. Every morning since they arrived in Chicago, Tesla had gone there to feed the ducks and pigeons.

Czito started off in a run up the street toward the shining domes and towers of the World's Fair. He looked about all the while, hoping to see a cab or a carriage pass by, but the street ahead and behind was empty.

Czito reached the southernmost boundary of the fairgrounds: a board fence some eight feet high. At the top of the fence ran two coils of barbed wire. He thought for a moment of trying to climb the fence, but in another moment realized that he couldn't. So he ran along the fence the length of several blocks, stopping a couple of times to rest the burning sensation in his lungs. He kept going and finally reached the fairground's south gate. Czito went up to the sentry and held up his ground's pass.

"I've got to find Mr. Tesla quick!" Czito said to the sentry. "Is there a mounted police nearby?"

"No," the sentry said. "But I can call one up on the telephone. It'll probably take a few minutes for him to get here."

"I don't have a few minutes!" Czito shouted. "Never mind. Just let me through!"

The sentry lifted the wooden arm barring the way, and Czito ran into the fairgrounds.

Czito ran across the Court of Honor and on toward the exhibit halls.

Now everything seemed to slow down for Czito. The cement pavement over which he ran seemed to pull and stretch away from him, while his legs seemed to grow heavier with each passing second. He thought of what Tesla had once told him about Zeno's Paradox: the faster Achilles ran, the further he had to go, because the series of points ahead of him was infinite. Czito was now Achilles running with leaden legs through an infinite, unending space.

The buildings of the World's Fair loomed over Czito. It seemed to him that they were rising up to crush him, that the pavement before him and the buildings above him were stretching out and pulling away only to collapse again in a moment and engulf him in a smothered eternity.

Then Czito caught sight of Tesla at the edge of the lagoon. The world pulled in and snapped back, with Tesla at its center. Czito felt a rush of energy and ran forward in a new burst of speed.

"Mr. Tesla!" Czito shouted. "Mr. Tesla!"

Czito was running toward Tesla as fast as he could. He ran over a bridge spanning a canal and on up to Tesla who was standing on a grassy shore. As Czito approached, pigeons scattered away from Tesla in a whirlwind cloud of gray and white.

"Czito!" Tesla said, "Look what you've done!"

Czito stopped in front of Tesla, and gasped out, "They've taken it!"

"Who? Taken what?"

"The Crystal. The Master Crystal."

The expression on Tesla's face shifted from irritation, to shock, to a grim determination—all in the space of three seconds. Then Tesla's expression solidified—as if his face had turned to stone.

Czito saw a blur; it was Tesla moving past him. Czito took a deep breath and plunged forward, following.

Tesla's long legs now worked like the pistons of a locomotive, the white cement pavement of the fairgrounds rushing beneath his feet, becoming a road bed for upright rolling stock.

Tesla shot by the Transportation Building where workers on scaffolding stopped and stared at his streaking passage—a demonstration in space, color, and motion questioning the proposition that human legs had been outpaced by faster forms.

Now Tesla darted to the left and cut past the building for Mines, his blurred passage taking on the aspect of molten gold and mercury rushing up from secret volcanic regions.

Now Tesla darted to the right, the echo of his footfalls crackling against the walls of the Electricity Building.

Now Tesla was in front of the Administration Building; now he was not—an unaccountable flash and disappearance—impossible to trace or govern.

Tesla was in front of the Machinery Hall Annex. He went through the door. In front of him steps lead up to a giant dynamo. He ran up the steps, leapt on top of the dynamo, and then down again to another set of steps on the other side. Mechanics turned their heads, believing the blur they saw out of the corner of their eyes was a machine flying apart and exploding. Before they could turn to see what had passed, Tesla had gone out through a small machine shop, and out its back door.

Ahead of Tesla lay an open pasture, cleared for the construction of livestock sheds. Beyond the pasture stood a board fence—the same one that Czito had thought of climbing. Tesla raced across the pasture, reached the fence, made a leap, and caught the top edge of the fence with his fingertips. He pulled himself to the top, sat on its edge, and then stood upright, one foot on the top of the fence, one foot pressing on the coils of barbed wire attached at its top. Tesla slowly crouched low, and then sprang off the fence and jumped for the ground. He landed on both feet. He was outside the fairgrounds.

Now Tesla ran east along 67th Street, the southern perimeter of the fairgrounds. Several blocks he ran, the board fence whizzing by him on his left, trees waving past him from across the street on his right—and below him the freshly laid macadam street receiving a precise impression of Tesla's shoeprints in the asphaltum with every stride he took.

Now 67th Street came to an end and Tesla turned south on to the street fronting Lake Michigan. Tesla's warehouse loomed up ahead on the left a block and a half away.

Tesla reached his warehouse, inserted a key into its front door, and went inside.

The moment Tesla entered the front work room, a strange calm overcame him. He had a sudden realization that he had to move with absolute clarity and precision, and that the least amount of haste would bring with it confusion and error. Everything in the front room looked normal and untouched. Tesla saw Czito's workbench, and Czito's tools scattered just as he had abandoned them. He went into the hall, passing the splintered door frame.

Tesla passed into the hallway and turned into the room with the vault. He went up to the vault's open door and looked in at the empty pedestal that had once held the Master Crystal. He stared at the space where the crystal once sat. Then he turned and went to a cabinet in the corner.

The cabinet had a combination-lock wheel on its door. He spun the wheel back and forth and then opened the door. Inside, several shelves were filled with small electrical devices. He removed one of these devices—a little rectangular tin box with a tiny incandescent light bulb mounted on its top—and also a tool box. He closed the cabinet door, and brought the device and the tool box to a table.

Tesla took a small screwdriver from the tool box and unscrewed two bolts on the back of the tin box.

Kolman Czito appeared in the doorway breathing heavily. He had managed to catch a ride back to the warehouse on a freight wagon. He put the flat of his hands on the top of a table and bowed his head, drawing breaths in deep gasps, trying to find his voice.

Tesla searched through the toolbox, then went to the cabinet, looked, and found two tiny cylinders and brought them back to the table.

Finally Czito managed to say, "The thief escaped before I realized the crystal was gone. I shot at him, but missed."

"What did he look like?" Tesla asked, taking one of the tiny cylinders and pushing it into the back of the tin box.

"He was dressed all in black with a beard and dark spectacles."

"Yes," Tesla said, "of course."

"The crystal gone," Czito said, "and three years to grow another!"

"We don't have three years," Tesla said, "I'd say we don't have three minutes before the crystal is out of our reach and our work stopped permanently by those who have it."

Tesla had inserted the other tiny cylinder into the back of the tin box, and had closed up its back and was now tightening the two bolts back into place with the screwdriver.

Tesla finished the job and then pulled out from the top of the tin box an eight inch long telescoping steel rod mounted next to the little incandescent light bulb. He held the rod pointed outward and flipped a switch on the front of the box. He pointed the steel rod about the room, swinging it east toward Lake Michigan, then south, southwest, west. . . .

The little incandescent light bulb on the top of the tin box flashed. Two seconds passed and it flashed again. Two more seconds—and it flashed yet again.

"The crystal is still in Chicago," Tesla said.

"Do you want me to go with you?" Czito asked.

"No," Tesla said. "Stay here and guard the ship."

Tesla felt in his inside coat pocket for his revolver; it was missing, and he suddenly realized that he had left it in his hotel room that morning. There was no time to go back and retrieve it, and he knew that Czito would need his own Navy revolver.

Tesla dashed to the door.

"And telephone President Cleveland," Tesla said, stopping in the doorway. "Tell him we need guards outside. Our secret is no longer secret."

Tesla turned and rushed out the door.

Out on the street, Tesla knew exactly which direction to go. The little tin box he held in the palm of his hand told him the exact direction in which the crystal lay, also its distance from him. The telescoping steel rod received invisible electrical pulses emitted by the crystal, registered the intensity of the pulses, and, from that, calculated exactly how far the waves had traveled from their source. The distance was interpreted and expressed as a sequence of flashes in the little incandescent light bulb. The faster the bulb flashed, the closer was the source of the electrical pulses—the crystal. The little tin box was nothing less than an electric bloodhound.

Tesla held the steel rod out toward the west and began walking, first at a steady pace, then faster. Then he was running. The bulb continued to flash, now every second and a half.

Tesla ran along 68th Street until he reached Stony Island Avenue. There he turned right and went north toward the fairgrounds. Another block and he turned west again, but at the next corner he turned back to the north. The little incandescent light bulb was now flashing once every second.

Tesla was now running along a sidewalk through a suburban neighborhood just west of the fairgrounds. He saw a row of frame houses up ahead with people sitting out in their front yards and on their porches. He slowed down to a brisk walk and pocketed his little tin box. The people in their yards looked up from their conversations and watched Tesla go by. He continued on up the street, passing shops and small warehouses.

Tesla stopped on a street corner and took out the tin box. The bulb on its top flickered rapidly. Tesla extended the steel rod and swept it in an arc. When he pointed the steel rod at a three-story boarding house across the street, the bulb shined brightly. When he pointed the steel rod in any other direction, it went dark.

Tesla retracted the steel rod and put the tin box in his coat pocket. He strolled across the street and stopped in front of the boarding house, and saw that it was a theatrical hotel, one of many that had just went into business to house performers working on the fair's Midway Plaisance. Tesla went up the steps to the boarding house, opened the door, and went in.

There was a dim hall, two doors to the right, and a flight of stairs on the left. Tesla took out the tin box and pointed it around the hall. It shined only when its steel rod was held up to the ceiling.

Tesla went up the stairs on tip-toe, got to the second floor, and went on up to the third floor. He reached the top floor, and moved silently along a hall. He pointed the tin box at a door. The little incandescent light bulb shined steadily. Tesla slid the tin box back into his coat pocket, approached the door, and knocked.

A moment passed of complete silence. Then the door opened.

A man appeared in the space of the half-opened door. He was a large bearded man, wearing a strange high-crowned hat and spectacles with lenses the color of a patent medicine bottle.

"Excuse me," Tesla said. "I seem to be lost. If you would be so kind as to tell me—"

The bearded man started to close the door. Tesla lunged forward, blocking the door with his foot and shoulder. The bearded man pushed the door closed from inside. Tesla fell back into the hall; then rushed forward, battering the door with his shoulder and arm, driving the bearded man back into the room.

"Who are you?" Tesla shouted.

The bearded man studied Tesla a moment; then lunged and grabbed Tesla by the lapels, drew him close, and then shoved him away. Tesla stumbled back and crashed against the plasterboard wall, cracking it.

Tesla sprung toward the bearded man, grabbed his arms, and threw the man to the floor. The bearded man clung to Tesla, and brought Tesla down with him. The two men rolled across the room, now the bearded man on top, now Tesla, now the bearded man again. Tesla shoved the bearded man aside, and a cylindrical case fell out of the man's heavy overcoat and rolled across the floor. Both men reached for the case, but the bearded man grasped it in his left hand; with his right, he swung back and struck Tesla in the face. Tesla fell back to the floor.

The bearded man dived through a window and rolled out on to a landing of a fire escape.

Tesla shook his head, got up, and dashed to the window in time to see the bearded man descend the fire escape and drop to the sidewalk below. The bearded man started down the sidewalk but turned, looked back up at Tesla, and drew his revolver. Tesla stepped back inside the window just as a bullet whizzed past his head and penetrated the ceiling. The bearded man turned and ran on down the sidewalk.

Tesla climbed through the window, descended the fire escape, and dropped to the sidewalk as well. He saw the bearded man run north up the street and turn right at the next corner. Tesla went after him. When he got to the corner, Tesla looked to his right expecting to get a clear sight of the bearded man running down an empty street. But this he did not see.

Instead, when Tesla reached the corner and looked to his right he was confronted with the vision of a street swarming with people. Carriages lined the curbs, guarded by liveried coachmen. Tesla entered the crowd, looking over men's shoulders and their hats, and over lady's fans and their hats decorated with artificial flowers. There were people and more people, and beyond them some more people. There weren't just hundreds of people filling that street and moving along it at an easy, leisurely pace; there were thousands. And not one single individual among them wore a beard, not that Tesla could see.

Up ahead, Tesla saw two policemen, and a saw-horse set up in the middle of the street to keep any more carriages with people in them from coming down that way. Beyond them were, yes, some more people.

Tesla went past the policeman, and looked up, and then he understood where he was and why this crowd was so filled up with so many people.

Down the street a little further, the red and white board fence came to an end and opened up on a great, arched entranceway. The words on the arch read: "Buffalo Bill's Wild West and Congress of Rough Riders of the World." On one side of the arch was a large portrait of Columbus limned by some talented sign painter and designated by the caption "Pilot of the Ocean, the First Pioneer." On the other side of the arch was another portrait done by that same Midwestern Michelangelo, this one of Buffalo Bill and captioned "Pilot of the Prairie, the Last Pioneer."

Tesla looked down and studied the crowd. He turned on his heel and looked all about in a three-hundred-sixty degree arc. He did not see the bearded man, only thousands of smiling people slowly moving toward the main entrance of the big show. There were rich people, poor people, and people who were neither rich nor poor. There were young people, old people, and people who were neither very young nor very old. There were fat people, thin people, and people who were neither very fat nor very thin. There were foreign people, American people, and people who looked to be neither foreign nor American. There were all kinds of people, in all kinds of shapes, and sexes, and apparel. Except there were no people with a beard, a high, black hat and spectacles made out of a patent medicine bottle.

Tesla took out the little tin box and extended the steel rod an inch. The light flickered faintly in the direction of the show entrance. But when he turned the steel rod to the right, pointing it at a high board fence, the little bulb lit up brightly.

Tesla walked along with the tin box cupped in his hand and glanced at its light bulb every few seconds. He kept a sharp lookout on the speed of the flicker in the light. Whenever he turned the steel rod in the direction of the board fence, the little light bulb would shine brightly and steadily. Beyond the board fence, the bearded man was not much more than thirty yards away.

The crowd flowed toward the main entrance. Tesla stepped out of the flow, and approached a gate in the fence. A big cowboy stood at the gate smoking a cigarette.

Tesla went up to him.

"Excuse me. My name is Nikola Tesla. I'm the electrical consultant for the World's Fair."

Tesla took out his ground's pass and showed it to the cowboy.

"That don't cut no mustard 'round here," the cowboy said. "You fair people wouldn't let us set up our show on your grounds, and now we don't want nothin' to do with you. So, git! Or I'll fill ya full of lead."

Tesla pulled the cowboy's revolver from its holster, twirled it on his finger, and then flipped the cylinder out and looked at the cartridges.

"Blanks," Tesla said, slipping the revolver back into the cowboy's holster. "Let me see Buffalo Bill."

"Who'd you say you were?" the cowboy asked.

"Tesla. Colonel Cody knows who I am."

"Tesla, eh? Jest a minute," the cowboy said, going through the gate.

"Make it quick," Tesla said. "It's urgent. And if you don't make it quick, you won't have a job in five minutes."

At that comment, the cowboy smirked, flipped his cigarette on the ground, and said, "Wait here."

Tesla waited for the cowboy to shut the gate, and then tried to go in behind him, but the gate had locked.

Tesla watched the flicker of the light as he moved the tin box back and forth. The location of the crystal seemed to be moving around beyond the gate only a few tens of yards away.

Tesla looked both directions along the length of the fence in front of him. In one direction the fence ran all the way to the wall of the arena; in the other it ran to the street entrance. Tesla looked at the top of the fence and thought of climbing it. Just as he was preparing to do so, the gate opened, and the cowboy came out.

"This way, Mr. Tesla," the cowboy said.

Tesla went through the gate. The cowboy closed the gate behind them, and said, "This way."

Tesla followed the cowboy into the campground of Buffalo Bill's Wild West Show. Ahead, on a carpet of circus-sweet tanbark, lay several acres of canvas tents and Indian tepees. The place immediately struck Tesla as an emblem, a symbol, a hieroglyph of peace. Here, stretching before him lay the tents of two peoples who had fought a series of bloody wars. Now, the wars had ceased and these same peoples lived side by side, if not in friendship, certainly in complete unanimity of commercial purpose. How strange and unreal, Tesla thought. Why had these people fought in the first place? What stirred them to battle? And now the Indians, after their people had been bloodied, crushed, and decimated, stood around their tents chewing tobacco, eating Crackerjack from the box, and playing horseshoes.

The cowboy and Tesla approached a tent surrounded by a garden of flowers. Standing in the door of the tent was Buffalo Bill and Annie Oakley.

"Mr. Tesla!" Buffalo Bill said. "Such a delight to see you again! It's my pleasure to introduce you to Miss Annie Oakley."

"Miss Oakley," Tesla said, bowing.

"Mr. Tesla," Annie Oakley said with a curtsy. "I'm sorry I didn't see you when you came to the show the other day."

"You were magnificent, Miss Oakley," Tesla said. "Colonel Cody, I am afraid I must be abrupt. A piece of very valuable property has been stolen from me. An extremely rare jewel. I have traced the thief here to your camp."

"My camp?" Buffalo Bill asked. "Surely you don't think one of my people is the thief?"

"No," Tesla said. "I have no reason to think that. I believe, however, that the thief has come here to escape my pursuit. I request permission to search your camp."

"What does your man look like?" Buffalo Bill asked.

"He was dressed in black, had a beard, and wore dark spectacles."

"We've seen no one like that, have we Annie?"

Annie Oakley shook her head. "I would've remembered somebody like that."

"Pete," Buffalo Bill said, "go with Mr. Tesla and help him turn the camp inside out."

"Yes, sir," Pete said.

"If it is just the same," Tesla said, "I prefer to do this by myself."

"As you wish," Buffalo Bill said. "Good luck. And if you find your man, come on back when you're finished and see the show. I'll put you up in a box."

"I shall do that," Tesla said, starting off.

Buffalo Bill and Annie Oakley watched Tesla march off toward a line of Indian tepees.

"He shore looks mad," Annie Oakley said.

"He shore does," Buffalo Bill replied with a smile.

Tesla passed the Indian tepees without looking inside any of them. He kept up his march straight through the Indian camp. The light bulb on the tin box was telling him to go straight ahead.

In the arena, Buffalo Bill's Cowboy Band struck up the "Star-Spangled Banner." The notes rose up into the air, crashed, and rose again, filling the campground with their struggle, crisis, and triumph.

Tesla passed out of the Indian camp, and through the camp of the U.S. Army, the French Army, and the German Army. He stopped in front of the tents of the Russian Army.

A troop of Cossacks were mounting their horses, getting ready for the big opening parade which presented the "Grand Review of the Rough Riders of the World." These Cossacks were fur capped, bearded, and armed to the teeth. Tesla ran his eye over their bearded faces.

Just then, thundering behind Tesla came what seemed to be the cavalry of half the industrial world—the United States, the French, and the Germans. They swept around the campgrounds and toward a big open gate leading to the arena, their flags flying and trumpets blasting. The Cossacks raised their rifles in the air and started off in the equestrian train.

Bearded face after bearded face whizzed by in front of Tesla, all distinctly Russian faces, broad-cheeked and steely-eyed. A cloud of dust rose up, obscuring the scene. The last of the Cossacks came charging by, three cavalrymen spurring their horses to top speed. The first one glared at Tesla as he passed. The second one looked straight ahead. The third one was looking the other way—Tesla could only see the back of his fur cap.

"Hey, you!" Tesla shouted.

The last Cossack rode forward, keeping his head turned away.

Tesla took off running alongside the Cossack, and shouted again, "Hey, you! Turn around!"

The Cossack's head turned. He was wearing bottle glass spectacles.

Tesla reached out and tried to grab the dark-spectacled rider's boot. The rider reined his horse around in a tight circle, and then brought the horse up on its hind legs, with its front legs kicking out. Tesla jumped back. The horse came down, spun about, and horse and rider charged forward and galloped through the open gate that led into the arena.

Tesla looked about. Buffalo Bill approached on horseback holding the reins of a second horse that trotted beside him.

"Mount up, Mr. Tesla," Buffalo Bill said, holding out the reins of the second horse.

Tesla took the reins and mounted the horse, and Buffalo Bill and Tesla urged their horses into a gallop and through the gate to the arena.

The cavalries of the world were charging around the arena leaving behind them a great cloud of dust. Twelve thousand people in the grandstand cheered the horsemen.

As Buffalo Bill entered the arena, the crowd of twelve thousand leapt to their feet. Buffalo Bill charged forward to the center of the arena, while Tesla broke into a fast gallop after the last rider of the Cossack troop.

Tesla came up behind the dark-spectacled rider, got even with him, swung one leg over so that he was riding side-saddle, and then leapt on to the back of the dark-spectacled rider's horse. Tesla reached around, grabbed the reins of the horse with one hand and the rider's beard with the other, and the beard came off in Tesla's hand! Then the dark-spectacled rider punched Tesla in the ribs with his elbow, trying to knock Tesla off the horse. Tesla didn't budge, but the horse started to panic, and broke ranks with the other riders. Then the horse began to buck and kick. Tesla and the dark-spectacled rider were thrown into the air and landed on the ground. The horse ran off and out of the arena.

Tesla lay on the ground, the wind knocked out of him. He took two deep breaths, got his lungs inflated, and stood up.

The dark-spectacled rider was no longer dark-spectacled. In the fall from the horse, those bottle glass spectacles had flown through the air and landed several yards away from the rider. Now the rider covered his face with his forearm as he stumbled to his feet.

The cowboy named Pete came running up.

"Are you all right, Mr. Tesla?" Pete asked.

Tesla nodded.

The rider dressed as a Cossack shielded the sun from his eyes with his hand and began running toward the gate.

"Stop him!" Tesla shouted.

Pete and Tesla started off in pursuit of the man dressed as a Cossack.

The crowd of twelve thousand did not notice the altercation out in the arena. It occurred as Buffalo Bill sat astride his horse and the cavalry of the world's armies came thundering by behind him. A few people may have noticed Tesla, Pete, and the other man run out of the arena, but it meant nothing to them. They did not realize that when Tesla and the Cossack imposter fell to the ground, they and the whole city of Chicago came within a hair's breadth of being incinerated off the face of the earth. An instant after this, the planet Earth itself would have been split into two parts—one half careening in toward the sun, the other spinning out of its orbit toward the dark, cold regions of the solar system. Such a real possibility was unthinkable to everybody in the crowd, but Tesla and the imposter were well aware of it.

Tesla and Pete came through the gate but the man who was dressed as a Cossack was nowhere to be seen. Pete continued in a run toward the Russian camp, but Tesla stopped and took out his little tin box. The man who had stolen the crystal was up ahead to the left beyond the Russian tents. Tesla ran forward, passed around the tents, and came to another board fence at the back side of the camp. He approached the fence and saw where a hole had been chopped through it. An axe lay on the ground. Pete came running up.

"Damn his worthless hide!" Pete said.

"Thanks for your help," Tesla said to Pete. "I'll

take it from here." Tesla went through the hole in the fence.

Once through the fence, Tesla spied the Cossack imposter running down the street. The imposter turned a corner and disappeared from sight. Tesla went after him, turned the same corner, and saw the imposter going into the door of a warehouse. Tesla got to the warehouse, opened its door and went in. A flight of stairs to the right led up into darkness. Tesla went up the stairs to a second floor, looked out, and saw that the whole floor was empty. The flight of stairs continued on up to the roof. Tesla went on up, went through the door at the end of the stair way, and emerged on the roof.

The imposter stood at the rooftop's edge; he raised his revolver and aimed it at Tesla, and Tesla jumped back inside the door. Tesla heard the report of the revolver and saw the inside of the door split open from the passage of a bullet. The imposter jumped from the edge of the roof and across a narrow alley to a neighboring rooftop. Tesla came out and saw the imposter go through another rooftop door and down into the neighboring building.

Tesla jumped across to the other rooftop, landed on it, and went through the same door that the imposter had just entered.

Tesla went down the stairs and entered the floor of a warehouse filled with barrels. He removed his little tin box. The light bulb on its top showed that the man had gone down to the ground floor and possibly out of the building. Tesla went on down the stairs.

On the ground floor a man wearing a shop apron turned around and said, "Hey, what are you fellows doing in here?"

"Did the other man go out?" Tesla asked.

"Yes, he went out!" the man in the shop apron said.

Tesla went out the door and saw the imposter run down the street and turn a corner to the left.

Tesla got to the same corner and saw the imposter running away under a railroad bridge and to the neighborhood on the other side. There, on the other side, the imposter turned right into an alleyway. Tesla went after him, reached the alleyway and turned.

The imposter was running toward the end of that block. Beyond that block was a street, and beyond the street, another high board fence.

The imposter reached the fence, jumped, caught its top edge, pulled himself up and over it, and went down on the other side.

Tesla reached the fence and jumped, caught the top edge of the boards, and pulled himself up to the top. He saw the imposter running between two wooden buildings. Tesla dropped to the ground and continued his pursuit.

Tesla and the imposter had just entered the Midway Plaisance. Up ahead several men stood around the fair's Captive Balloon. The Balloon was fully inflated with hydrogen and fitted with its passenger gondola. Two men were just about to get into the basket to test it when the imposter approached in a run with his revolver drawn.

"Back!" the imposter shouted, "Back! Or I shoot!"

The men working with the Balloon stood their ground too dumbfounded to move.

The imposter fired his revolver and the men dropped back.

"Are you crazy?" roared one of the balloon workers.

The imposter climbed into the Balloon's passenger gondola.

Tesla approached in a run.

The imposter leveled his revolver at Tesla and pulled the trigger. The hammer clicked; his revolver was out of bullets. The imposter tossed his revolver aside, brought out a big knife and cut one of the ropes that held the Balloon to the ground.

The Balloon workers came forward, but the imposter held up his knife and growled, "Back! Back! I kill!" The Balloon workers fell back.

The imposter slashed through the second rope that held the Balloon fast. The gondola began to lift off the ground. The Balloon workers rushed forward again, but the imposter swung out with his knife, driving them back again.

The gondola was up in the air five feet from the ground. Tesla reached the gondola and grabbed hold of its side as it rose in the air—seven feet—ten feet—fourteen feet—twenty feet.

The Balloon workers looked up to see Tesla dangling from the side of the Captive Balloon as it continued to rise in the air over the Midway Plaisance—forty feet—fifty feet—sixty feet—

The Balloon now began to move to the east, blown by a brisk wind, and as it rose in the air, it picked up speed very rapidly.

From the ground, people everywhere began looking up. The crowds at the Wild West arena could see the Captive Balloon moving up over the distant domes of the World's Fair. Those out on the street a block or so closer could make out the silhouette of a man in the passenger gondola, and the silhouette of another man hanging on the gondola's outside edge, his feet dangling in the air.

In the rapid ascent of the balloon the imposter could not sense the imbalance of weight on the gondola created by Tesla hanging on the outside. So Tesla was able to pull himself over the side of the basket as the imposter stood looking out the other side with his back to Tesla. Just as Tesla managed to get inside, the imposter turned around. The two men stood looking at each other. Below them, the gondola barely cleared one of the towers of the Electrical Exhibition Building.

Then the imposter lunged forward with his knife slashing the air. Tesla grabbed and twisted the imposter's arm which held the knife; the knife flew up from the imposter's hand and out over the side of the gondola. Tesla shoved, and the imposter fell back against the ropes. Then the two men rushed each other. The imposter grabbed Tesla by the throat. Tesla gripped the imposter's wrists, trying to pull the imposter's hands away. The imposter kept his grip. Tesla reached up and gouged at the imposter's face. The pink, papery skin of the imposter's face gave way and peeled off; it was nothing but a mask of rubber and glue. Beneath that the imposter's real skin was revealed to be a deathly white! Tesla tore away the rest of the mask, completely exposing the imposter's face and head—a bald head, a hairless head with the skin so pale, pinkish-white that it might have been that of a circus clown's. Tesla looked into the squinting eyes of the imposter, and saw that his irises were a pale pink, the pupils—almost imperceptible dots. Tesla was not looking into the eyes of a man—they were the eyes of some kind of inhuman monster.

"*What* are you?" Tesla gasped.

"He who kills you," the imposter said.

Down below in the streets near the Midway Plaisance crowds gathered here and there. They were watching the Captive Balloon moving through the sky and the silhouette of two men struggling with each other in the Balloon's gondola.

The crowd grew quiet as one silhouette in the gondola seemed to overpower the other. One black figure rose up over the edge of the gondola and fell to its outside edge. The silhouette's legs could be clearly seen dangling in the air.

The Captive Balloon drifted behind the domes and towers of the World's Fair. The people below in the streets lost sight of the two struggling silhouettes in the gondola. Now only a few workers on the fairgrounds and on the rooftops of the exhibit buildings watched as the Captive Balloon drifted out over Lake Michigan, ascending rapidly through the blue sky.

To the workers watching from the rooftops of the exhibit buildings the silhouettes on the gondola now seemed to be struggling with a fury. The silhouette on the outside held on by one arm. The one on the inside tottered on the gondola's edge. The Captive Balloon was now far out over Lake Michigan, perhaps a thousand feet in the sky. The silhouettes on the gondola could hardly be seen by the workers on the rooftops of the fair's exhibit buildings.

Then—a worker on the rooftop of an exhibit building thought he saw one of the silhouettes on the gondola fall off—straight down toward the lake.

Nikola Tesla was holding to the side of the gondola, his hands in a cold sweat. The imposter had tried to kick Tesla's hands free of their grip on the basket's ropes. But Tesla had reached out and pulled the imposter's boot with a sudden tug, sending his white-faced assailant down over the side and out into space. Tesla had clung to the gondola in cringing expectation of the death-flash from the exploding crystal. But there was no flash.

Tesla looked down and saw the imposter floating in mid-air some two hundred feet below. The imposter was enveloped in a shimmering sphere of white light, and he seemed to waver like a heat mirage in the desert. Tesla could see that the white light came from a beam shining from above, and his glance followed the beam up to its source near the zenith of the sky. The beam was coming from a little black speck, a little black cylinder. Tesla looked back down. The imposter, now white-faced and bald, was slowly rising up in the air enveloped in the beam of shimmering light; then he ascended faster; he passed by where Tesla hung on the Captive Balloon's gondola and kept going straight on up into the sky. Tesla looked up. The imposter was shrinking away toward the little black cylinder at the zenith; he shrank until he was only a point that faded away and disappeared. A moment passed while the little black cylinder hovered at the sky's zenith. After another moment, the little black cylinder moved away slightly to the north and faded into the blue of the sky.

Tesla climbed back into the gondola and pulled the rope that released the Hydrogen gas. He took out the tin box and pointed it straight up to the sky. Its light bulb was dark for five seconds, then—it flashed! Tesla looked up to the zenith of the sky. He saw nothing but blue, but he knew that somewhere up there, about five miles above Chicago, the foreign airship hovered, and inside that ship the Master Crystal pulsed with life.

Tesla also knew that he had very little time. He could almost visualize the interior of the foreign airship. He knew that those who took the Master Crystal were looking it over, peering into its lattice structure, testing its characteristics. As soon as they were certain they possessed what they had set out to capture, the men of the foreign airship would depart. And where would they go? If Tesla did not act immediately the men of the foreign airship would depart for unknown regions, the power of the crystal would be theirs, and there would be no way of finding them again or defending the world against their hostile designs.

Tesla flipped to "off" the tin box's electrical switch, retracted its steel rod, and slipped the box back into his pocket. He slumped against the edge of the gondola and pulled harder on the rope that released the Balloon's gas.

As Tesla descended toward the surface of the lake he looked back toward the shore and saw an electric launch approaching from the fair.

Lillie West, George Ade, and Houdini stepped out of their express train arriving from downtown Chicago and into the terminal station of the World's Fair. Their trip had only taken twelve minutes.

The three of them strolled through the station, its polished floors suggesting to Lillie the possibility of a railroad station dance. They glanced up at the white-arched rotunda. Houdini's gaze fell upon the wall ahead, which was mounted with clocks—twenty-four of them—one for each time zone in the world.

"When it's daytime here," Houdini said, "it's nighttime on the other side of the world. Not only that. Everybody over on the other side is upside down."

"To them we're upside down," Lillie said.

Houdini nodded. "It don't make no sense if you think about it," he said.

"That's what they said to Columbus," Ade said.

"Guess nothin' is the way we think it is," Houdini said with a shrug, and the three of them descended the stairs and went on out of the terminal.

Outside, Lillie West looked up along the crowded street, trying to see beyond all the people on their way to Buffalo Bill's "Wild West Show."

"Whatcha lookin' for, Miss West?" Houdini asked.

"A cab," Lillie said.

"Uh-uh," Houdini said, shaking his head. "No cab. Those cab drivers will blab to anybody, especially the coppers. I don't want any witnesses around. We'll walk."

"Won't we be all the more conspicuous on foot?" Ade asked.

"Yes, but I am no slave to fashion," Houdini said.

"I mean," Ade said, "won't we be more *visible* on foot?"

"Oh," Houdini said, throwing up his hand in dismissal. "I knew what you meant. Sure—we'll be more visible, but I ain't worried about visible. Visible is good. Accountable is not."

Ade's sense of condescension toward Houdini took a pause. Perhaps Houdini didn't know the definition of "conspicuous," but what, Ade asked himself, did Houdini mean in using the term "accountable"?

"What exactly do you mean?" Ade asked.

"A man notices his own business. If we take a cab, the driver will remember us. If we walk, we will probably be seen by somebody. But will that somebody remember what he saw? And if he remembers, how much will he remember?

I can tell you: not much. People almost never pay attention most of the time. They're sleepwalkers."

"I know what you mean," Ade said. "Sometimes I see out on our suburban crossings a dozen vegetable truck wagons with the drivers of each nodding on their seats and allowing the reins of their horses to hang loose. If the horses didn't know the way home, they'd all be lost."

"Exactly," Houdini said. "But a fellow need not be nodding off to be asleep. Lots of sleeping gets done with the eyes wide open."

Both Lillie and Ade began to realize that, despite Houdini's tangled and ungrammatical speech, there was a sense conveyed by it that went beyond mere "horse sense."

They were about to get a glimpse of Houdini's unique way of looking at things. All three of them walked along the sidewalk until the crowd began to thin out.

"I'd like to see the skeleton key," Ade said.

"What for?" Houdini asked.

"I'm just curious," Ade replied.

"And you know what they said about the cat," Houdini said.

"All the same. Let me see it," Ade said.

"Hate to disappoint," Houdini said, "but I ain't got no skeleton key."

Ade stopped walking. Houdini and Lillie stopped and looked back at Ade.

"What do you mean you 'ain't got no skeleton key'?" Ade asked.

"I'll tell you what I mean," Houdini said, "but come on. Let's not keep standing here."

Ade started forward again with Houdini and Lillie.

"I ain't got no skeleton key because I don't need no skeleton key. My mind is the key. And I'll tell you something: There really ain't no such thing as a skeleton key, at least as most people think it to be. There ain't no one key that can open everything. You see. . . . Wait a minute, wait a minute."

Now Houdini stopped on the sidewalk.

"Before I go any further," Houdini said, "we have to have an understanding. We have to do a pledge."

"A pledge?" Lillie asked.

"An oath of secrecy and loyalty to the secrets of Houdini. Do you have anything to write with?"

"Why?" Ade asked.

"To write out the oath," Houdini said.

"We don't have time to be writing out oaths," Lillie said.

"All right," Houdini said, rubbing his chin. "Your word will do. You will swear by the honor of your mother and father and under the eyes of Almighty God that you will never betray the secrets of Houdini to another living soul, not so long as you both shall live!"

Houdini was holding his right palm up with great solemnity.

"Swear it," Houdini said, "or I cannot help you."

"We swear," Lillie said, somewhat irritated.

"No, no, no," Houdini said. "You cannot say 'we.' You must say 'I.' Say 'I swear etc., etc., etc.'"

"I swear etc., etc., etc." Lillie repeated.

"No, no, no," Houdini said, "You must say the whole oath."

"Now look here—" Lillie started to say.

"You must say it, or I will not help you."

Lillie looked at Ade.

"I think he means it," Ade said.

Lillie looked back at Houdini, raised her right hand, and said, "I swear by the honor of my mother and my father that I will never—"

"And under the eyes of Almighty God," Houdini said.

"And under the eyes—" Lillie said

"Start again," Houdini said. "From the beginning."

Lillie looked at Ade and let out a sigh.

"Start again!" Houdini snapped.

Lillie raised her right hand again, and said, "I swear by the honor of my mother and father and under the eyes of Almighty God that I will never betray the secrets of Houdini."

"To another living soul so long as you live," Houdini said.

"To another living soul so long as I live," Lillie said.

"Now you," Houdini said to Ade.

"I swear by the honor of my father and mother—"

"My mother and father. Mother comes first."

"I swear by the honor of my mother and father and under the eyes of Almighty God that I will never reveal the secrets of Houdini to another living soul so long as I live."

"Give me your hands," Houdini said, holding his right hand out with the palm down.

Lillie and Ade extended their right hands. Lillie placed her hand over Houdini's, and Ade put his hand over Lillie's.

"Now," Houdini said, "under the eyes of God, do you doubly affirm your oath to be true to Houdini?"

"Yes," Lillie said.

"Yes," Ade said.

"So mote it be," Houdini said solemnly, dropping his hand and bowing his head.

After a moment, Ade said, "Now. Will you please tell me how you expect to get into that warehouse without a damn skeleton key?"

Houdini looked up, and said, "Patience, Mr. Ade, patience. You are not very patient are you?"

"Not very," Ade said.

"I'm going to explain it all to you. But you just relax. All that tightness around your shoulders is your worst enemy. Relax. Both of yez relax. Don't you understand by now? Don't ya get it? You're in the hands of Houdini. Now, come on."

They all started down the sidewalk again. Houdini took his time to speak. Finally he said:

"Now, about that skeleton key. Ain't no such thing. Not really. What people call a skeleton key is really just a master key. A master key is cut so that it can open a number of different locks. The locks are always similar. Take a pair of regulation handcuffs. Nearly all the handcuff locks in the United States are made exactly the same and can be opened with the same key. A lot of locks are made the same way. A lot of times you can open a lock with a piece of wire."

"I know all about that," Ade said. "I did that last night."

"A monkey can open a lot of locks with a wire or a hair pin or a little piece of metal," Houdini said.

"But the locks on this warehouse are not like that," Ade said. "They are very sophisticated."

"Uh-huh," Houdini said, "and if they weren't, wouldja be comin' to me? Don't think so. Let me tell you somethin'. I'm not worried about *any* locks. I never worry about any locks. Locks is the *last* thing I think about when I approach a container."

"What do you mean?" Ade asked.

"Openin' locks ain't my game. I told you that out front at the start. I'm an artiste who specializes in escape. The first mistake people make when they think about escape is to put all their worry and time into the lock on the container. That ain't my way. I look for other ways out. I want to get out of the container without even touchin' the lock. Let the lock be, I always like to say. No need to disturb its rest. I look at the other parts of the container: How is it put together? What is it made of? Most of all, I see the container as a system of links, 'cause that's all it is. A chain is the simplest container. How do you get out of a locked chain? Open the lock? Probably not. You look for the weakest link. You break through there. Usually the lock is *not* the weakest link, so I don't bother with the lock. A fellow gives me a handcuff the make of which I have never seen before. Couldn't get out of it if my life depended on it. Not in a million years. What do I do? I say to him, 'I'm going to make it really tough on myself. I'm going to snap a whole bunch of handcuffs on my wrists—and then I'll put yours on top of 'em! Whaddaya say to that?' Fellow can't believe it. Wants to see me do that. I snap on four or five pairs of handcuffs—goin' all the way up my wrists. Now—he snaps his cuffs on up here above all the rest. I go into the cabinet, slip off all my rigged cuffs, and then when I get to his, well, they are snapped on way up here around my forearms! All I have to do is slide them down my arms and over my wrists and off my hands! Am I goin' to worry about the lock on that pair of cuffs? No way, no how, no, sir! Locks! I do not bow down to locks! I give them no respect! I let all those 'sophisticated' locks go right on being 'sophisticated.' I'm busy getting out of the container."

Ade and Lillie had listened to Houdini, all the while walking beside him. There was a silence as they turned his words over in their minds.

Finally, Lillie asked, "So Tesla's warehouse—how do you propose to get into *that* container?"

"Won't know 'til I see it and study it," Houdini said. "You can tell me all about it as we go along. No two containers are alike in the whole world. They may look alike, they may feel alike, they may smell alike. But don't let that fool ya for one second. Every container is unique, and it always has a trap for ya. It *always* has a trap! And you never know what it's going to be 'til it grabs ya."

"If you never know," Ade asked, "how will you know what to do in advance?"

"Mr. Ade," Houdini said, "if you want to know what to do in advance, take up bookkeeping, take up stamp collecting, take up ballroom dancing, even. But if you're going to practice the art of escape, you *never* know what you're going to do in advance, no matter how much you study, no matter how much you prepare. And believe me, you *do* prepare. You never know what is coming. And when what's coming comes, you deal with it; you think, you fight, you feel—most of all you feel—you feel everything but fear. Fear you can't afford. You're never rich enough for that. No, no two containers are alike. They're just like people, and just like people, they always have a trap."

A little later that morning, Fred Hall and I stepped out of a cab in front of the Great Northern.

"You know, Hall," I said, "this is the best I've felt since I've come back to America."

"Does this call for a celebration?" Hall asked.

"Yes," I said. "Yes, it does. I'm going right up to my room—and take a nap."

"A nap? That's your idea of a celebration?"

"Well, we could get drunk, but I had too much to drink last night, and I'm still working on sleeping that off. Truth is: it feels like I have a cold coming on."

Hall and I went through the entrance of the hotel.

"Go ahead," Hall said. "You've earned a rest. We both have."

"What are you going to do?"

"I'm going shopping."

"Oh, yes. For the wife."

"That's right."

"Well, you go on and buy up all the stores. To hell with economizing and to hell with the bank panic. We're already rich."

"Not as rich as Carnegie."

"Richer."

"Not as rich as J.P.?"

"Ri—Well, we'll see about that. Yes, sir, we'll see about that one. This time next year, we may be giving ol' J.P. a run for his money."

"Wouldn't that be a run!"

"It'd be a marathon! And by then we'll be able to hire a whole team to run it for us."

I gave a wave to Hall and stepped into the elevator, closed its scissor-cage doors, and found I was alone without even the company of the elevator operator who was absent from his post. I pulled the lever and the car started up for my floor. Suddenly my elated mood began to deflate. Something about being closed up inside that little moving closet did not set right with me.

The elevator reached my floor. I pushed the lever back against the wall, jerking the car to a stop, snatched the door open, and stepped out into the hall. I fished in my pocket for my hotel key, brought it out, put it in the keyhole of the door to my room, turned the key, opened the door, and went inside.

I came face to face with Tesla.

"Mark," Tesla said.

Tesla's hair was all askew; perspiration beaded his forehead; the right side of his face appeared swollen; he looked pale, drawn—sick, actually.

"Tesla!" I said. "What the hell are you doing here?"

Tesla did not reply. I felt someone looking at me out of the corner of my eye. I turned, and there was Cleveland seated at my writing desk, completely calm and composed.

"Come in, Clemens," Cleveland said. "We have some disturbing News."

I came into the room.

Cleveland stood up, looked down at me, and said, "Mr. Tesla's crystal has been stolen."

I stood there a moment looking at Cleveland, and then turned back to Tesla. I could see that Tesla was actually fighting back tears in his eyes. I looked away, feeling ashamed and embarrassed.

"Do you understand what I have just said?" Cleveland asked.

"Yes, sir. Yes, Your Excellency. I do. And I am very sorry to hear of it. Do you know who took it?"

"It was the men of the foreign airship. One of them broke into Mr. Tesla's warehouse this morning."

"Have you sent the army after them?"

"No," Cleveland said.

"Pinkerton's men, then?"

"No," Cleveland said. "No one. Tesla tried to capture the thief. It was a desperate attempt. He was almost killed."

"What are you going to do?"

"The crystal must be retrieved at all costs," Cleveland said, "but we cannot involve the Army, the Navy, or Pinkerton. This matter is too sensitive. No word of what has happened can be allowed to reach the general public. Under no circumstances whatsoever."

"What about the Treasury Department? The Secret Service?"

Cleveland shook his head, and said, "No department of the government yet exists which is equipped to deal with a matter this sensitive."

"Then what will you do?"

"Contain the secret by containing the number of people who know the secret. That means it is up to us to retrieve the crystal."

"Us?" I asked uneasily. "What do you mean 'us'?"

"Tesla, myself—and you."

"Me? I don't understand. There's nothing I can do to help you."

"I need you, Mark," Tesla said. "I need you to pilot the airship."

"Pilot it? Where?"

"After them."

"What are you saying?"

"We have to go after them."

"Go after them? Where?"

"Wherever they are."

"Wherever they—! I think not. I think not, Tesla. That is not your solution. I mean, I—I am not—I cannot be—I would be of no use to you."

"You won't help?"

"I'd like to, Tesla, I'd like to. Of course I'd like to help any way I can, but going after that airship? And—what? Fighting with it? Where? In the sky? My God. I couldn't do anything like that. I simply couldn't. We'd all get killed in two minutes. I'd be of no help to you whatsoever. I'd be in the way. I'm just an old riverboat pilot. I am not your man."

"You are the only one who can help me, Mark," Tesla said. "With your assistance—and Mr. Czito's—we can go after them."

Cleveland said, "There is no other solution, Clemens. You must pilot the airship."

"No, no, no!" I said, pacing away from Cleveland.

"It's the only way," Tesla said, his eyes dry and steady now. "We have to move fast."

Cleveland said, "If they've taken the crystal, our adversaries know much more about us than we do about them."

"I agree," I said. "And I wish you luck."

"Tesla has to go after them," Cleveland said.

"I agree."

"Retrieve the crystal or destroy it along with their own ship."

"I agree."

"And you must pilot Tesla's ship."

"There! That part—I *don't* agree!"

"Clemens!"

"Your Excellency! You are asking the wrong person! I am a worn out old man."

"You're the only person besides Tesla and Czito who has ever piloted the ship."

"Get Czito to pilot it."

Tesla said, "I will need Czito to monitor the induction coils and capacitors."

"Then *you* pilot her."

"I'll be up top—manning the guns," Tesla said.

"Your Excellency! This is preposterous! Get one of your balloon aeronauts to pilot the ship!"

"No time!" Cleveland said. "The only balloonists in Chicago are the carnival workers at the fair. And I will not entrust this operation to such people."

"Why, those carnival workers are good people! Salt of the earth!"

"Clemens! We must act *now*! And in absolute secrecy! With as few people involved as possible!"

Tesla came up to me holding his tin box.

"Mark, this device is a kind of wireless telegraph receiver. It intercepts the electric pulses radiating from the crystal, and thus acts as a tracker, constantly indicating the position of the crystal by this flashing light bulb. Watch."

Tesla pointed the steel rod on the tin box slowly around the room, sweeping it in a complete circle. The incandescent light bulb on the box remained dark.

"Nothing," Tesla said. "But—watch!"

Tesla turned the steel rod straight up to the ceiling of my hotel room. A few seconds passed, then—a flash!

I looked at Cleveland, then back at the incandescent light bulb on the tin box; the bulb was dark, but then—again—a flash!

Tesla said, "By the intervals between the flashes of light, I estimate that the crystal is in the foreign airship some six miles above the city."

Tesla collapsed the steel rod back into the top of the tin box, and said, "With the crystal, they could do anything."

Cleveland said, "Mr. Tesla tells me that they could incinerate the whole city of Chicago in a single instant."

"Your Excellency," I said, "I am a certified coward. You *do* know I deserted the Civil War?"

"You deserted the Confederacy. It doesn't count."

"Your Excellency! I have a family!"

"No more excuses!"

"A wife and three daughters!

"You *have* to go!"

"Who'll support them when my bones are spinning around out there in the intergalactic void?"

"Clemens!"

"Answer me that!"

"Clemens!"

"Who'll support my wife and children?"

"Clemens! If you do not act *now*—you, this city, this country, this world—*your family*—may soon be nothing but dust in the intergalactic void!"

"I'm a coward! And a liar! And I won't follow orders!"

"Clemens! I'll admit: you're—not—much! But you're all I've got!"

"That's exactly what my wife tells me."

Cleveland had my lapels gripped in his big hands. I looked into his eyes; they were two little slits, lit beyond by an inscrutable fire.

I dropped my head down. Cleveland dropped his hands. I turned and looked out the window and down at the street.

Everything looked normal. That's what was so terribly, insanely wrong. Everything *looked* normal.

Chapter Six

The Oyster Is Served

> I see a bird setting on a limb of a high tree,
> singing with its head tilted back and its mouth
> open, and before I thought I fired, and his song
> stopped and he fell straight down from the limb,
> all limp like a rag, and I run and picked him up
> and he was dead, and his body was warm in my hand,
> and his head rolled about this way and that, like
> his neck was broke, and there was a little white
> skin over his eyes, and one little drop of blood
> on the side of his head; and, laws! I couldn't
> see no more for the tears; and I hain't never
> murdered no creature since that warn't doing me no
> harm and I ain't going to.
>
> — Huck, *Tom Sawyer Abroad*

Lillie, Ade and Houdini had walked along 67th Street beside the fence that enclosed the south perimeter of the fairgrounds until they were within a block of the street that fronted the lake shore.

As they walked, Houdini glanced down at the road bed and took note of the impression of Tesla's shoeprints in the fresh asphaltum. He had noticed that the shoeprints had started suddenly as if the person who had made them had dropped from the sky, and, as he walked along, he studied the length of each stride.

Finally Houdini said, "Big man."

"Who?" Ade asked.

"Whoever made those," Houdini said, pointing down at the shoeprints. "Look at the length of the stride. And he was in a hurry. I think he came over

The bolt of electricity reached out like the claw of some bird of prey.

the fence back there. And not too long ago, either. Those prints are real fresh. Looks like they just laid the gravel and tar on this road this morning or maybe yesterday afternoon."

"So what?" Ade asked.

"So what? Ain't you ever read Sherlock Holmes or Poe?"

"Certainly," Ade said.

"Well, you gotta notice things. If you don't notice things, you're just one of the sleepwalkers. *Oy*! Turn around."

Houdini had turned around suddenly, walking back in the direction that the three of them had come. Ade and Lillie stopped and followed him.

"What's wrong?" Ade asked.

"Psst! Coppers," Houdini said in a low tone.

"Where?"

"About a block and a half down that next street."

"That's where the warehouse is," Lillie said.

"They were in front of a big building," Houdini said.

"That has to be Tesla's warehouse," Ade said. "Are you sure it was police?"

"I can spot the boys in blue a mile away," Houdini said. "This changes everything. I'm out."

"What do you mean you're 'out'?" Ade asked.

"It means I'm gone, I'm done, I'm out of sight."

"What about your claim?" Ade asked.

"What about it?" Houdini asked, but then he stopped. "What claim?"

"That you can get out of anything," Ade said.

"And I can," Houdini said, starting up again. "Getting *into* anything is another matter. Especially with coppers standing around."

"All right," Lillie said. "Your word is no good, so
our word is no good."

"Whaddya mean by that remark?" Houdini asked.

"The Secrets of Houdini Revealed," Lillie said. "Nice title for a Newspaper article."

"Splendid!" Ade said. "We can work in his jump off the State Street Bridge. Explain the whole thing. What we can't explain, we make up."

"Wait a minute! Wait a minute!" Houdini said. "You can't do that! You made an oath! An oath on your mother and father!"

"Yes," Ade said. "It will be a terrible thing to break that oath. It will haunt us, day and night, night and day, for the rest of our natural lives, won't it Lillie?

"Night and day," Lillie said, nodding.

"Yes," Ade said, "it will be a heavy burden to live with, but live with it we must. Unless you can see your way clear to helping us."

"Yer bluffin'."

"Come along, Lillie," Ade said. "I believe if we hurry we can have our exposé ready in time for the evening edition."

"Wait a minute, wait a minute, wait a minute. Come back here, both of yez. Come back here. Yez two are the lowest, lousiest, scum of the earth! You break a oath you made to Houdini and you're no good and I'll take care of yez both! And I mean you too, Miss Lillie West Wisenheimer! Ya ain't no lady! I'll clean the floor with the both of yez!"

"Come along, Lillie," Ade said. "The reading public is waiting for our story."

"Wait a minute, wait a minute! Yez two wouldn't do this to me, would yez? Yez ain't that low. I didn't read yez two that way."

"Houdini," Ade said, "we are reporters, and you will find out reporters get their story one way—or another."

Lillie and Ade started back up the street.

"Wait a minute, wait a minute, wait a minute!"

Lillie and Ade stopped.

Houdini looked back toward the street fronting the lake.

"All right," Houdini said. "All right. We'll give it a try. We'll give it a try. It's going to take some doing, but we'll give it a try."

"That's all we ask," Lillie said coming up beside Houdini.

"All you ask," Houdini said. "All you ask is all I got. All I got and a lot more. That's all you ask. You stay here. Both of yez stay right here and don't budge from this spot."

"Where are you going?" Ade asked.

"I'm going to go case the container. It ain't going to be easy with those coppers loitering around out front. You say you went up to the rooftop of this building?"

"That's right." Ade said. "There's a skylight up there."

"That skylight is our weakest link," Houdini said. "Windows are always the weakest link. That's why burglars go through 'em most of the time. Did ja notice burglar alarm wires on those skylight windows?"

"No," Ade said, "but I wasn't thinking of looking for them at the time."

"You wasn't thinking of looking," Houdini said. "Sleepwalkers! I'm dragging along a couple of sleepwalkers with me. What a mess Houdini has gotten himself into! Yez two wait here. Right here. I'm going to case the container."

Houdini adjusted his derby over his eyes, turned around and went back up the street to the next corner. He turned left and walked two blocks until he got to 69th Street. There he turned left again and walked east toward the lake. As he approached the street fronting the lake, he slowed his pace and peered around to his left, and looked back up north along the street toward Tesla's warehouse. He got a clear view of the south wall of the warehouse and the fire escape stairs running up along its side. He noticed a metal door near the foot of the fire escape. The door was set into the wall about half the length of the building from the street. He saw the two policemen standing in front of the building. One stood in a slouch; the other stood erect and twirled his club around in the air. The club twirler seemed to be talking. The sloucher seemed to not be listening.

Houdini looked at the area surrounding the warehouse. To the north of the warehouse was a fence that seemed to enclose a storage area, possibly a lumberyard. On the south side of the warehouse he saw that there was a little park, a patch of grass, and a few trees and bushes. Beyond that was the shore of the lake. Further up the street, closer to Houdini, the policemen's wagon stood at the curb in front of the little park with its horses still hitched up.

Houdini's eye ran over the whole scene, rapidly sketching in space a path, a sequence of actions, to be carried out by himself, Lillie, and Ade. It only took a few seconds for him to do this, and as soon as he had, he turned around and retraced his steps back to 67th Street.

Lillie West and George Ade stood where Houdini had left them. They were surprised to see him return so soon.

"That was quick," Ade said.

"I took my time," Houdini said. "I always take my time. That's why I'm quick. I got the whole thing cased, wrapped, and tied up with a shiny new ribbon."

"You can get us in?" Ade asked.

"It's a cinch," Houdini said. "I got a look at those two coppers. Somebody scraped the bottom of the barrel pickin' those two to be guards. They're dillies. Tell ya how we're going to deal with 'em. We need what we magicians call 'misdirection.' That's you, Miss West. You are plenty of misdirection. You got a pocket watch?"

Lillie held up a locket she wore around her neck, opened it up and showed Houdini her little watch inside.

"Nice," Houdini said. He took out his own watch from his vest pocket, and said, "We synchronize. I have eleven twenty-two. What do you have?"

"Eleven twenty-four," Lillie said.

"Eleven twenty-four it is," Houdini said. "I set my watch to your time just like that. There. We're the same.

At eleven thirty exactly you come around the corner there and walk toward the warehouse. When you get a little ways down the street where the coppers can see you, stop, turn around, and take a picture of the fair buildings with your Kodak."

"What for?" Lillie asked.

"Misdirection and cover story," Houdini said. "You're going to be misdirecting the coppers and settin' up yer story that you are out sightseein' and takin' pictures. When ya get up close to the coppers ya smile real big like you think they are the most handsome devils you have ever laid your eyes on.

That'll rattle 'em good. Just when you've got 'em rattled, you trip and fall on the ground. Ya gotta trip for real. Make it look good. Now the two knights in blue hafta come to yer rescue. Now they're out of the picture completely. We've got 'em shelved and on ice. They're completely dead from the neck up. Now you gotta do this trippin' act when you get even with the south corner of that warehouse. You gotta do that so you can look back to the south side of the warehouse. You gotta face the warehouse at all times and keep the coppers' backs to the warehouse. That's absolute, or we're all cooked. Now I see there's a door there on that south wall. When you see it open, that's your cue to beat it out of there. Head south down the street. About half a block down the street, the coppers have their patrol wagon pulled up next to the curb. The horses are still hitched. Go around the wagon and wait ten seconds, but whatever you do, don't spook the horses. Wait ten seconds, count the seconds in your head, then turn around and peek back to see if the coppers are still watching you. I know they'll be watching you until you get to the wagon. If they lose sight of you after you go past the wagon, they'll lose interest fast. Party's over, as far as they're concerned. If they ain't lookin' down the street at you, then go around the wagon, slip through the high bushes there, and go all the way out to the shore of the lake. Then come back up to the warehouse along the shoreline. When you get to the warehouse, wait by that door on the south wall. It will open very soon, and we will let you in."

"And what are you going to be doing all this time?" Lillie asked.

"Gettin' in," Houdini said. "Mr. Ade and I will be coming around from the south almost in plain view. If you wasn't there, we would probably be seen. With you there, we will be invisible. Now. Any more questions?"

Lillie and Ade looked at each other, then back to Houdini and shook their heads.

"All right," Houdini said. "Mr. Ade, you come with me. Remember, Miss West, eleven thirty. Eleven thirty exactly."

Houdini threw his head back, beckoning Ade to follow him; he then turned around and began walking back up the street. Lillie and Ade looked at each other. Then Ade turned and followed after Houdini. They reached the next corner, turned right and disappeared down the street. Lillie turned around and looked toward the street fronting the lake.

"An' I say to the sniveling blaggard, 'On your feet ye worthless beggar, or I'll shy your lean carcass into the river an' dhround ye!' An' the spider-legged divil sprang up an' ran out o' there, coward that he was."

These words belonged to Officer Malone who had just finished recounting the one, shining moment of his career when he had bullied a harmless tramp down on the loading docks of the Chicago River. Officer O'Hara had heard the story several times before, and had been unimpressed with the first telling of it. He now felt somewhat sickened by the tale.

"Faix, an' did the captain pin a medal on ye for that one?" asked Officer O'Hara.

"A medal? 'Course not. Jus' doing me job, jus' doing me job."

Officer O'Hara jabbed Officer Malone in the ribs with his forefinger, and said, "Now would you look up the street there, lad?"

Officer Malone turned to his right and caught sight of Lillie who was standing in the middle of the street and taking a photograph of the fair buildings with her Kodak.

At that exact moment Houdini and George Ade quickly walked across the stretch of street that lay south of the policemen. As Houdini had predicted, the attention of the policemen was directed north up the street toward Lillie; in fact, the policemen had their backs turned to Houdini and Ade.

Lillie stood looking back at the fair a moment longer; then began slowly strolling down the street toward the policemen. When Lillie got within speaking distance, she smiled at the policemen, and said, "Good morning, officers."

The policemen lifted their helmets and said in unison, "Morning, Miss."

Officer Malone said, "Fine morning it is too, wouldn't you say?"

"Oh," Lillie said, "it is a beautiful day! Just look at the sky up there. Have you ever seen such blue in your lives? It looks just like—"

Lillie had reached the south corner of Tesla's warehouse. She was looking up to the sky in a spring-time reverie that teetered and tottered at the edge of ecstasy.

Her feet moved across the pavement of the street with a languid carelessness. One foot did not seem to know what the other was doing; her right foot went in front of her left, her right heel coming down on her left toe. It was a perfectly natural motion. Lillie continued forward, her left foot starting to lift up, but unable to budge from the weight of her right toe. Her left ankle wobbled, bent, and her whole left foot went on its side to the pavement. Her body followed, her hands flying out, her skirt flying up, the policemen flying forward—but not in time. Lillie hit the pavement hard.

"Oh, my!" Lillie cried. "Oh dear!"

Lillie turned her head. She could see the side of the warehouse and Houdini and George Ade standing next to it.

The two policemen rushed to Lillie's side, their backs to Houdini and Ade.

"I. . . I've twisted my ankle," Lillie said.

"Allow me, Miss," Officer O'Hara said, extending his hand.

"I don't know if I can get up," Lillie said.

"Take your time, Miss," Officer Malone said. "We'll help you."

As soon as the policemen came up next to Lillie, Houdini sprang up on the iron grillwork covering the two lower flights of stairs on the fire escape. Ade, holding Houdini's coat and hat, watched from behind a bush as the young magician climbed the grillwork of the fire escape like a monkey climbing a tree. Houdini reached the top of the grillwork, slid over its edge like a snake, and shot up the steps in a silent tip-toe. In a few seconds, Ade lost sight of Houdini.

Up on the roof, Houdini took in the place in a single glance. He went straight up the slanting roof and peered down into the windows of the skylight. Through the windows he could see the top of Tesla's airship, about thirty or forty feet below, and below the airship by another twenty-five feet or so lay the cement floor of the warehouse.

Houdini studied the windows which composed the skylight as a long gable running the length of the rooftop. Each face of the gable was made of thirty-six rows of window panes. Each of the panes was about eight inches square and set into a wooden frame, and against the inside surface of the glass pane near the bottom of each row of frames ran a thin insulated wire which Houdini knew was connected to a burglar alarm bell somewhere below in the warehouse.

Houdini peered down through the windows, now no longer looking at the airship, but at the arched iron trusses that ran directly beneath the skylight by a few feet. Below, on the opposite wall, Houdini could see iron columns which he knew were connected to the trusses. He studied the iron columns and saw that at intervals of a few feet there were bolt screw heads projecting down along their length. Those screws held the iron columns to the outside wooden frame of the building.

Houdini had seen enough. He knew what he had to do. He took out a little pen-knife, opened it up, and slid the blade along the edge of the glazing on the window pane before him. He carefully scraped and peeled back the glazing on all four edges of the pane. Having exposed the edge of the glass pane, he began working on the nail heads that held the window pane in its frame. He slid his knife blade under the nail heads until each one was bent all the way back. This done, he pried down under the edge of the glass. He kept carefully prying all around until the glass came free. He lifted the whole window pane out of its frame and set the sheet of glass carefully aside. Next, he wedged the tip of his blade under a little nail which held the insulated burglar alarm wire across the bottom of the opening of the window frame. With delicate pressure, he pulled the nail halfway out from the wood. He went to the other nail on the other side of the frame and worked on it in the same fashion as he had the first nail. In a moment, the second nail came up, and the wire dropped loose. He carefully pushed the burglar alarm wire down until it touched the bottom edge of the window frame. Houdini closed his pen-knife, slipped it back into his pocket, and buttoned a flap down over the pocket.

Now the wooden frame surrounded a square opening about eight inches across. It would appear to a casual observer that a grown man—or even a full-grown boy the size of Houdini—could not pass through that space, but Houdini began to do just this very thing. He lay on his back, put his head and arms through the opening, squeezed his shoulders together, but the opening was not large enough for him to pass through. He squeezed his shoulders a second time. Still, his bulk was too large. He had hoped it would be easier, but it was not going to be easier. He squeezed his shoulders together again, and then continued putting pressure on his left shoulder until he completely dislocated his upper arm bone from his shoulder socket. The pain was sharp and searing. Another person would have screamed, but Houdini didn't scream. His jaws were locked tight, his lips sealed, his breath passing through his nostrils. He was slowly wiggling through the opening, hanging upside down about sixty or seventy feet up from the concrete floor with a dislocated arm. The only thing holding him up was the friction between his body and the surrounding wooden frame. He was through the opening up to his chest. He got his arms free and he tried swinging his left arm to snap it back in its socket. Every movement was fiery agony to him.

Now Houdini felt his feet go up in the air. The full weight of his body was on the wooden frame. He heard a creaking, and knew that the wood was getting ready to crack and split; in another moment the frame would crack; the opening would widen; his body would slide through the opening and fall straight down head first to the cement floor sixty feet below.

Houdini kept swinging his arms, but he could not relocate his left arm in its socket. He suddenly stopped wiggling. He could feel the weight of his body begin to drive him down through the opening at a faster, uncontrollable rate.

Then the wooden frame cracked. Houdini plunged downward—head down—toward the cement pavement.

President Cleveland had a hansom cab waiting for us downstairs in front of the hotel entrance. Tesla and I jumped into it, and we sped off to the train station. There, we boarded one of those twelve-minute express cars that Houdini, Lillie, and Ade had just taken ahead of us. Neither Tesla nor I said a word to the other. I sat next to the window and watched the buildings flash past us, then a street crossing, then more flashing buildings, then another crossing, then more buildings. Our track rose up along an earthen embankment, passed the Midway Plaisance, and then began a long loop until we came into the terminal station of the World's Fair.

Tesla got up and rushed out of the car, glancing back only once to be sure that I was still behind him. As we went through the station, I had to break into a little trot to keep up with Tesla's brisk stride.

"Tesla," I said, trying to catch my breath. "Slow down a little."

Tesla said nothing, but kept up his brisk pace as I raced after him down the stairs and all the way out of the station. Up ahead I saw a hansom cab. Tesla raised his long arm, the driver raised his hat, and Tesla grabbed me by my arm and dragged me along in a run toward the cab. We piled into it, I, gasping for breath.

"I told you I wasn't up to this!" I groaned.

Tesla said nothing, but the driver touched up the horses and we were off like a bullet.

"Who's the driver up there?" I asked.

"A Pinkerton man," Tesla said.

"He drives like a Pinkerton man," I said.

Houdini hung from the wooden frame of the skylight. The lip of the frame had splintered, and Houdini had plunged through it until he caught his fall with the back of his legs hooked around the frame's outside edge. He hung this way for a moment, like a circus acrobat on a trapeze swing, slowly swinging back and forth by the crook of his legs on the bottom edge of the wooden frame.

Kolman Czito had heard the crack of the window frame while he was inside the airship checking the engine, and he had charged out of the ship with his revolver drawn. He looked everywhere for the source of the sound, everywhere but straight up. He circled the airship twice, peering about, while Houdini hung overhead watching Czito's every move.

Czito stood for a moment, looking to his left, then to his right, trying to listen for a sound. He heard nothing. Finally, Czito turned with his revolver held high, and walked stealthily to the front of the building.

Houdini slowly and silently released his breath. He had stopped breathing when Czito appeared below. Now Houdini began breathing in long, slow draws. At the same time, he slowly swung his left arm around in circles until he felt the sudden, relieving "pop" of his upper arm bone snapping into his shoulder socket. After this, he continued to hang there for a few seconds, breathing slowly. Then he began to swing back and forth in his upside down position. After a couple of swings, he reached for the top of the iron truss a foot or so away to the right of his hands. On his first try, his hands missed the truss by a few inches. He swung back again to the left, then to the right, reached, and his hands touched the top of the truss, but slipped off; his palms were drenched in sweat.

Houdini stopped and hung still. His whole body was drenched in perspiration. It was trickling down his chest and back, running along the front and back of his neck, covering his face, soaking his hair, and, from his dangling hair, falling in drops down to the cement floor sixty or seventy feet directly below him; there, it splashed, and formed a little puddle.

Houdini listened to the little splashes, and expected to see the man with the revolver return any second; he was sure the sound was echoing throughout the whole warehouse.

Now he began to swing again, utterly exhausted; the strength in his knees was beginning to go. Houdini's face was blood-red, glistening wet, his gray-blue eyes wide with the agony of his tortured knees, the agony of his dizziness and nausea. He was fighting—fighting Fear—and behind Fear stood Death. And he saw Death laughing.

Houdini was swinging fast now: left, right, left, right, a pendulum of flesh and human will. His mind put up the "closed" sign. He was no longer thinking; he was only feeling; he was feeling everything, everything he had ever felt in his life all in this one, swinging instant—everything but Fear. His hands were ahead of him. He saw his fingers moving toward the iron truss, moving very, very slowly. He saw his fingers and thumbs opening wide, two fans held out over the truss. The fingers and thumbs began to close as they hung in space. Houdini noticed the hair on the back of his thumbs, faint slender hairs. He saw that his fingers were coming close to the truss, and closing upon it.

Then—it was as if Houdini came up out of water—and at the same instant everything around him sped up. He heard the rasp of his breath in and out. His palms gripped the iron truss with every ounce of strength left in his body. He pulled his body toward the truss, and his legs came out of the window frame and dropped straight down. Now he was hanging from the truss, his legs swinging in the air. Houdini kicked his legs forward and hooked them into the cross-bracing of the truss.

Houdini began climbing down along the upper arched beam of the truss until he reached its end, and then put his foot down on the first bolt projecting from the iron column. He moved down the column, stepped to the next bolt, moved down, stepped again to another bolt, and kept going slowly and steadily downward until he climbed all the way down the column to the floor of the warehouse, just as if the column had been a ladder.

When Houdini reached the floor, he stood up, slowly bowed at the waist with his arms extended, and then came back up with his arms extending and stretching high over his head. He slowly lowered his arms, breathing deeply, and stood that way for several moments. Then he smiled; he was looking at the open door of Tesla's airship; it was wide open, just the way Czito had left it when he had charged out of the airship.

Houdini took a step to the left, looked toward the front of the warehouse, then turned to the steel door on the south wall. It was a simple affair locked with only three steel bolts. Houdini carefully slid the bolts back and opened the door. He saw George Ade crouching next to a bush. Ade saw Houdini at that same instant and got up and rushed to the door, handing Houdini his coat and hat. Houdini stepped back into the warehouse and Ade waved to Lillie who was still standing out on the street talking to the two policemen.

Lillie was saying, "I think I just need to walk it off."

"Are you sure you're all right, Miss?" Officer O'Hara asked.

"I think so," Lillie said. "Thank you. You've been very kind."

Lillie limped away. Ade saw that the two policemen were watching her. He retreated back inside the warehouse and carefully closed the door.

Lillie kept limping down the street at a slow but steady pace. When she reached the patrol wagon, she came along next to it, went past the horses, and then stepped toward the curb and out of the line of sight of the two policemen.

Lillie stopped at the curb and looked back. She couldn't see the policemen from where she stood; her view of them was blocked by the patrol wagon. And this, of course, meant that the policemen could not see her. She began to count to ten slowly, just as Houdini had instructed, and, when she reached ten, she took a small step out to the street and looked around the edge of the patrol wagon. She saw the policemen talking to each other and gesturing broadly with their hands. Lillie realized that they were describing to each other what had just happened; in a minute or two they would be disagreeing on some detail and this would serve as subject matter for conversation for the rest of their watch.

Lillie stepped back and went between two bushes, and then made her way out to the lake shore. From there she marched north along the shore until she reached the south wall of the warehouse. There, she came up along the wall, passed the fire escape, and stopped at the door.

Lillie pulled at the handle of the door and it swung open. George Ade came out from behind it with a big grin.

"Well?" Ade whispered, "Come on if you're coming," and he took Lillie by the arm, pulled her inside, and closed the door.

Lillie, Ade, and Houdini stood looking at the airship.

Lillie raised her Kodak, and aimed the box camera at the airship which shined brightly from the rays of the noonday sun pouring in from the skylight windows directly overhead.

Lillie was about to snap a picture when she felt a hand on her back shoving her forward. She looked around and saw that it was Houdini, and that he was shoving Ade forward as well; all the while Houdini was shaking his head. Houdini raised a finger to his lips, and then pointed to the front of the warehouse. Just at that same moment Lillie heard the footsteps.

All three of them—Lillie, Ade, and Houdini—rushed up the steps of the airship and through her open door.

Kolman Czito approached the airship with his revolver held in the air. He was sure he had heard footsteps—several footsteps. He looked about carefully, listening all the while. All within his sight was stillness and silence. Then he heard a creak of metal. He spun about.

Czito pointed his revolver at the open door of the airship, slowly ascended the steps, and peered through the ship's door. The lower deck was still and quiet. Czito stepped inside, looked about, and then went to the steel ladder and looked up through the hatch to the top deck. He listened again, heard nothing, but decided to ascend the ladder anyway. He went up slowly, climbing the ladder with his left hand on each rung, and his right hand holding and aiming his revolver up toward the open hatch.

Czito's head emerged through the hatch. He stopped on the ladder and looked up and down the length of the upper deck. He saw nothing; he heard nothing. He listened a moment longer, and then descended the ladder.

Lillie, Ade, and Houdini had made it up the ladder to the upper deck. There, Ade spied a closet door near the steps leading up to the pilothouse. He slid the door open, pushed Lillie into it, and went in behind her. He turned back to slide the door shut and saw that Houdini had disappeared somewhere. Ade slid shut the door of the closet.

Now Lillie and Ade stood face to face in the closet. A little grilled window in the closet opened out on to the pilothouse. From this grilled window, they had a partial view of the pilothouse interior; they could glimpse part of the pilot's wheel and a few levers and controls. They stood there waiting for a moment, then heard a clang of metal below followed by the metallic clatter of rapid footsteps entering the lower deck of the airship and ascending the ladder to the upper deck.

It was Tesla and me; we had jumped out of the hansom cab; the Pinkerton man had pushed the two policemen aside, Tesla had opened the front door of the warehouse with his key, and the two of us had rushed into the warehouse and past Kolman Czito—to whom Tesla barked as we passed, "Prepare for flight!"

As Tesla and I raced up the steps to the pilothouse, I heard a clang below and knew that Czito had closed and locked the door of the airship. I came into the pilothouse and stood before the wheel. Tesla stood by my side. In a moment, Czito came running in and closed the switch that opened the big sliding doors of the warehouse.

Out beyond the pilothouse windows the big doors of the warehouse began sliding open, revealing the waters of Lake Michigan and the blue sky above them.

Tesla said to Czito, "Set the coils for half power. We want to disable their ship and bring it down in a controlled landing, not destroy it. We can't risk exploding the crystal while in Earth's atmosphere."

I looked over at Czito. He looked pale as a poached egg, and his head was trembling. It made me wonder what I looked like.

Tesla said, "Anytime, Mark."

I stood before the wheel, looking down, shaking my head, and said, "I've got to be the craziest ass on the planet to agree to this!"

I let out a long sigh, and looked over at Tesla. He was watching me with great intensity in his eyes. I turned and closed the starter switch to the airship's engine and began to hear the engine's undulating hum.

"Take her below the surface of the lake," Tesla said.

I touched the wheel with my fingertip and the pedal with my toe, and the ship started through the doors. I let her clear the warehouse completely, and then took her straight down to the surface of the lake. We began submerging rapidly. The waters of the lake splashed in front of the pilothouse windows, engulfed them, and then we were under in a gray haze streaked with beams of sunlight. I pushed the ship forward. Up ahead, schools of fish darted away in front of the pilothouse windows. I pushed the ship on forward at a slightly faster rate. Now there was only a grayish haze. We moved through the haze for a minute or two.

In a moment Tesla said, "We're far enough out from the city. Take her up."

I steered the ship upward, and we broke the surface of the lake in a great splash.

Above us were white clouds and blue sky. I aimed the prow of the airship for the clouds. Then we were upon the clouds, then inside of them; it was a sudden gray world, a mist thicker than any London fog. I pushed the airship on up through the cloud and we broke through to its top. Here was a vast bed of cotton laid out under the bright glare of the sun with clear, blue sky overhead.

Tesla took out his little tin box, drew out its steel rod, switched it on, and said, "This will be your compass, Mark. Follow the flashes of light."

Tesla took the tin box and mounted it upon a pedestal in front of the pilot's wheel.

"If it stops flashing," Tesla said, "pivot it about until it picks up the position of the crystal again."

"And what's its present indications?" I asked.

"Straight ahead," Tesla said.

I pushed the airship forward. Up ahead was a cloud that was shaped like a fish. We flew toward the cloud, and as we approached it, the appearance of its shape changed from a fish to that of the body of a giant woman pouring out a bucket of wash water. We entered the gray interior of that cloud and broke out its other side to the bright sunlight.

Then we saw it—far away in the sky—a black cylinder!

"Well, I'll be damned," I said.

Tesla went aft of the pilothouse and came forward again with a spyglass in his hand; he raised it to his eye and looked through it out the pilothouse window. In a moment, the black cylinder of the foreign airship came into the circle view of Tesla's spyglass. Tesla gazed upon the cylinder with great intensity, as if he were trying to memorize its every detail. All the while I was slowly approaching the object of Tesla's scrutiny.

Tesla handed me the spyglass. I took it, looked through it, and found the black cylinder in the circle view. The thing was a black, featureless, windowless cylinder; it was not cigar-shaped, but flat on both of its ends. And even I noticed something that was very meaningful to Tesla. The foreign airship had two metal rods on its top, just like the fancy lightning rods or "aerial conductors" on Tesla's ship. I thought this was mighty strange.

I said, "The thing has lightning rods just like ours."

"Yes," Tesla said. "I know. I'm going up to the gun tower. Maintain your course."

Before I could say a word, Tesla was flying up the steel ladder that went up to the gun tower, a little one-man room mounted atop the dome of the pilothouse.

I brought our airship on toward the black cylinder. It seemed to be hanging there in the sky by an invisible thread, the bait on the fishing line of a giant. I slowed us down and stopped our airship in the sky.

The foreign airship hung in the sky not more than a hundred feet from the bow of our ship. I could see the texture of her hull, a rough, black something; it could have been metal, it could have been soot-blackened stone. The thing just hung there in the blue sky.

Then from some point on that rough, black hull shot a white bolt of electricity; it reached out like the claw of some evil bird of prey and grabbed hold of the bow of our airship and shook us with a thunderclap.

[*Fzt! - boom -beroom - boom!*]

I was nearly knocked off my feet. I tightened my grip on the pilot's wheel.

"Hold her steady, Mark!" Tesla shouted from the gun tower.

"I'm trying!" I shouted back.

Just as I got our airship steadied, Tesla fired a ray of electricity from the gun tower.

[*Fzt! - boom - beroom!*]

I saw a bright, white beam of undulating light shining from above the top edge of the pilothouse windows. The beam of light struck the side of the foreign airship, making a circle of blinding light on its dull, black hull. From that circle of light radiated countless fingers of crawling electric bolts girdling the foreign airship round about. The foreign airship shuddered in the sky, then shot straight up, breaking free of Tesla's beam.

"Go after them, Mark!"

I pulled back on the pilot's wheel, and our airship turned her prow to the zenith. I could see the foreign airship moving away straight up through the sky. It looked like it was falling in the wrong direction.

I followed the black speck of the foreign airship straight up.

After a moment, I noticed something most peculiar. The sky was changing color; it had been a bright blue, but now it was a deep, dark blue, and growing darker by the second.

Then I saw a star—then another one.

"My God!" I shouted. "The sun's going out!"

"It's not the sun," Tesla shouted down from the gun tower. "We're leaving the atmosphere of Earth and entering the interplanetary vacuum!"

The sky became a deep, dark blue, just as it appears after sunset when the stars come out. And then the dark blue flashed away. The sky was suddenly a solid black, a cold, solid black studded with stars more brilliant than I had ever gazed upon in my life, even those I had viewed from the peaks of high mountains. Every star was a pure, clear, bright point of white, and there were millions upon millions of these white points out there, and, through it all, the Milky Way stretched overhead and earned its name; it was a river of milky liquid frozen in its flow through the infinite, dead blackness of airless space. All sense of earth-bound existence ceased; I felt we were lost amid a vast, endless sea of stars and black space.

Tesla shouted, "The foreign airship is starboard thirty degrees!"

I managed to turn the pilot's wheel starboard. The airship responded; the starry night sky shifted larboard. Then what came into my view from beyond the windows of the pilothouse made me gasp for air and blink my eyes. I saw the black cylinder of the foreign airship silhouetted against the glowing blue and white globe of the world!

We had actually traveled out into the great dark of interplanetary space and were *looking back at the world*!

I did not have time to study this uncanny view. The foreign airship was hurtling toward us. Tesla fired—[*Fzt!*] —and the white ray coming from our airship struck the foreign airship on its bow and deflected its course away from us. The foreign airship fired back.

[Fzt! - boom!]

A wall of white light filled the windows, and I was thrown back across the pilothouse. I dove back to the wheel, grabbed it with both my hands, and steered our airship in a tight circle around the foreign airship. Tesla started firing a barrage of electric rays, and these struck the foreign airship at various places on its hull. With each strike the foreign airship seemed to shudder and be pushed back. It seemed as if Tesla was nudging the foreign airship in a series of pushes that was sending it back down to the earth. Tesla was not engaged in a military attack, but a cold act of mechanical engineering aimed at bringing the foreign airship down to the ground and all in one piece.

Suddenly, a bright ball of red fire shot from the foreign airship and struck us somewhere below the pilothouse.

[*Fzt! - boom - beroom - boom! Bumble - smash!*]

There was a brilliant flash of light and a vibration so powerful that it shook me to my bones. I was knocked off my feet and thrown across the pilothouse. I was an instant from falling on my back, to be killed, or at least crippled for life. But I did not hit the floor, nor did I hit anything.

For a moment I felt like I was falling. I thought a hole had opened up in the floor and I was falling back to the earth to my doom. But after a moment, I managed to turn my head. I was not falling, at least not falling through any floor, for the floor was below me and was not going anywhere; neither was I. It was then that I realized that I was actually floating above the floor and at that moment I truly believed that I was dead.

I looked out the pilothouse windows and saw that the blue and white globe of the world was orbiting around us once every three seconds!

Then I saw Czito coming toward me. It looked like he was swimming underwater. But he was not swimming in water—he was swimming in air!

Somehow I managed to get my jaw to move and my lungs to breathe, and I shouted, "Hey! Hey! What's happening? Are we dead?"

"Not dead," Czito said. "Weightless."

Tesla came out of the gun tower and swam through the air toward us.

"Czito!" Tesla said. "Check for a short circuit in the coils."

Czito swam away. It seemed to me that Czito had some expertise in swimming in air, and it occurred to me that he and Tesla had been up this way before. Czito swam out of the pilothouse and down into the upper deck. In a moment he shouted:

"Mr. Tesla! There are people back here!"

Tesla swam down near the steps leading out of the pilothouse and looked down the length of the upper deck. I tried a couple of breaststrokes and found that I could swim in the air, too. If I wasn't dead, I surely was flying like an angel.

I came up behind Tesla and peered down into the upper deck. Down there—or up there—or wherever there—for all up and down had become meaningless—*out* there was Czito floating like Montpelier's balloon. Next to him were two other human balloons: Lillie West, holding her skirt with some awkwardness, and George Ade, reaching into the air trying to grab his hat which was floating in front of him.

"Stowaways," Tesla said.

"Damn it to hell," I said.

"The coils!" Tesla shouted to Czito.

Czito slid open the door of the ship's engine and reached inside to the machinery.

I felt something click inside my head, and a pop in my ears, and thousands of invisible fingers pull me down in the direction of the airship's floor. My innards lagged behind the way that innards always do when you take a sudden plunge.

All of us hit the floor at the same instant. I landed on my right knee, and felt a sharp, sudden pain shoot up my leg from my knee to my hip.

"Ow!" I shouted. "Oh! Damn it all to hell and back! What in the hell kind of tumble jug is this?"

"Sorry, Mark," Tesla said, getting up off the floor.

"I thought this ship had its own gravity!"

"We had a slight disruption."

"Disruption? Eruption, you mean! I landed on my good leg. My *good* leg! Now I'm a cripple with *two* bad legs!"

I lay there in agony, rolling about. Tesla helped me to my feet. I rubbed my leg. It didn't seem to be broken, but it hurt like plumb perfect hell. I turned about and saw Lillie West and George Ade coming up the steps of the pilothouse with Czito behind them.

"And what the hell are the two of you doing here?" I shouted.

Ade started to open his mouth, but I held up my hand, and said: "Wait. Don't answer that. Don't answer that. I don't know what the hell I'm doing here."

"Friends of yours?" Tesla asked me.

"Not by a damn sight," I said. "They're a couple of snooping Newspaper reporters."

"George Ade, *Chicago Record*."

"When I said you were persistent I was expressing only a pale representation of the truth! You two have no idea what you've gotten yourselves into!"

"Some idea," Ade said. "We're in a war."

"Damn right we're in a war," I said. "And you've brought your lady friend here to the front lines."

"I am not his lady friend," Lillie said, "nor has he brought me anywhere. I'm here entirely of my own accord."

"Well," I said, "your own accord is trespassing on private property—no—Federal Government property! This here ship has been commandeered by the President of the United States! And we're all under sealed military orders! When we get back home—*if* we get back home—both of you will be locked up in solitary confinement in the Federal Penitentiary for a hundred years!"

There was a sound of crashing coming from the upper deck. Czito went down the steps of the pilothouse and stopped before the open door of the engines.

"It's another one, Mr. Tesla," Czito said.

Tesla went down the steps and stopped in front of the engines.

"Ehrich!" Tesla said, "What are you doing in there?"

I came down the steps, stopped next to Tesla and Czito and looked into the engine. I saw Houdini hanging upside down inside the engine, his arms and legs all tangled up in the machinery.

"Friend of yours?" I asked Tesla.

Tesla said, "Ehrich used to be my messenger in New York."

"I was blackmailed," Houdini said. "They blackmailed me, Mr. Tesla. I didn't want to do it."

"Come out of there," Tesla said, "before you electrocute yourself."

"Yes, sir, Mr. Tesla, yes, sir," Houdini said, climbing out of the engine.

"Watch that wire!" Tesla shouted.

Houdini came on out, stood up, and looked up at Tesla.

"Come with me," Tesla said, and we all went back up to the pilothouse.

I looked out the windows. There was no sign of the foreign airship anywhere. If it was out there, it was not visible against the blackness of the starry night. And it was a very strange starry night; for all around us was a starry black sky, while our pilothouse was flooded with sunlight.

Tesla went to the little tin box mounted on the pedestal near the pilot's wheel. The box's bulb was dark. Tesla pivoted the box around on its pedestal.

"Czito," Tesla said, "do you see anything in the viewing glass?"

Czito went to the control board at the aft of the pilothouse and bent over a square of glass set into the board. The glass glowed with incandescent electrical light, showing up as a number of flashing points on its surface to form some kind of diagram or map. I came closer and looked at it, and recognized that it was a diagram of our solar system.

Czito said, "The foreign airship is moving off rapidly—in the direction of. . . Mars!"

Tesla came up next to Czito and looked at the diagram made of incandescent light. He studied the diagram a moment and then turned to me, pointed at the tin box mounted on the pedestal next to the pilot's wheel, and said, "There's your compass, Mark."

I said, "You don't really intend for us to chase those varmints any further, do you?"

"As you said, Mark, we are under sealed orders to retrieve the crystal—or destroy it."

I turned away from Tesla and went to the window. The blue and white globe of the world was no longer circling our airship, or, that is to say, we were no longer spinning around in space.

I said, "I didn't sign up for service to leave the planet."

"Mark!" Tesla cried, and he came up next to me, and led me away from the others as far as he could. Then he said in a low tone:

"I do not know the extent of the Martians' knowledge. They seem to have applied electrical principles similar to those which I have discovered. Perhaps they know more than I do, perhaps less. But one thing is certain: They have the Master Crystal in their possession, and within a short time they will understand and use its power. And its power is majestic. It is capable of splitting the Earth in two and hurtling it into the sun. Now. Do you want to go home?"

I looked into Tesla's face and saw a great fear and dread in his expression, especially in his eyes. His face was definitely swollen now, but he was no longer sweating.

Uncertainty tore at my insides. If I took us back to the ground, I might be sentencing everyone in the world—including my wife and children—to a dark and uncertain future—a future of devastating war with an otherworldly people who, perhaps, held human life of no value and no consequence whatsoever. If I went forward, I was risking my life and the lives of everyone on board, and there was no guarantee—indeed, little hope—that through that risk we might rescue our world from the grasp of those otherworldly hands. I weighed our little hope against our dark uncertainty, then turned, grasped the pilot's wheel, turned the airship about so that her prow was aligned with the steel rod of the tin box—and pressed the accelerator pedal with my foot.

"Thank you, Mark," Tesla said.

"Don't thank me. I'm taking us to a funeral—our own."

I looked over at the tracking machine mounted on its pedestal; its light bulb was dark. Then there was a feeble flash, then darkness again.

I pressed the accelerator pedal with my foot. I had no sense of forward motion; the stars before me didn't move. I pressed the accelerator down harder.

"Nothing's happening," I said. "We're not moving."

"On the contrary," Tesla said, "You have us moving along at a speed of ten thousand miles an hour."

Tesla pointed to a speed indicator on the panel in front of the pilot's wheel. The indicator's little numbered wheels lined up to form the figure of "10,000."

Tesla said, "Pay no attention to the fixed stars. You will not see them move, not on this flight."

Tesla took Lillie, Ade, and Houdini all the way aft along the upper deck to the stern of the airship. Here was a room encased above and around by mullioned windows like those of the pilothouse. It was a bright little parlor, lit by the blazing sun shining through a starry night sky. This strange combination of night and day which is the eternal shade of interplanetary space was a sight to which none of us would become accustomed.

Three sides of the parlor were walled in with mullioned windows from waist high up, and the windows curved upward to form something of a dome overhead. The fourth wall of the parlor was fitted with bookcases and a writing desk. The books were locked into the shelves with a covering of wire mesh doors.

The parlor was furnished with armchairs, a center table, and a settee. The chairs and settee had been overturned, but the table had somehow landed upright on its feet. Tesla went about the room turning the chairs and settee upright. When he had finished, he went and stood before the mullioned windows at the stern of the airship. Behind him hung the brilliant blue and white globe of the world, slowly shrinking in size against an unchanging, star-scattered blackness.

"Come in," Tesla said to the others who had stood in the doorway watching him. "Come in and sit down. All of you."

Lillie came in, followed by Houdini, and then Ade. Lillie sat in a chair and Houdini slumped down on the settee. George Ade remained standing.

"Mr. Ade, is it?" Tesla asked. "Please be seated."

Ade came over and sat in the chair across the table from Lillie.

Tesla looked at Lillie, and asked, "How did you gain entry to the airship?"

Lillie started to speak, but then nodded her head toward Houdini who, in turn, held his palms to his chest in an expression of total innocence.

"Ehrich? How did you get in here?" Tesla asked.

Houdini said, "Through the window."

Tesla inclined his head. "Through the window? You mean, the skylight on the roof?"

"That's right," Houdini said.

"I see," Tesla said. "And why exactly did all of you do this? Why did you break in?"

Houdini shrugged, "Like I said, Mr. Tesla, I was blackmailed—by them two people sitting there. They made me do it. They said if I didn't help them, they'd reveal my trade secrets—or phony something up and say those were my secrets. I made a mistake, Mr. Tesla, a mistake, that's all. A mistake in trusting."

"It seems you are not the only person who has made a mistake in trusting," Tesla said. "I never thought you would do this to me, Ehrich, even under the threat of blackmail."

"You don't understand, Mr. Tesla. They were going to do a number on me in the papers, a big write-up about the secrets of Houdini being revealed. If they had done that, they would've ruined me, ruined me before I even got my foot all the way in to the show business! Then what would I have? Nothing! A whole lot of nothing and me with a widowed mother and sister to support! And they meant it! I know they meant to do me one and good. And then they were talkin' a lot of high-falutin' lingo about democracy and freedom of the press and the rights of the people and how I was a gutless coward and liar! *That* was what they was talkin', Mr. Tesla! Sounding so high and mighty and full of airs! And mockin' the name of Houdini, Mr. Tesla, mockin' the name of Houdini! I wasn't going to let them get away with that! I had to show 'em, Mr. Tesla, I had to show 'em! And I *did* show 'em. I did. And now here we are, and there it is, and that is that. I made a mistake, a mistake in trusting. But, Mr. Tesla, I never meant you no harm. Never. You was always square with me, and I'm sorry for this mess I made, but I can't unmake it. I can't unmake it."

Houdini sat, slowly shaking his head back and forth.

"No, Ehrich," Tesla said, "you certainly cannot unmake it." Tesla turned back to Lillie West and George Ade. "And what about you two people? What do you have to say for yourselves?"

"It is not for us to justify our actions," Lillie said, "but for you to justify yours."

"Ya see what I mean, Mr. Tesla?" Houdini asked. "Have you ever heard such airs?"

"Your statement is most interesting, Miss," Tesla said. "You break into my private property. You put lives at risk, yours as well as countless others. And then you say it is for me to justify my actions. By what logic do you support your position?"

"Your question is most interesting, sir," Lillie said. "You carry on a secret war with weapons of incredible power. You put lives at risk, yours as well as countless others. And then you refuse to acknowledge your responsibility. By what logic do you support your position?"

Tesla blinked.

"I see," Tesla said. "You believe I have been reckless in this conflict with the Martians?"

"I believe," Lillie said, "that you have not only been reckless, but tyrannically unjust. Unjust to the people of the United States, unjust to the people of the world. The people of the world have a right to know of the existence of the Martians. A right, sir. And I intend to do everything in my power to see that their rights are upheld."

"I see," Tesla said. "And so you broke into my warehouse to—do what?"

"Photograph your airship and find whatever other evidence that I could to prove that the Martians exist."

"I see," Tesla said. He went to the window and looked out at the globe of our world which was growing smaller and smaller.

After a moment, Tesla turned around, and said, "You will never be allowed to print any photograph of this airship in your newspaper or in any newspaper or in any book anywhere in the world."

"And," Lillie asked, "what about Freedom of the Press?"

"An admirable institution," Tesla said, "one I support wholeheartedly, along with another institution—survival—without which nothing else is possible. A public revelation of the Martian's existence would shock mankind and shatter the premises of six thousand years of secular and religious history."

Lillie said, "It is time that the people of the world learned the truth about their world's history."

"Perhaps," Tesla said, "the thought of the existence of the Martians does not unsettle your mind, Miss West, but I judge you to have a mind that is somewhat above the average of our race. You are educated. You have given thought to both the high things as well as the low. I can see in your eyes that you have lived. You are a woman of unusual will and determination. I state the obvious, but for a reason: Do not assume because you are so that others are so. They are not. Much greater minds than yours have wrestled with this issue of what the mass of men should know and what should be withheld from their knowledge. I will tell you what the greatest minds whom we have consulted believe would happen should the existence of the Martians be suddenly revealed to the mass of humanity: People would flee the cities of the Earth. Industry would grind to a halt. The stock markets of the world would collapse. Governmental authority would crumble amid the chaos. The chain of military command would be broken. Political assassinations and coups would push aside the rule of law. Mass chaos and mob rule would follow—a chaos no army could contain or overturn. There would be rioting mass migrations, food shortages, and mass starvation, followed by the bloody genocide of millions and hundreds of millions. The Martians would have destroyed us without firing a shot."

"You really believe that would happen?"

It was George Ade who had asked that question.

"Yes," Tesla said, "and so does President Cleveland."

"So Cleveland will order our editors to kill the story," Ade said.

"Yes," Tesla said. "He will most certainly do that."

"And does this mean that we are your prisoners?" Lillie asked.

"I do not consider you my prisoners," Tesla said. "You are my guests. I ask only that you do not interfere with the operation of this ship."

"We have no intention of interfering with anything," Ade said.

"And," Tesla said, "I ask that you keep the secret of our conflict with the Martians between us."

Lillie said, "You ask us not to interfere with the ship. You ask us to keep the secret of the Martians' existence. You ask. Why? Why ask us anything? Why not be honest and put it all in the form of a direct order?"

"Because," Tesla said, "I seek your rational understanding and voluntary agreement, not your obedience. In this situation, your obedience is of very little value. In most situations, obedience is of very little value between rational, thinking people. I want to convey to you the understanding that our situation is desperate. The Martians have stolen a crystal from me. The crystal is a device of great power, of tremendous energy."

"Is it a bomb?" Ade asked.

"It could be used as a bomb," Tesla said. "It has many uses, some wonderful, and some so terrible as to be beyond your imaginations."

"I see," Ade said. "I understand the secrecy."

"I don't," Lillie said. "Nothing Mr. Tesla has said justifies keeping the existence of the Martians a secret from the public. Quite the contrary. It argues for their exposure."

"And how is that?" Tesla asked.

"What happens if the Martians attack our cities and the public has not been told? What would be the effect then? It is then you would have the mass panic which you so fear. Do you think so little of your fellow man that you feel you must shelter him from the truth like a child?"

"I think a great deal of my fellow man, Miss," Tesla said.

"Then why don't you give your fellow man a chance?"

"There are some things that, for the sake of my fellow man, must be kept secret. The theft of my crystal proves that."

"I'm not talking about your crystal—or any military secret. I'm talking about the fact of the Martians' existence, a fundamental scientific, political, historical fact. The kind of fact that the authorities have always attempted to suppress from the days of Socrates to Galileo to now. Why don't you live up to the ideals which you proclaim?"

"What do you mean?"

Lillie stood up and looked back to the blue circle of the world. When she spoke, she was reciting from memory:

"'I came to America because it was here where I could most fully develop my ideas. It is here in America where every man has a chance to know the truth about all things. And this is the noblest ideal; for every man has the right to know and live the truth.' Nikola Tesla, New York Times, 1892. Why, Mr. Tesla? Why don't you live up to the ideals which you proclaim? Or are you just another Edison? Another P. T. Barnum of electricity? A shoddy lightning rod that bends at the slightest breeze?"

Lillie stood looking up into Tesla's eyes, and Tesla stood looking down into Lillie's. Tesla did not answer her, but stood slumped, his hands hanging at his sides.

Then Lillie turned abruptly, and started out of the room.

"Lillie!" Ade cried, rising to his feet. But Lillie had gone through the door.

"I'm sorry, Mr. Tesla," Ade said. "Miss West can be headstrong at times, and—"

"Please," Tesla said. "Do not apologize for her."

Tesla continued to stand there for a moment. Then he turned and went through the door.

Ade looked over at Houdini, and Houdini shrugged, got up, and went out the door as well.

George Ade was left alone. He turned and looked out through the mullioned window at Earth which was becoming a small blue disk in the cold, black night of space.

Up in the pilothouse I stood before the wheel, watching the incandescent light on the little tin box and making slight adjustments to it and the wheel every few moments. We were pursuing the foreign airship on an almost straight trajectory across the solar system to the planet Mars, and had already traveled nearly 500,000 miles into space, for I kept my foot on the accelerator pedal and so our speed was constantly and steadily accelerating. Tesla warned me not to accelerate too much at one time; he was uncertain how much heat the engine's wiring could actually take. This was one detail he had not yet thought out completely.

There we were, hurtling along at about half a million miles an hour, yet, standing at the pilot's wheel, it felt as if we were not moving at all. Our solar system was so immense that you could travel and travel at the most unimaginable speeds and still not have traversed a fraction of it.

I stood there, gazing at what seemed to be unmoving stars, and reflected upon who I was, where I was, and what I was. I was only a man. And man, the species, is only an incident in a scheme. He is not sure where he came from, and he is not sure where he is going. He is like the oyster. The oyster believes that the world was made for him, that all those millions of years of evolution were just so he could get *his* rights. Then along comes the maitre de, and the oyster is served.

Chapter Seven

A Good Imitation of Hell

What's a desert good for? 'Taint good for nuthin'.
Dey ain't no way to make it pay.

— Jim, *Tom Sawyer Abroad*

The distance between Earth and Mars at their closest approach is about 35 million miles, give or take a few million. If we use Man as the measure, following the example of the ancient Greeks, I estimate that it would only take about 10,000 years to walk that distance between the two planets, if you kept up a steady pace and only observed the Sabbath and all the regular holidays. Anyone can see that it is not that far.

Of course, no one person would ever live long enough to go the whole distance. It would have to be done in relays; about 142 life-long relays would reach to the finish line. One man would start out, go on walking for about 70 years more or less, and then let his great-grandson take a turn. That next generation would march for another life-span, or thereabouts, retire from the field, and hand the business over to its descendants, just as it is done here on Earth, only these people would be walking through the vacuum of interplanetary space, and that ought to be easy enough, seeing that there is nothing to get in the way, except maybe an asteroid or two.

Upon reflection however, maybe there would be a few difficulties. Tesla informs me that interplanetary space is just chock-full of what he calls "cosmic rays," "fields of force," and "domains of intensified ether." These things do not sound very inviting. You would not want to stroll through that kind of weather without thoroughly bundling up. If you did not suffocate for lack of air—and you would—you would most assuredly get fried from the inside out as all that "intensified ether" and all those "cosmic rays" passed through your internal

It seemed a black velvet carpet spangled brilliantly with stars.

regions. It is strange that all that empty space could be so filled up and crowded, but that is the way it is out there in the eternal night between the planets, and one must either take it or leave it; one can no more change the nature of outer space than one can reform a congressman: one will clambake you from the inside out, the other will coddle you from the outside in; either way, your goose is cooked.

We in our airship did not have to be concerned about any of those things. Our airship protected us just fine. Surrounding the hull of our airship was a very strong magnetic field which kept out all that weather that was blowing around out there in all that empty, filled-up space. Tesla says that the magnetic field surrounding our ship functioned just like the magnetic field surrounding the Earth: it was a shield that absorbed or reflected etheric and cosmic rays.

Yes, we were snug in our airship, and we did not have to proceed at a walking pace, either. No, we did not have to depend on any relays. We would all go to Mars together, and go without any lolly-gagging or dawdling.

The six of us aboard Tesla's airship were not a crew; we were only a collection of individuals, and, with the exceptions of Tesla and Czito, we knew nothing about airships or the interplanetary ether or even general science, for that matter. I knew my multiplication tables up to twelve times twelve; Houdini knew a little something about locks and a little bit more about sleight-of-hand; Lillie West had an impressive knowledge of musical theory and could speak French like a Frenchman; George Ade had a Purdue University education in literature and a Chicago newspaperman's education in civic mendacity, petty crime, union riots, professional pugilism, baseball, and Chicago weather. None of these skills and talents was of much use on board an airship that was gradually accelerating through interplanetary space to a speed of ten million miles an hour.

Yes, I had been a steamboatman on the Mississippi River. But that was before the Civil War, and the Mississippi is not anything like interplanetary space. For one thing, there is much more water on the Mississippi, and the scenery has more variety. I did understand the art of steering a vessel, and that counted for something, that is, if anything counts. But piloting an airship was really nothing like piloting a steamboat. With a steamboat you worry all the time. With an airship you hardly ever worry any of the time, but when you do worry, it's nothing like steamboat worrying; it's a kind of worrying that comes to you like a clap of thunder and grabs you and shakes you and won't let you go; it's a kind of worrying that has no direction, no up or down, no forward or backward, it's just there, and yet you still don't know where it is.

At least I had something to do. Lillie West, George Ade, and Houdini found themselves at loose ends.

Lillie West sat in a little room situated behind the ship's engines on the starboard side of the upper deck. She sat looking out of a porthole at the unmoving stars. Several times Tesla stuck his head into the room to look in on her. When he did this, Lillie refused to acknowledge him; she said not a word, nor even turned her head.

George Ade remained in Tesla's library at the stern of the ship, mesmerized by the sight of our planet shrinking away from us. He kept watching it as it shrank to a small blue disk, and then to a brilliant blue star. Finally Ade sat down in an armchair, gazing off into a field of stars where Earth had once been visible. The stars had not changed at all, but Earth was gone, or perhaps that was Earth, that little faint blue star that shone there among all the others. Ade tried to comprehend what was happening, but he couldn't really do it. It all seemed like a magic lantern show. He sat there trying to make it real; then he thought of the Great Chicago Fire when he was a boy, and how he watched its glow in the sky from a distance of eighty miles. The Chicago Fire did not seem real to him then, either. But it was real—and so was this.

Houdini was not in a reflective mood as he moved through the airship; it was not his nature to be so in times of crisis. He saved his reflections for long walks at night through cities and along rivers and lakes. He always walked alone when he reflected. He would speak to no one, and would tell no one where he was going. Houdini was a creature of secrets, but these were not the secrets of locks and chains; they were secrets of the human heart and will. Unlike the rest of us, Houdini had made it a daily practice to place himself in crisis—a self-made crisis. Then he would watch himself as if at a distance. He would see a man struggling under water, fighting not just for breath, but for courage to endure the immediate moment. That man was not "Houdini," he was "Ehrich Weiss"—Houdini's real name and real person. Houdini was the person watching from a distance. But now, Houdini was not in crisis. No, his heart was light, and he was congratulating himself. He had made it "inside the container," and even now he was working on how to get out. He had gone to the lower deck of the airship and was looking over everything that was there: the air pressure suits hanging on the ship's bulkhead, the escape craft gleaming with its clear dome of glass. His eyes twinkled in delight, and he could not help but reach out to. . .

"Don't touch that!" Czito barked.

Houdini jumped back and thrust his hands behind his back. Czito had descended the ladder and had caught Houdini trying to lift the dome of glass up off the craft.

"I was only lookin' at it," Houdini said.

"Don't touch anything down here," Czito said. "Don't touch anything anywhere on this ship unless you are given permission by Mr. Tesla or me."

"Aw," Houdini said, "I ain't doin' nothin'."

"Watch yourself!" Czito said, and went back up the ladder.

"Aw," Houdini said, scratching the back of his head. He went over to a door with a porthole and peered through the little round window. Czito came back down the ladder.

"What did I tell you?" Czito barked.

"Aw, can it!" Houdini said. "I told you I was just lookin'."

"Don't tell me to can it!" Czito shouted.

Czito came down the ladder and went up to Houdini and stood face to face with him.

"When I give an order," Czito said, "you obey it, or you'll get locked up!"

"So?" Houdini said. "You think I care? What is this anyway?"

"It's an airlock," Czito said.

"You mean, like a water lock on a submarine?" Houdini asked.

"That's right," Czito said. "When the door closes it forms a hermetic seal. Then the chamber has all the air pumped out of it and is compressed into storage tanks."

"What for?"

"Never mind what for," Czito said. "Just keep your hand off that handle. Fool with that and you'll suck all our air out of the ship."

"No kiddin'! Say, that's dangerous. You should put a lock on that to keep it from being fooled with."

"Up until now we didn't need to because on this ship we haven't had any fools. You come with me."

Czito took Houdini by the back of his coat collar and pulled him over to the steel ladder.

"Hey!" Houdini shouted, "Hands off the fabric! You're stretchin' the threads!"

"Get up there," Czito said, shoving him up the steel ladder. "I'm going to keep my eye on you."

Houdini went up the ladder with Czito following up behind him. When they got to the upper deck, Czito pointed to a metal box and said, "Sit!"

"There?" Houdini asked indignantly.

"There," Czito said. "And don't move until you're given permission."

Houdini sat down. Czito started up the steps to the pilothouse. Houdini said, "I wasn't doin' nothin'. Nothin'!"

We had been moving along on a straight course for quite some time when Tesla came into the pilothouse, approached Czito, and said, "Go rest. I'll take over."

Czito got up from his chair and went down the steps and out of the pilothouse.

I said, "They've been going at a steady clip for some time."

Tesla said, "I suspect that they have achieved an optimum acceleration for the particular energy system which drives their ship. Interestingly, if this is their optimum acceleration, it falls within the specifications for the optimum acceleration of our ship."

"Do you think that's a mere coincidence?"

"What do you think?"

"I think their ship is too much like your ship."

"Very good, Mark."

"How do you think they stole your designs?"

"We have suspected that the Martians have been visiting our planet for a number of years, perhaps several decades. We think they first came to Earth by a large rocket propelled by some kind of chemical fuel. This is suggested by the size of the ship we have observed orbiting Earth. It is a tenth of a mile in length. Most of the mass of that ship probably consists of a fuel supply."

"So what are you saying? That they sent spies to your laboratory?"

"Of course. I have always assumed that anyone in my employ is a potential industrial spy."

"Does that include Mr. Czito?"

"Mr. Czito is an exception to my rule. Him, I trust implicitly."

"And so you think you have actually employed Martians in your laboratory?"

"That is highly unlikely. I believe the Martians are a very sophisticated and subtle people. They know how to work through intermediaries. These intermediaries probably have no idea that they are working for people from another world. There is some indication that the Martians are involved with some large-scale counterfeiting operations. We think that most of their activity on Earth has been financed with counterfeit bank-notes. The United States Treasury Department has been trying to trace the source of these operations. Of course, the Treasury agents have not been told that the people they are pursuing are probably beings from another world."

"If the Martians sent paid spies from among our own people to steal your designs, why did they send one of their own to steal the crystal?"

"I have been extremely circumspect with the crystal. No one besides Czito even knew that it existed. I kept the crystal in an electrically shielded lead-lined vault. There was no way that any of my employees could know anything about the crystal at all."

"Then how do you think the Martians knew what you had and how to get at it?"

"I have been running that very question over in my mind since the crystal was stolen. I know this: my sources for the metals which went into the making of the crystal were secret, but now I realize their secrecy was not unassailable. Let's assume the Martians had some fragmentary, imperfect knowledge of the crystal. If this were so, they would be able to make some inference as regards the nature of my activities by the kind of metals I was working with, most particularly those metals of the platinum group."

"But how could they have a fragmented knowledge of what the crystal was made of?"

"Because the crystal existed long ago on both our world and theirs, but the making of it was lost on Earth long ago, as it was probably lost on Mars. On Earth, the process has been sought by alchemists for thousands of years."

"Is the Master Crystal the Philosopher's Stone?"

"The Philosopher's Stone is used in the Master Crystal; it is the 'new element' which I've discovered; actually it is gold in a highly energized state. The making of the Philosopher's Stone was never lost, only held as a secret among a very few. On the other hand, the Master Crystal was entirely lost."

"So the Martians could not directly spy out your crystal making operation, so they were forced to steal the Master Crystal itself."

"Yes. And I fear that they know enough that once they study the Master Crystal, they will very quickly unravel the secrets of its making."

That thought gave me pause, and I fell into a silence. After a minute or two of thinking upon the whole situation, it occurred to me that we should lose no time in catching up with the Martians. So I asked:

"You say we are going at about the optimum acceleration the engine can sustain?"

"We are close to its limit. You must understand that this ship is only a prototype, and is really quite crude. With the proper engineering, a ship could be made that could travel from Earth to Mars in a blink of an eye."

"So you don't think we *should* try to catch up with them—or you don't think we *can*?"

"We could most certainly put on a short burst of speed and catch up to them. We can safely do that. Indeed, we *must* do that before they reach Mars, and I do believe that is their destination. But for now we must wait."

"Why? Why not do it now and be done with it?"

"The destruction of the Martian ship is going to be extremely problematical. It must be a precise operation if we ourselves are to escape alive."

"By all means. Escaping alive is at the top of my list."

"But these Martians are formidable adversaries. The electric rays I fired upon them had little effect. It seems that their ship has an electro-magnetic field surrounding it, just as our does, and that field acts as a shield, tending to deflect anything that comes within its path.

"So how will you destroy their ship?"

"I have been working on one of our sets of auxiliary capacitors. They were partially damaged in our battle with the Martian ship. I am now in the process of re-charging them. I'm charging them slowly and carefully by a special process to avoid a sudden dielectric break-down. When the capacitors are fully charged, we shall close in on the Martian airship and hurl at it a single, intense ball of electricity. That ball will blast their ship into a cloud of super-heated gas."

"That sounds like a workable and practical plan, and one I endorse enthusiastically."

"There is only one problem. When we destroy the Martians, we risk destroying ourselves as well; for when the Master Crystal is broken, it will release enough energy to destroy a planet. The moment I fire upon the Martians, you must reverse direction and accelerate to the speed of light within one or two seconds. To do that, you must engage this special switch here and slam the accelerator pedal to the floor. Do you think we can carry out such an operation?"

"We can. We can and for one reason only: we must."

Tesla nodded grimly, and then turned back toward the control board.

Suddenly Tesla shouted, "Czito! Come here!"

Czito came running up the steps of the pilothouse, and rushed to Tesla's side. I went to where they stood and peered over Czito's shoulder. The diagram of the solar system showed several new flashing points of light where there had previously been only the one indicating the Martian airship. Tesla was able to magnify the view of these points of light until they filled the whole viewing glass.

"What do you think they are?" Tesla asked.

"Ships maybe?" Czito asked.

"No," Tesla said, "not ships. Look at the arrangement of their positions: too irregular, too random. Ships would be spread out in a symmetrical formation more or less. This is a collection of objects moving at random through space."

"Maybe the Martian ship exploded," Czito said.

"Think, Mr. Czito!" Tesla said. "If their ship had exploded, we would have witnessed an intense flash of light from the disintegrating Master Crystal. No. This is something else. Asteroids. They are asteroids."

"Of course!" Czito said. "But where did they come from all of a sudden?"

Tesla said, "It may have originally been a single asteroid just out of reach of our electric echo-beam. The Martians could have broken it into pieces by firing an electric ray at it."

"Why would they do that?" Czito asked.

"To accomplish precisely what they have accomplished," Tesla said. "Confuse us in our pursuit. Which one of those lights represents the Martian's ship?"

"I don't know," Czito said.

"And there is no way to know," Tesla said. "The Master Crystal is so far away from us, the wireless tracker cannot accurately locate it. How big do you think those asteroid fragments are?"

"Hard to say," Czito replied. "They must be at least as large as the Martian airship."

"At least," Tesla said. "Mark, do you think you can steer your way through them?"

I said, "I suppose we are going to find out very shortly."

I turned forward and saw a white streak of light shoot over the top of the pilothouse.

"Looks like we're going to find out in about two seconds," I added.

I went to the wheel and took hold of it.

"Back us up," Tesla said. "Back us up."

I hit the pedal to stop the ship, looked at the number counter that told our speed, and saw that we had stopped dead still in space. I then pressed the reverse pedal. The counter started forward again, only a negative sign rolled into place in front of the other numbers.

In a moment, I saw the first of several asteroids tumbling toward us; it looked like a locomotive gone off its tracks.

"Try to match our speed to the asteroids," Tesla said.

I pressed the reverse pedal a little more. The asteroids rolling toward us seemed to slow down a bit. Tesla and Czito stood by me; all our eyes were glued to the objects speeding toward us. I watched one big rock spin by the starboard bow of the ship and on aft of us so close that I felt that I could've reached out and touched it.

As I looked behind for that instant I caught sight of Houdini, Lillie West and George Ade coming up the stairs and into the pilothouse. I turned forward again with a jerk; more fragments of rock were headed straight at us. I swung the prow of the ship larboard and the fragments flew past our starboard side. I glanced back again and saw that our three stowaways still clung to the railing of the stairs leading up into the pilothouse.

"What are all of you doing up here?" I said, turning forward again. "You three go aft and start practicing your solitaire."

Tesla said, "We must consider them a part of the crew. We may have need of their help."

"Help!" I said, "The only thing they can do is help get us all killed!"

I kept increasing the speed of our reverse motion. Two spinning chunks of rock that looked like gray lava sped directly toward us. I steered our ship around them, only to find behind them a potato-shaped rock the size of a mountain. It grew in size with terrifying rapidity, and I steered our airship up to avoid it, only to realize that we were doing nothing but climbing up the asteroid's face. Here was the main body: a cruel and pitted gray surface that grew to such monstrous proportions that it nearly filled the view of the pilothouse windows. I pulled the wheel back and turned the bow of our ship straight up and hit the forward accelerator pedal. The asteroid continued toward us, threatening to crush us like a fly. We seemed only a second away from being smashed against its surface when we cleared its last, craggy peak, and the whole mountainous rock passed beneath us in a wink and a flash.

As we came up over the asteroid, I brought our airship back to its original orientation in relation to the fixed stars. It was then that we saw the great tail of the asteroid spread out before us: hundreds—perhaps thousands—of asteroid rocks and fragments along with tons upon tons of pulverized rock dust hurtling toward us from the blackness of starry space. There was no time to avoid this sea of fragments, only time to plunge through it and steer from one near disaster to another. I brought the ship down, up, starboard, larboard. Every turn of the wheel saved our lives from one threat while at the same time placing us at risk of dying from another.

I asked Tesla, "You said this ship has a magnetic shield, didn't you?"

"Yes," Tesla said. "It will deflect or vaporize the smaller particles."

"What about the larger particles?" I asked.

"I would advise you to avoid the larger particles," Tesla replied.

"I was afraid of that," I said.

Lillie came up beside Tesla and asked him, "What happens if one of those large fragments hit the ship?"

Tesla said quietly, "The ship will split apart. And if the impact doesn't kill us, we will all suffocate in the vacuum."

"Oh," I said, "don't sugar-coat it for her, Tesla. Just give her the raw facts."

Up ahead I spied an opening in the field of debris, a great black 'O' with only stars beyond it. I aimed the bow of our ship for the center of the 'O.'

"This is almost as bad as the bend around Hat Island on the Mississippi River," I said.

"Almost as bad?" Czito asked.

"On the Hat Island bend it'd be pitch black with a fog so thick you couldn't see the back of your hand."

"And this. . . is. . . better?" Czito asked.

"I can still see the back of my hand," I replied.

We went through the oval. It was something like a great smoke ring of dust and rocks. Several fragments struck the prow of the airship, or, that is, struck the magnetic field surrounding us; the fragments flashed away in streaks of light and sparks. Occasionally one of the striking fragments would make a sound exactly like that made by a ricocheting bullet.

"We're almost through it," Czito said. "We're going to make it!"

"Of course we're going to make it," I said.

Then suddenly we were clear of the debris field. Ahead was only black sky and stars. I looked back at Tesla. He was standing at the control board, looking aft through the pilothouse windows. I turned all the way around and saw the field of asteroid fragments which we had just come through, and felt a great relief to be out of it.

"What a show!" Houdini said.

Tesla came over to the little tin box mounted on the pedestal and studied it for several seconds, all the while pivoting its steel rod all around in front of us. The incandescent light bulb on top of the tin box remained dark.

"Something's wrong," Tesla said.

"With your machine?" I asked.

"No," Tesla said. "I doubt anything is wrong with this device."

Tesla kept pivoting the tin box around at various angles, but the light bulb remained dark. I watched him do this awhile longer, and then an odd, sick kind of expression came across his face. He started turning the tin box around on its pedestal until it was pointing back in the direction we had come.

That was when we all saw it.

The light bulb flashed very faintly. Its steel rod was pointed directly back at the asteroid debris field.

"The crystal!" Tesla whispered. "They have jettisoned the crystal into the asteroid."

I stopped our ship and turned her about 180 degrees.

"They must have realized we would overtake them before they reached Mars," Tesla said. "They know we will turn back for the crystal."

"They just showed their hand," I said, "and it warn't four aces!"

"Yes," Tesla said. "They seem to have folded."

"So I'm going to have to take us back through the rock quarry," I said.

"I'm afraid so," Tesla said.

"Well. . . hold on, then."

I touched the accelerator pedal and we rapidly approached the debris field of the asteroid. Actually, it looked as though the debris field had reversed direction and was moving toward us again, instead of us moving toward it.

Tesla was adjusting the position of the little tin box on its pedestal again. I took us back through the big 'O' of rocks and dust and plunged us deeper into the asteroid field. As rocks and dust began whizzing around us, I slowed us down and tried to approximate the speed of the hurtling asteroid fragments. There was only one problem: none of the fragments were moving at exactly the same speed. I even saw a couple of fragments collide with each other and explode into still smaller fragments, and these scattered every which way before us. I steered up and around this collision and managed to dodge most of the flying rock; some of the small pieces reached the vicinity of our ship but were thrown away like pebbles from a sling-shot by the electric force field surrounding us.

"Go down a bit, Mark," Tesla said.

I obeyed his order, and passed by several rocky fragments. Up ahead was the main asteroid body.

Tesla said, "I think they have planted the crystal on or inside that asteroid."

I slowly brought our airship toward the surface of the asteroid; the great, pitted mass grew in size until its surface filled the pilothouse windows. I could've stretched my arms out straight on either side, and my view of the asteroid would've stretched from my right finger tip to my left.

We stood there looking at the pitted, cratered surface of that immense gray rock. Tesla pivoted the tin box's steel rod toward the asteroid's surface, and moved it about until the little light bulb got to flashing with some enthusiasm.

"It is down there," Tesla said. "Right down there, probably somewhere in that crater."

Tesla pointed out the crater to me; it was a little black spot on the surface of the rock. He took the spy-glass and looked through it, then gave the spy-glass to me. I looked through it and saw that the black spot was a crater, although I had no clear idea how big it was.

"I will have to go down to the surface of the asteroid," Tesla said.

"Go down?" I asked. "How? In that lifeboat down on the lower deck?"

"No," Tesla said. "The crystal may be lodged in a space where the emergency craft could not enter. I will have to go out on to the surface of the asteroid dressed in an anti-gravity pressure suit. Keep the ship in this position. Mr. Czito, come with me."

Tesla descended the stairs with Czito following behind him. I looked over at Lillie, Houdini, and Ade.

"Well?" I said. "You three wanted to see an airship. Now you're getting to do that and a little bit more."

"We meant no harm, Mr. Clemens," George Ade said. "We were only doing what we thought was right."

"Said the burglar to the man with an empty house," I replied.

"Who is the burglar, Mr. Clemens?" Lillie asked. "I would say the man who steals the truth is the greatest burglar of them all."

"Why, certainly, young lady!" I said. "If you are only discovering that, you are a very slow learner. Our world has always been ruled by thieves and burglars and liars and murderers. And they have always corrupted us, their subjects. Anyway, personally, I do not really object to your burglary, I only object to your self-righteous justification of it. You did not do it because it was 'right'."

"No?" Lillie asked. "Then why do you say I did it?"

"Damned if I know," I said. "And I don't think you know the real reason you did it, either. I'd say we rarely know the real reason we do any of the things that we do."

"I'd say you are an expert at lying to yourself," Lillie said.

"Now that," I said, "is a truth. How rare. I shall stand here and contemplate it."

Down below on the lower deck, Tesla put on one of the pressure suits that had been hanging from the ship's bulkhead. Czito helped to buckle Tesla into the suit. Then Czito slipped the straps to a box-like device over and around Tesla's shoulders, so that it was secured to Tesla's back like the knapsack of a mountain climber or a soldier. The box-like knapsack contained a tank of compressed air and an electrical anti-gravity machine—a miniature of the engine that powered the airship. Two little lightning rods or "aerial conductors" rose from the top of the knapsack by several inches. Then Czito crowned Tesla with one of those glass-bubble helmets, and fitted and screwed it into a metal ring-collar made into Tesla's air pressure suit; this gave Tesla's whole garment a hermetic seal.

Tesla flipped a little switch on a control panel attached to the chest and belt of his suit. There was a faint whine, the sound of the suit's electrical system going to work.

Tesla spoke to Czito through a telephone-type speaker built into the base of his glass helmet:

"Stand by the wireless telephone in the pilothouse. If anything happens to me or the crystal, I will give you the order to depart for Earth instantly. You will carry out that order no matter how much Mark Twain objects. Do you understand, Mr. Czito?"

"Yes, Mr. Tesla. I'll do exactly as you say."

Tesla nodded, and then stepped through the door of the air-lock chamber. Czito closed it behind Tesla, and then nodded at Tesla through the porthole window on the door. Tesla threw a red-handled switch and a great rush of air passed out of the chamber and through a vent into the wall. A gauge next to the switch showed that the chamber was empty of air.

Tesla pressed the handle that opened the door in the chamber which led outside the airship. The door's seal released and he pushed the door open all the way and looked out. Directly ahead was the rocky wall of the asteroid, shining gray and white in the brilliant rays of the sun. Below and above was the black void of space spangled brilliantly with stars.

Tesla stepped out of the airship and the door automatically closed behind him. The artificial gravity field of the airship pulled Tesla back. He turned a knob on his belt and the anti-gravity field from his knapsack pushed him away from the ship and out toward the asteroid. Tesla looked beyond his feet; it seemed to him that he was standing on a black velvet carpet decorated with stars.

I watched Tesla fly toward the asteroid. He looked like a little white rag doll or snowman. He shot away and shrank in size, and it was only through that shrinkage that I began to get some understanding of the size of the asteroid; I began to realize this was not a big rock, but a mountain, perhaps three-quarters of a mile in length and half a mile in breadth. Features on the face of the asteroid which I had estimated to be ten or twenty feet across had to be re-estimated as Tesla flew toward them; for as Tesla grew smaller, those features grew larger, and it became clear that they were not ten or twenty feet across, but closer to one hundred to two hundred feet across. Tesla became a white dot against the gray mountainous face of the asteroid.

I looked through the spy-glass and located Tesla. He was speeding along like a shining white bird, the rocky surface below him only a gray blur of horizontal lines in the circle view of the spy-glass. I took the spy-glass away from my eye and could see Tesla as a little white dot approaching a black spot that I now realized was a hole about 50 feet across. I watched the white dot that was Tesla slow down and circle about the circumference of the black spot. I put the spy-glass to my eye again and saw that Tesla hung above the big gaping hole, his hands held out in front of him. He was pointing the tin box down at the hole in the asteroid. He hung there like a little white rag doll a moment longer, and then started down, shrinking in size a little, and then—he vanished! He simply blinked out and was gone.

"He's disappeared," I said, handing the spy-glass to Czito.

Czito took the spy-glass, looked through it, and said, "I see him. He's in the shadow of the crater. Now he's out of sight. He's gone down inside the crater."

Czito handed the spy-glass back to me and went to the control board behind me. He picked up the earpiece from the telephone there, and listened.

"What are you doing?" I asked.

"Listening for Mr. Tesla on the wireless telephone," Czito said.

"You mean," I asked, "Tesla has a telephone in that suit he's wearing?"

Czito nodded, and said, "The speaker and earpiece are built into his helmet."

I looked through the spy-glass again. I could see nothing but the black mouth of the hole or crater, but I kept looking anyway.

Tesla had gone deep into the crater. Actually, it was not a crater; it was just a very deep hole. What formed the hole, Tesla did not know for certain. He has speculated that it was the result of a gas bubble which was expelled some time in the distant past when the mass that formed the asteroid was in a molten state. The asteroid itself Tesla believed to be composed of nickel and iron, and he was fairly sure that it had come from the asteroid belt that circled the sun beyond Mars. Somehow it had been pulled from its course by the gravitational tug of some other cosmic body and thrown on a course passing between the Earth and Mars. As the Martians sped along in their airship, they must have encountered the asteroid and broke it apart to create a wall in space separating them from us.

An electric torch mounted on the top of Tesla's glass helmet threw a strong beam of light into the recesses of that rocky tunnel or lava tube through which he now drifted. The whole passage was filled with floating debris: rocks, pebbles, and dust. Tesla passed through all this, sweeping it aside with his left hand, pointing the tin box and its steel rod with his right.

Up ahead the walls of rock converged to a narrow tube about thirty feet in circumference. The incandescent light bulb on the tin box flickered rapidly.

Tesla flew on forward and came to a fork in the tunnel; one cave going off to the left, the other to the right. He pointed the steel rod of the tin box toward the cave to his left. The bulb stopped flashing; it was glowing with a steady brightness.

Tesla plunged forward into the cave on his left, the electric torch on his helmet washing the rocky walls with a white, glaring light. He moved through an increasingly thick cloud of sand, dust, and small rocks. He kept reaching out with his left hand to sweep his path clear. With every stroke of his hand the rocks and dust moved away, responding to the magnetic and anti-gravity field surrounding his body. He reached the dead end of the cave. The place opened up to a cavern room about fifty feet across and fifty or sixty feet deep.

Tesla saw nothing on the surface of the cavern some twenty feet down, that is, beyond his feet. Between Tesla and this floor was nothing but a swirl of dust and rocks. Tesla looked up through the glass dome of his helmet, and spun his body back to cast the beam of his electric torch toward the dark regions over his head. His light beam flashed upon a metallic box spinning around in a cloud of dust and rocks. It was about twenty feet beyond his head.

Tesla flew upward slowly to face the spinning box. He collapsed the steel rod of the tin box and slipped the tracking machine into a pocket on the leg of his air-pressure suit.

Tesla reached out to the spinning metallic box and closed his hands around it, arresting the box's spin. He studied the box a moment in the glare of his electric torch.

The box had a hinged lid, but no lock or keyhole to allow access. It was shut tight and Tesla could not try to pry it open while wearing the awkward gloves of his pressure suit. He knew he would have to risk bringing the box back into the airship.

I stood at the pilothouse windows looking through the spyglass at the black opening on the asteroid. Every second that passed seemed too long a wait, but I waited and waited, and then waited some more. Every second I was about to yank the spyglass away from my eye, and every second I was crazy to keep on watching.

Finally, when I had almost given Tesla up for dead, he appeared. He was only a white dot on the edge of the black opening.

"He's out!" I shouted.

Czito came up and I handed him the spyglass. He looked through it, and said, "He's carrying something under his arm—a box!"

Czito gave me the spyglass and shot out of the pilothouse and down the hatchway to the lower deck.

Tesla was growing larger by the second. He sped by the windows of the pilothouse, his right hand raised, his left cradling the box. He swooped toward the lower deck.

Czito waited for the air to fill the chamber where Tesla stood. When the needle on the gauge next to the door moved to *full*, Czito opened the door.

Tesla stepped out of the chamber and handed Czito the metal box. Czito set the box down on a workbench built into the ship's bulkhead, and then helped Tesla unscrew and remove his helmet.

As soon as the helmet had cleared Tesla's head, he said, "Do not touch the box any further. It's a trap."

Houdini came clambering down the ladder.

"Go back up, Ehrich," Tesla said. "Tell the others to remain above as well."

"Yes, sir," Houdini said, and he climbed back up the ladder.

With Czito's help, Tesla removed the anti-gravity machine and the air-pressure suit, and then Czito hung the suit, helmet, and knapsack on their hooks attached to the ship's bulkhead.

Tesla held the steel rod of the tracking machine over the box; the light bulb on the machine shined brightly. Tesla took from a drawer in the workbench another small machine, threw its switch and held it over the box that he had retrieved from the asteroid.

Tesla said to Czito, "The magnetic field of this box is more intense than it should be if it only contains the crystal. If the crystal is in the box, there is some other kind of electrical device inside there with it."

"*If* the crystal is inside the box?" Czito asked. "The wireless tracker shows that the crystal *is* in the box."

Tesla said, "The wireless tracker shows that something is in the box that radiates electric pulses of the same frequency as the crystal. That does not mean necessarily that it *is* the crystal."

Tesla stepped away from the box and thought for a moment. Then he turned to Czito.

"We cannot open the box," Tesla said. "It is most likely that this box is rigged with a bomb. It may also contain the Master Crystal, but I doubt it. It may possibly contain only a wireless transmitter that mimics the signal of the crystal."

Czito said, "But the wireless tracker did not pick up a signal from the direction of the Martian ship, so this box must contain the crystal."

"No," Tesla said. "Not necessarily. They probably accelerated beyond the range of the wireless tracker while we slowed down to pass through the debris of the asteroid."

"Then what are we to do?"

"We must treat this box as if it contained the Master Crystal and a bomb. We must make that assumption. Given that, you know what we have to do."

"Jettison the box, explode it with an electric ray, and get away from here very fast."

Tesla nodded. "Bring the box up to the pilothouse."

Czito went up the steel ladder, and Tesla came up behind him. When the two of them got to the upper deck, Tesla took the box, and they went on up to the pilothouse.

"So that's it," I said.

"This is 'it', perhaps just as the Trojan Horse was 'it'," Tesla said.

"You think this is some kind of fancy mouse-trap?" I asked.

"With the Master Crystal as the cheese," Tesla said, "or something that smells like the Master Crystal."

"So you think your electric bloodhound has been fooled," I said.

"It is possible."

"So what are we to do?" I asked.

Tesla looked about at all of us, Lillie, Ade, Houdini, Czito, and me. He explained, "This box is probably a trap. If we open it, it will probably explode, killing us all. If we leave it behind here in this asteroid field, it might actually contain the Master Crystal, and the Martians could return, retrieve it, and deactivate the bomb somehow. Taking it with us or leaving it behind, either way is unacceptable."

"Are there no other alternatives?" George Ade asked.

"Only one," Tesla said. "We can jettison the box, and explode it with an electric ray."

"Then why don't we do that?" Ade asked.

"If the Master Crystal is in the box, it would explode, and the explosion would be immense. It could engulf and destroy our ship, unless we moved away rapidly at the instant of the explosion. It would be a precise maneuver. Mark Twain and I have discussed this and believe that we can do it. However, there are no guarantees. What do you all say? Should we try it?"

I said, "We must try it."

"I agree," Lillie West said.

"I agree, as well," George Ade said.

"Ehrich?" Tesla asked.

Houdini shrugged. "Do it, don't do it, sounds like we're all going to get fried no matter what. What are you askin' us for, Mr. Tesla? You know we gotta do it."

"Very well," Tesla said, and he walked over to the jettison tube, opened its door, shoved the box into it lengthwise, and closed the door again.

"Mr. Czito," Tesla said, "wait for my word, then push the jettison tube button. Mark, bring the stern of the ship around toward the asteroid, and stand by for my order to move. When I say, 'move,' throw this switch and floor the accelerator pedal, and keep your foot down on it. Don't concern yourself with the asteroids. Just have the prow of the ship pointed at that circular opening out there in the debris field. We will be moving so fast the electric field surrounding the ship will instantaneously vaporize anything in our path. Are we all clear?"

"All clear," I said.

"Mr. Czito," Tesla said, "come over here and stand ready to push the jettison button."

Czito did as he was ordered, and Tesla climbed the ladder up to the gun tower.

I swung the airship around to face the 'O' in the asteroid debris field, and got the prow pointed precisely at its center. On either side of the 'O' a great number of rock fragments floated and drifted about, but directly in front of us was a clear path all the way to the 'O'. How long it would remain clear was uncertain; at any moment one of those fragments could drift into the open path. Could the field of our ship deflect one of those large fragments? Or would we all be instantly vaporized by the collision?

From the gun tower Tesla shouted, "Get ready, Mr. Czito! On my word 'eject,' you will push the jettison button. Mark, on my word 'move,' you will throw the switch and floor the accelerator pedal. Are you ready, Mark?"

"Ready!" I shouted.

"Ready, Mr. Czito?" Tesla shouted.

"Ready!" Czito shouted.

There was silence in the pilothouse. Houdini, Lillie, and Ade stood back against the stair railing.

I grasped the pilot's wheel, and my palms broke out into a cold sweat. I brought my right hand down over the special switch which Tesla had pointed out to me—the switch that would allow me to accelerate the airship to the speed of light in one second. I looked up through the pilothouse windows at the gray specks floating in front of a pitch-black sky.

"Eject!" Tesla shouted.

I heard a click and a metallic shifting of machinery, followed by a rush of air. That sound was immediately followed by Tesla shouting:

"Move!"

I slammed the switch-handle down and stamped my foot on the accelerator pedal.

A flash of white light flooded the pilothouse, and then everything went black. I kept my foot on the accelerator pedal, but I began shaking all over and could not stop the shaking. In a few seconds, the dim outlines of the pilothouse's interior became visible, and, in a few more seconds, things brightened further until I could see the stars beyond the pilothouse windows—and the stars had shrunk to a circle ranged out in front of us!

"Mark!" Tesla shouted. "Stop the ship!"

I removed my foot from the accelerator pedal and slammed my foot on the pedal that stopped the ship. There was a second burst of white light, followed by utter blackness, and then the stars in front of us flared up and moved back, and stretched themselves out over the blackness of space to their original positions.

Tesla came down the ladder from the gun tower.

"Turn the ship about," he said.

"Back to the rock quarry again?" I asked. "This is beginning to get monotonous."

"Back again," Tesla said. "That was not the crystal."

"No?"

"No. Turn the ship around. I want to see what was in that box."

I turned the ship around, and Czito helped direct me back to the field of asteroids. It took several minutes to get back from where we came, for we were traveling well below the speed of light this time.

We approached the asteroid debris field once again, and I piloted us through the now-familiar 'O' of rocks and dust. I steered our ship through the spinning rocks toward the main asteroid, and as we approached that gray space mountain, it occurred to me that I was really learning how to pilot an airship—the hard way.

We now all recognized the features of the main asteroid, including the black crater where Tesla had found the box. Then next to that original crater I spied a new one.

"Tesla!" I said, "Do you see that?"

I turned and saw that Tesla was looking through the spyglass. He handed the spyglass to me and said, "It's a new crater, created when the box was hit by the ship's electric ray."

I looked through the spyglass. It was definitely a new crater, about one hundred feet across.

I handed the spyglass to Czito. He looked through it, and then handed it to George Ade who looked through it, and then the spyglass was passed among everyone in the pilothouse until we all got a good look.

"It was a bomb," I said.

"Yes," Tesla said. "And if we had opened the box inside the ship, we would've all been killed."

"But it was not the crystal," I added.

"No," Tesla replied, "Not the crystal. If the Master Crystal had been in that box, this asteroid and all of this debris would not be here. There would be nothing here but super-hot gases."

All of us, Tesla, Czito, Lillie, Ade, Houdini, and I stood in the pilothouse, staring at the asteroid.

Then Tesla finally said, "Take us away from here, Mark."

I asked, "To where?"

"To Mars," Tesla replied.

I brought the prow of the ship around so that it pointed at the big 'O', and then took us through the field of floating rock and dust again.

As soon as we were clear of the asteroid debris field, Tesla pointed out Mars to me; it was a red point of light that looked like a star. I lined up the prow of our ship with that red point and carefully pressed the accelerator pedal.

"Take us up gradually to a speed of ten million miles an hour," Tesla said.

"Aye, aye," I replied.

Tesla turned to the others in the pilothouse and said,

"When we engage in battle with the Martians we're going to need as many hands and eyes monitoring the coil flucuations as we can get, or we may very well sustain another power surge and short circuit. Can I count on the three of you to help Mr. Czito?"

"I'll be glad to help any way I can," George Ade said.

"Both of us will," Lillie West added.

"And what about you, Ehrich?" Tesla asked.

"Sure," Houdini said with a shrug, "whatever you need."

"Mr. Czito," Tesla said, "I leave their training to you."

"I'll do my best," Czito said.

Tesla said, "I'm going to check the engine."

Czito looked at Lillie, Ade, and Houdini, and said, "I assume none of you know much about electrical engineering."

"Not a thing," Ade said.

"Nothing," Lillie said.

"I've studied many a tome on the subject," Houdini said, "and have carried out experiments in my own laboratory."

"Certainly," Czito said dryly. "We will start with the basics of electrical conduction. Electricity runs on a wire from a power source to a load."

"A load of what?" Houdini asked.

Czito looked over at me, then back to the others.

"We will begin at the beginning," Czito said with a sigh. "The very beginning. Let's get a couple more chairs up here."

George Ade and Houdini went down the steps of the pilothouse, came back up with two chairs, and sat them down in front of the control board.

"Please be seated," Czito said to Lillie, Houdini, and Ade.

The three of them sat down in front of the controls.

Czito said, "Before you are the controls of a switching system."

Lillie said, "It looks like a telephone operator's switching board."

"Yes," Czito said, "there is a certain similarity. But instead of telephone reception lines, this system controls the circuits that electrify the ship's outer steel hull. It is the resonance between the electric field of the ship's hull with the electrical skin-wave coming from the aerial conductor which determines the speed and direction of the ship. The primary adjustment of resonance is made by Mr. Clemens at the pilot's controls: the wheel, the pedals, and the primary switches. The control switches before you control the electrical surges which occur with any sudden change of speed and direction. You do not need to understand the technical reasons for these power surges. Basically, they are the result of interactions with the surrounding ether which causes not only inertial effects, but electrical ones as well. Power surges also occur when the ship is struck with energetic rays, such as those we sustained from the Martian airship. These power surges can cause short circuits and a loss in electrical power. Therefore, it is important that all these electrical surges are monitored at all points on the ship's hull. When the surges occur, the affected circuit must be switched to an electrical dump or virtual ground located inside the lower deck. The red lights at the top of the column of switches indicate a surge when they are lit. When you see one of these go on, you must take the cord directly below it and plug it into its corresponding receptacle below it here. That connects it to the ground. When the light goes off, unplug the cord. In a series of sharp turns or changes of speed, you may need to plug and unplug the cords every second or two. Now, I am going to give Mr. Clemens some instructions, and as he carries them out, I want all of you to watch the lights on the board. We will start with a simple maneuver and proceed to the more complex."

I said, "If this was a steamboat, they would be the engineers watching the pressure gauge on the boilers."

"The analogy is an over-simplification," Czito said, "but I suppose it will serve."

Czito began having me take the ship through a series of maneuvers, speeding up, slowing down, stopping suddenly, starting up again suddenly, and then he asked for loops, corkscrew spins on a straight course, and finally corkscrew spins on an undulating course that no snake could follow. The stars beyond the pilothouse windows moved up and down, starboard and larboard, and spun about like a pinwheel on the Fourth of July.

These maneuvers went on for quite a while. Finally Tesla came in and said that we had done enough. I was glad, because all that spinning was beginning to make me dizzy.

I put us back on course to Mars, and began increasing our speed gradually until we were back up to ten million miles an hour.

I had been standing watch at the pilot's wheel for quite a while and shaking from head to foot all the time. I could not stop shaking. It was strange; I did not feel all that nervous, but something down deep in me had been terrified at our sudden acceleration to the speed of light. In that strange and terrible moment, it seemed as if the universe had blinked out of existence; not that I had died, but that everything else had ceased to exist. When the stars slowly reappeared again, they were all pushed forward in front of us to form a sort of ring. Tesla has told me that this was caused by light being distorted through an etheric bow-shock wave that had formed in front of our ship. The wave was in the shape of a funnel and all the light around us was bent toward it and passed through it before reaching us. The stars had not really moved ahead of us at all, they had only appeared to do so.

Well, that all should have been comforting to know, but something down deep in me wouldn't stop shaking. Whatever that thing was, it couldn't be reasoned with. I took out the only cigar I had on me, and brought out a match to light it up. Just then, Tesla reached out and took hold of my hand that held the match.

"Sorry, Mark," Tesla said, "I can't allow you to smoke."

"Why not?"

"The air filtering system can't handle it. We have a limited supply of air and we must keep it breathable."

"You mean to tell me that you have designed a ship that can travel faster than light, but you can't smoke on it?"

"If we were on earth, I wouldn't be concerned. But as things stand, I'm not sure when we can get another supply of air."

"And if I don't smoke, how long will our air last?"

"Long enough. The filtering system re-circulates the carbon dioxide and converts it back into oxygen. But smoke particles might jam the system."

"Well, if I can't smoke, do you have anything to drink?"

"Water. Only water."

"Water and air. Is that all we have on board?"

"That's all."

"Nothing medicinal?"

"There's a bottle of wood alcohol in the medical kit."

"That's all? This ship is not properly provisioned. Not for an ordinary human being. You should have a cargo of Scotch whiskey on board, or at least some rum or grog or something. Look at my hand. I'm all used up."

"Take a break, Mark. I'll stand watch for you."

"All right. But if I can't smoke or drink the only break I see coming is my nerves breaking all apart."

"Mr. Ade," Tesla said, "take Mr. Clemens back to the library. Perhaps you can find him a book to read."

"Oh," I said, "you have storage space for a Christian Science Reading Room, but none for a little aged libation? Tesla, I have found a flaw in your engineering, and you must have it corrected!"

I started out of the pilothouse.

"Mark," Tesla said. "I'll take that cigar and match."

I handed the contraband over to him.

I said, "Don't you destroy that cigar, Tesla. It's a Moos and only improves with age."

I followed George Ade down the steps and out of the pilothouse, leaving Tesla to steer the ship. Houdini followed behind me, and said, "That was some piloting back there!"

Ade and I stopped and turned around and looked at the boy.

I said, "Yes, well, that was some swimming I saw you do."

"Swimming?" Houdini asked. "When did ja see me swimming?"

"When? I don't know. I've lost track of time. How long have we been aboard this ship?"

"Four hours," Houdini said.

"Four hours? Are you sure?"

I took out my pocket watch and Houdini held his watch up next to mine. The hands on both watches were getting close to four o'clock.

"See?" Houdini said, "It's been four hours. How long did ja think it had been?"

"I don't know. Four days, maybe."

"Naw, four hours. That's all. So when did ja see me swimming?"

"Oh. You swimming. Let's see, it must've been yesterday—Friday morning."

"You saw me jump?"

"That's right. I saw you go over the side of the bridge there on State Street."

"Well, whaddaya know! Say! I remember! I saw you go by in a cab, didn't I? When Jacob and Mike were carrying me on their shoulders!"

"That's right," I said.

"Of course!" Houdini said. "At the time I said to myself, 'That man looks just like Mark Twain!' But then I said, 'Naw! Couldn't be. What would Mark Twain be doing in Chicago of all places? He's gotta be on the Mississippi piloting a boat or something.' You know, I read that book you wrote."

"That book I wrote? Now what book was that?"

"Why, *Tom Sawyer*, of course! I read the whole thing. And you know what? I went to your hometown, Hannibal, Missouri, and I went to the cave where Tom and Becky got lost, and it was just like your book! You sure nailed that one. And guess what? I stood right in front of your house."

"Now isn't that fine," I said, and started to turn away.

"And look at this," Houdini said, and he unbuttoned the pocket on his trousers, reached into it, and brought out a little pebble in the palm of his hand. "You know what that is?" he asked.

I looked at the pebble, and said, "Can't say that I do."

Houdini said, "It's a rock from in front of your old house. Here, take a look at it."

I took the pebble and looked at it, and said, "By George, I believe I do recognize this. I used to pass it every day when I was a boy! Only thing is, it has grown considerably since then. When I knew it, it was only a grain of sand, and it didn't seem that it would ever amount to much. But look at it now, so round and full and prosperous, and who knows what the future will bring? Why, it might grow up some day to be another Plymouth Rock, if not a Washington Monument!"

Houdini looked at me a moment with his head cocked to one side, like a hound dog that can't get the scent; then he straightened up and broke into a laugh.

"Aw, ha, ha, ha! Yer makin' a joke! Aw, ha, ha, ha! I just got told a Mark Twain joke by Mark Twain himself! Aw, ha, ha, ha! A rock that grows up! Aw, ha, ha, ha! That's a good one! Ha, ha, ha! That's rich!"

"I'm glad you enjoyed it," I said, handing him back the pebble. "Here's your souvenir."

"Thanks," Houdini said. "Now that you have touched it, it's worth a lot more. I'm going to keep this the rest of my life and have somebody place it on my tomb when I die."

"When you die?" I said. "You're too young to be thinking about dying."

"Why do you say that?" Houdini asked. "Everybody dies. Dyin's just a fact of livin'."

"Well, that's true enough," I said. "And considering the situation we're in, I suppose dying is on all on our minds right now."

"My father always said, 'The day of one's death is more important than the day of one's birth.' And he knew what he was talkin' about. He was a scholar and a rabbi.

Can I shake your hand, Mr. Twain?"

I held my hand out. "Clemens," I said. "Just call me Clemens."

Houdini took my hand. "And just call me Houdini."

Houdini shook my hand in an attempt at a Masonic clasp—the Lion's Paw. I did not respond to his gesture. He dropped his hand and looked at me.

"Ain't you on the square?" Houdini asked.

"Yes," I said. "Are you?"

"Well, not yet. I'm not old enough yet. Not for a couple more years."

"Yes," I said. "Well, you're not doing that right. Give me your hand."

Houdini extended his hand and I showed him the proper way to do the Lion's Paw.

"Like that," I said. "And then you do this. See?"

"Yes," Houdini said. "I get it."

"Where did you learn that grip?" I asked.

"Like I said, my father was a scholar. He had a lot of books. I read it in one of them. I used to read a lot of his books, but then he had to sell them."

"Yes, well," I said, "that's the way you do the grip, but I'd advise you not to do it again until you're initiated. You understand?"

"Yes, sir, Mr. Clemens," Houdini said grinning.

I nodded to him, and then Ade and I turned about and went on aft to the library.

Lillie West stood in the pilothouse watching Tesla steer the ship. She watched his tall figure stand still at the wheel, looking at a red star that lay straight ahead of the ship's prow.

"You called him 'Mr. Clemens,'" Lillie said.

Tesla kept looking straight ahead.

"That's the first time I heard you do that," she said.

Tesla turned and looked over at Lillie.

"To others," Tesla said, "he is 'Mr. Clemens.' To me, he will always be 'Mark Twain.'"

"He means something to you," she said.

"A great deal," Tesla said. "When I was a boy I was very sick. Dying, actually. I felt the will to live leave me. Cholera does that to a person. But then I managed to read Mark Twain's Jumping Frog story. It made me laugh so much, I forgot all about being sick and dying."

"So that is why he means so much to you."

"For making me laugh when I was sick? No, that's not it."

"Then why?"

"For making me laugh whether I'm sick or well. Just for making me laugh. Just that alone. It is more than sufficient. Few people appreciate the importance of laughter. What about you, Miss West? Do you still remember how to laugh?"

For once Lillie's eyes averted Tesla's gaze; she looked away toward the red star that seemed to be growing brighter.

"I do not see anything to laugh about at the moment," Lillie said.

"That," Tesla said, "is when one needs to laugh the most. And to be able to find the point of laughter at such a time—ah, that is the work of genius."

George Ade and I had settled down in the library at the stern of the ship. We were seated in the armchairs and a stack of books lay on the center table where Ade had put them. I had glanced through the pages of several of them and had set them all aside. I was in no mood for reading; neither was Ade. We just sat there looking out at the stars.

"Books," I said. "To the making of many books there is no end, as Solomon wrote when he was making another book. So many books are so like each other it is a marvel that we authors should continue manufacturing the things, but I suppose it beats working for a living."

"We seem to be trapped in a book right now, one by Jules Verne."

"Yes, Verne could have authored this trip, the main outlines of it, that is. But he couldn't have thought up this airship of Tesla's, and he sure as hell couldn't have thought up Tesla. Verne gets all his character sketching secondhand from some very bad French literature and Walter Scott. The result of all that pawnshop kind of literature is deadly boredom. War talk by a soldier who has been in a war is likely to be interesting, but moon talk by a poet who has not been in the moon is apt to be dull."

I had not realized Tesla had come in behind me while I had been speaking, and now he came around in front of us and said, "Mark and I do not agree on the literary merits of Monsieur Verne. I believe he is a remarkable writer and unappreciated by the many, even by some of those who enjoy him most. Have you ever read *Hector Servadac*?"

"No," I said, "but I have heard of it. It's something about Earth being struck by a comet, isn't it?"

"That's right," Tesla said. "In it Verne encodes much knowledge that has long been held secret."

"Well," I said, "that's all fine. But when I read a story, I want it to flow along in an understandable way so that I don't have to stop and cipher it all out every other paragraph."

"You just don't like French literature," Tesla said.

"I just don't like the French," I amended.

Tesla laughed, but then looked at me with concern and asked, "How are you doing?"

"I'm all played out, Tesla, all played out. What I need is some real rest. Some solid sleep."

"There are crew quarters on the bottom deck," Tesla said. "Go on down there."

"Well," I said, getting up, "you do have some practical accommodations on board after all. I'm going down there right now. You and Czito can handle things for a while, I'm sure."

"I'll call you when I need you," Tesla said.

I went down the ladder to the lower deck and turned toward the bow of the ship. There was a door going into a narrow hall. I went through the door. There was another door on the right. This was a four bunk crew's quarters. On the left was another door. This was a bathroom. I went into the crew's quarters and lay down on a bunk built into the bulkhead of the ship. I listened to the steady drone of the ship's engine and in a few moments I drifted into a troubled doze. In another stretch of immeasurable time I fell into a deep, exhausted sleep.

It was during this sleep that I had a curious dream. I was walking through a strange city. It was not like any city I had ever seen before. I walked along looking in shop windows. Not a soul was out on the streets, nor was there any sound of birds, nor did I hear the rustle of the wind. Everything was deadly still, but the sky was bright blue. I walked along wondering where I was and what I was doing there. Then I turned a corner and came upon a familiar sight: it was my house in Hartford, Connecticut. My daughters, Susy and Clara, came running toward me; they were little children again.

"Papa! Papa!" they cried.

"What is it, my dears?" I asked.

"What happened to the sky?" Susy asked.

I looked up to where they were pointing. The blue sky had a black hole in it showing stars, and the whole city spread out over the distant horizon was being broken apart piece by piece and drawn up into that black void.

Susy asked, "Is it heaven or hell?"

I woke up in a cold sweat, breathing heavy. I rubbed my face and reached for my pocket watch, took it out, and tried to see the time. It was too dark to read the watch's face, so I got up from the bunk and went out to the hall, which was lit by a single bulb, and looked at my watch again. It read seven fifty-five. I had been sleeping over three hours.

I went to the ladder and climbed it to the upper deck. I found Tesla standing in front of the ship's engine. He had the doors slid open and was studying the engine as it operated. The drive crystal filled the interior of the airship with a rainbow of light.

"Mark," Tesla said, "I was just about to come wake you up. How was your rest?"

"Uneasy," I said. "How's the engine?"

"It is doing as well as can be expected," Tesla said. "The ship has never operated for this long at these electrical potentials before. I was concerned about some of the wiring. But it seems to be holding up. Let's go up to the pilothouse."

Tesla slid the cabinet door closed and we ascended the stairs to the pilothouse. As I came up the steps, I caught sight through the pilothouse windows of a small, glowing, reddish-orange disk hanging ahead of us in space, just beyond the prow of the airship.

Tesla said, "I have instructed Mr. Czito to make a relatively slow approach to Mars so we can throw out our electric echo-beam and detect any surprises that the Martians might have in store for us."

Kolman Czito stood at the pilot's wheel, and at Czito's position at the control board at the aft of the pilothouse sat Lillie West, George Ade, and Houdini.

I approached the control panel where Lillie and Ade sat and looked at the diagram of the solar system which was all lit up under that square sheet of glass. Two points of light flashed near the glowing point of light on the diagram labeled *Mars*.

"Do you think that little flashing point is the Martian airship?" I asked.

"Yes," Tesla said. "The two moons of Mars are presently on the opposite side of the planet."

I approached Czito, and said, "I'll take over now."

Czito nodded and went back to the control panel.

Tesla said, "We will arrive on Mars shortly. I had hoped the auxiliary capacitors would be charged by now, but the damage they sustained was greater than I realized."

"What does that mean for us?" I asked.

Tesla said, "I am not sure that we will have enough power to destroy their ship, but we cannot wait any longer. We must try to stop the Martians before they reach their home planet."

I said, "That means we must stop them right now."

"That's right," Tesla said.

I pressed the accelerator pedal down. The disk of Mars began expanding and taking on the aspect of a rusty-looking sphere.

"Mars," Tesla said. "Or as it was once called in the antediluvian tongue: *Khahera*, 'Word-in-Flesh.'"

I continued our 'slow' approach to Mars. The planet was still about two million miles distant, but it stood out against the black of space as a salmon pink disk with streaks and spots of blue and green. Creeping along at the rate of four million miles an hour as we were doing now, it would take us at least a good thirty minutes to reach the planet's surface. I had the strong urge to press the accelerator pedal again, but I resisted. I knew Tesla was right; there could very well be a trap up ahead.

In a few minutes we began to get a better view of the planet. The disk of Mars had grown large enough to make out a few details. These meant nothing to me, but Tesla and Czito knew the surface features well, and began to call out their names and describe what they thought those features might actually be in the way of mountains and valleys.

By and by we began to perceive the so-called canals of Schiaparelli. They seemed real enough at the time, and foreboding. A people who could design and construct the engineering marvel of a world-wide canal system would be a formidable adversary. Perhaps they had a fleet of airships—or several fleets. Perhaps they could encircle us with a thousand airships and smite us with an electric bolt which would smash us as the flyswatter smashes the fly. Perhaps they had even more powerful weapons, unimaginable to our minds, weapons which would gather us up and sweep us to the surface of their world—and there we would remain their captives and slaves for the rest of our tortured lives. These and a myriad of other imagined dangers passed through my mind as the flat disk of Mars continued to grow and stretch itself out against the black curtain-drop of interplanetary space.

Then, after a little while longer, when the disk of Mars looked about the same size as the Moon does from Earth, I began to notice something: some of those canals began to break up in my field of vision; instead of a dark line stretching itself across an expanse of salmon-pink, I now saw a series of dark spots disconnected from each other, and only roughly aligned. In a few more minutes some of the other lines began to resolve into spots, splotches, and streaks—nothing but discreet patches of light and shadow. What had seemed to be straight lines earlier were now only a rough alignment of separate craters and blotches of variegated color. I blinked and squinted, but it did no good; the canals were gone. I looked over at Tesla. He was studying Mars through the spyglass.

"What happened to the canals?" I asked.

"There are no canals," Tesla replied. "They are an optical illusion. And look there. There are no seas, either. See how those blue-green areas are turning grayish-brown as we draw closer?"

"Yes," I said, "yes, I do. But how can that be?"

Tesla said, "Those blue-green colors are an optical illusion."

I suddenly felt a surge of relief. No canals! My confidence rose. I looked back at Mars. It was larger than ever, and with every second that passed it was stretching itself out further and further, growing rounder and rounder, filling itself out, bulging toward us, transforming itself from disk, to ball, to planet—to world.

I now spied something that looked like a vast crater on the northern hemisphere of the planet. The whole Martian world had a broken, abandoned, discarded aspect to it. It was nothing like the blue and white globe of our world. I realized that Earth was a joyous, living thing, but Mars looked dead. I thought about the nightmare that I had just had during my nap, and what Susy had asked me in it. As I looked upon the face of Mars, I knew that this place was not heaven. It could have very well been hell, for all I knew. If it was not hell, it was a very good imitation.

Czito said, "The Martian airship is approximately five thousand miles ahead of us. They are directly on a line between us and the region of *Thaumasia Felix* on the surface of Mars."

"Where is this region of 'Them Asians' located?" I asked.

"*Thaumasia*," Czito said.

"Yes," I said, "where is it?"

Tesla handed me the spyglass. I looked through it and saw an even more detailed view of the surface of Mars.

Tesla said, "It is that oval circle there fifteen degrees south of the equator. The dark area at its center is called *Solis Lactus*."

The circle which Tesla had pointed out to me was a mixture of yellowish and pink colors. The dark area, which at a distance looked blue-green, now appeared to be a gray, ashen color.

Czito said, "The Martian airship is definitely moving toward *Thaumasia Felix*."

Tesla said, "Aim the prow of the ship directly at *Solis Lactus* and accelerate by another ten thousand miles an hour."

I did as Tesla ordered. In a moment, he was at my side again. He was adjusting the tracking machine on the pedestal. He pivoted the steel rod back and forth. In a moment the light bulb on the tracking machine flashed.

"There!" Tesla said. "Straight ahead, Mark, straight ahead. We are within only a few miles of their ship."

Tesla picked up the spyglass and looked through it. He stood there a minute or two without moving, and then said, "I believe I see them."

The electric bloodhound mounted on its pedestal was flashing once every three seconds.

"I'm going up to the gun tower," Tesla said. "We must destroy them before they reach Mars. If they get much further, we will be forced to try to bring them to a controlled landing on the planet's surface. We cannot risk the destruction of Mars. Get ready to move in reverse at the speed of light on my order."

Tesla shot up the ladder to the gun tower. Suddenly I caught sight of a black speck against the glowing red face of Mars. I steered toward it, and in a moment I could clearly see that it was the Martian airship.

I put on a little speed and the Martian airship grew in size to a clearly visible black cylinder silhouetted against the red, brown, and yellow expanse of Mars spread out beyond the pilothouse windows.

Just as I was planning on moving in closer, Tesla fired an immense, white ball of fire; it sped toward the Martian airship and crashed against it in a silent explosion of fire and lightning bolts. A sphere of shimmering light surrounded the Martian airship after the explosion, but the ship appeared undamaged.

"Hold position, Mark!" Tesla shouted from the gun tower.

Then suddenly, the Martian airship turned about and shot a red ball of fire directly at us. I put our ship into a dive and the ball of fire sped over the top of the pilothouse. Then the Martian airship turned back around and sped away toward Mars, becoming a black dot in five seconds. I hit the accelerator pedal and went after the black dot.

"They've developed a powerful shield around their ship," Tesla shouted from the gun tower. "We won't be able to destroy them in space. We'll have to try to ground them on the Martian surface."

"Now why did I think that was exactly what you were going to say?" I shouted back up to Tesla.

I pressed the accelerator pedal and piloted our airship on toward Mars; the planet spread out before the pilothouse windows, pushing back the starry night sky of space. We hurtled toward the planet's surface, a desert wasteland of red and black, yellow and gray. Then, looking straight ahead, the night sky of space was gone; ahead was only a great tan and yellow plain covered in craters like those on the Moon, and, to the north, a vast canyon of red rock cleaving the plain asunder.

In another five seconds we reached the upper atmosphere of Mars. The interior of the pilothouse took on the ruddy glow of the Martian skies beyond our windows.

The Martian airship had slowed, and I now piloted our airship down toward it, and then, in a swooping arc, under it, so that I could see the belly of their ship through the uppermost panes of the pilothouse windows.

Tesla fired a beam at the belly of the Martian airship, then another.

[*Fzt! Boom! Beroom!*]

The Martian airship seemed to shudder, but continued on its course.

I brought our airship closer to the Martian airship as all the while both of our ships descended through the atmosphere of Mars and into a great cloud of dust rising several miles above the rusty wastes of the planet's surface. We pierced the wall of the dust cloud, and, for a moment, the dust was so thick that I lost sight of the Martian airship. But then we came out of the dust, and I saw that the Martian airship was still directly above and ahead of us, and just as I looked up and saw it, the Martians fired another ball of intensely bright red fire. The ball of fire hurtled directly toward the pilothouse where I stood.

I took our ship into an immediate dive, and the ball of fire passed within a few feet of our gun tower where Tesla sat, and sped aft where it barely missed the stern of our ship by what seemed only inches.

I was feeling relieved at having dodged the fire ball, when there was a flash of light so bright it nearly blinded me. Then we heard and felt a terrible, rumbling explosion somewhere from below—an explosion that was so powerful that it knocked me off my feet and threw me back against the control board where Lillie, Ade, and Houdini sat. I blinked and got my balance and could see that Lillie, Ade, Houdini, and Czito were flying about plugging and unplugging switches on their control board, trying to keep up with the flashing red lights.

I staggered back to the pilot's wheel and saw that we were plummeting in a corkscrew trajectory straight to the ground. I wrestled with the pilot's wheel, pulling it back and stopping our downward spin. A blur of rocky ground swept by in front of us, and then the sky flashed up in front of the ship's prow again.

Tesla came bounding down from the gun tower.

"Mark!" he shouted. "Turn her about! Retreat!"

"Retreat?" I shouted, "I'm an expert at that!"

Blinking and rubbing my eyes with my left hand, I tightened my grip on the pilot's wheel with my right and yanked the wheel starboard. Our airship pivoted 180 degrees and we shot away in the opposite direction.

"Get us out of here, Mark," Tesla said. "The Martians have attached the Master Crystal to their airship's electrical system. If they hit us with one of those balls of electricity, they will vaporize our ship."

"Vaporized, eh? Well, if I'm going to get killed I might as well get vaporized. No funeral expenses."

I glanced aft through the pilothouse windows and could see a cloud of smoke rising from the planet's surface where the ball of fire from the Martian's airship had exploded. The cloud was shaped like a mushroom; it had a central column of smoke rising up thousands of feet, and above it spread a gray smoke cloud in the shape of a gigantic cap spreading out over the pink sky for miles around.

Suddenly, another ball of fire shot by the gun tower and sped by in front of us.

"Get down!" Tesla shouted.

We all hit the floor. I squinted my eyes shut, but there was still a flash of white light shining through my closed eyelids, followed by a sickening "boom." I raised up on my knees, grabbed the pilot's wheel, and looked out over the prow of the ship. We were careening over a firestorm rising up from the surface of the planet. I slammed my knee on the accelerator pedal, and we sped over and out of the twisting billows of black smoke and tongues of red fire. I staggered to my feet and looked aft through the pilothouse windows. We had just passed through another one of those mushroom clouds of smoke and fire. I turned back around and tried to accelerate our ship over the surface of Mars.

Czito shouted, "They're right behind us!"

It was at that moment that I realized that our airship's controls were not functioning properly. They were working, but the ship was sluggish in her response, and growing more sluggish by the moment. As I struggled with the wheel and the pedals, our ship continued on her way speeding above the surface of Mars.

I said, "Something's happening to the wheel. The ship's not responding."

"It's the explosions below," Czito said. "They've disrupted the ship's field."

"The wheel's freezing up!" I shouted. "Help me turn it!"

Tesla reached out on my left side, and grabbed the pilot's wheel. A second later, George Ade appeared on my right. The three of us strained to get the wheel to turn; it had taken the touch of a feather to turn it earlier; now it required the pull of an ox. Lillie, Czito, and Houdini stood bent over the control board, their hands flying from one switch to the other. There were too many red lights for them now, or they had too few hands.

As we struggled with the wheel, I looked up beyond the prow of the ship and saw the edge of a crater looming toward us. We were on a direct collision course.

"Pull her up!" I shouted, "Up! We're going to hit!"

With the finesse of a lumbering elephant, our airship lifted up and away from the crater's edge as Tesla, Ade, and I pulled back on the pilot's wheel. We cleared the crater's edge.

"We're not going to hit," I said.

On the other side of the crater rose another craggy range of undulating land. In an instant, another crater loomed before us, its rocky walls higher than the last.

Our airship was now plummeting sideways down into a canyon. Tesla and Ade braced their legs back along the floor and pulled with all their might, while I hung on and did the hoping. We got the prow of the ship up in the air and I pressed the accelerator pedal as hard as I dared.

The airship jerked forward in the sky and passed over the crater's edge.

But just as quick, another crag on a crater's edge flashed before us—this time the crag seemed the size of a mountain.

"We're going to hit!" I shouted.

All three of us kept pulling on the wheel. We rushed up to the mountain so close that I could see a blur of individual rocks on its cliffs. We turned the wheel hard to starboard, and our airship banked away from the mountainside at a 90 degree angle. We flashed over a cliff and left the mountain behind. I looked back to see its retreat.

"We're not going to hit!" I shouted.

I turned around. We were headed straight for the face of yet another broken crag; its top loomed over us.

"We're *not* going to hit!" I shouted.

I slammed the brake pedal with my foot, and our airship slowed, but not enough. We were climbing straight up the face of the crater wall, a blur of reddish-brown rock filling our view of the pilothouse windows. All of us—Tesla, Ade, and I—leaned back with all our might, pulling on the wheel.

"*We're not going to hit!*" I shouted.

The prow of our airship skimmed along the surface of the mountain face, inches from colliding. Then there was a flash of yellow sky. We were passing over the mountain.

"We—"

[*Ka-boom!*]

"We hit!"

It was a rumbling, cracking, scraping vibration which stopped my voice. Sparks and rays of light shot in front of the pilothouse windows. Then I caught a glimpse of a jagged rock flashing by the larboard side of the pilothouse windows. I realized the belly of our airship was sliding along the shoulder of the mountaintop!

The rumbling and cracking and scraping ceased and we came out over to the other side of the mountain.

Now our airship seemed to lose almost all of its power. The prow pointed back down to the ground again, and the whole body of the airship rocked to and fro as if it wanted to turn over on its back. We started losing our internal artificial gravity field, and I began to feel the pull of centrifugal force on my arms and legs.

Our airship was descending in a wild wobble toward an immense plain of white—an enormous ice field—the edge of the southern polar ice cap.

Tesla shouted, "Everyone! Pull up on the wheel!"

Lillie, Czito, and Houdini sprang from the control board and rushed to join the rest of us.

Now all six of us clustered around the pilot's wheel; pulling on its uppermost rim, grasping its handles, yanking desperately at its spokes.

The plain of ice filled the view of the pilothouse windows, a white, streaked blur; a rushing, solid torrent, promising instant death.

My foot hit the brake pedal hard. Our airship slowed, and her prow rose up. The view of the plain of ice was pushed down by a horizon of yellowish-orange sky.

"Up! Up! Up!" Tesla shouted.

There was a low rumbling vibration and scraping sound. Then a "boom" that shook us to the marrow. The view through the pilothouse windows was engulfed in sparks and the shimmering blue glow of electrical fire and great chunks of ice flying up in front of us striking the pilothouse windows in a fusillade. The yellow-orange horizon rose up directly ahead above the linen ice plain of Mars. Our airship was plowing into that plain, digging a trench into its surface as we went.

The control board in front of the pilot's wheel exploded in a shower of sparks. Then there was another explosion: an electrical "boom" and flash of white light.

An instant later everything went pitch-black and we were all thrown off our feet.

No one is certain what happened immediately after that.

CHAPTER EIGHT

In Realms of Power

> Away off on the edge of the sand, in a soft, pinky
> light, we see three little sharp roofs like tents,
> and Tom says: 'It's the pyramids of Egypt.'
>
> — Huck, *Tom Sawyer Abroad*

Night had descended on Chicago. In the streets of the city, gas and electric lights flared up and obscured the starlight shining from above. No one thought to look up to the sky. Chicago was not a city of poets, but of merchants. Everyone kept their gaze level, looking for the next dollar and the next deal.

Over on Congress Street carriages driven by liveried coachmen lined up to unload their elegant passengers under the glare of the electric lamps in front of the Auditorium Building; along State Street pedestrians strolled in front of shop windows on their way to theatres and restaurants; and in front of the Great Northern Hotel on Dearborn a steady stream of people flowed in and out of the main entrance, the air around them vibrating with the strains of "After the Ball" coming from an orchestra in the hotel's ballroom. If anyone had stopped to listen they would have been annoyed, for that sentimental ballad had already worn out its welcome with the people of Chicago. But nobody stopped to listen. That is the way it was in Chicago: the people there were always too busy to listen, and so they passed by, neither liking nor disliking, on their way to the next thing just because it was the next thing.

An hour after this flurry of activity, the traffic on the streets of downtown Chicago thinned out and slowed down. Everyone was inside the theatres and restaurants and hotels; city life had transferred from the outdoors to the indoors. The city's sidewalks had become almost as quiet as those of a country village.

Racing along one of these quiet sidewalks was a messenger boy who had been told that a fast delivery would bring a big tip. He approached the entrance of the Great Northern in a burst of Olympic speed, slipped breathlessly through the entrance of the hotel, went up to the desk clerk, and announced: "Telegram for Robert O'Brien!"

The desk clerk wrote down a room number on the messenger's envelope, handed the envelope back, and the boy bounded away to the elevators. There, the boy said to the elevator operator: "Fourteenth floor!" and up the two of them went. When the elevator operator stopped at the hotel's top floor, the messenger pushed back the door, and bounced out into the hall, looking up and down its length. His gaze fell upon the room number for which he had been looking; it was only a few steps away. He went up to the door and knocked. Shortly, the door opened.

"Robert O'Brien?" the messenger asked.

"Yes."

"Telegram."

O'Brien signed for the telegram, tipped the messenger, took the envelope, and closed the door. He opened the envelope and looked at the telegram message. It was an apparently meaningless series of numbers. He went to the door of an adjoining room and knocked. The door swung open, and behind it stood Dan Lamont, Secretary of War.

"It just came in," O'Brien said.

"Get on it," Lamont said, "and let me know the moment you're done." Lamont closed the door.

O'Brien went to the desk in his room and sat down with the telegram in hand. He took out a sheet of hotel stationery and began writing, his pencil scratching along the surface of the paper. In a few minutes O'Brien was finished. He got up and knocked on Lamont's door again.

Lamont answered the door and O'Brien held out the sheet of stationery. Lamont took the sheet, looked at O'Brien's pencil scratchings, said, "Burn the telegram," and then closed the door.

With the sheet of stationery in hand, Lamont went across his room and through a door into a spacious adjoining suite, and on across this second room to another door where he stopped and knocked. He listened by the door a moment, heard a steady rasping, and then cracked the door open and put his head inside.

Lamont saw that President Cleveland was still heavily asleep, snoring like a bear.

"Mr. President!" Lamont said sharply.

Cleveland made a sudden horrific gasp that sounded like tearing cloth and sat upright in bed.

"Goddamn sonovabitch I'll gut you like a fish!" Cleveland roared with his eyes tightly shut.

The tallest pyramids were nearly half a mile high.

"Mr. President!" Lamont shouted, "It's me, Dan Lamont! Wake up! Mr. President!"

Cleveland slowly opened his eyes. "What?" Cleveland asked, looking around the room.

"Mr. President!" Lamont said.

"What?" Cleveland asked, rubbing his eyes. "What the hell is it? It better be important!"

"It's the telegram," Lamont said. "From Asaph Hall at the Naval Observatory."

"Oh," Cleveland said. "Oh, that. All right. All right. I'll be out in a minute."

Lamont pulled his head back and closed the door. He heard Cleveland coughing in the next room. The coughing went on for more than a minute; then it turned into a gagging sound. The sound stopped, a minute or two passed, and then Cleveland came out of his bedroom wearing his dressing gown and slippers.

"What do you have?" Cleveland asked, taking the sheet of paper from Lamont's hand.

Cleveland looked at the sheet of paper and read the following:

"Dear Mr. President,

Achieved clear viewing tonight. Mars clear disk on western horizon above horns of Taurus. At 9:24 pm Washington time observed bright lights on or near surface of Mars flashing at intervals of five seconds or less. Unable to determine exact location of lights on Martian globe due to distance of planet from Earth and local atmospheric conditions. Will continue to monitor skies as per your instructions. Asaph Hall."

Cleveland studied the message a moment longer after reading it aloud.

"What does it mean?" Lamont asked.

Cleveland looked up at Lamont, and said, "Tesla and Clemens have reached Mars—but they may be dead."

Lamont said, "We need to start work on a cover story for both of them. Tesla's no problem. We can say that he was electrocuted in a laboratory accident. Mark Twain will be more difficult. Do you know if he's been sick lately?"

"He coughs a lot from those cheap cigars he smokes," Cleveland replied.

Lamont thought for a moment, and then said, "We could say he caught cold—pneumonia."

"Don't say anything—yet," Cleveland said. "Just keep Clemens' suite closed. Allow no one in there."

"Yes, sir."

"Especially Fred Hall. Have a man keep an eye on him."

"Yes, sir."

"Round up the hotel's doctor and tell him that it has already been determined that Clemens is seriously ill and is to have absolutely no visitors."

"Yes, sir."

"And if anybody asks where Clemens is—Hall or anybody else—have the doctor tell them he's in bed with a cold—with a cold, nothing more."

Now, do you see what I mean? Do you see how skillfully Cleveland constructed this lie? He was careful, and modest, and extremely economical in his claim. I was sick with a cold, nothing more, nothing less. This claim allowed maximum flexibility. If he needed me to get a little sicker, he could arrange that; if he needed me to get well all of a sudden, a cold was just the thing that could allow that development also. And if he needed me to die, he could turn up my temperature, give me the chills, the whooping cough, the double pneumonia, all in due course, and then when the situation required it, he could make me gasp my last breath, and maybe even supply me with some dying words; but then, he would probably forego the dying words; that would be overdoing it, and would violate Cleveland's principle of economics. The President knew how to lie, and he taught me something about how to tell a lie that will live, but I still lack his talent. You see, I would have got up an enthusiasm and would have wanted to supply some dying words, and I would've supplied them; and then, by and by, somebody would notice something in those dying words; it would be a clue that would, when traced out to its logical conclusion, prove with irrefutable logic that I had not died at all and that I could have never spoken those words at the time claimed, or at any earlier time. Yes, the lesson I learned from Cleveland was: lie, yes, lie, but only lie as much as is absolutely necessary. The rest of the time, tell the truth. It will all go much better if you do so, for both you and the lie.

What had really happened to us? What was the truth? Were we alive or dead? Cleveland did not know, and neither did we.

In the confused pitch-black of the airship time stood still. There was no light, no sound, no motion; there was nothing by which to judge the passage of time, so, for us, there was no time. But then I felt the urge to emit a sort of low groan, so I emitted it. After that, I knew I was alive to one extent or another, whether I wanted to be or not. I sort of groaned again, and I think I said something like:

"Is anybody there?"

I heard a stirring somewhere in the pitch-black, then the fricative scratch of a Lucifer match—[*s-suf-ff!*]—and Tesla's face appeared in front of me floating in the pitch-black.

"Mark," Tesla said quietly, "are you injured?"

"I don't know," I said, "I hardly know if I'm alive."

"Czito!" Tesla said.

"Here, Mr. Tesla!" Czito replied.

"Get the electric torch," Tesla said.

I heard Czito rustling past me, and then a moment later, the pilothouse was flooded with electric light.

Lillie and Ade lay on the floor of the pilothouse. Houdini sat on the floor with his back leaning against the bulkhead aft of the pilothouse; he was rubbing his face and squinting at the light. Lillie and Ade began moving about on the floor.

"What happened?" Houdini said. "Did they get us? Did they get us?"

"Where are we?" Lillie asked, rising up on one elbow.

Ade put a hand over his face, and said, "We crashed."

"We crashed," Houdini repeated. "We crashed. They got us. They got us."

"No one has us," Tesla said. "I believe our ship is buried in ice. How deep, I cannot say."

Tesla took the electric torch from Czito and threw its beam on to the pilothouse windows. Beyond the windows was only a solid white wall—around us and above us. We all began slowly dragging ourselves up from the floor, feeling for broken bones as we staggered to our feet.

"Is anyone injured?" Tesla asked.

"I'm all right," Lillie said.

"Me too," Ade said. "Just shook up."

"Ah," Houdini said, "it was nothin'. A bump in the dark, that's all, a bump in the dark."

"What about you, Mark?" Tesla asked.

"I am sure that I am mortally wounded with internal injuries, but at the moment I don't feel a thing. Perhaps I am internally paralyzed and don't know it."

"Let me see you," Tesla said shining the electric torch at me. He studied me a moment, and said, "You seem all right. Are you in pain anywhere?"

"Oh," I said, "I'm in pain everywhere, I suppose, but no more than usual. Don't worry about me. What about the airship?"

Tesla motioned Czito to the control switches in front of the pilot's wheel, and handed Czito the electric torch. Tesla tried the switches. Everything on the board was dead.

"It must be the coils," Tesla said. "Come along."

Tesla descended the stairs of the pilothouse, and Czito followed, illuminating their way with his electric torch. I followed them, and behind me, Lillie, Ade, and Houdini came along in the gloom.

Tesla slid back the door to the ship's engine and looked in.

"Yes," Tesla said, "the coils are fused. And all the capacitors appear to have completely discharged, and the pulse has extinguished the drive crystal."

"What can be done?" I asked.

"Fortunately," Tesla said, "We have extra wire down on the lower deck. I believe we can affect a repair."

Czito handed me the electric torch, and went back toward the pilothouse. In a second, he came forward with another electric torch, its beam falling upon the floor of the upper deck.

Tesla said to Czito, "Go below and begin uncoiling the conduction wire from the big roll. Mr. Ade, you and Miss West go below and help Mr. Czito. Erich, I want you on the ladder to guide the wire up through the hatch."

"What shall I do?" I asked.

"You stay here with me and supervise," Tesla said.

"Yes," I said, "I imagine you are in great need of my expert supervision."

The others went below while I held the electric torch on Tesla so that he could see inside the engine cabinet. He began snipping away on the coil of wire with a pair of wire cutters. He managed to cut out a long section of wire and pull it off the coil. I could see where several wires had been melted into one lump of copper.

"That looks to be your problem," I said with an air of expertise.

"Yes," Tesla replied, "one of them."

Tesla continued for several minutes tediously unwinding the big coil of wire. Occasionally he would find sections where the wire was fused and he would cut those sections out. When he finished with the primary coil, Tesla went to the other cabinet and started all over again inspecting the secondary coil.

After much tedious work, the coils had been thoroughly inspected and all the fused sections removed. Tesla rewound all the coils by hand, noting as he did so that they had to be wound just so or they would be "out of tune" and the airship would not work properly.

When all the remaining wire had been wound back around the armatures again, each coil was short by a certain amount. Now the wire came up from below threaded through the hatch by Houdini. I peered down through the hatch and saw Lillie holding the other electric torch, trying to illuminate at turns both the work of Czito and Ade below and Houdini up on the ladder, each of them getting just enough light to guess at what they were doing. As I watched this, I suddenly noticed that Lillie's electric torch was getting dimmer and dimmer. I looked at mine; it was going out, too.

"Quickly!" Tesla said.

Houdini quickened his pace in feeding the wire up through the hatch and on to the floor of the upper deck. Tesla's fingers worked rapidly inside the cabinet.

"Hold the light a little closer," Tesla said.

I asked, "Will these lights hold out until your work is done?"

"Let us do our work, and let the lights do what they will," Tesla replied.

I took that to mean "no." It was not at all reassuring. When the lights went out again, it would be totally dark, and I had no idea how Tesla would finish his work under pitch-dark conditions.

The worst happened. Both electric torches —the one I held and the one that Lillie held—went out—and at just about the same time.

"Are there no other lights or lanterns on the ship?" I asked in the blind blackness.

"None," Tesla said.

"What about the electric torches on those glass helmets down on the lower deck?" I asked.

Tesla said, "The power for the torches on the helmets and the equipment on the pressure suits is transmitted wirelessly from the ship's main engines. The only other source of power is the capacitors in the emergency craft. We must leave those alone; for if the airship cannot be repaired, the emergency craft is our only hope of returning to Earth alive. All our other systems are out and they will not come up again until this coil has been finished. Keep working."

Keep working? Yes, that's what Tesla said. Now he reminded me of Horace Bixby, the master riverboat pilot who had the river courses of the Ohio, Mississippi, and Missouri memorized so well that he could steer a steamboat with his eyes closed. Tesla was doing something like this. I could hear him working with the wire as fast as ever in the pitch-dark. He worked on for many more minutes, working only by touch and memory. Then I recalled the strange nature of Tesla's memory, and wondered if by some unfathomable power he was summoning a vision of the coil and engine before him, a vision of what they would look like if the ship had been illuminated with electric light. I fully believed and believe that he was seeing the unseeable by the strange power of his memory and imagination. Then—

"It's done," Tesla said.

He said this in such a way that he conveyed an absolute certainty. I did not have to ask him if he *thought* the engine would work, or what the odds of its working might be. No, I could tell that Tesla knew with absolute certainty that the ship's engine had been repaired.

I heard the snap of a switch where Tesla stood, and the airship's interior was suddenly flooded with bright electric light and the drive crystal began to flash with a rainbow of colors. Tesla was standing inside the machinery of the engine. I felt a draft of cool air and realized that the system that filtered and circulated the air inside the ship was working again as well.

"Some of these capacitors have exploded," Tesla said. "We can manage without them. Mr. Czito, come up here and reroute the circuits." Tesla stepped out of the engine, and said to me, "Now let's check the pilot's wheel."

We went up to the pilothouse. In a moment Czito appeared with a tool box and then went out again. Tesla unscrewed a metal plate on the panel in front of the pilot's wheel and looked in.

"More fused wiring," Tesla said.

Tesla went to work. Every few minutes I would peer over his shoulder to see what he was doing. He was cutting out some wires and fusing other wires together with a little rod.

I said, "I tell you, when we hit ground, I was sure we were headed for the hereafter."

"Yes," Tesla said. "Fortunately, the electro-magneto-gravitic field surrounding the ship acted as a shield, a field of force. Our artificial gravity field, or that is, what was left of it, further protected us from the inertial forces of the impact."

"But do you think we can get out of this hole we've dug ourselves into?"

Czito came back up the stairs of the pilothouse and said, "I've rerouted the circuits around the damaged capacitors."

Tesla said, "Mr. Czito has just answered your question. We may not have full power, but we have enough to blast our way out of this impact site. Perhaps enough to blast through solid rock if necessary."

"In that case," I said, "a little bit of ice over our heads shouldn't be a worry."

"It shouldn't be," Tesla said.

Tesla closed up the panel in front of the pilot's wheel and screwed it back tightly into place.

"The wiring is finished," Tesla said, handing Czito the tool box. Then he turned to me and said:

"The wheel is yours, Mark. Take her up."

I went to the switch that started the ship's engine.

"Straight up through the ice," Tesla added.

I closed the switch. The solid wall of ice covering the pilothouse windows lit up with blue electric light.

"Here goes," I said.

I pushed the accelerator down and steered the ship up. There was a great cracking sound and the ice in front of the windows churned and thrashed as we began moving upward. In a moment daylight broke through, the ice outside fell away in chunks, and the yellowish skies of Mars shone through the pilothouse windows. I heard gasps of relief from everyone behind me.

"Take her all the way up," Tesla said.

I steered the airship up toward the sky, but the ship's prow would not follow. We bumped and skidded along the surface of the ice field for about three hundred yards, and then I brought the ship to a halt.

"The ship won't respond," I said.

Tesla stood there for a moment, thinking, and then he happened to turn around and look aft through the pilothouse windows.

"Czito!" Tesla said. "The aerial conductors have been damaged!"

I turned around and looked out through the pilothouse windows. The aerial conductors—those fancy flagpole things—were bent back and flattened against the roof of the airship.

"Oh, no!" Czito said.

"It could be worse," Tesla said. "They could have been broken off completely. I think they can be bent back into position. I'll have to go out there and work on them. What kind of atmosphere do we have out there?"

Czito looked at a gauge on the control board, and said, "The atmospheric pressure is seven millibars, and there's about ninety-five percent carbon dioxide out there with small percentages of nitrogen, argon, oxygen, and water."

Tesla said, "Completely unbreathable. It's practically a vacuum. I'll have to go out in a pressure suit. Mark, open the switch for the main engine. Mr. Czito, come with me."

I opened the engine switch and Tesla and Czito went below to the lower deck. Tesla got into a pressure suit again. In a few minutes I heard a rush of air on the lower deck and a metallic mesh of gears. Then a clang sounded throughout the airship and we saw Tesla dressed in his pressure suit float out over the top of the airship. He landed on the ship's roof and stood before one of the bent aerial conductors, and then he flew back to the airship's door.

"What's he goin' to do?" Houdini asked.

I shrugged my shoulders. "Damned if I know. I just hope to hell he does *something*."

Once again I heard a metallic clang and mesh of gears below. In a minute Tesla came up the stairs of the pilothouse. He was still dressed in the pressure suit, but he had removed his helmet and knapsack. Czito came in behind him.

Tesla said, "The conductors have sustained severe damage, but I think I can get them straightened back up and functioning again. I'm going to need some help. I want Mr. Czito to remain here in the ship. Mr. Ade? Would you care to accompany me outside?"

"In one of those diving suits?" Ade asked. "All right. You'll have to tell me what to do."

"Certainly," Tesla said. "Come with me."

Tesla, Ade, and Czito started out. Houdini came up behind them.

"What about me?" Houdini asked. "Don't you need me to do something?"

"Yes, Ehrich," Tesla said, "I need you to remain inside."

Tesla turned and went down the steps, followed by Ade and Czito.

"Aw," Houdini said, scratching the back of his head. He looked over at me.

"Mr. Tesla still thinks I'm a little kid," Houdini said. "Well, I ain't no little kid. I ain't! Look at this!"

Houdini took off his coat and rolled up his right sleeve all the way up his arm and pointed to a place on his shoulder.

"Ya see that?" Houdini asked.

"No," I said, "I don't see anything."

"Right there," Houdini said. "That little white scar."

"Maybe," I said. "I guess, if you say so."

"It's there. You could see it if you'd look closer. That's a gunshot wound. I've been shot—shot and shot at."

"Do tell."

"I was running for my life."

"Why?"

"Some people said I'd stolen some chickens."

"Had you?"

"Not me. No. I never stole nothin' my whole life. I was just passin' through, just passin' through, lookin' at the scenery."

"What happened to the chickens?"

"I have no idea. Somebody else must've pinched them. But they tried to lay it on me. Now tell me honestly, Mr. Clemens, don't you think a fellow who can out-run a bullet is someone who can stand the test of danger?"

"I should certainly think so. I wish I could out-run bullets like that. But perhaps it's just as well. I might have gone down the wrong road and become a chicken thief—not that I'm saying you were a chicken thief—I just probably lack your forbearance."

"My what?"

"Your strength of will."

"Oh."

I looked over at Lillie. She was looking out the pilothouse windows with an anxious look on her face. I turned back to Houdini.

"So," I said, "Houdini. That is an unusual name."

"It's a stage name," Houdini said. "My real name is Weiss, but I don't use it anymore. I'm Houdini now. Houdini means 'Like Houdin.'"

"Houdin?" I asked. "You mean, the sculptor?"

"I don't know nothin' about no sculptor. Houdin was the world's first modern magician. Robert Houdin."

Lillie looked over at us and said, "That is pronounced Robert-Houdin."

"Yes," Houdini said, "that is the French way of saying his name—Ro-bear Hoo-dan. I know, I know. I know lots of languages: French, German, Hungarian, English."

"You've studied?" Lillie asked.

"Oh, yes," Houdini said. "And taught."

"And where was that?" she asked.

"In my father's college," Houdini said.

"Your father had a college?" I asked.

"Yes," Houdini said. "It was a small religious college. You wouldn't have heard of it."

"I see," I said. "So you want to be like Houdin?"

"Like and not like," Houdini said. "I'm going to be greater than Houdin. Houdini is a master not just of magic, but all things mysterious. But in magic, Houdini is the King of Cards. For example: Houdini can do this."

The boy magician reached out in the air with his right hand with his right sleeve still rolled up to his shoulder. He wiggled his fingers, closed his hand into a fist, and when he opened it again—there was a deck of cards! He spread the cards out to form a fan, and then closed them up again, closed his hand over the deck, opened his hand—and the deck was gone!

I said, "I've seen magicians and card sharps disappear *one* card, but never a whole deck!"

"That's a new wrinkle in the trick that is all Houdini. Nobody ever catches wise to where I get the deck."

"There they are!" Lillie gasped.

Something of far greater interest than a card trick appeared outside the windows: it was Tesla and Ade flying up over the airship, both of them dressed in air pressure suits. Ade waved to us in the pilothouse and we waved back. Tesla carried a box of tools in one hand, and he descended to the roof of the airship and stood up on it.

Ade came down slowly and stood beside Tesla. They began bringing out a steel cable from the tool box and a metal device with a windlass attached to it. Ade walked back along the rooftop of the ship reeling out the steel cable, and then stopped. Tesla came up next to him, and the two of them attached the windlass to the roof of the ship. This done, Tesla took the loose end of the steel cable and brought it over to the top of the aerial conductor and attached the cable to it with a metal hook. Tesla waved his hand and Ade began winding up the windlass. The aerial conductor began being drawn and bent upward by the retracting steel cable. Tesla watched the place where the aerial conductor was mounted on the top of the ship and kept waving his hand at Ade who kept winding up the windlass. The aerial conductor continued to rise; it had reached an angle of about forty-five degrees. Ade stopped turning the windlass, and then started up again. In another minute, the aerial conductor stood straight up once again.

Tesla removed the steel cable, flew over the rooftop with it, and attached the cable to the other aerial conductor. Ade began turning the windlass again until he had brought the second aerial conductor to its original upright position. Tesla removed the cable and flew over to Ade. The two of them removed the windlass from the top of the ship, drew in the steel cable, and then flew back to the door of the airship.

"That was slick!" Houdini said.

"Yes," I said, "let's hope it was slick enough to get the ship flying again."

Again we heard a metallic clang, a meshing of gears and a rush of air. A few moments passed and then I heard the excited voice of George Ade. He was saying something to Czito, but I couldn't make out what it was. Lillie went down the steps of the pilothouse and went to the hatch on the upper deck and looked down through it. Czito came up through the hatch, followed by Ade still dressed in his pressure suit with his helmet and knapsack removed.

"It's amazing out there!" Ade said to Lillie. "You wouldn't believe it! And that flying machine of Mr. Tesla's—it's incredible!"

Houdini said, "I wish Mr. Tesla would let me try it out!"

"Mr. Houdini," Lillie said.

"Houdini—just Houdini! Didn't I already tell ya?"

"Mr. Houdini!" Lillie said, "This is not a game! This is not a holiday! This is not one of your magic tricks!"

Lillie went back up to the pilothouse.

Houdini looked over at Ade, and asked, "What'd I say? What'd I say?"

"Nothing," Ade replied. "It was nothing you said."

Tesla came up through the hatch; he was also still dressed in his pressure suit.

Tesla said, "I think the conductors will operate. Let's give them a try, Mark."

We all came up into the pilothouse and I closed the switch for the main engine. The familiar undulating hum from the ship's engines vibrated throughout the ship. I pulled the pilot's wheel back and pressed the accelerator pedal.

The airship shot up into the sky, and I could see the ice plain drop away. I looped the ship back around and we looked down at the site of our crash: a long trench—perhaps a quarter of a mile long—ending in a dark, gaping hole in the ice. No one said anything as we looked down.

We searched the skies north, south, east, and west for some sign of the Martian airship, but there was none; we presumed that the Martians had left us for dead down there in the ice and gone on for wherever they were bound. Tesla believed it was somewhere underneath the surface of the planet.

After I circled the ship about the crash site, I turned us north. In a short while, we left the ice field behind and began flying back over that vast field of craters where we had nearly crashed. Now those craters seemed far less menacing. I took us up a little higher, about five thousand feet. The craters seemed to flatten out at that height. The land itself seemed unvarying in its flatness. Below, we were flying over a reddish field of volcanic rock broken up everywhere with craters formed by some unknown process. At that time, I did not know whether the craters were volcanic cones or the impact holes created by the collision of asteroids. In a short while, Tesla would explain that they were the latter. I did not stop to speculate on geology, but sped over the planet's surface, all the while watching the tracking machine, hoping to see its light bulb let out a single flash.

I pushed the airship forward at a speed of ten thousand miles an hour. Czito would give me course corrections just about every minute, for Tesla wanted us to travel due north up the zero degree meridian of the planet. I followed the meridian in a sinuous trajectory, veering off course by no more than ten degrees at any point.

After a few minutes we came upon a vast field of blackish-gray rock. This was unmistakably volcanic and reminded me of regions on the Island of Hawaii, but this volcanic floor stretched on and on for what seemed to be endless miles; it rolled and undulated to the horizon's edge.

Now the sky, which had been a pale blue, turned yellow-red again on the horizon. We were approaching another dust storm.

"I'm afraid Schiaparelli will be disappointed," Tesla said, looking down on the starboard side of the pilothouse. "Dawes' Forked Bay is not a bay at all—only the end of this outcropping of rock."

Just as Tesla said that, we left the volcanic rock field behind and passed over a sandy desert that was colored gray, ochre, and rust-red. I watched the tracking machine; its light bulb remained dark.

"Still no sign," I said to Tesla, nodding at the tracking machine.

Tesla said, "Continue on to the North Pole. Then shift sixty degrees longitude and return to the south."

We flew onward across the ruddy desert. A few more silent minutes passed—then: away off on the edge of the sand, in a soft, pinkish light, we saw several shapes that looked like the sharp roofs of tents, and George Ade said, "Look! Pyramids! Just like the pyramids of Egypt!"

"Bring the ship about!" Tesla shouted with a sudden, tremendous excitement.

I stopped the ship in mid-air, turned her around back to the south, and then stepped away from the wheel and joined everyone at the windows. We all looked down.

The pyramids were about five thousand feet below us and rising up out of the desert sand off to the east. There were about seven of them grouped together in a kind of city plat. Some of them were immense and looked to be about a mile long on each of their sides. The others were probably about the size of the Great Pyramid at Giza, but they were dwarfed by the giants looming over them. Tesla took out the spyglass and looked through it.

"Ruins," Tesla said sadly. "They are all ruins."

Tesla gave the spyglass to Czito, went to the tracking machine, and pointed its steel rod downward in the direction of the pyramids. The light bulb on top of the tracking machine remained dark.

"Nothing," Tesla said in an empty, hollow voice. He looked over at Czito and asked, "What is our position?"

Czito went over to the viewing glass on the control board and looked down at it.

"We are at forty point six degrees north latitude, ten point four degrees west longitude," Czito said.

Tesla stepped to the center of the pilothouse. He looked straight ahead, and did not say a word. He held this attitude for about a minute, and then I felt the urge to say something.

"Tesla?" I asked, "Are you all right?"

"Sh!" Czito whispered at me. "He's thinking!"

Tesla continued to stand there. One by one, Lillie West, George Ade, and Houdini turned to look at Tesla, and then we all looked back and forth at each other.

Finally Czito said in a low tone, "Mr. Tesla is visualizing."

Another minute or two passed. Tesla did not move one muscle, did not blink one eyelid, did not twitch one hair on his mustache. It seemed that he had turned into a wax-works figure. Yet, somehow, uncannily, I sensed that his brain was rapidly processing great volumes of information.

I asked Czito, "How long does this go on when he strikes one of these attitudes?"

Czito said, "I have seen him stand like this without moving for a whole day and night without eating or drinking a thing."

"And what are we to do in the meantime?" I asked.

"Wait," Czito said, "wait. I do not advise disturbing him while he is in this state."

I went up to Tesla and tried to look up into his eyes and noticed that his pupils were dilated so that they looked very large and black. Houdini came up beside me and also looked up at Tesla.

"I saw him go into one of these trances once when I delivered a telegram to him," Houdini said. "I went away and came back two hours later, and he was still starin'."

Czito said. "All we can do is wait and hope he comes out of it soon."

We stood there a few moments longer, and then we all turned back to the windows to look down at the distant pyramids looming up from the sands below. And then, as I stood there studying the pyramids through the spyglass, Tesla finally came up for air.

"Mr. Czito!" Tesla said, instantly coming out of his trance, "This is extraordinary! We have come upon the ancient temple grounds of *Khahera*, the very place from which the planet derived its name, 'Word-in-Flesh'. This place was carefully sited upon the surface of the Martian globe to produce a number of physical and spiritual effects. Mark, take us down toward those pyramids. I want a closer look."

I went over to the pilot's wheel and steered us down toward the surface of the desert. As we descended toward the pyramids, the place opened up and spread out toward us. I took our airship down between the structures that lay ahead. The tallest pyramids were nearly half a mile high; at our 2,500 feet altitude, their tops were abreast the pilothouse windows. I slowed the airship down so that we passed by the great stone masses at a walking pace. Tesla stood at the pilothouse windows studying the surface of the pyramids through the spyglass.

These immense pyramids were somewhat similar to the Egyptian ones on Earth; but there were striking differences. Most notably, some of these pyramids appeared to have five sides. Like the Egyptian pyramids, these were constructed of stone blocks, but the sizes of these stone blocks were much greater than their earthly counterparts. I would estimate that the average size of the stone blocks making up the largest Martian pyramids was one hundred feet across! Some of the blocks were even larger. These blocks dwarfed the giant stone blocks of Baalbek on Earth. Unlike the Great Pyramid of Giza, these Martian pyramids still retained their outer casing. I cannot say of what kind of stone this outer casing consisted. At certain angles of viewing the stone of the pyramids took on an almost metallic sheen. The color of the stone itself was probably a dullish gray like the color of lead, but I cannot say for certain because most of the stone surfaces seemed to be almost entirely covered over with a thin layer of reddish-brown sand. In places where the sand was blown away these patchy areas revealed the dull-gray sheen of the stones underneath. Although these outer casings were intact on the pyramids, they were not without damage. Covering all the pyramids were countless pock markings of craters large and small. The great drifts of sand massed along their bases and over their walls gave these structures the appearance of natural sandstone mountains. The bases of the pyramids were all buried in sand and the uneven desert floor suggested that long ago none of the sand was there, but rather some kind of pavement, and no doubt that pavement was still there now, somewhere below the sand.

I brought the airship down into the very midst of the Martian monuments. Directly below us in an open space between the pyramids lay a mound with four or five rectangular openings cut into it.

I looked off the larboard bow of the airship and caught sight of an immense structure that had been severely damaged by some great force. I motioned for Tesla to look at it, and, when he turned to train his spyglass on it, everyone else turned to look larboard as well.

This structure was not a pyramid exactly, but something similar; exactly what it was originally would be hard to say. The two sides of it that we could see had been exploded, collapsed, and then melted away be erosion. I could glimpse a crater on its eastern side. The outer casings had been torn away by some unimaginable force revealing here and there in deep crevices of overhanging cliffs the interior structure with stone beams some fifty feet thick! We could look down through this vast structure of stone beams, and, except for its scale, imagine that we were looking down into the steel beam construction of a Chicago skyscraper.

Beyond the pyramids a few miles distant to the east lay a hill about a mile and a half long and perhaps 1,000 feet high. At first I paid no attention to it, but Tesla turned his spyglass to it and stood there looking at it.

"Mark," Tesla said, still looking through the spyglass, "take us out over that prominence."

I brought the airship on across the sandy plain at an altitude of about 2,000 feet. As we approached the hill, I noticed that the outline of its crest had an appearance that was vaguely similar to the reclining profile of a human face. I thought nothing of this; for I have seen many hills and mountains on Earth that looked like a face or an animal or some other recognizable thing. These kinds of features on Earth I always found to be a freak of geology, so I assumed this hill to be one more of these accidental formations. But as we drew closer to the hill, it became suddenly obvious that this was not the work of nature. This hill was a mile and a half long sculpture of a face. At just a little over 1,000 feet above the surface of this colossal sculpture we were so close to it that we could see the details of its stony eyes staring back up at us, the iris of the right eye shaped like a cone composed of facets. It seemed that this sculpture was made out of the same leaden gray material as the pyramids, and, like the pyramids, this sculpture was covered over with a thin layer of reddish-brown desert sand. The whole face of the colossus was scatter-shot with tiny craters and in many places its surface was broken with chasms, collapsed, and eroded. This colossal head was made wearing a helmet that resembled to me the cap of a French Foreign Legionnaire without the bill; that is, it seemed to be a hat with a curtain hanging down on either side of the face, or maybe it wasn't curtains, maybe it was long hair, or something else. There were carved details in the headdress which suggested that it was once encrusted with some kind of jewels—and what jewels they must have been, for they each would have been the size of a house—or perhaps a castle! The mouth of the figure seemed to have fangs rather than human-looking teeth. The expression of this colossus was fierce, and I found it unnerving to look eye to eye with the lifeless form.

"Take us up higher," Tesla said.

I took the airship up in a corkscrew spiral. Around 10,000 feet I stopped the ship and joined the others at the window. At this height we had a very good view of the colossal head below us; we were able to see the whole thing in a glance. Distance lent a kind of focus, and some of the places that had appeared to be at close viewing only rocks, lumps, and hillocks, now formed part of a total pattern and single expression: a mind gazing out through time itself.

"It's a monster," Houdini said.

"Some kind of mythological beast," Lillie added.

"A sphinx," I said.

"Yes," George Ade said, "but what does it mean?"

"It is the sun god, *Helu*," Tesla said, "the ancient god symbol revered on both Earth and Mars. The right side of the face is a baboon, known to the ancients as *Babi*; the left side of the face is a lion, known to the ancients as *Rey*. The ancient Egyptians pictured *Babi* as the doorman of *Set*, the god of the material realm of power. It was *Babi*'s symbolic function to hold the bolt to the door of heaven and prevent the unperfected soul from entering. *Rey*, the lion, was a symbol of the soul perfected through the transforming fires of material experience. It was through the union with the sun god, *Rey*, that one became the perfected *Helu*, which literally meant 'faces,' but esoterically meant 'the two faces of the god made one.' When this union was accomplished, the perfected soul was able to command *Babi* to open the door of heaven. With the door opened, the perfected soul mounted to heaven on an electric ray focused on a particular star. This star would act as a doorway between the realm of matter and spirit. Thus we find that the ancient Egyptian word *sba* meant both 'star' and 'door.' *Sba* suggests its esoteric meaning as a 'soul gate' in that it contains the word *ba* 'soul.' This esoteric meaning can also be found in Babylonian where *bab* meant 'gate' but esoterically implied 'soul.' This transcendence of the soul beyond the temporality of the material realm of power to the permanency of the spiritual realm was the aim of the ancient civilizations on both Earth and Mars. In every generation, this transcendence was always attempted by a single individual who would act as an alchemical seed for the whole of humanity. Rarely were the attempts successful. When an attempt did succeed, the transcending individual would open the way to heaven for himself while spiritually developing the rest of his species. When the transcending individual physically died, the energy sent out from his body would be transmitted throughout the world as a spiritual effect. The pyramids were designed for this purpose to act as an oscillator coupled to the vibrations of the planet. The physical vibrations transmitted information which would be absorbed in the brain of the recipient at a subconscious level. This whole complex here is an alchemical laboratory; its purpose was nothing less than the spiritual liberation of a world, and that purpose has been the basis of every religion on Earth as well. We find the myth of *Helu* or *Horus* imbedded in the story of Mithras, in the ritual of animal sacrifice among the Hebrews, in certain concepts of Buddhism, and in the story of Jesus. These are all human conceptions of God experienced as a solar myth."

Lillie said, "I distinctly recall reading that you are a materialist, that you believe the universe has always existed, and that man is nothing more than a 'meat machine.'"

"Yes," Tesla said, "I have said those things. But you of all people, Miss West, must now know that not everything a person says in public corresponds precisely with what that person knows to be so in the privacy of his own mind. Ours is an age of materialism. Since the time of Sir Isaac Newton no reputable scientist has been allowed by the powers that be to speak publicly of the spiritual realms of power. Yet, Newton was an alchemist throughout his whole life, as are we who have succeeded him in the golden chain. The materialist believes that everything is dead; the alchemist knows that everything is alive and that in the material realm of power all spirit is expressed through functions of material bodies. Thus, the materialist sees only the veil of Isis, but the alchemist pierces the veil and sees the spirit which animates the world."

"How did you come to know all of this?" George Ade asked.

"All of what, Mr. Ade?" Tesla asked in reply.

"Well," Ade said, "about the Martians, for instance."

"Come now, Mr. Ade," Tesla said, "surely as a newspaperman you must be well acquainted with the many sources of secret and arcane knowledge."

"We have our little fraternities and societies," Ade said, "Sigma Chi, Masonry, the Whitechapel Club. But all our skullduggery is mostly fun and games."

"It is in fun and games," Tesla said, "where much is hidden. Among Earth's secret societies at their highest levels much is known about the history of the solar system, not just Mars, and you will certainly never find this information in the curriculum of any university."

"So much for free inquiry," Lillie said.

Tesla said, "The secrets you would have attempted to reveal in a single Newspaper article, Miss West, have been held by the most powerful men on Earth for thousands of years. Many before you have fought the battle for free inquiry, some dying in their battle. Do you believe a single Newspaper article will accomplish what the philosophers of the last ten thousand years have failed to accomplish?"

"I believe," Lillie said, "that for me to surrender the battle is to betray all who have fought before me."

"I am no advocate of surrender," Tesla said, "but a victorious battle must be strategic, and, unfortunately, so far, your battle has had no strategy whatsoever. As the ancient knowledge has been guarded with subtly and power, so its revelation to mankind must be carried out with even greater subtly, even greater power. This is a fact which I offer for your consideration, Miss West."

"And so the history of Mars came to you through some secret source?" Ade asked.

Tesla said, "The story of the civilization of Mars and how it came to ruin is described in legends transmitted orally and with secret documents through numerous secret societies: the Knights Templar, the Rosicrucians, the Freemasons, the Knights of the Golden Circle, the Bavarian Illuminati—and other groups whose names are hardly known to the world—the Priory of Sion, the Sons of Heliopolis, the Golden Chain of the Magi—the Order of the Flaming Sword."

"And what do these legends describe?" Ade asked.

Tesla said, "The legends tell of two world civilizations: one on Earth, the other on Mars. Two brilliant yet contentious brothers who destroyed both of their worlds in an interplanetary war. The story begins millions of years ago when our ancestors came to this solar system from other stars. For millions of years there was a stable, high civilization on Earth and Mars. The aim of the civilization was the advancement of souls from this material realm to the spiritual realm. Then a war broke out among the people of our solar system and those of another. This ended with the destruction of the cities of Mars and the loss of its atmosphere. The effects of that first Martian destruction can still be observed in the field of craters which we flew over in the southern hemisphere. A group of asteroids pass through our solar system at regular intervals as the sun passes back and forth through the galactic plane in its orbit around the center of the galaxy. During one such entry into the galactic plane, asteroids were directed toward Mars in an ancient war. Coming in from the south, they pummeled Mars until its seas were vaporized and its atmosphere was scattered into space. The civilization on Earth was destroyed as well, but with much less devastation to the planet. The few survivors on Earth managed to destroy the last of the invaders, but, a few generations after the last battle, the civilization on Earth had been reduced to the most primitive level. Then, five hundred thousand years ago, other beings came to this solar system and began developing the human race again. Over the many thousands of years, other high civilizations arose on Earth. Eventually, man returned to Mars and reconditioned the planet, restored its atmosphere, its seas, its plants, its animals.

Then, just thirty thousand years ago, intelligences who worshipped power came into our solar system and once again war broke out. These intelligences divided the people of Earth and Mars. The art of alchemy which had been established to advance the spirit of man became subverted to the control and enslavement of man's mind and spirit. The pyramids were perverted into machines which could dominate and control the individual mind and will. Another war was waged between the two planets causing great destruction. Another war on Earth sank the continent of Atlantis over twelve thousand years ago and on Earth, they sank half the continent of Atlantis and shifted the geographic poles by ten point five degrees. This was accomplished by the tangential strike of a large body with the surface of the Earth. The scar of that devastating event can still be observed as a crater lake on the surface of our globe: it is Lake Victoria on the African continent. The great spiral rift emanating from Lake Victoria and the three great mountains to the east of the lake are all the result of the impacting body wrenching the planet from its original direction of rotation and reestablishing a new equator and axis. Here on Mars, the devastation was even greater. Once again, the planet's atmosphere was blown from its surface and consumed in a great flash-fire."

"What kind of weapons could create that kind of destruction?" Ade asked.

"Artificial crystals which converted cosmic rays into electricity," Tesla replied.

"You have rediscovered their science," Ade said.

Tesla nodded, "And the Martians who exist on this planet today are about to do the same."

"So," Ade said, "the ones who built these structures are the ones who fought the interplanetary war?"

"No," Tesla replied, "it was the descendants of the builders who betrayed their elder's legacy. And that legacy survived in a fragmented form among what was left of the Atlanteans. After the second destruction of Atlantis a little over twelve thousand years ago, the legacy was transmitted to Egypt, and from there it has survived on Earth down to this very day. From the Atlantean legacy I can determine a number of things. For example, we know that the ancient civilizations used the sexagesimal number system, that is, a system based upon the number sixty. This was no caprice or chance, but was a choice informed by very profound knowledge. The ancients knew that the material universe is constructed upon the base sixty system of numbers. My sixty-cycle polyphase system of alternating current exploits this knowledge to achieve maximum efficiency in electrical systems. The foundation of the base sixty system in three-dimensional geometry is the tetrahedron. The underlying structural force of all planets and stars can be described geometrically as a tetrahedron inscribed within the surface of a sphere. The site of these pyramidal constructions here is determined by the geometry of a tetrahedron inscribed within the surface of Mars and suggests likely points where other constructions may be sited. Relating this to what I know of the ancient Martian legends, I strongly suspect that the center of the present Martian civilization lies beneath the planet's surface somewhere in the vicinity of *Nix Olympica*, the largest mountain on the planet. And somewhere near that mountain is the most likely place where the Martians have taken the crystal."

"Why there?" Ade asked.

"That is the site of the most intense tetrahedral vertex in the planet's stress-energy system, and therefore that mountain is the one place on the surface of the planet where the Master Crystal can draw the greatest energy."

"And where is this big mountain?" I asked.

"West of here," Tesla replied, "on a latitude of nineteen point four seven degrees."

I went to the wheel and turned the airship toward the southwest, and said to Czito, "Let me know when we reach that latitude," and I pressed the accelerator down.

We moved away from the stone face and the pyramids, and in a moment that work of gigantic power disappeared under the horizon behind us, leaving ahead of us only the endlessly rolling sands of Mars.

Chapter Nine

Exceeding Capacity

> The fastest man can't run more than about ten miles an hour—not much more than ten thousand times his own length. But all the books says any common ordinary third-class flea can jump a hundred and fifty times his own length. . . .
>
> — Tom, *Tom Sawyer Abroad*

We had traveled over the surface of Mars for only a few minutes when I saw a glint of sunlight reflecting up from the surface of the planet.

"Did you just see that?" I asked Tesla who was standing next to me.

"Yes," Tesla said. "Turn the ship about and let's see what it is."

I turned the ship 180 degrees and went slowly back along the trajectory we had just traveled.

"Bring the ship down another thousand feet," Tesla said.

I obeyed Tesla's order and brought us down to within a thousand feet of the planet's surface. We floated along slowly at about fifty miles an hour with everyone at the windows studying the rocky surface below.

"There!" Tesla said. "Stop the ship."

I brought the ship to a halt and went to the windows with the others and looked down. About a thousand feet below I saw a structure of glass, a sort of undulating, snake-like glass tube, built into a wall of rock about two thousand feet in length.

"Is that one of their cities?" I asked.

"No," Tesla said. "Bring us down closer, Mark."

I went to the wheel and slowly edged the ship down toward the wall of rock. In a moment the top of the rocks seemed to push their summits up

Tesla flew down toward the doomed tower, and the others followed behind.

directly beyond the pilothouse windows. I brought the airship down about fifty more feet and the giant glass tube hove into sight directly beside us on our starboard bow.

"I can see through the glass!" Lillie said. "There are plants growing in there!"

"A giant glass-enclosed conservatory!" I said.

"There must be many such structures on the planet's surface," Tesla said. "This is how they grow their food. It's a Martian farm."

"Mr. Tesla!" Houdini shouted. "I can see men down there through the glass!"

"Where?" Tesla asked, bringing the spyglass to his eye.

"Down there!" Houdini said, pointing toward the end of the tube.

Tesla looked through the spyglass in the direction Houdini pointed, and said, "Yes. They are men, wearing hooded robes and dark spectacles. And. . . they are looking back up at *us*. Take us out of here, Mark."

I went to the wheel and accelerated the airship up and away from the wall of rock.

"We must move fast now," Tesla said. "We have been seen. If our presence is reported, the Martian airship crew will know that our ship has not been destroyed and they will come to find us again."

"How fast can I fly this ship in the planet's atmosphere?" I asked.

Tesla said, "Take us up to fifty thousand feet and accelerate to twenty thousand miles per hour."

I took the ship up as Tesla had instructed. In a few moments Czito said, "We have reached nineteen point four seven degrees latitude."

"Turn the ship due west," Tesla said.

I turned the ship toward the sun which was now down toward the west throwing out its afternoon light. Somewhere out there, millions of miles back beyond the sun, Earth sped along on its orbit, and our home world's existence now seemed as unreal and fanciful as Mars had once seemed.

"You are now pointed due west," Czito said.

"Stay this course and maintain your speed," Tesla said.

After a few more moments the red horizon seemed to bulge up and a scattering of white clouds slipped into view from over the bulge. I watched as the bulge grew closer, and as it spread out in size so did the vast umbrella of white clouds that hovered directly above it. Then we began passing over the clouds, and through their breaks I could see the surface of the planet below. At the summit of that bulge of land was the caldera of a volcano that was so big that its floor must have been fifteen or twenty miles across.

"That's not a mountain down there," I said. "It's a volcano—and it makes the Kilauea Crater look like a carbuncle."

Tesla said, "That is *Nix Olympica*, the central volcano of Mars, and the central node of the planet's lateral gravitational field. Do you remember the legends?"

I said, "The Martians built an underground city inside a giant dormant volcano."

"Yes," Tesla said, "and it was there that they made their last stand against the warships of Earth as this planet's atmosphere was blasted from its surface."

"You know," I said, "years ago on the Island of Hawaii, I had a kahuna take me down into the lava tubes that run beneath the volcano. Those tubes ran for miles and opened up into gigantic caverns. The kahuna told me that some of those tubes extended underneath the sea floor to the other islands of the Sandwich chain. If the Kilauea has lava tubes like that on Earth, just imagine what must be under that piece of real estate down there."

"Yes," Tesla said, "and not only the tubes and voids that are natural formations, but imagine the ones cut by artifice thousands of years ago. A people who could build half-mile high pyramids on the planet's surface could build on the same scale underground. Bring the ship back down to five thousand feet and stop it in position above the edge of the caldera."

I brought our airship down toward the edge of the volcano—a sheer vertical wall of rock rising several thousand feet from the crater floor. As I got us to the altitude of 5,000 feet, I looked out across the floor of the caldera and saw that it stretched to the horizon; I could not see the opposite wall of the volcano. I stopped the ship and we floated directly above that sheer wall of rock.

Tesla pivoted the tracking machine downward. A moment passed and then—the bulb atop the tin box flashed—the electric bloodhound had found its scent!

"There!" Tesla said. "The crystal is down there! Not more than two miles below!"

Tesla removed the tracking machine from its pedestal and slid the little tin box into a pocket on the leg of his pressure suit.

"I'm going down into the Martian city," Tesla said.

"I'm going with you," Ade said.

"Are you sure you want to come with me?" Tesla asked.

"If the two of us go," Ade said, "we'll have twice the chance of all of us coming out of this alive."

"Some might argue with your statistics," Tesla said, "but not I. Do you know how to handle a gun?"

"I have a passing acquaintance with a Chicago Palm Protector," Ade answered.

"Ah," Tesla said, "the voice of experience. Try this."

Tesla drew a strange looking gun from a holster attached to his pressure suit and held the weapon out to Ade who took it and held it in his hand.

"Where do the bullets go?" Ade asked.

"It doesn't use bullets," Tesla said. "It fires electric rays."

"Does it have a battery in it?" Ade asked.

"No," Tesla said, "its power is received wirelessly from the airship's engine. You won't be running out of bullets with this electric ray gun. You keep it. I'll get another one."

"I'm going with you, too," Lillie said, stepping forward.

"Oh, no you're not!" Ade snapped.

"It's not for you to say, George," Lillie said.

"Like hell," Ade said.

"George," Lillie said, "you know I'm a crack shot."

"Oh," Ade said, "you're a regular Annie Oakley—shooting at clay targets. The targets down there are going to be shooting back."

"Mr. Tesla!" Lillie protested.

"Miss West!" Tesla said. "I have only one question: Are you prepared to die?"

"And to live," Lillie replied.

Tesla smiled faintly.

"Then follow me," Tesla said, "and I will introduce you to the operation of an anti-gravity pressure suit."

"What about me?" Houdini asked.

"What about you, Erich?" Tesla asked.

"I want to go, too," Houdini said.

Tesla shook his head, "No, Ehrich. You stay here."

Houdini stepped up to Tesla and looked all the way up at him. "I'm going, Mr. Tesla," Houdini said. "You need me. You need all of us. I ain't a kid no more. I ain't a kid, Mr. Tesla!"

"And if you get killed," Tesla asked, "what am I to tell your mother?"

"That I died for my country," Houdini said. "That's what you'll tell her. That I died for my country. She wouldn't have it any other way."

"I see," Tesla said. "Very well. Very well, Erich. Come with me. All three of you, come with me to the lower deck."

Tesla and the others started out of the pilothouse.

I said, "Now, Tesla, wait a minute."

Tesla turned about, stepped up to me, and said, "If we do not contact you by wireless telephone in two hours, head straight for Earth and report to President Cleveland. Mr. Czito will give you the bearings."

"Damn it, Tesla!" I said. "You better be *back* in two hours!"

Tesla looked at me, then said quietly, "Take care, Mark," and he extended his hand.

I looked at Tesla's hand, then back up at his face, and said, "I always mind my p's and q's," and I shook Tesla's hand.

Then Tesla, George Ade, Lillie West, and Houdini all turned and went down the pilothouse stairs. I looked over at Czito who looked back at me uneasily, and then he followed the others out.

Down on the lower deck Tesla explained to Lillie and Houdini how to don the air pressure suits.

Tesla said, "Step into the trousers and the attached boots, pull the suit up, slip your arms into the sleeves and then into the gloves attached to the sleeves, pull this little tab up in front, and then pull these two tabs together at the neck ring. This will close the suit up with an airtight seal."

Lillie went to the crew's quarters to change into her pressure suit. Houdini removed his coat, vest, shoes, trousers, collar, tie, and shirt, and handed each of these in succession to Czito. At last the boy stood there with nothing on but a red flannel undershirt, a pair of red flannel drawers, and black cotton socks.

"Don't wrinkle the fabric," Houdini said.

"Don't wrinkle the—" Czito said indignantly. "There isn't an inch on this suit without a wrinkle on it!"

"Those ain't wrinkles," Houdini said, "they're contours. That suit is just broke in good."

Czito shook his head and took Houdini's clothes away. Houdini held out his air pressure suit and stepped into its legs.

"This thing is too big for me," Houdini said.

"It will have to do," Tesla said, "and it will fill out a bit when it is pressurized. Mr. Czito, help Erich with his air tank and gravity generator."

"It's Houdini now, Mr. Tesla. My name is Houdini."

"All right," Tesla said, "Houdini. Mr. Czito, help Houdini with the machinery in his knapsack."

Czito came forward with a knapsack containing an air tank and a gravity generator, and strapped it on to Houdini's back.

Lillie came out of the crew's quarters dressed in her air pressure suit.

"Very good," Tesla said. "Turn around."

Lillie turned around and Tesla buckled a knapsack containing an air tank and a gravity generator on to her shoulders.

"Tighten the belt in front," Tesla said to Lillie.

Ade said to Houdini, "You put the helmet on this way," and Ade slipped his glass helmet over his head and twisted its base into the metal neck ring attached to his air pressure suit. There was an audible "click" as the helmet's edge slipped into a spring-loaded slot that provided a hermetic seal to the whole suit. Houdini slipped his own helmet over his head, twisted it into the neck ring on his suit, and "clicked" it into a locked hermetic seal.

"Now you," Tesla said to Lillie, and he raised her helmet in both his hands, brought it down over her head, and twisted and locked it into the neck ring of her suit.

"Now me," Tesla said, and he put on his own helmet, and then turned on the valve that let the air flow out from the compression tanks in his knapsack and into the interior of his suit. He went over to Lillie and turned on her air valve, and then did the same for Ade's and Houdini's. He then turned on another switch on the control panel attached to his belt.

"You should all be able to hear me," Tesla said, and Lillie, Ade, and Houdini heard Tesla's voice inside their helmets; it was a clear aural transmission just as if it had come over a telephone.

"Hey!" Houdini said, "How are you doing that? Where are the wires?"

"There are no wires," Tesla said. "You are hearing a wireless transmission of my voice through the ether as an electric wave. And I can hear each of you. This switch on your belt controls your wireless telephone. Mr. Czito can hear my voice outside the suit through a speaker at the base of my helmet. This switch opens a channel to the wireless telephone up in the pilothouse. And this switch," Tesla flipped a switch on his belt and he rose up off the floor of the deck and floated in the air, "this switch controls your anti-gravity unit. Turn it on now to the second position."

Lillie, Ade, and Houdini all flipped the anti-gravity switch on their belts, and they all simultaneously rose up an inch or two from the floor of the deck.

"Now," Tesla said, "turn the switch to the lowest position."

They all did so, and they all descended back down to the deck.

Tesla said, "Now your anti-gravity units are still functioning, but not enough to give you any lift. Keep them turned on like this at all times when you are not flying. The anti-gravity unit provides a field of force around your body which will act as a shield which will tend to deflect any rapidly moving incoming projectiles. Such projectiles create an etheric bow-shock as they approach the artificial gravity field, and it is this bow-shock which becomes a field of force."

"Will this force deflect bullets?" Ade asked.

"It should," Tesla said. "But I must admit that I have never tested the system for shielding against bullets. It should also shield against electric rays up to five hundred thousand volts in power."

"And above that power?" Ade asked.

"Above that power," Tesla said, "a ray will break through the field, and, depending on its magnitude, it could do anything from giving you a mild shock, to burning out the coils in your anti-gravity unit—to killing you. Do not assume your force field will protect you under any circumstances. If you are fired upon, take cover wherever you can. Is that understood?"

Lillie, Ade, and Houdini nodded their heads.

"Now," Tesla said, "as to flight control: it is very simple. This single switch here on your belt controls your vertical lift. It is the only switch for anti-gravity control. It has six settings: low, at which you are now set; nodal fixation, that is to say, flotation at whatever altitude you happen to be positioned; slow vertical lift, at a rate of about two feet per second; slow vertical descent also at about two feet a second; fast vertical lift at about twenty miles per hour; and rapid acceleration."

"What is the limit of acceleration?" Ade asked.

"There is no limit," Tesla said. "I would advise you to be careful with the rapid acceleration mode. We will be passing through lava tubes and caverns. If you are not careful, you could dash yourself against a wall of rock. At extremely high speeds your force field will protect you, bouncing you away from whatever obstacle you might hit, but at somewhat lower speeds you would be crushed."

"How do we move forward or side to side?" Houdini asked.

"Very simply," Tesla said. "You lean your head and shoulders in the direction you wish to move. This will tilt the anti-gravity field, and you will then be pushed in the direction in which you are leaning. This technique of control is so simple and efficient that you will instantly and intuitively feel your way with it as soon as you make your first level flight. While in flight, keep your left hand on your control switch at all times. And in your right hand—"

Tesla went to a cabinet in the bulkhead, opened it, and took out another electric ray gun.

"In your right hand," Tesla said, "will be your ray gun."

Tesla handed the ray gun to Lillie, brought out another ray gun and gave it to Houdini, and then took a third gun from the cabinet and slipped it into the holster attached to the right leg of his air pressure suit.

"Holster your guns for now," Tesla said. "And keep them holstered until you are ready to shoot. And when you shoot, shoot to kill. That means you will aim for the chest. Now: Are there any questions?"

Lillie, Ade, and Houdini stood looking at Tesla saying nothing.

"Very well," Tesla said. "We will each in succession exit the ship through the air lock. I will go first. Mr. Czito!"

Czito opened the door of the air lock and Tesla stepped through it. Czito closed the door. The others could still see Tesla's helmeted head through the door's porthole.

Tesla said, "I will be waiting for all of you outside. Remember, whatever you do, do not turn off your anti-gravity unit. I do not think any of you should be troubled by fear of heights. The feel of your anti-gravity field will dispel all vertigo. Remember! You all know how to fly! You have done it countless times before—in your dreams!"

Tesla nodded, and Czito closed a red-handled switch. There was a sound of rushing air inside the chamber where Tesla stood, followed by silence. Then Tesla moved away from the porthole and could no longer be seen. A moment later the bulkhead of the ship vibrated with a single metallic "clang!" Czito closed another switch. There was a sound of air rushing back into the air lock chamber. Czito waited a moment, and then opened the chamber's door. He turned about, holding the door, and Lillie stepped forward and into the chamber.

"Good luck, Miss West," Czito said, and he closed the chamber's door. Again, Czito closed the red-handled switch and the air rushed out of the chamber.

"Push the door handle all the way down," everyone heard Tesla say in their helmets.

Lillie pushed the door handle down, and then was able to push the outside door of the airship open, revealing a vista of red desert, streaks of white clouds in a pale blue sky, and Nikola Tesla floating mid-air in his helmeted anti-gravity pressure suit.

"Do you have your anti-gravity switch turned on to the second position?" Tesla asked over his wireless telephone.

"Yes," Lillie gasped, "I do."

"Then lean forward, Miss West," Tesla said, "lean forward and you will be pushed out of the airship by your anti-gravity field."

Lillie bowed her head and curled her shoulders forward. She suddenly felt herself falling, not downward, but sideways out of the airship! She went through the open door. As she passed the door, it swung shut behind her on an automatic spring and closed with a faint, dull snap. Inside the ship, this snap reverberated as a loud "clang!"

"That's it," Tesla said. "Fall toward me here."

Lillie moved toward Tesla.

"Now straighten up," Tesla said. "Straight up."

Lillie raised her chin and pushed her shoulders back. Her motion was arrested and she stopped three feet in front of Tesla, floating in place.

"We're standing upon something," Lillie said. "It feels exactly like we're standing upon a floor!"

"And we are," Tesla said, "we are standing upon a gravitational node. Even under ordinary conditions on the surface of a planet, one always stands upon a gravitational node. Only now in our atomically energized state, we can stand upon a much higher, denser node than usual."

Lillie glanced downward. She could see the distant sands of a desert below, as if she stood upon a mountain top thousands of feet high, but now there was nothing below her feet. Out to the west, she could see the blackish-gray plain of the volcano's floor stretching away to the horizon. To the north, she could glimpse a vertical wall of rock reaching from the rough, sandy highlands to the black floor of the volcano thousands of feet below.

The door of the airship opened again. Houdini stood inside the airlock chamber looking out at Lillie and Tesla.

"Do you have your anti-gravity switch in the second position?" Tesla asked Houdini.

"Yes," Houdini said, breathing heavily, "second position."

"Then bend forward," Tesla said, "bend forward and come out."

Houdini bent forward and shot out of the airship like a bullet, the door slamming shut behind him.

"Hey!" Houdini shouted as he shot by Lillie and Tesla, and kept going.

"He's going into a tumble!" Tesla said, and he flew off after Houdini, grabbed him by the arm, and the two of them spun around in space.

"Get your orientation!" Tesla said. "Head up! Head up!"

Houdini bent upwards and came to a stop.

"That's it," Tesla said. "Head up. Your head and your shoulders are your rudders. Now, carefully and slowly move over toward Miss West."

Houdini twisted his shoulders and felt a falling sensation as he moved toward Lillie. As he approached her, he raised his chin, and he came to a stop.

"Hey!" Houdini said, "This is easy!"

"Yes," Tesla said, "in a few moments you will be able to feel your way. Just keep your switch on position two for the moment."

Now George Ade emerged from the airship. He came all the way out and the door of the airlock sprang shut behind him.

Tesla removed the tin box from the pocket of his air pressure suit, drew out its steel rod, and flipped the switch on the front of the box. He pointed the steel rod downward and the light bulb on top of the box flashed. Two seconds passed and the light flashed again.

"We have a signal," Tesla said. "We will descend to the wall of the caldera below. Follow me. And be prepared for anything. Carefully turn your anti-gravity switches to the fifth position—slow descent."

Tesla flipped his switch and began to slowly drop away from the other three floating aeronauts. Lillie followed Tesla downward, then Houdini, and then George Ade came along following the others.

Czito came up through the hatch to the upper deck and ascended the stairs of the pilothouse.

"They're on their way," he said.

We went over to the windows and looked down. A hundred or so feet below us we could see the four of them descending toward the edge of the crater wall, four little white figures, flying away like four white birds.

"Miss West has a lot of pluck," Czito asked, "hasn't she?"

"Why," I replied, "I'd say she's all pluck."

Lillie, Houdini, and Ade followed Tesla in his descent toward the volcano's wall. As they came within a few hundred feet of the top edge of the crater, a pathway half-buried in sand came into their view. Tesla descended toward it and waved for the others to follow him on down.

As they continued in their descent, it became apparent that the pathway below them was a broad avenue some one hundred-fifty or two hundred feet wide. Most of it had been completely buried in sand and rock, but, at intervals, enough of it was exposed to give an impression of what it had once been: a road leading to the edge of the crater coming from who knew where way out there on the surface of the planet.

They were within a hundred feet of the roadbed now, and could see that it was made of individual paving stones, each stone measuring about twenty-five feet across and cut at odd angles so that all the stones interlocked each other like pieces of a gigantic jigsaw puzzle. The road went to the edge of the crater. They flew toward the crater's edge and then passed over it and out over the sheer vertical drop of the caldera's wall going down thousands of feet to the floor of the volcano. A flight of stone steps cut into the wall of rock led down from the crater's edge to a platform built into the rock two thousand feet below.

They followed the stone steps down to the platform, flying down beside the wall of rock as stone landing upon stone landing of the massive staircase whizzed by them. They reached the platform and found that it was a balcony of stone and in front of it was a single door also made of stone and set into the volcanic wall of the crater.

Tesla went down and landed feet first on the stone platform, and the others came behind him and slowly landed in the same way.

"Put your flight control switch in the first position," Tesla said.

They approached the stone door. It appeared to be a single, massive stone some thirty feet high by about twenty feet wide. Inscriptions were carved upon the door in an unknown language. Thousands of years of wind-blown sand had nearly eroded these carvings into a smooth surface. Tesla studied the inscriptions for a moment, and then said:

"It is a memorial to the dead—and a warning to the living—to us."

Tesla approached the seam where the edge of the stone door fitted into its stone casing set into the volcanic rock. The seam was so precise a knife blade could not be inserted into it.

"Now how are we going to get that opened?" George Ade asked.

"That," Houdini said, "is going to take some doing."

"Indeed it is," Tesla said. "Look up there, and down here."

Tesla pointed to two recesses cut into the top of the door and two others cut exactly the same way about four feet up from the door's bottom edge.

"What are those?" Ade asked.

"Drawer handles," Lillie said. "They're drawer handles!"

"Couldn't be," Ade said. "Not on a thing that size."

"I think Miss West is correct," Tesla said.

"Sure," Houdini said. "I can see it. Those slots are designed for pulling that rock straight out. But we'd need a crane to pull it."

"Perhaps not," Tesla said, and he took hold of the bottom slot with his gloved hands. "Yes," he said, "these slots were designed as handles for human hands."

"How could a human being move a thing that size?" Ade asked.

"I will show you," Tesla said, and he turned on his anti-gravity machine and flew up to one of the top slots in the door.

"Mr. Ade," Tesla said, "come up here to the other slot. Miss West, you take the slot below me. Houdini, you take the slot below Mr. Ade."

They all followed Tesla's instructions: George Ade flew up to the slot next to Tesla; Lillie and Houdini reached out and slipped their hands into the slots on the stone door in front of them.

"Now," Tesla said, "with your left hand on your anti-gravity switch and your right hand grasping the slotted handle, turn your anti-gravity switch to the fourth position and lean back away from the door as you do so."

They all followed Tesla's instructions and they all felt a force tugging them away from the door, but nothing else.

"Keep your right hand firmly grasping the slot," Tesla said. "Don't lose your grip. Now turn your anti-gravity switch to the sixth position—and hang on."

Once again they all did as Tesla instructed, and once again they felt a slight tugging force, but still nothing else.

"I don't think this is going to work," Ade said.

"Just a moment, Mr. Ade," Tesla said. "Hold your position and watch."

Several more seconds passed and then—

"Hey!" Houdini said, "We're moving! The door's moving!"

"Hold your position, all of you," Tesla said. "Our combined anti-gravity fields have permeated the stone door and now its mass is equivalent to ours. We will carefully draw the door all the way out as far as we can. I believe it is fitted on a sliding track."

The four aeronauts held tight to the stone door as it slid straight out from the wall of rock. The door came out of the rock like a gigantic filing cabinet. As it slid out, another door opening was revealed on the side of the massive block of stone.

"Stop," Tesla said. "Turn your flight switch back to the first position."

Tesla descended and Ade followed him down. They all looked at this second, smaller door on the side of the larger block of stone. The smaller door was recessed into the stone and affixed to it was a kind of wheel also made of stone.

"Mr. Ade," Tesla said, "help me turn the wheel."

The two of them grasped the stone wheel and tugged at it. The wheel gave way and began to slowly turn. Tesla and Ade had got the wheel to turn about a half revolution when the door to which it was attached slid open, revealing a dark interior.

Tesla drew his electric ray gun from his holster, turned on the electric torch mounted atop his helmet, and went through the opening in the stone. From inside the stone block, Tesla said:

"The rest of you come on in."

Lillie, Houdini, and Ade went through the opening in the stone. Inside, all four of them stood in a small stone chamber, its walls, ceilings, and floor perfectly cut and polished. They all turned on the electric torches mounted atop their helmets. There was nothing in the chamber but a single stone lever protruding from a slot in the wall.

Tesla slid the door of the chamber back to its closed position, and then turned a second wheel which was mounted on the door's interior surface.

"We are in an air lock chamber," Tesla said, "and this lever will either open the way to the interior for us or kill us all where we stand. Shall I pull it?"

"Pull it," Lillie said.

"Pull it," Houdini said.

"Go ahead," Ade said. "Pull it."

Tesla took hold of the stone lever and pulled it all the way down along its slot in the wall. When the lever reached the end of the slot, a sliding, grinding sound began, and the floor of the chamber began to vibrate.

"What's happening?" Houdini asked.

"I think the entire stone is automatically retracting back into the wall of the volcano," Tesla said.

The grinding and vibrating ceased and was immediately followed by the sound of rushing air. Then another door, which no one had noticed up until then, slid open. Beyond this door was a black void.

"Draw your guns and follow me," Tesla said, and he drew his own gun and went through the open door, the electric torch on his helmet lighting his way ahead.

Lillie, Ade, and Houdini followed Tesla through the door which led into a long tunnel cut into the volcanic rock. They all walked along, their electric torches on their helmets lighting the stone passage with the white glare of electric light. The shadows on the rough cut stone walls drew toward them as they moved along the passageway. The floor of the tunnel was smooth, but covered with a thick layer of fine powdered dust. They continued down the tunnel for several hundred feet and then came out into a large room cut into the rock; it was about one hundred feet high, fifty feet wide and seventy-five or one hundred feet long. In the center of the room stood a fifty foot tall stone statue of a woman seated in a cross-legged position. She was wearing an elaborate headdress and had three faces and six arms. One face looked to the right, another to the left, and the third straight ahead. The statue's six arms were poised in various positions, the hands shaped into gestures suggesting some kind of sign language.

"Get a load of her," Houdini said. "She can't decide what to do."

They circled about the statue and came to a fork in the tunnel. Tesla pointed the tracking machine's steel rod ahead and the light bulb on the top of the tin box flashed rapidly in the direction of the tunnel on the left.

"This way," Tesla said, going forward and into the left tunnel.

Now they moved along this other long tunnel which was also cut into the stone. This tunnel twisted and turned. After going about a hundred feet, they came upon three more forking tunnels and they all realized they were in the midst of a labyrinth.

"We follow the signal," Tesla said, and he continued forward, taking the tunnel going off to the left.

They kept walking down this tunnel for about a hundred yards, and then it opened out to a large lava tube with an underground stream. The beam of Tesla's electric torch swept the streambed and something moved in it; a white shape broke the water's surface and a pair of wicked yellow eyes shined back up at them.

"It's a crocodile," Tesla said, "a white crocodile."

The beast opened its jaws and showed a pale pink tongue and a line of needle sharp teeth.

"Looks hungry," Houdini said.

"Flight switches in the second position," Tesla said, floating out over the stream.

The other three aeronauts followed Tesla in mid-air.

"No dinner today," Houdini said, passing over the jaws of the crocodile, the beast's white snout snapping shut.

They all landed on the opposite side of the stream and went into yet another tunnel. This tunnel began leading downwards at an angle, and then, after only a few feet, abruptly turned left. The tunnel narrowed, and then opened up into another, larger chamber of rock.

The beam of Tesla's electric torch fell upon a big heap of brown fur. The heap rose up to a height of seven feet and turned around; it was a bear-like animal, perhaps some kind of sloth. It had a tiny head, glittering black eyes, a long snout, a thick neck corded with muscle, and powerful forepaws with long, sharp claws.

The animal let out a high-pitched scream and charged forward. Tesla fired upon the beast with his electric ray gun and the beast's forward motion was instantly arrested as it was enveloped in a blaze of fire and lightning bolts. The beast dropped to the floor, quivered for a moment, and then lay still as smoke rose in a thin column from its blackened fur.

Tesla slowly approached the dead animal and looked about the cavern.

"Keep your ray guns drawn," he said. "We are in a wilderness."

Beyond the beast, the cavern opened up further, and, as they proceeded on into it, the beam of their electric torches only dimly reached the opposite wall of rock. Above them, from the ceiling of the cavern, hung a great number of stalactites, glittering like chandeliers in the beams of their electric torches. In front of them, stalagmites rose up from the floor of the cavern like the columns of a gothic cathedral. Beyond the columns lay an underground lake. Along the edge of the lake they saw large white rats skittering away from the beams of their electric torches. They all walked along the edge of the lake and saw finger-sized fish swimming in thick schools and leaping up above the surface of the water. A creature that looked like some kind of crab crawled along the rocky edge of the lake.

They continued on along the shore. Looking down, they noticed that the sandy surface over which they walked had given way to a floor of paving stones set in a tessellated pattern of black and gray rock. The paving stones led up to a wall of rock and another door with a wheel.

Tesla took hold of the wheel and tried to turn it.

"Mr. Ade," Tesla said, and Ade came up beside Tesla and tried to help him turn the wheel.

"It won't budge," Ade said.

Tesla and Ade stepped back and looked at the door.

"If only we didn't have to wear these clumsy gloves," Ade said.

"Mr. Tesla," Houdini said, "let me try it."

"All right," Tesla said, waving Houdini toward the door. "Have a go."

Houdini approached the door and grasped the wheel with both of his hands. He stood there for a moment and did not seem to be making any progress.

"That's enough," Tesla said.

Houdini didn't budge. Then slowly, the wheel moved a fraction of an inch—then another fraction.

"He's turning it," Ade said.

The wheel in Houdini's hands slowly began turning an inch at a time, then, suddenly, Houdini yanked it all the way around in a single motion, and the door slid back, and a gust of air came through it, blowing dust and sand all around them.

"Very good," Tesla said, "very good—Houdini."

Tesla stepped through the open door.

The others followed Tesla through the door: Houdini, Lillie, and Ade who slid the door closed behind them. They had come out upon a stone platform with a low wall; it was a sort of balcony, and as they looked down over this balcony they saw before them a cavern of gigantic proportions—and 'gigantic' can hardly convey the scale of that place. The floor of the cavern lay below them by perhaps as much as a mile! It was as if they stood on the ledge of a mountaintop and looked down upon a valley thousands of feet below, a valley slumbering in the night and dimly lit by moon glow. But there was no moon here. Rather, it seemed that some of the upper walls of this underground world were encrusted with what appeared to be a kind of phosphorescent rock. Or perhaps the Martians had devised some way to electrify portions of the cavern walls to render them incandescent. Whatever the method, cause, or mechanism, this whole vast Plutonia glowed with a faint, blue light, and, far below on the cavern floor, points of lights blazed up in patterns of rectangles and circles which suggested the blocks and streets of a city!

Crossing level upon level thousands of feet above the city, numerous bridges spanned a space that was nearly a mile wide in places, connecting the distant walls of the cavern to those near at hand. And far below the bridges, rising up from the floor of the cavern city was a slender tower; it was perhaps a thousand feet high and its summit was crowned by a dome. Atop the dome was a pinnacle tower, and surmounting the pinnacle tower was set yet another, smaller dome. Coming out of and leading away from this smaller, uppermost dome were four bridges, each of the bridges leading off in a cardinal direction toward the cavern's walls.

Tesla held out the tracking machine and slowly swept its steel rod across his view of the underground city. When the tip of the steel rod pointed directly at the domed tower, the tracking machine's light bulb increased the tempo of its flashes.

"Follow me," Tesla said.

Tesla flipped the anti-gravity switch on his belt and rose up over the wall and out into the space of the giant cavern. Lillie, Ade, and Houdini each rose up into the air and followed Tesla in his flight.

Tesla flew down toward the domed tower, and the others followed behind. As they descended, they passed over several foot bridges, but saw no one. They reached one of the four foot bridges leading to the tower. Tesla descended to the surface of the bridge and landed on it feet first. Lillie landed beside him, then Houdini, and then Ade.

Tesla held up the tracking machine and pointed its steel rod at the tower's door that lay straight ahead of them about a hundred yards away. The light bulb on the tracking machine flickered rapidly. Tesla turned the tracking machine off, retracted its steel rod, and slid the little tin box into a pocket on the leg of his air pressure suit.

"Keep your guns aimed straight ahead," Tesla said.

"No guards. No one in sight. They appear to be expecting us and laying a trap."

Tesla began walking with his gun aimed ahead at the closed door. Lillie, Houdini, and Ade walked behind him with their guns drawn.

When they got within one hundred feet of the door to the domed tower, the door slid open, and from inside the tower a flashing rainbow of light flooded out toward them. Tesla did not break his stride, but kept moving toward the door. He reached the door and went through it, and the other aeronauts came in behind him. Tesla stopped inside the threshold of the door and looked up.

"My crystal," Tesla said.

In front of them was a circular room with an upper, circular balcony and domed ceiling. In the center of the room was a round three foot high metallic platform. At the center of the platform was a pedestal about five feet in height. Mounted atop the pedestal was Tesla's crystal—the "Master Crystal"—flashing out brilliant rays of light in a rainbow of colors. The light played upon the walls and upon the domed ceiling, pulsing, shifting—yellow, red, purple, green. . . .

"What are you waiting for?" Ade asked Tesla. "Take it!"

"And be electrocuted?" Tesla asked. "Look at the platform. Do you see the glow? It's surging with thousands of volts of electricity, with probably very high amperage. We have to find a way to cut its power source."

"That will not be necessary, Mr. Tesla."

The voice that spoke those words was deep and resonating with an accent of Yankee America mixed with a sound that was foreign even to Tesla's ears.

Tesla turned about and looked up to the balcony railing. A large man stood there looking down with a faint smile of amusement on his lips. The man was completely bald, his skin was pale, almost white, and his eyes—his eyes were as pink as a rabbit's. He wore a simple long white robe and therefore looked like a marble statue of a Roman emperor, except that this was a statue that moved and breathed. The man stood leaning on the railing, looking directly at Tesla as if Tesla were the only person in the room, and Tesla looked back up at the man and did not glance away from him for even a second.

"Have we met before?" Tesla asked.

"Let's say we haven't been formally introduced," the man said, and he began to walk the circuit of the upper balcony.

"You speak English very well," Tesla said.

"So do you," the man said. "You come from Croatia originally, don't you?"

"You know a great deal about me."

"No, I know everything about you."

"This interest you have in me—should I be flattered?"

"Oh, definitely," the man said, stopping and looking down again. "Of all the people of your world, I have found you the most worthy of my interest."

Houdini stepped forward with his electric ray gun aimed upward.

The man at the balcony smiled, and said to Tesla, "Please ask your associates to lower their weapons. They are unnecessary. I have no intention of harming anyone."

Tesla motioned for Houdini and the others to holster their guns, and Tesla holstered his as well.

"So much better," the man said. "So much more civilized."

The man on the balcony had circled around to an elevator platform. He stepped upon it and descended to the lower level.

Stepping forward off the platform, the man said, "Allow me to introduce myself. I am Kel, High Priest and King of *Khahera*—this planet which you know by the name of Mars. Come. Come with me and I will show you my world—the world of *Khahera*."

Kel turned and strolled through one of the four doors leading out of the domed tower. Tesla turned to the others, nodded slightly, and then turned and followed Kel. Lillie, Ade, and Houdini looked at each other, and then followed behind Tesla.

They all came out upon one of the bridges spanning the gigantic cavern. The bridge stretched five hundred feet ahead of them and terminated under a great arch of stone set into the cavern wall. Tesla looked at the railing of the bridge as they walked along and Kel took notice.

"The metal fascinates you," Kel said. "These bridges and this tower—all were built thousands of years ago. The formula for their metal has been lost and our greatest sages have been unable to analyze or duplicate it. But then, that should not be surprising."

"You have been watching Earth a long time," Tesla said.

"For centuries, Mr. Tesla, for centuries. Our royal astronomers have long been fascinated with your blue world, and of the sea of space beyond with its suns and planets. Only we royals knew of the existence of *Erta*, our name for your planet Earth. Most of the people of *Khahera* believe the universe is solid rock extending into infinite space, and they the only inhabitants at the universe's center. The great royal plan has long been to return to Earth and conquer it. For centuries the plan was only a dream. But like the development on your world, we here on *Khahera* have slowly rediscovered the old knowledge. One hundred years ago our people came upon a sealed chamber filled with ancient writings. Our greatest sages could not understand much of what they had found. But they understood enough to begin a great work. It was the building of a ship propelled by a thunderous fire, a ship that could carry a man out of our universe of infinite rock to a universe of infinite space—and floating in that infinite space a blue world rich in water and air."

"You lived secretly among us," Tesla said, "watching us, walking among us—"

"Studying your languages, your ways. Every two years as *Khahera* swung close to *Erta*, we would send out an expedition of eight men. The first expedition descended from the main ship to *Erta* in a special winged rocket craft and landed on a desert plain in the western regions of your North American continent. The men of that expedition secreted their craft in a remote canyon on the edge of that desert plain and set out on a march of several days until they reached a small settlement. There they presented themselves as men from a foreign land who had been lost in the desert. Soon they learned the rudiments of your English language, acquired some of your money, and moved on to larger towns and cities, always observing, always learning, always remembering. They reached San Francisco, traveled by train to New York, and then by ship to London. A few months later they returned to the western desert of North America and departed in their ship. Some seven months later they reached *Khahera* in their main ship. This first expedition was carried out in your year of 1876, and it set the pattern for all expeditions that followed. In the last ten years I have been on two such expeditions. You are surprised?"

"I would think," Tesla said, "that a king could not afford to leave his kingdom unattended."

"Ah," Kel said, "a weak king cannot afford to turn his back for a moment. A true king has no back. A true king does not delegate his vision; he sees all for himself, and thus is never deceived. And I saw all that was worth seeing of your world, but I was most interested in the city of New York and spent most of my time there. It was there one day at the New York Stock Exchange that I first heard the name of Tesla. And I heard of the work of Tesla. And I knew it was Tesla whom I would most fully come to know."

"Your airship is not a rocket," Tesla said.

"No," Kel said, "it is not a rocket."

"It was built from my designs," Tesla said.

"Of course," Kel said, "my airship was made from your designs down to every vacuum tube, magnifying coil, and spark gap. My spies followed your every move, your every thought, and as your workers built in your secret New Jersey laboratory, my workers built in mine only ten miles away. For every stroke of the rivet gun, for every turn of the screw made by your workers, my workers would follow with a stroke of the rivet gun, a turn of the screw of their own. And as your airship became assembled and completed and real, so also did my airship, in turn, become assembled and reach its completion, its reality. But when my spies began following your purchases of materials they found something most interesting. The same metals and minerals you were acquiring were also to be found in ancient documents here on *Khahera*—documents relating to the making of a crystal of infinite power. Our sages could never understand these documents, but now, with our spies studying your methods, we realized that you had rediscovered the secret of making the Great Crystal of Power, the long-lost ancient wonder which even our wisest sages believed to be only a myth. The Great Crystal. It changes everything, doesn't it?"

"And how is that?" Tesla asked.

"Its power, Mr. Tesla, its power. The crystal *is* power. Infinite power. The power of the gods."

"The power that destroyed both our worlds."

"The ancient ones? They were not equal to the power. That was why it destroyed them. But you and I, Mr. Tesla—we do not fear the power. If you had feared the power you would not have come here. You would not have created the crystal."

"I created the crystal for mankind. To free the human race from the slavery of physical toil."

"Slavery of physical toil? Now, do not disappointment me. Please do not disappointment me with such naïve statements, Mr. Tesla. The masses are capable of nothing but the slavery of physical toil. Come. Let me show you something. Come. Bring your associates with you."

Kel led them through the stone arch set into the wall of volcanic rock and through a tunnel that extended about one hundred feet and opened out into another region of the cavern. Ahead, another bridge extended out over the cavern to another wall of rock about two hundred feet distant. Kel led them all out on to this bridge and stopped and waved his hand over the yawning gulf below. The others stopped and looked down.

A hundred feet below, a bridge spanned from one outcropping of the cavern to another about a hundred yards away. A great crowd of people walked slowly over the bridge, each carrying a lighted object, a lamp of some kind, or perhaps a candle.

"The people of *Khahera*," Kel said.

"Where are they going?" Lillie asked.

"Nowhere," Kel said.

"What are they doing?" Ade asked.

"The perambulation," Kel said, "The Walk of Rememberance."

"What is it?" Lillie asked.

"A religious ritual," Kel said, "performed three times a day. It reenacts the destruction of *Khahera* thousands of years ago and the great surface evacuation that was made when only a select few were permitted to flee here below to escape the horrors above—slow death by starvation and freezing—then quick death by fire and suffocation in the vacuum. The people today do not understand the meaning of the story. They do not know the meanings of such things as 'planet,' 'asteroids,' and 'space.' They know only that the world was convulsed and the good were sent below here to the center of the universe and the bad were left far above in the rock somewhere to die—to die in the wilderness of rock above our heads where no one but our high priests dare go today. And so they walk and walk and walk. The perambulation. Mr. Tesla, do you know why our priests invented this silly, pointless, disgustingly stupid ritual? Do you know why? Can you guess? It was to give these idiots something to do! Something to do! Some physical toil! Come with me!"

Kel led them across the bridge to the opposite wall of rock and through another tunnel that curved to the right and emerged upon a balcony overlooking another section of the vast cavern. There they all stopped and looked down. They gazed down upon monstrously large steam engines, their pistons slowly moving back and forth.

"Ancient steam engines," Kel said, "running on natural volcanic heat, running virtually without stop for thousands of years, with almost no repairs—

ancient machines, providing all our food, all our clothing, all our necessities, year in, year out, generation upon generation without end. And during all those hundreds of generations, no one understood how the machines operated and no one cared to know."

Kel turned away and walked back in the direction they had come. Tesla walked beside Kel now, with Lillie, Ade, and Houdini following behind.

Kel said, "The people of *Khahera* were content to graze upon the products of the machines, graze like cows. But they were a growing population, spreading through all the tunnels girdling the planet, and, in sum, they were an almost useless population. So the kings of *Khahera* contrived periodic civil wars to reduce the population, and, through conflict and synthesis, reinforce the remaining populace's obedience to their king, and, with empty ritual and make-work and religious slogans extolling the virtue of labor as an end in itself, rob the people of the hours and days of their lives, dulling their minds into a raw material which could then be shaped according to the king's will. Now, according to my will."

Kel turned to Tesla. They had stopped on a bridge spanning the cavern. The Martian King's pink eyes glowed with a fire that Tesla had seen before in the eyes of the richest men on Earth.

"Are the people of your world any different?" Kel asked. "Oh, yes, I know. I have read your John Locke and your Federalist Papers. I have studied your adopted American Constitution and your so-called Declaration of Independence. I have seen your sham 'democracy,' your sham 'people's elections' made with bought votes and bought counters of votes. I have seen your elected officials, mere puppets of the world's real rulers who are unelected and unknown to the masses who they rule. Yes, I have seen your supposed democratic government and I have laughed. And I have studied the usury of your money system and your supposedly free economic competition carried out with secret threats and lies and murders. I have seen half your planet slumbering in the smoke of opium and the other half bowing before the whip, the club, and the gun. I have seen your labor strikes and their settlements with the laborers still enslaved, still bowed down before their masters. Should this astonish? The last thing the laboring masses of your world desire is to set down the burdens of their labor. You can see their devotion to their slavery in their hostility to the machine—the machine which will labor for them and thus make their very existence superfluous to their masters—the machine which will transform the useful laborer into the useless eater. Instinctively the masses of your world sense that their rulers intend to replace them with the machine, and, that when the machine age dawns upon your world in full, their rulers will dispense with them because they, the idle masses, will have become a useless excess population which can no longer serve or amuse their masters. I ask you, Mr. Tesla, are the people of your world any different than the people of mine? Do they not spend their lives in meaningless, empty, toil—in mindless, repetitive actions? In their own perambulations? Slavery? Slavery is all of which they are capable. Slavery is their desire. Slavery is their destiny. Slavery is their salvation. And you, Mr. Tesla, you would free them. Free them to do *what?*"

"To live," Tesla said. "To live as they have never imagined. Never dreamed."

"Of course they've never dreamed!" Kel roared. "And they never will! Dreams and imaginings are for men such as you and me."

"You have dreamed?" Tesla asked. "You have imagined? No. You have imitated. You have stolen, like every mediocrity that has ever existed."

"I?" Kel asked, "A mediocrity?"

"Mediocrity is not stupidity, it is malice. Mediocrity is not ignorance, it is tyranny—the lust to rule the will of another."

"Platitudes!" Kel shouted, "Swill! Flattery for the masses! Words fit only for the ears of cattle being led to the slaughter!"

"No, they are the epitaph of a tyrant. It is not that the people cannot be free, but that the tyrant does not want people to be free. It is not that the people are 'useless,' but that they do not exist for the purpose of being used at all. It is not that resources upon which human life depends are scarce, but that the tyrants stand at the door of the infinite flow of energy which permeates the universe and say to the laboring masses: 'This fountain of life is not yours, but ours, and we will parcel it out to you according to the degree of your obedience to our will.' No, you tyrants do not want people to be free, for in a free world, you would have nothing upon which to feed. The malice in your soul would turn in upon itself and eat you to death."

"Ah! Ah, ha, ha!" Kel laughed. "The electrician attempts psychology, normative philosophy, and teleological criticisms while lacking any comprehension of high policy and royal consciousness! The great minds know that civilization itself is tyranny. The whole universe is ordered upon the principle of predation. It is nothing less than a pyramid of power. At its apex—the masters—at its base—the slaves—in between—the fools who believe us when we tell them they are free."

Tesla said, "A pyramid with power flowing only to the apex cannot stand. The universe is a circuit of power. The power flows to all parts, great and small; yet the greatest is only a finite part. Whenever any part attempts to draw to itself infinite power, it will exceed its capacity and be destroyed. Such is the destiny of all tyrants: destruction—by the very power at which they grasp."

"You are a disappointment," Kel said. "I had hoped that you could be of use to me, and so I have indulged in this little chat. But now I see you are nothing but a silly fool. An electrician. A mechanic. A slave. You have no concept of policy. You cannot grasp the genius of pure will."

"Yes," Tesla said, "pure will. That's what it always comes down to with tyrants. As I knew it would with you. That is why I have this."

Tesla suddenly drew his electric ray gun and aimed it at Kel.

"Of course," Kel said, "You prove my point. It always comes down to pure will. It is the universal principle. The beginning of all things—and the end."

"Put up your hands," Tesla said.

Kel did not move.

"Shoot me, Mr. Tesla?" Kel asked. "Think again. Look up there."

Kel had nodded upwards to the wall of rock rising up in the distance behind Tesla.

"See what he's talking about," Tesla said to Ade, and Ade turned about slowly and looked up.

"Two men above us with some kind of weapons," Ade said.

"My royal guards," Kel said. "They are deadly shots."

"So am I," Tesla said, and he, Lillie, Ade, and Houdini began backing away from Kel.

"Please, Mr. Tesla," Kel said, smiling, "don't make me kill you."

Tesla spun about on his heel and fired his electric ray gun at one of the guards peering out over a balcony ledge on the wall of rock. The electric ray of Tesla's gun struck the guard in a blaze of fire and lightning bolts. The guard screamed and toppled from the balcony and down out of sight into the dark space of the cavern below.

Instantly, other guards appeared from balconies and openings in the distant cavern walls; they all took aim at the aeronauts and fired. Both bullets and rays of electricity exploded on the bridge. Tesla fired his ray gun at the cavern walls and ran back toward the domed tower. In an instant, the other aeronauts were running behind him, firing their ray guns at the guards peering out from the distant walls of rock.

Tesla reached the entrance of the domed tower and went through it. Ade came in behind him, then Lillie, and then Houdini who stopped at the door and fired back at a guard running toward them on the bridge. The ray of electricity from Houdini's gun struck the guard in an electrical explosion, and the guard was thrown back off his feet and landed on the ground, dead. Far at the other end of the bridge, Houdini could see Kel standing with his feet spread apart, and he seemed to be laughing.

Tesla glanced at the Master Crystal pulsing upon the pedestal attached to the electrified platform and knew he had no time to find the conduit of power and cut its circuit.

"We must draw all the guards away from here," Tesla said. "Make your way back to the cavern entrance."

"What are you going to do?" Ade asked.

"Lead them on a merry chase through the bowels of the planet," Tesla said. "Now go."

Lillie, Ade, and Houdini ran out the door that opened on to the bridge that led back to the way they had come from the cave entrance.

Tesla turned around and saw guards coming on the run from another bridge to his left. He turned and ran out the door on his right, and crossed the bridge that stretched ahead to a wall of rock.

As Lillie, Ade, and Houdini approached the end of the bridge upon which they ran, guards sprang out from the arched entrance to the wall of rock and fired upon them.

"Up!" Ade shouted to Lillie and Houdini, and the three of them rose up over the heads of the guards and flew away into the cavern as rays of electricity shot past them in their flight.

Tesla had made his way to one of the many balconies overlooking the cavern, and he now ran along its length, firing at guards stationed upon bridges below and above him. He reached the end of the balcony, flew up over its railing, and then dropped down into the open space beyond. Tesla fell ten stories, and then slowed his descent, flew on forward, and landed on a bridge. Before he could be seen by any guard, he ran across the bridge and into an opening in the cavern wall.

Tesla came upon an elevator, entered it, and threw a switch. The elevator began to descend rapidly. At intervals, through the window of the elevator door, he could see flashes of the cavern below. The elevator came to a stop, its door slid open, and Tesla stepped out.

He was now in a narrow tunnel with a flight of stairs leading further downward. He took the stairs, and descended sixteen flights. At the fifteenth landing, Tesla heard voices and footsteps coming from above. He stopped for only an instant to listen. The footsteps were descending toward him. Tesla ran down the last flight and there he entered a tunnel cut roughly into the solid volcanic rock. He walked slowly for about one hundred yards and then stopped. He saw guards ahead approaching from the other end of the tunnel. He turned around. Guards were also approaching from behind him.

Tesla turned forward again and began walking to meet the guards ahead, his ray-gun held level.

Then Tesla came upon a metal-gated archway set into the stone tunnel on his right. He turned a switch on his ray-gun and fired at the gate. The metal instantly heated to incandescence, melted and vaporized away, leaving a gaping hole with red-hot edges. Tesla plunged through the red-hot hole, disappearing from sight of the guards.

Tesla now found himself in a labyrinth of rock tunnels, a pitch-black, tomb-like place lit only by the electric torch on his helmet. The labyrinth twisted and turned, forked into two, then into three, then into six tunnels. Tesla counted his steps as he went and noted where he turned. Another person would have been lost, but Tesla drew a map in his head as he went. He realized he was moving in a circle through the labyrinth. He could hear the footsteps of the guards coming from behind. He now realized the pattern of the labyrinth and knew that he was moving in a spiral toward a central room—a central room which he believed would lead the way back out. And in a moment he did reach that central room, and when he did, he was greeted by a storm of bats fluttering up and around him.

Tesla looked up. The bats were flying up into a circular shaft that extended upwards vertically hundreds of feet. Somewhere far above, Tesla could see a pin-point of light punctuating the upper opening of the shaft.

Tesla looked down and around and realized that this room was a dead end, that there was no way out but straight up, and so he flipped the anti-gravity switch on his belt and rose straight up through the shaft.

Below him, the guards appeared and fired up at him. The electric rays of their guns missed Tesla, or, perhaps, it was Tesla's anti-gravity field that deflected the rays. The only thing that Tesla knew for certain was that he could see the electric rays coming from the guns of the guards below; some of the rays shot past him straight up through the shaft, while others struck the side of shaft as he rose upward in his flight.

The guards continued to fire up into the shaft in a continuous barrage. The stone walls of the shaft began to glow red, and the air in the tunnel spun about, until it formed a super-hot whirlwind. The shaft became a furnace and the whirlwind became a tornado of flame twisting upward to meet Tesla in his flight.

Tesla could feel the fire approaching him, the soles of his boots burning his feet, the air in his pressure suit suddenly too hot to breathe. He turned his anti-gravity switch to the sixth position—and held his breath.

The tornado of flame spun itself into a whirling ball directly under Tesla, almost licking his heels. The walls of the shaft were a streaked blur. Tesla was moving upward at a rate of nearly two hundred miles an hour and going faster every instant. The ball of fire twisted at his feet, reaching up, its tongues of flame licking his knees.

The opening out of the shaft loomed directly above Tesla. He darted through it and out into the main cavern.

At that same moment, the fireball exploded.

Chapter Ten

Sober, Sanctified, and Stercoranated

> We clapped on the power, and went for them a-biling. We was there in no time, and come a-whizzing down amongst them, and they broke and scattered every which way, and some that was climbing the ladder after Jim let go all holts and fell.
>
> — Huck, *Tom Sawyer Abroad*

I sat at the control board in the pilothouse of Tesla's airship, watching the telephone, waiting for it to ring. It had been nearly two hours since Tesla, Lillie West, George Ade, and Houdini had flown out over the edge of the volcano, disappearing to our sight. I knew it had been two hours, for I held my watch in my hand and saw its second hand sweep along its face until it had completed another circuit, adding another dreadful minute to all the others that had already passed.

I looked over to Czito who stood by the windows, looking down toward the edge of the volcano. He had been standing there nearly the whole two hours, only to step away at intervals to pace back and forth and then return to the windows again.

There was a very thick, unpleasant silence in the pilothouse, punctuated only by the low rhythmic hum of the airship's engine and the ticking of my pocket watch.

I slipped my watch back into my vest pocket and looked back to the telephone and fixed my stare upon it once again. It stared back at me, obstinately silent. I picked up the telephone's earpiece and spoke into the mouthpiece:

"Hello? Hello? Tesla? Are you there? Are you anywhere? Damn it, Tesla, answer me!"

There was no answer, only a crackling, rushing sound of air. I slammed the earpiece down on the pedestal, stood up, and looked over to Czito. He had turned around and was staring at me, his face white with shock and fear.

"Well, Czito," I asked, "where are they?"

"They'll show at any moment," Czito replied.

"Well," I said, "I'll tell you now: I have no intention of leaving them here."

I went over to the window where Czito stood and looked out. Below us lay the rim of the giant volcano, silent and gray-black. Beyond the rim was a broken plain of volcanic rock stretching off into a hazy covering of distant white clouds tinted pink at their edges with the setting sun.

I took out my pocket watch and looked at it again. The two hours were up—and then some.

"Damn it!" I said, "I can't stand this!"

I put my watch back in my vest pocket, and started off toward the pilot's wheel.

"We're going down there," I said.

Czito stepped in front of me, and said, "Mr. Tesla said to wait here!"

"I'm in charge here," I said, pushing Czito aside. "We're going down."

"You can't," Czito said, and I felt his hand on my shoulder.

"I can and I will!" I said. I reached for the wheel, but didn't grasp it, for Czito grabbed hold of both of my arms and pulled me back.

"Damn it, Czito!" I shouted. "Let go of me!"

I broke free of Czito's grasp, spun about, and grabbed Czito by the lapels of his vest.

"Don't you get it?" I shouted. "Don't you understand? Tesla's just trying to save our necks!"

"He ordered us to report to President Cleveland!" Czito shouted back.

"Report?" I shouted. "Report *what*? That we left him to *die*? Cleveland can't do a damn thing! Nobody on Earth can do a damn thing! It's up to us!"

I released Czito's lapels, and added: "And you know it."

Czito looked at me a moment, his eyes flashing in anger and fear. Then the fire in his eyes died down and they went empty and hollow. Czito bowed his head down, and nodded.

Six and a half thousand feet below us, George Ade, Lillie West, and Houdini flew on a circuit through the giant cavern, firing their ray guns at guards stationed on the upper balconies. The guards fired back with both electric rays and bullets. The force fields surrounding the air pressure suits of the three aeronauts acted like invisible bubbles of steel, deflecting everything in their path.

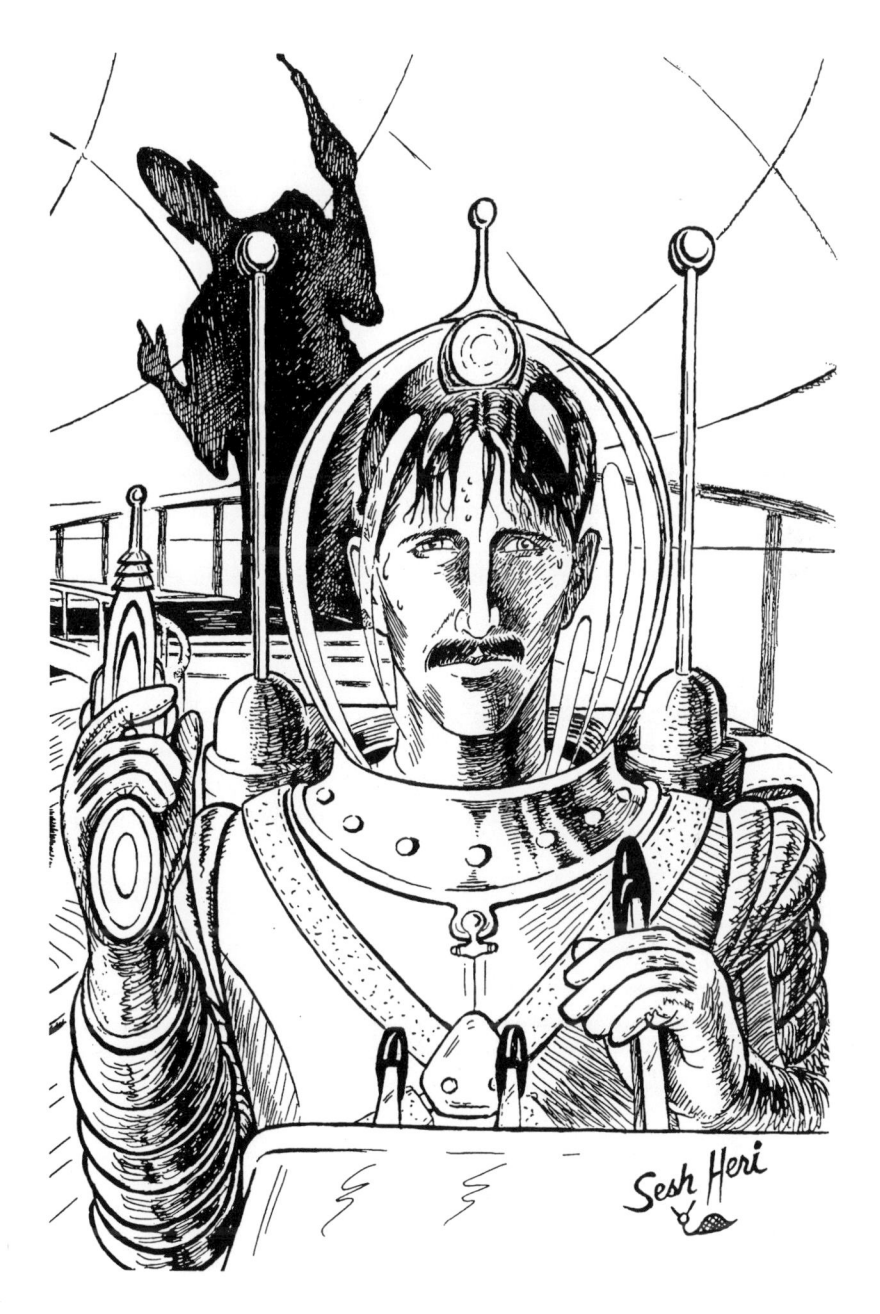

"Drop your gun."

Then several of the guards rolled up something to the edge of one of the balconies that looked like some kind of cannon. They fired a ball of fire from this cannon and it struck Houdini in mid-air. The boy magician's knapsack erupted in sparks, his whole body was enveloped in a shimmering green haze, and he began dropping downward in sudden jerks.

"Ahhh!" Houdini screamed.

Houdini flipped the anti-gravity switch on his belt, but he continued to descend like a falling leaf. Then he began going down in a rapid spiral. He leaned forward, swooped down over a bridge, and tumbled to its surface.

A crowd of Martian guards ran out on to the bridge and converged upon the spot where he lay.

"George!" Lillie cried.

"Come on!" Ade shouted, gesturing for Lillie to follow him to another bridge one hundred feet below them.

Another ball of fire sped out into the cavern, this time toward Ade who shot to one side as the ball passed within feet of him. The ball continued on its course and exploded against a distant wall of the cavern with another shattering electrical 'boom!'

Ade and Lillie landed on the bridge and ran to an entrance in the cavern's wall of rock. They reached the entrance and stopped inside the threshold, leaning against its stone wall.

"George," Lillie cried. "We have to go after him! We've got to try to save that boy!"

"He's dead, Lillie," Ade said, his voice hard and even. "We both know he's dead."

A fusillade of bullets exploded on the floor in front of them. Lillie and Ade flattened themselves against the stone wall. Ade waited a second, then leaned around the corner of the stone wall and fired his ray gun. He could see a group of guards on the bridge drop down and scurry for cover. Ade drew back behind the wall.

"I'm going out firing straight ahead," Ade said. "As soon as I'm out, take off over the heads of the guards and fly directly to the cave entrance."

"What are you going to do?" Lillie asked.

"Don't worry about me," Ade said. "Just head for the entrance."

Ade fired his ray gun around the corner of the stone wall, and then drew back again.

"You're going back," Lillie said. "To help Tesla. Aren't you?"

"I'm going back," Ade said.

"George—"

"No arguments!" Ade snapped. "Not this time!"

"George!"

There was another fusillade of bullets followed by a flash of fire; a ball of electricity exploded on the ground in front of them. Ade lunged forward, firing his ray gun in a continuous blaze, incinerating several guards charging forward on the bridge. Ade drew back behind the stone wall.

"Lillie," Ade said, "You may think you're Helen of Troy, Betsy Ross, and Susan B. Anthony all rolled into one. But I know what you are."

"What am I, George?"

"Just one woman. You're Lillie West—and that's all who you need to be."

Lillie reached up to Ade with her gloved hand, but he turned, lunged forward around the corner, and ran forward with his ray gun blazing out right and left.

An instant later, Lillie West swooped over the head of George Ade and hurtled up above the Martian guards, firing down on them in her flight.

I had steered the airship down along the wall of the volcano, following the staircase cut into the rock. Czito stood by the windows, peering down.

"It ends down there," Czito said. "There's a stone platform and some kind of slab set into the wall."

"Do you see any sign of them?" I asked.

"No," Czito replied. "Nor of anyone or anything else."

I brought us all the way down to the bottom of the staircase and stopped the airship so that we hovered there in front of the stone door.

"They must've gone in there," Czito said.

We looked blankly at the stone door for a moment, and then I picked up the spyglass and looked through it to the wall of the volcano where it diminished into the distance toward the north. About a mile away I could see another gray rectangle in the black wall of volcanic rock.

"Look at this," I said to Czito, and gave him the spyglass.

"It's another door all right," Czito said, looking through the spyglass. "A big one."

Czito kept looking through the spy glass, and then, in another moment, he said, "Uh-oh."

"What is it?" I asked.

"It's opening," Czito said, and he gave the spyglass back to me.

I found the giant door again in the circle view of the spyglass and saw that it was slowly sliding back, revealing a dark interior beyond. Then out of the shadows of the door's threshold the blunt prow of the Martian airship slid out into the ruddy sunlight. I felt a crawly sensation on my scalp and my knees began to go weak.

"Jesus!" I whispered.

"What?" Czito asked.

"It's the Martian airship," I said. "It's coming out of its hell-hole."

"They've seen us," Czito said.

"Of course they've seen us!" I said. "They're coming to finish us off."

I looked around the pilothouse and then glanced above at the gun tower. "Do you know how to man that electric Gatling gun up there?" I asked.

"I do," Czito said.

"Well then," I said, "get up there in the cat-bird's seat and get ready to blow a hole through that goddamned flying tin can out there!"

Czito made no reply, and when I turned my head to look at him I saw that he was clambering up the steel ladder to the gun tower as fast as he could go.

I looked back through the spyglass and found the big door in the circle of its view again. The door was still open, but the Martian airship was gone!

I turned the spyglass out to the north and the Martian airship flashed into view. It was hurtling straight toward us! I tossed the spyglass aside, grabbed the pilot's wheel, and tapped the accelerator pedal with my foot. We shot upward toward the Martian airship while it barreled down toward us.

"Czito!" I shouted.

An electric ray shot out from above on our airship's gun tower and hit the front of the Martian airship with a big boom. The Martians fired back with a ball of fire, and it hit directly under the prow of our airship.

[*Keer-rack-a-rackle SMASH!*]

"That was a weaker electric charge than what they were shooting at us before!" Czito shouted. "A lot weaker!"

"They must not be hooked up to the crystal," I said.

The Martian airship was moving in an arc to come in at us from behind. Czito fired again and hit the Martian airship with another ray.

[*Fzt! Boom!*]

"We're not even scratching them!" Czito shouted. "We need more power or we're finished!"

"And how in the hell can we get more power?" I shouted back.

[*Beroom! Boom! Bumble-SMASH!*]

A big ball of fire had struck our airship and knocked me backwards. I fell against the control board aft of the pilothouse and saw that several bulbs on it were lit up.

"It's all lit up down here on the board!" I shouted.

Czito shouted, "We're going into overload—dielectric breakdown!" He slid down the ladder and bounded to my side. His hands flew up over the board, plugging several cords into sockets. The lights on the board flashed off.

"We can't take another hit!" Czito said.

I lunged for the pilot's wheel and pulled us up; we were about to crash on the floor of the crater. I steered us back up into the sky, and, just as I got our airship straightened out, the Martian airship shot a ball of fire at us. I brought our airship hard to larboard and the ball shot by the starboard windows of the pilothouse.

"If you know a way for us to get more power, now's the time to tell it!" I shouted to Czito.

"There is no way," Czito said, "unless. . . "

"Unless the hell what?"

"Unless we put all the power of the ship's engine into the ray-gun," Czito said. "But we can't do that."

"Why the hell not?"

"We need the engine for flight."

[*Boom-be-room SMASH!*]

We were hit by another big jolt of electricity; the whole ship shuddered and vibrated.

"I'm taking us down for a landing," I said.

"You can't surrender!" Czito shouted.

"Surrender, hell," I said. "We're going to kill every single one of those goddamned sons of bitches in that goddamned tin can. If I land and shut off the engine can you use all its power to fire the gun up there?"

"Yes!" Czito gasped. "But with the engine off we'll have no shield—we'll be sitting ducks!"

"Only for a second," I said, "and a second is all we need. I'm taking us down there and landing and when I say fire, you sure as hell better fire—or we're both dead! Now get up there! We're going down!"

Czito shot back up the ladder to the gun tower and I brought the airship down to within a few feet of the crater floor and hit the landing switch. Our airship's landing struts let out a vibration and whine as they came out of the belly of the ship. There was a metallic 'clunk,' and I knew the landing struts had locked into place. I brought the ship all the way down, and a grinding sound told me we had made hard contract with the ground. The Martian airship swooped in an arc in the sky and came down toward us. I opened the switch to the ship's engine, instantly felt our interior gravity shift to the natural pull of the Martian surface, and at the same moment shouted:

"Fire!"

A blue-white ball of fire shot out from our gun tower and plowed into the prow of the Martian airship. There was a terrific flash of light and a deafening rumble—[KA-BOOM-BA-BOOM-KLA-BLAM!]—and the Martian airship exploded in a fiery spray of particles and fragments. Half the airship was utterly obliterated and the other half dropped straight down and crashed against the crater's floor and billows of black smoke poured out of the crushed and twisted remnant.

I brought us up into the air and circled the site of the crash and Czito came down the ladder and went to the window and looked down. The black smoke spread out and blew away and all that was left behind was a crushed half-cylinder of metal lying embedded on the crater floor.

"You got 'em, Czito," I said. "You got the goddamned sons of bitches."
Czito said nothing, but just kept looking down at the wreck.

Down inside the cavern Tesla flew over the underground city and rose up toward the bridges spanning above him. He had barely escaped being roasted alive by the fireball and now the inside of his pressure suit had become an oven. His lungs felt like they were on fire and he could only manage short, sharp breaths. Beads of perspiration stood out on his face and rolled down from his wet hair to his forehead, cheeks, nose, and chin. Despite this, he kept a firm grip with his left hand on his anti-gravity switch, and in his right hand he gripped his electric ray gun.

Tesla saw Martian guards grouping again on the bridges and at the balconies of the cavern's walls. He began spinning as he rose in the air, raised his ray gun, and began to fire. He kept firing as he rose, and the electric ray from his gun began describing a deadly spiral swath of electric fire cutting through all space around him. The swath struck through crowds of guards on the bridges and on the walls, and the guards fell back and scattered for cover, leaving their dead behind.

Above Tesla loomed a bridge. He flew up and around it, saw that it was empty of guards, and landed upon it. He looked at one end of the bridge and then the other. No one was in sight. Tesla felt his head trembling involuntarily. He took a deep breath of hot air and slowly exhaled. His head stopped shaking. Then Tesla walked forward across the bridge, his ray gun held steady. Below, he could hear the thunderous explosions of ray guns, bullets, and ball lightning.

Houdini could hear those same explosions, but he was far below in a pit of rock covered by a barred window twenty feet over his head. Another window looked down upon a lower level where a great crowd of people stood and milled about.

How did Houdini get into this predicament? Well, when he had tumbled down on to the surface of the bridge, the Martian guards had grabbed him, tore away his pressure suit, bound him in chains, and marched him to an elevator. He and the guards sped downward, somewhere far below the main cavern, and there, in the lower tunnels, Houdini was marched in his chains to a door, shoved through it, and the door slammed shut behind him.

In the pitch darkness of his cell his eyes adjusted. In a minute, he realized that he was surrounded by other people. They were all standing around him in complete silence and staring at him. These people were all wearing robes and were pale and bald, just like their king, Kel. Unlike Kel, these people were all cadaverously emaciated—they were not much more than living skeletons. They all stared at Houdini with their hollow pink eyes. Each of them bore upon their forehead a tattoo, a line of figures that looked like some kind of hieroglyphs, letters, or numbers.

Houdini stared back at the people. His arms were bound behind his back and chains crossed around in front of his chest.

Houdini kept looking at the people, and then finally said, "How ya doin'?"

The Martians looked at each other and then back to Houdini.

"Any of you speak English?" Houdini asked. "*Sprecken ze deutch? Parlez vous Francais?*"

The Martians said nothing.

"Naw," Houdini said, "I didn't think so. But—who knows? You can never tell."

All the while Houdini spoke he had been wiggling his shoulders back and forth. He stopped, slowly let out his breath, and then he began wiggling out of the chains like a snake shedding its skin. The chains slipped down, and fell to his feet. His hands were still bound behind his back.

"This is the tough part," Houdini said. "I'd like to swear all of youse to secrecy, but I kind of doubt you'll ever talk to anybody I know."

Houdini sat down on the stone floor and then lay on his side. He began straining his arms downward until the chains binding his wrists together came down and passed under his buttocks. The Martians did not move or make a sound, but they all watched Houdini's struggle with great intensity. Houdini squeezed the chains over his toes which were flattened against his buttocks.

"Don't think I can do it, huh?" Houdini gasped out. "This ain't the dime show—this one's the dollar!"

The chain was up on his ankles. He bent forward, pulled the chain along his shins—his knees—and then his hands came out in front of him.

Houdini sat up and looked at his chained wrists. The chain was held fast with some kind of metal lock.

"I come a hundred ga-zillion miles," Houdini said, "a hundred ga-zillion miles—and the locks—the locks are all the same!"

Houdini stood up.

"I got no respect for locks!" Houdini said. "No respect! But don't ever tell anybody that!"

Houdini reached down to the waistband of his red flannel under drawers and pulled out a thin wire. He then bent the wire a little and inserted it into the keyhole of the lock on his wrist. The lock sprung open and the chains fell to the floor. The Martians let out a gasp in unison.

"Never saw that one before, huh?" Houdini said. "Well, you ain't seen nothin' yet!"

There was a scream from below and the Martians all rushed to the barred window and looked down. Houdini pushed his way to the edge of the window and looked down as well. Down below he saw a crowd of other emaciated

Martians being shoved into a white-hot stream of volcanic magma and being burned alive! The people were being herded forward from behind by two armed guards and shoved into the fiery stream by a seven foot tall metallic automaton!

"Don't you worry, folks," Houdini said, "don't you worry. We're gettin' out of here and we're going to stop those *mumzers*—stop 'em for good!"

Houdini went to the door of the cell. It had no knob, no keyhole, no opening of any kind.

"Well," Houdini said, "that door ain't the way, it ain't the way. Think! Think!"

Houdini looked straight up at the barred window directly overhead. His glance trailed downward along the stone walls. He could see the stones were rough hewn, and that, if he were careful, his feet and hands could find purchases on them that would allow him to climb the wall all the way up to the window twenty feet overhead. He went to one of the walls and began climbing up along it, stone upon stone, until the top of his head was only an inch or two below a corner of the barred window. He reached up and put his right hand around one of the bars and tugged at it. The bar was set solidly into the stone.

"That ain't going nowhere," Houdini said. He climbed back down to the floor of the cell. When he got back down he reached into the waistband of his under drawers and carefully pulled out a long slender roll of white kid leather. He knelt down and laid the roll of leather on the stone floor and opened it out flat. The leather contained a number of very small tools: a miniature ratchet, screwdriver, and a hacksaw blade with a handle designed to be held between one's forefinger and thumb.

Houdini picked up the hacksaw, and said, "When you can't squeeze your way out, when you can't pick your way out, when you can't bribe your way out, when you can't dig your way out—you cut your way out!" He rolled the other tools back up in the piece of leather and then stuffed the leather tube back into the lining of his waistband. Then he put the tiny hack saw blade between his teeth and began climbing up the stone wall again. He got back up to the window, took the hacksaw blade from between his teeth, and, holding its handle between his thumb and forefinger, he began sawing into a metal bar.

"Huh!" Houdini said. "This stuff cuts like cheese! Sit tight down there! I'll have you all out in a minute!"

Houdini's hand moved back and forth in a streaked blur, while metal filings dropped from the bar.

Czito stood at the pilothouse windows looking through the spyglass.

"It's cracked," Czito said.

"What's cracked?" I asked, turning the pilot's wheel larboard and taking us north toward the crater's wall.

"The lens in this spyglass," Czito said. "It's cracked."

"I must've dropped it while ago," I said. "Can you see anything out of it?"

"Yes," he said, "they're closing that big door in the wall of the crater."

"Not very friendly folks," I said, "are they? I'm taking us over there anyway."

I brought our ship toward the crater wall and we passed by in front of the big door where the Martian airship had come out. That door was made of some kind of metal and it was about one hundred-fifty or two hundred feet square. It was now shut tight, and, of course, the Martians inside were not about to open it.

I asked, "Any suggestions, Mr. Czito?"

We both stood there looking at the metal door and the wall of volcanic rock in which it was set.

"We could blast a hole through that door with the electric ray-gun," Czito said.

"That would get us in," I said, "but what would happen to all the air inside?"

"It would all get sucked out here into this near-vacuum," Czito said.

"All of it?" I asked.

"There has to be another door beyond this one here in order to form an air lock. All the air in the first chamber would be sucked out. If our electric ray penetrated through the second door of the air lock, the air inside their cavern city would start to be drawn out as well."

"Would all their air come out?" I asked.

"Eventually—yes," Czito said.

"And that would suffocate everybody inside," I said.

"That's right," Czito said.

"Well," I said, "I am not going to murder a city full of civilians—even Martian civilians. I would bet the people inside that city don't know any more about this fight of ours than the citizens of Chicago do. We are not about to fire a hole through that door. How else can we get in there?"

"There is no other way," Czito said.

"Goddamn it, Czito, don't tell me that! We have to get in there! We will get in there! Nothing else is acceptable! Now, you tell me how!"

"Me?" Czito asked. "How should I know?"

"You're the scientist," I said.

"I am not a scientist," Czito said. "I am only a mechanic! I make cabinets. I put in wiring. I just put in wiring, Mr. Clemens!"

"Don't give me that, goddamn it! You are not just a mechanic! You are the mechanic for the greatest scientist in the world! You know things—you've seen things that nobody else on earth has ever seen! Now, I want you to think and think hard: Have you ever seen Tesla do anything or heard him say anything that could give us just the slightest clue as to how to get inside of that volcano? Think, Czito—think!"

"Nothing!" Czito cried, "There's nothing! You're asking the impossible! You want magic—not science! Well, let me tell you—not even the Houdini Erich Weiss could just pass through that wall of rock like a ghost—and that's what you're asking me to figure out: how to go through that wall of rock like we were—"

Czito stopped speaking. He was looking straight ahead at the wall of volcanic rock that was spread out before us about two hundred feet beyond the pilothouse windows. Czito continued to stare at the wall of rock without moving a muscle.

"Czito?" I asked. "Czito? Have you gone into one of Tesla's trances?"

"I'm beginning to understand Mr. Tesla's trances," Czito replied. "I'm beginning to understand a lot."

"What are you talking about?"

"I think I know how we might get through that rock," Czito said. "But we might just as well get instantly killed."

"We might just as well get instantly killed if we stand here and do nothing," I said. "Now tell me what you're thinking."

"All right," Czito said, "all right. Here it is: I just remembered something Mr. Tesla said when we were testing the airship one night. He told me to be careful when adjusting the circuit controller and the valve to the aerial conductor. He said that if I opened the valve on the aerial conductor all the way and set the frequency of pulsation too high on the circuit controller we could get some very unusual and unwanted effects."

"What kind of effects?"

"I'm trying to remember. I'm not absolutely sure, but I think he said that we might become invisible and pass through the Earth just like a ghost. I think that's what he said, but it was so strange, I just ignored him. Maybe I thought he was exaggerating or joking or speaking figuratively."

"Does Mr. Tesla ever exaggerate or joke or speak figuratively when he speaks to you about his inventions?"

"No," Czito said, shaking his head. "Never."

"Now," I said, "I want you to think about this idea of opening the aerial conductor valve and setting the circuit controller too high. Why would that make us invisible or make us like ghosts?"

Czito looked down, removed his spectacles and wiped the lenses with his handkerchief.

"The circuit controller," Czito said, "controls the frequency of electrical pulsations. It has a certain range of variability and the specific frequency at any moment is determined by the positions of the pilot's controls up here in the pilothouse."

"I think I already understand all that," I said.

"I'm reviewing," Czito said. "Mr. Tesla has said that sometimes a problem can be solved by reviewing those elements which are already known."

Czito paced away from me.

"High frequency electrical pulsations polarize the atomic structure of the airship and allow the lines of gravitational force to pass through its structure, in other words, make the airship gravitationally transparent."

"So," I said, "perhaps higher frequency pulsations of greater power would allow light to pass through us like it passes through a window pane."

"That could be," Czito said.

"And maybe," I said, "even higher frequencies and greater power would allow the atoms of other bodies to pass through us the way light rays and gravitational forces do."

"Yes," Czito said, "that could be so as well. But if that's true, trying to actually interpenetrate solid matter with the airship could be very problematic, very dangerous."

"What could happen?" I asked. "What could go wrong?"

"If the frequency was not maintained at a steady rate throughout the whole airship, the atoms of the airship could get scrambled. The ship's hull could join and fuse into machinery. We ourselves might become fused into the ship's bulkhead. Or maybe the atoms of our bodies might disintegrate. We might collapse like a heap of sand—or just go up in flames."

"All right," I said. "That's the worst. What's the best we could hope for?"

"If we can maintain a steady, extremely rapid pulsation," Czito said, "we would be able to pass through the atomic structure of the wall of rock in front of us and come out on the other side."

"And how would we return to a normal state of solidity?"

"Simply by reducing our electrical power and rate of pulsation."

"Do you know how to adjust the aerial conductor valve and the circuit controller?"

"Yes."

"And do you know how much power and how high the frequency should be to turn us into ghosts figuratively speaking? And I do mean figuratively speaking!"

"No, but there is a practical way to determine all that."

"How?"

"When everything around us—including ourselves—looks like the image of a double-exposed photograph—that is, semitransparent—that will be the correct setting."

"That means you would have to adjust the aerial conductor valve and the circuit controller with the engine turned on. Can you do that?"

"It would be extremely dangerous, but yes, I could do that."

"Then do it."

Houdini had cut through the bar in the window, and had carefully removed it and tossed it to the floor of the cell. He was now squeezing through the opening in the window made by the missing bar. He pulled himself on through the window grasping the other bars and then clung to the outside wall for a moment, looking down. He was inside a long hall with a high ceiling that went up about twenty-five feet. Below, he saw the outside of the door of the cell from which he had just escaped. He started down the outside wall, carefully feeling his way with his toes on the rough stone. Down he climbed a stone at a time. He got to the floor of the hall and went to the door of the cell and inserted his piece of wire into its keyhole. The door sprung open.

"Come on," Houdini said, "before somebody sees us! Come on out! You're free!"

The Martians stood staring at Houdini a moment, and then one of them came forward timidly, looked around through the door, and then shouted back to the others inside:

"*Em! Em!*"

The Martians poured through the door and went running down the hall.

"That's what I was saying!" Houdini called after the Martians, "*Em! Em!*"

Houdini then turned and looked back down the hall. There were at least a dozen more doors like the one in front of him, a dozen more doors probably holding behind them many more starving captives. It did not matter to Houdini that those captives were Martians. He went down the hall and in rapid succession opened all the doors, shouting at every one as it sprung open: "*Em! Em!*"

The Martians poured out of the doors, all of them ragged and starving just like the others, all of them with the same blue tattoos on their pale foreheads.

Just as Houdini opened the last door in the hall, the sound of gunshots rang out from below. He ran with all the others down a stone stairwell. When they reached the first landing all the people scurried into a tunnel that led off into darkness. The sounds of the gunshots were coming from the stairwell another flight below. Houdini went down the stone steps and came upon the chamber he had seen from the barred window of the cell, the place where people were being thrown into a river of molten lava.

The two guards were shooting into a mob of attacking prisoners. Each time a shot rang out the mob would fall back, only to rush forward again. There was a final surge and the mob fell upon the two guards and dragged them down into a sea of heads and arms.

A piercing scream cut through the air. Houdini looked up to see one of the Martians being carried in the arms of the seven-foot tall automaton. The metal monster was carrying the Martian toward the river of molten lava.

Houdini ran forward through the crowd and climbed up a jagged embankment of volcanic rock and got to the top ledge that overlooked the flowing stream of molten rock. The automaton had almost reached the edge of the lava.

Houdini sprang forward and jumped on to the automaton's back. The giant monster of metal seemed to sense the added weight and turned about. It paused for a moment, dropped the Martian it held in its metal arms, and then began reaching up over its shoulders at Houdini who clung to the giant's back.

The automaton kept reaching up, trying to pull Houdini off its shoulders. Houdini hung on, his left arm around the neck of the automaton, his right hand trying to pry open a door in the automaton's back. The automaton spun about and flung Houdini to the ground.

Houdini lay sprawled upon the ledge directly above the stream of lava. The automaton lumbered forward to pick Houdini up and cast him down into the liquid fire below. Houdini lay still. The automaton approached and bent down with its metal hands reaching out. In another second all would be lost, the automaton would have Houdini in a grasp stronger than a steel vice. The monster's hand came within an inch of Houdini's face. The boy magician flattened himself against the ground and rolled toward the automaton, grabbed hold of the monster's metal ankles, and pulled back with all his strength.

The automaton tottered on the ledge of rock, and then pitched forward head-first into the white-hot river of lava. Houdini jumped back as molten rock splashed upward, the automaton's head and shoulders striking the surface of the molten river.

In a moment, Houdini looked back over the ledge of rock. The automaton was being consumed and melted away into the flow of lava.

"*Em!*" Houdini said, looking down over the ledge, "*Em!*"

I stood next to Czito where he worked on the circuit controller inside the airship's engine. He had turned a valve at the top of the engine machinery and had then opened up a metal housing next to the big coil of wire, and he was now slowly turning a little slotted wheel with a screwdriver. The light from the drive crystal washed over us with its rainbow colors, and I now found that pulsing light to be very nerve racking.

"Nothing's happening," I said.

"Not yet," Czito said, and he stopped turning the little wheel with the screwdriver.

"That's it," Czito said. "That's as far as I'm going."

"But nothing's happening," I said.

"Not yet," Czito said again, and he waved for me to step back. I obliged, and then Czito stepped out of the engine too, but left the door of the engine cabinet open.

"Why do you keep saying, 'Not yet'?" I asked.

"Because," Czito said, "it will take a minute or so for us to achieve complete atomic polarization. Come on, we should be up in the pilothouse when that happens, and we shouldn't be moving about."

Czito and I hurried up the steps of the pilothouse and we stood in front of the pilot's wheel.

"Now stay right where you are," Czito said, "and don't move from the spot where you're standing! If we get to moving around in here too much we may go through the wall or the floor!"

"I'm stock still and I ain't about to budge one inch!" I said.

We stood there looking out the pilothouse windows. In a moment a green haze or fog formed all around the outside of the airship.

"What's happening?" I asked.

"The atoms of the outside atmosphere are becoming stressed. The magnetic field around the ship is pushing them away, and the secondary field being set up above the magnetic field is holding them in."

"What about us?" I asked.

"Everything within the field surrounding the ship is becoming atomically polarized—from the outside in. The complete and even atomic polarization outside crystallizes inward toward us at a steady rate. The atoms of our bodies are lining up in rows to form a complex crystal lattice."

"I don't like the idea of my innards turning into a crystal," I said. "I don't like that idea at all."

I looked over at Czito and realized that the green fog wasn't just outside the airship, but was permeating the inside of the pilothouse as well.

"That green fog is in here," I said.

"Yes," Czito said, "I noticed that, too."

"Are we breathing that stuff into our lungs?" I asked.

"Mr. Clemens," Czito replied, "our lungs are turning into that green stuff."

"Mr. Czito," I said, "is it my imagination, or are you turning green yourself?"

"Mr. Clemens," Czito said, "I believe that both of us are turning green. I believe that everything is turning green."

"We're stuck in a green fog," I said.

The pilothouse suddenly got so thick with that green fog that I could scarcely see Czito. Then the fog started to fade away, and when it did, Czito and the interior of the pilothouse where we stood were almost completely transparent. It seemed that I was just floating in mid-air above the floor of the volcano. I could see the rocky surface below and the wall of rock in front of me with complete clarity. But the floor of the airship had nearly disappeared. I looked down at my own feet and legs and found that there was nothing much to look at; I had become more transparent than a glass of water!

"My God," I said, "we're fading away into thin air!"

"We're still here, Mr. Clemens," Czito said, "it's just that all the light is passing right through us. Try bringing the airship toward the wall of the volcano."

Czito's voice had become faint, as if he were far away from me. I felt for the accelerator pedal with my foot. I could feel that it was still there under the sole of my shoe, but I couldn't see the pedal any longer, or the sole of my shoe, for that matter. I gave the accelerator pedal a tap and we began moving toward the wall of rock in front of us.

"This is it," I said. "We either crash or we pass through."

"We either crash or we pass through," Czito said.

We were now only fifty feet in front of the wall of rock—then twenty-five feet—any second the prow of our airship should have been plowing into solid rock. We kept going. We heard nothing. We felt nothing. We were just moving straight forward into that wall of rock. We were fifteen feet away—ten feet.

"Goodbye, Mr. Clemens," I heard Czito say, and then we were enveloped in total blackness.

"Mr. Czito," I shouted, "can you hear me?"

In response I heard a faint call, as if coming from a great distance: "I hear you!"

It was Kolman Czito's voice, all right, but I could barely hear it. I didn't try to move, except that I tried looking around by moving my eyes. I could barely see a faint, glowing white outline of the pilot's wheel and my hand grasping one of its knobs. I turned my head and saw the outline of Kolman Czito's profile, spectacles and all. I turned my head to the front again. There still was nothing but blackness ahead. Then, all of a sudden instant, a scene flashed in front of us; it was the interior of the cavern city of the Martians—a world of twisted and oppressive rock spanned by glittering bridges and arches, and below, towers rising up from thousands of feet on the cavern floor. I drew in my breath sharply, and cried out as loud as I could, "Mr. Czito, we're inside! Turn down the circuit controller!"

I looked over to where Czito had been standing and could no longer see any trace of him. I kept standing by the pilot's wheel, looking down upon the cavern city, waiting for Czito to reach the circuit controller.

Czito was behind me trying to do just that very thing, but having a difficult time trying to do it. He could hardly see the inside of the airship at all. He shuffled his feet along the floor, reached the railing to the stairs, and slowly began descending the steps.

"Czito!" I shouted. "Are you there?"

"I'm going down the steps!" I could barely hear Czito shout back. He crept down the stairs and shuffled along the top deck until he reached the open door of the engine cabinet. He couldn't see any of the machinery inside, but, strangely, he could see the light coming from the drive crystal. He reached into the engine cabinet and felt his way up to the valve on the aerial conductor and turned it down. Then he felt his way across the engine's machinery until he touched the circuit controller and found its slotted wheel. He brought the screwdriver that he held in his hand up to the slotted wheel, inserted it, and began turning the wheel back to its original position. When he had the wheel adjusted, he withdrew the screwdriver and stepped back.

"I've made the adjustment!" Czito shouted back up to me, but I did not hear him. I stood at the pilot's wheel feeling very helpless and frightened.

But then the green haze appeared in front of me. I looked down at my feet, and saw that it was below me as well. It grew thicker, just as it had done before, but this time, as it started to fade away, the interior of the pilothouse came into view. In a moment, the green haze was gone and everything in the pilothouse looked as solid and real as it always had. I turned around and saw Czito coming up the steps.

"You did it, Mr. Czito," I said, "by God, you did it!"

Czito nodded, looked about, and said, "Before this is over we may both wish that I hadn't done it."

I steered our airship through the cavern. About half a mile below us the Martian city glowed with incandescent light. We passed under a bridge which spanned the uppermost reaches of the cavern. This bridge had no support beneath it or above it, and had a span of perhaps three-quarters of a mile.

"What kind of steel could hold up over a span of that distance?" I asked Czito.

"There is no metal I know of that could sustain an unsupported span of that length," Czito said.

We passed on around an outcropping in the volcanic wall of rock and came upon the central part of the underground city. Far in the distance we could see the central domed tower rising up from the floor of the cavern and the many bridges spanning overhead. It was then that we saw the flashes of light and heard the rumbles and cracks that we now readily recognized as the sound of artificial electric rays.

"That's got to be them over there," I said, and I steered the airship over the top of one of the bridges and headed over to where I had seen the last flash of light.

As we approached, I caught sight of a group of men in uniforms and helmets shooting up toward a ledge of rock in the cavern wall about two hundred feet above them. I steered our airship up to the ledge and Lillie West hove into sight, crouching on the ledge with her back against the cavern wall. She was still in her air pressure suit, and, at intervals, she would lean over the ledge, fire down at the guards, and then draw back to her position against the wall.

"Czito," I asked, "can you hit those varmints down there?"

"I can try," he said.

"Well, try! And hit 'em hard!"

Czito shot up the ladder to the gun tower. I looked down at the Martian guards and saw them wheeling out an object that had the disagreeable appearance of a cannon.

"Czito," I said, "you had better hurry it up. It looks like they're breaking out their heavy artillery."

Below, the cannon fired and I saw a ball of fire shoot straight toward us. I steered our airship down in a plunge and the ball of fire shot over the top of the gun tower.

A second later Czito fired a ray of electricity at the Martian guards. The ray struck the guards and enveloped them in a sphere of white fire. I could see the guards waver like they were in a heat mirage and then disappear from the bridge.

"What happened to them?" I asked.

"They were vaporized," Czito shouted down from the gun tower.

The moment Czito fired upon the guards, Lillie had spun about and spied us coming through in the airship. She raised her hand to me, and then flew away into the cavern.

"Come back here right now, young lady!" I shouted to her, even though I knew she could not hear me.

George Ade had not made it back to Tesla. He had made it to a bridge leading to the laboratory that held the crystal, but a guard ran forward and fired a bullet at Ade. The bullet whizzed by Ade, and he fired back with a bolt of electricity, striking the guard dead. A moment later, another guard came up from behind and grabbed Ade's right arm. Ade tried to turn around, and as he struggled with the guard behind him, a third guard came running forward and began trying to remove Ade's helmet. In another moment, a crowd of guards converged upon Ade.

Ade swung out with his left fist and batted the hands of the guards away, and then he reached down with one swift motion and flipped the antigravity switch on his belt, and he and two other guards—the one behind him and the one in front—rose up in mid-air, breaking free from the crowd of guards below on the bridge.

Ade pushed the guard in front of him away, breaking the guard's grasp upon his helmet. Kicking helplessly in mid-air, the guard moved out of the influence of Ade's artificial gravity field and fell downward into the cavern.

The guard hanging on Ade's back now reached around in front of Ade and unbuckled his knapsack, and, with a sudden tug, pulled it off of Ade.

Ade suddenly felt a sickening rise in his stomach and knew he was beginning to fall to his death. As he began to drop, Ade glanced up through the glass dome of his helmet and saw the guard above him spin about and the knapsack slip from the guard's grip. The knapsack rose up into the cavern like a toy balloon. The guard was pulled upward by the knapsack's ascent for a moment. Then, slipping outside the area of the knapsack's gravitational influence, the guard began to fall, and Ade knew that he and the guard would die together.

Ade looked down. The floor of the cavern, two thousand feet below, seemed to rise up toward him. It was a dark expanse sprinkled with countless pin-points of light.

Ade felt his body begin to spin and he instinctively held out his hands to stop that motion. He arrested the spin, but now his body began to flip with his head pointing down, his feet swinging up. He could see the floor of the cavern rush toward him much faster now. Ade swung his arms and his head and shoulders came upright.

Then George Ade saw a blurred flash of white; it was Lillie West. She had swooped down from above and grabbed Ade under his arms. Now they were both falling in a dizzying spin—a hopeless whirlwind of lights spread out below them. Then Ade felt them slowing, and he looked down and saw that Lillie had reached for the antigravity switch on her belt. The floor of the underground city loomed before them. Ade could see a dark square structure and something that might have been a road or path. They continued to slow—and then stop—perhaps two feet above the surface of the road bed. There they floated for a moment, and then Lillie said:

"Well? Come on if you're coming!"

And she flipped her gravity switch to the sixth position—rapid acceleration—and that's what the two of them did—straight up through the cavern.

Tesla flew in a circle around the domed tower. As he passed over each of the four bridges leading to the tower's uppermost dome, he dropped a small metal ball. When one of these balls would land on a bridge, it would erupt into a fountain of crackling lightning bolts, effectively blocking all access to the tower from the bridge. In a moment, all four bridges were erupting in fountains of lightning.

Next Tesla flew under the bridges and fired an electric ray at the elevator cables running along the side of the tower. The cables snapped apart; and an elevator car dropped from the side of the tower and crashed to the ground two thousand feet below. Then Tesla flew up to the domed tower and through one of its doors.

Inside, a guard instantly appeared at the railing of the upper balcony and fired at Tesla, and Tesla fired back, striking the guard with an electric ray. The guard shouted out and fell over the balcony. Tesla landed on the floor and saw movement to his upper right. He spun about, saw a second guard, and fired, blasting the guard back away from the balcony railing.

Tesla stepped forward and looked about. Everything was silent and still except for the Master Crystal pulsing a rainbow of light where it sat mounted on the pedestal.

Tesla flipped his anti-gravity switch and rose up in the air, passed over the balcony railing, and landed on the balcony. He saw a board of electrical switches and went over and looked down at it.

"Very good, Mr. Tesla."

It was Kel, stepping out from a sliding panel in the wall. He held a gun aimed at Tesla.

"Drop your gun," Kel said.

Tesla didn't move.

"Now," Kel said.

Tesla dropped his ray-gun on the floor.

"Now turn around," Kel said.

Tesla turned around, holding up his hands, and said,

"I have blocked all access to this room. Your guards cannot help you."

"What audaciously deluded words for a man with a gun pointed in his face," Kel said. "What need have I of guards? Of armies? I am Kel. I do not rule because I have armies. I have armies because I rule."

Kel motioned with his left hand for Tesla to move over to the balcony railing. Tesla warily took a step forward.

"Look down there," Kel said. "A million volts of electrical power are coursing through the plate at this very moment. You don't believe me?"

Tesla's eyes narrowed. "You—" he started to say.

"Yessiree Bob," Kel said in the accent of an Arkansas farmer, "that junk'll fry you dead."

"You!" Tesla said. "That was you—at the fair—in the crowd—at my exhibit!"

"Of course it was me," Kel said. "Didn't I tell you? I've been at your heels for years. I've been your shadow. Now you will become my shadow when you step upon the plate and one million volts of electricity burns through every muscle, vein, and bone of your body. And it won't be a cheap sideshow trick, either. You won't be wearing any cork-bottomed shoes this time. No insulation whatsoever. Take off the helmet! Take it off!"

Tesla reached up, pressed the button on his neck ring, and began unscrewing his helmet.

"That's it," Kel said. "Take it off. Take it all the way off."

Tesla removed his helmet and set it down on the counter of the electrical switch board.

"And the suit," Kel said. "Off with it!"

Tesla unbuckled his knapsack and dropped it to the floor.

"All of it!" Kel shouted.

Tesla pulled the tab down on the front of his air pressure suit, opened it up, and pulled his arms out of the suit's sleeves.

"The bottom as well," Kel said.

Tesla pulled his legs out of the bottom of the suit, and then dropped the whole suit on the floor in a heap. Tesla now stood in his stocking feet, wearing only his collarless shirt and trousers.

"That will do," Kel said. "Yes, that will be quite sufficient. You first, Mr. Tesla."

Kel pressed a button on the railing of the balcony, and a section of the railing slid back, and, below, a rectangular plank like a bathhouse diving board slid out from the balcony.

Kel said, "I read this in one of your old Earth books. Your old pirates executed their captives at sea by walking the plank. We have no seas on Mars. Not for thousands of years. We'll have to make do. Instead of walking the plank over water, you'll have to walk the plank over—electricity!"

Kel motioned for Tesla to step on to the plank. Tesla hesitated a moment, then took a step toward the plank, then another. He was in front of it. He lifted his foot over the plank—then suddenly spun about and grabbed Kel's gun arm. Tesla felt the tremendous strength of Kel as the two men struggled at the balcony's edge.

"Surprised at my strength, Mr. Tesla?" Kel asked, his eyes laughing. "You believed the low gravity of Mars would have weakened us! We are a people invigorated by cosmic radiation! We are the strongest and most willful humans in this solar system and we will conquer you weaklings of *Erta*!"

Tesla took advantage of Kel's speechifying and forced the Martian king's gun arm up into the air. The weapon fired, blasting a hole through the opposite wall.

"You fool," Kel shouted, "you'll kill us all! The crystal will explode!"

Tesla slammed Kel's gun hand against the balcony railing, and the ray-gun fell like a lost scepter and clattered to the floor below.

Kel struck out with his fist and hit Tesla square in the face. Tesla fell upon the projecting plank. Kel leapt on to Tesla, grasping Tesla's throat.

"Test my system, Mr. Tesla!" Kel shouted, his eyes wide and glowing with fury. "Test my system! As you did for your own at the fair!"

Kel tightened his grip on Tesla's throat and pulled him along the length of the plank to where it projected out over the electrified platform below.

"Must I. . . Must I," Tesla gasped.

Kel loosened his grip.

"Yes, Mr. Tesla?" Kel asked, smiling with contempt.

Tesla asked, "Must I always do everything myself?"

Kel's smile of contempt changed in an instant; his eyes widened, his mouth twisted open in shocked rage. The Martian king had felt a sudden force grab him at the back of his neck where the spine meets the skull, a pinching, paralyzing force, part physical pain, part nameless horror. Then, before any struggle was possible, the great king Kel felt a sharp dagger-like thrust to his abdomen; the thrust was Tesla's toe. Tesla's foot struck on forward into Kel's flesh and internal organs, while Tesla's right hand held Kel's neck in a vice-grip. Tesla saw Kel's face moving up and away from him, a face contorted by rage and horror.

The Martian king's body was pushed into the air, pivoting at the neck where Tesla held fast. Then Tesla released his grip, and Kel's head flew away, rotated above Tesla's face in mid-air, and followed its pivoting body up, over, and out from Tesla's line of sight.

There was a terrific boom and flash of light and heat. Tesla turned on the plank and looked down.

Kel had landed feet first on the electrified platform, and now stood upright, trembling in an electrically induced muscle-freeze. His entire body was enveloped in an electrical nimbus of spiked fire and lightning.

Tesla climbed off the plank, and rushed to the control board. He flipped switch after switch, but none produced any effect. He then picked up his ray gun from the floor, aimed, and fired, blasting the switch board into a smoking ruin.

The electrical power feeding on to the platform below was severed. The nimbus around Kel instantly disappeared. Released from his invisible electrical bonds, Kel teetered upright for an instant, and then collapsed on the platform.

Inside Tesla's airship, Czito exchanged fire with a group of Martian guards. I stood at the pilot's wheel trying to catch a glimpse of one of the aeronauts. In a moment I saw Lillie West and George Ade flying through the cavern toward us. As they approached, I could see that Ade was missing his knapsack and was clinging to Lillie. They flashed by the pilothouse windows and went flying toward the stern of the airship.

"That's the way," I said, "get back in here!"

Outside the airship, Ade reached for the door to the ship's airlock, opened it, and Lillie and he flew inside, shutting the door behind them.

I saw the airlock indicator light next to the pilot's wheel flash on.

"They're in!" I shouted to Czito. "They made it! Now where's Tesla?"

Tesla was still in the domed tower. He had just finished donning his pressure suit, buckling on his knapsack, and screwing his helmet back into its neck ring. He switched on his antigravity machine and flew over the balcony and down to the platform where Kel lay.

Tesla floated in mid-air above the Master Crystal, and, with a pair of insulated tongs, removed the flashing crystal from the pedestal. He brought a metal cylinder out of his knapsack, and inserted the Master Crystal into it, closed the cylinder's hinged lid, dowsing the crystal's light, and slid the cylinder and the tongs into a side pocket of his knapsack. With all these items secured, Tesla flew out over the platform and landed on the floor near one of the doors.

Tesla was about to go out the door when he heard a groan from behind. He turned and saw Kel's arm reach up into the air. Tesla went back and looked down at Kel.

The Martian King was a smoking, blackened scarecrow; the whites of his eye were blood-red. In a deep, gurgling voice, Kel croaked:

"You have the power now, Mr. Tesla. You have the power. But will they let you keep it?"

"They?" Tesla asked. "Who are 'they'?"

"J.P. Morgan," Kel replied, "and the men who pull his strings. Will they let you keep the. . . ."

Kel's face froze. A thin line of blood trickled from the corner of his mouth. His blood-red eyes continued to stare at the ceiling, but they saw nothing, for Kel was dead.

Tesla stepped back from the platform, and then turned and went out through the door.

Czito continued to fire at the Martian guards on the balconies of the cavern walls as I slowly piloted our airship above the underground city searching for some sign of Tesla.

Lillie West and George Ade came up the stairs of the pilothouse with their helmets removed. Lillie had also removed her knapsack.

"Am I glad to see you!" Ade said.

"Likewise!" I said, shaking his hand.

"Mr. Clemens!" Lillie said, hugging my neck.

"My dear," I said, patting her back. "Where's Tesla?"

"Back there," Ade said. "Where we left him."

"And Houdini?" I asked.

"He fell," Ade said. "They hit him hard."

I looked at Lillie and her eyes said it all.

"You did all you could," I said, "all that anybody could."

"What do we do now?" Ade asked.

I said, "Those varmints want a war, so let's give them the damnedest one they'll ever see!"

Below us, a group of Martian guards stood on a massive metal deck. They were adjusting cannon directly up at us. Suddenly they fired a ball of lightning at us that struck just below the pilothouse.

"They're breaking out their heavy artillery again!" I shouted to Czito. "Give them everything you've got!"

Czito fired an electric ray upon the guards with the cannon. The ray produced a brilliant flash of white light, and, when it cut off, guards, cannon, and metal platform were all gone! Those guards—like the others—had been completely vaporized out of existence by the electric ray!

Tesla was now flying above the underground city. He had seen our airship and was headed straight for it. As he passed over one of the bridges he heard a shout.

"Hey! Hey! Hey, Mr. Tesla! Mr. Tesla!"

Tesla looked down. He saw Houdini dressed in his red flannel underwear running on the bridge below and waving his arms.

Tesla swooped down to the bridge and grabbed hold of Houdini with his left arm, and then the two of them lifted back up into the air.

Now I saw Tesla and Houdini coming toward us in mid-air. Bolts of electricity from Martian ray guns shot past them in their flight. As Tesla flew along, he fired back to the right and left with his ray-gun.

Tesla and Houdini swooped by the pilothouse windows.

"Tesla's got him!" I shouted. "He's got the boy!"

Lillie and Ade ran to the pilothouse windows and looked toward the stern of the airship.

Tesla flew upward to the door of the ship's airlock. He grabbed the door handle, opened it, and swung Houdini through the door.

In the next instant a ball of electricity struck Tesla, and his knapsack erupted in sparks. Tesla was enveloped in a shimmering green haze and he began to jitter up and down in mid-air. He would drop, rise, and drop again. In one of these sudden plunges, Tesla's ray-gun slipped from his hand, floated in mid-air for a moment, and then tumbled and fell into the cavern. Tesla had managed to get back to the door of the airship when he saw a Martian guard on one of the balconies aiming electric cannon at him.

Tesla reached out in the green electric haze, spun his hand about, formed a ball of lightning, and threw it at the Martian guard. The ball struck the guard dead in a white explosion of electricity.

Tesla's anti-gravity machine went completely dead, and he began to fall past the open door of the airship. His hand shot out, grabbed hold of the door, and he swung himself inside the airship, slamming the door behind him.

"Tesla's in!" I shouted, seeing the airlock indicator light flash. "And we're getting the hell out! Czito! Get down here!"

Czito came sliding down the ladder.

I said, "Get back to the engine and turn up the juice! We're going back through the rock right now!"

Czito ran down the stairs.

"Lillie," I said, "Mr. Ade, you folks better brace yourselves. Czito's turning up the power on the engines and we are going to thin out, you might say. Yes sir, we are going to get so thin that we won't even be able to see each other. Just stand where you are and don't move around—and don't panic. We'll be back to normal just as soon as we get through all this rock here."

I had steered the prow of the airship right up against the wall of rock where we had come in. Lillie and Ade looked at each other and back at me; they must have thought I had lost my mind. In a second they might have thought they had lost their own, too; for that green haze started to fill the pilothouse, and in another second or two we all started to fade from sight.

I said, "The electricity is making us transparent. Now I'm taking us straight through that wall of rock. Everything is going to go black while we pass through, but just stay where you are and breathe easy."

I tapped the accelerator pedal and we sunk into the wall of rock. Everything went black, just as I promised, and in another few seconds, a twilight scene broke upon us. It was the exterior of the Martian volcano and the sun had just set.

"Turn down the juice!" I shouted back to Czito.

That green haze started forming around us again and when it cleared out, everything was sure and solid again, and I saw Lillie and Ade standing there, both of them white with shock.

"Now don't be concerned," I said. "We just got our atoms stretched out a mite so we could wiggle through the atoms of the rock. It was just a slight stretch—nothing compared to Ebner's Sponge Syndrome."

I took us out across the floor of the volcano, and then stopped the airship and looked back at the big door in the wall of rock. It remained closed and I did not think it would open again.

Czito came up the stairs of the pilothouse, followed by Tesla and Houdini. Tesla was still in his air pressure suit, but he had removed his knapsack and helmet. Houdini was wearing his shirt and trousers. Lillie and Ade rushed up to Houdini. Lillie threw her arms around the boy's neck while Ade grasped Houdini's arm and patted his back.

"All right, all right, yez wisenheimers," Houdini said. "Didja think they could hold Houdini?"

"Not for long," Ade said.

"Say," Houdini asked, "what kind of trick was that, I'd like to know? Were we invisible or were we invisible?"

"That trick was done by Mr. Czito, I believe," Tesla said.

"I remembered what you said about the circuit controller," Czito said.

"You shouldn't have done it, Mr. Czito," Tesla said.

"Blame me," I said. "I ordered him to do it."

"I'm blaming no one," Tesla said. "You shouldn't have done it. But if you hadn't done it, none of us would be standing here now."

Tesla came up to me by the pilot's wheel.

"Mark," Tesla asked, "how are you?"

"Sober, sanctified, and stercoranated!" I said. "Did you get it?"

"I got it."

"Then let's git!"

I hit the accelerator pedal and we went straight up and pierced the clouds. I steered us around to the west and put on some speed. In a second, the sun peeked out over the horizon. I kept going west until we got well into daylight and then I took us straight up through the blue and then into the night of space with all its stars.

Chapter Eleven

The Rip Van Winkle Wrinkle

> Now you begin to see, don't you, that *distance*
> ain't the thing to judge by at all; it's the time
> it takes to go the distance *in* that *counts*, ain't it?
>
> — Tom, *Tom Sawyer Abroad*

There is a kind of satisfaction that comes over a body when he has set out to do a deed and has done it and done it well; it is a sort of comfortable, self-important, self-satisfied feeling that settles on the legs and leaves the shoulders and arms feeling light, free, and easy. None of us in the airship had that feeling. We should have been rejoicing and praising God, but we did not feel so inclined. All of us had killed, all of us except me, and considering that I had directed a lot of the killing, it had to be concluded that I was responsible for the killing too.

Yes, we had been provoked. Yes, we had been shot at. Yes, we had killed in defense. Yes, we had killed as soldiers kill, under sanction of their government. But still we had killed. And that is not a light and simple matter, not simple at all until you do it. No one with any conscience at all can be indifferent to the matter of killing. The knowledge that you have killed weighs upon you; it does not settle in your legs, but in your neck and shoulders, and it is a taste in your mouth—bitter and acidic and dry. And so for quite a while none of us said a word. We all stood in the pilothouse together. We had survived. We had succeeded and gained possession of the crystal. But we had killed.

I piloted the airship beyond Mars. With Tesla's instructions, I got the prow of our ship pointed toward Earth. We could see our planet shining in the black void as a little blue star, a mere point of light which held the infinite spaces of human thought and feeling. All that had ever happened to mankind had happened on that one point; the rise of the Atlantean civilizations and their fall; the re-emergence of civilization in Sumer and Egypt; its development in Greece, Rome, and Europe; and now the birth of our industrial world. Millions upon millions of human lives lived on that blue point in brief joy and long suffering to be vanished and replaced with millions upon millions more. As my daughter Susy had once asked long ago when she was a small child: "What's it all for?" I did not have an answer for her then. As I piloted our airship toward the blue star that was Earth, I still did not have an answer.

Tesla gave Czito the metal cylinder containing the Master Crystal, and said, "Secure the crystal, Mr. Czito."

Czito took the cylinder and started down the steps of the pilothouse. Houdini followed behind him.

"I guess I'll get out of this contraption," Ade said, and he turned and followed Czito and Houdini down the steps.

Lillie was facing me. I looked over at her.

She asked, "Do you still hate persistence in a woman, Mr. Clemens?"

"Now did I say that? I'm always uttering one sort of foolishness or another. It's one of the pitfalls of being a humorist. You know what my mother always said about me? She said, 'Discount everything he says fifty percent. The rest is pure gold.' Anyway, I found out something about you. You're not just a woman. You are a lady. And a lady is nothing if not persistent."

"Miss West," Tesla asked, "are you all right?"

"I'm fine, Mr. Tesla," Lillie said. "Now."

"I've been thinking about what you said."

"Mr. Tesla—"

"You were right, of course. The people of Earth have a right to know about the existence of the Martians. But there are powerful men who are determined to keep the people from knowing the truth. Will you help me in a plan? A gradual release of the truth?"

"How?"

"I will start by giving a series of interviews in which I discuss Mars and the intelligent electric signals I have detected coming from there. Perhaps we can get such statements published in Newspapers such as yours—despite whatever pressures may be brought to bear on the papers' editors."

"I'll be glad to help."

"Thank you. For everything."

Tesla started to turn away, but Lillie stopped him.

"Mr. Tesla, what I said about you being a shoddy lightning rod—"

Tesla smiled down at Lillie, and said, "Do not concern yourself, Miss West, I have been known in my time to bend, but never to break."

Instead of growing smaller, it was growing bigger.

Down on the lower deck, Czito removed the Master Crystal from the canister with a pair of tongs. He placed the crystal on an insulated pedestal, and then stood watching the crystal pulsing with a rainbow of light.

Houdini came up beside Czito, and said, "So that's it."

"That's it," Czito said.

"It sure is a beaut," Houdini said. "Does it always flash like that?"

"Always," Czito said.

Lillie had gone below to the lower deck, and now only Tesla and I stood in the pilothouse. Tesla had removed his air pressure suit and had stowed it in the closet aft of the pilothouse.

We were humming along at a steady rate of acceleration. Every once in a while, Tesla would go back to the control board to make sure everything was running as it should.

I glanced aft through the pilothouse windows and saw that Mars hung behind us as a big, ruddy globe. Never before or since have I felt such relief to be out of a place as I felt to be out of that red planet. I had seen it once and once was far too much. I have no doubt everyone else on board felt the same way. In a few more hours we would all be back on Earth and our lives could return to normal, that is, if we could remember at all what normal was.

At the stern of the airship, Ade stood looking through the windows of the library, watching Mars shrink and recede in space. He had changed back into his clothes, and now the events that had transpired back on Mars seemed to him to be only a strange dream.

Lillie came into the library and stepped inside the threshold of the door.

"I wondered what I would do if you didn't come back," Lillie said.

Ade turned around and saw that Lillie had changed back into her dress.

"And what did you decide?" Ade asked.

"I decided that if you didn't come back, I didn't want to come back, either."

Ade stood looking at Lillie. The masked expression he always wore to protect himself from the world was gone.

"Well," Ade said, "I'm here. I've come back. What are you going to do now?"

"I'm coming back, too," Lillie said.

"Well," Ade said, "come on, if you're coming," and he held his arms out.

Lillie ran to him; their arms encircled each other, and they kissed.

Down below on the lower deck, Czito continued to watch the crystal. The relief and safety Czito had been feeling was suddenly interrupted with a stab of panicked uncertainty. It seemed to him that the intervals between the crystal's flashes of light were too brief. He took out his pocket watch and began timing both the duration of the flashes of light and the dark intervals between them.

"What's wrong?" Houdini asked.

"Sh!" Czito hissed sharply.

Czito held his watch up in front of him and counted off the seconds. Before two minutes had passed, Czito gasped, "Oh, no! The crystal!"

"What?" Houdini asked. "What's wrong?"

Czito said nothing, but removed the crystal from the pedestal with the pair of insulated tongs and shot up the ladder, with Houdini following up behind at Czito's heels.

Czito and Houdini rushed into the pilothouse, with Czito shouting, "Mr. Tesla! Mr. Tesla!"

"Czito!" Tesla snapped, turning about. "What is it?"

"The crystal," Czito gasped, "it's pulsing irregularly!"

"Let me see it," Tesla said, and he took the crystal in its tongs from Czito. In his other hand he brought out a jeweler's loop and looked at the crystal through it.

Tesla said, "The Martians have tampered with it. They've electrically altered the geometry of its lattice. It's drawing too much power."

Tesla looked up, and said, "It's going to explode. Czito! Open the jettison tube! Mark! Get ready to floor the accelerator pedal on my command!"

Czito opened the jettison tube. Tesla approached and inserted the Master Crystal into the tube, closed the tube's door, and pushed a button. There was a sudden sound of air rushing out.

"Now, Mark!" Tesla shouted. "Floor the pedal!"

I pressed my foot down on the accelerator. Immediately the field of stars in front of me began to move off to the right and left.

"Faster, Mr. Clemens!" Czito said. "Faster! We must attain light speed! Faster than light speed!"

"Hold on to your britches," I said. "We'll be going so fast, we'll get to where we're going before we get to where we got!"

I closed the light speed switch and slammed the accelerator pedal all the way to the floor. The field of stars in front of us began to distort and pucker together into a ring. I looked aft through the pilothouse windows and could see a pulsating source of rainbow colored light. We were rushing away from that light source, but instead of it growing smaller, it was growing bigger. In another instant, I could see that it was the crystal, growing bigger by the second. With each pulse of the light it expanded—now it was a spinning tetrahedron—now an octagon—now a giant faceted sphere the size of a moon.

I turned forward and kept my foot on the accelerator pedal. I could see the rainbow colored light wash over the prow of the airship. I turned back around, and saw that the crystal was bigger than ever and spinning rapidly on an axis.

It seemed to be rolling toward us! I glanced around the pilothouse and saw that Tesla was gone; only Czito and Houdini stood behind me, silhouettes against a flashing rainbow colored blaze. An instant later, I saw Tesla bound up the steps with Lillie and Ade coming up behind him.

I turned forward again. The stars in front of us had tightened their ring and had almost compressed into a ball of light.

Czito said, "Mr. Tesla, the—"

His words were cut off. The Master Crystal exploded behind us in an almost blinding burst of white light—almost blinding for none of us were looking directly at the crystal when it exploded. The explosion must have been titanic, but at first it made no sound. Then there came a terrible crackling electrical noise and it engulfed the whole ship and grew to an almost unbearable roar.

I kept my foot on the accelerator pedal. The field of stars in front of us shrank to a single point of light. Behind us, from the exploding crystal, came a storm of fire reaching out in great long arms to engulf our ship. I felt a tugging on the pilot's wheel and a vibration, but I kept my foot on the accelerator pedal. Suddenly, the point of light ahead winked out, as did the fire behind.

Czito said, "We are moving faster than light."

Tesla said," Yes, the starlight has shifted beyond the range of ultraviolet. You may slow the ship down now, Mark."

I took my foot off the accelerator pedal and hit the brake pedal. There was a burst of light in front of me; the universe opened up; the stars expanded apart, and, with them, the Earth came out as a great blue-white sphere hurtling toward us!

"Looka there!" I shouted. "We're coming in! We're coming home! Yee-how! Damned if I ain't a white-hot rocket from hell!"

I piloted the airship straight for Earth.

In a moment, Czito said, "Fire. I smell fire!"

Tesla and Czito rushed down the stairs to the ship's engines, with Houdini, Ade and Lillie following close behind.

On the upper deck, Tesla slid back the door of the engine. Black smoke rolled out of the cabinet. An electrical fire was raging inside.

Tesla said, "The explosion of the crystal must've destroyed the aerial conductors and instantly overcharged the drive crystal so that it is now drawing power uncontrollably."

"Can't you remove it?" Ade asked.

"No," Tesla said. "It would explode. We must abandon ship. Everyone to the lower deck—to the escape craft!"

Lillie, Houdini, Ade, and Czito began descending through the hatchway to the lower deck, while Tesla rushed forward into the pilothouse.

As Tesla approached me, I was steering the airship into the upper reaches of Earth's atmosphere.

"Mark!" Tesla shouted. "We must abandon ship!"

"What are you talking about? I can land this bird on a dime!"

"The drive crystal's going to explode!"

"Why'nt you say so? Let's get the hell out of here!"

Tesla and I ran down the stairs of the pilothouse and slid down the ladder to the lower deck.

Czito already had the glass dome of the escape craft hinged open. We all climbed inside, Tesla at the pilot's wheel with me beside him, Czito and Houdini in the seat behind us, and, in the back seat, Lillie and Ade.

Tesla pushed a button on the board in front of us, and the glass dome pivoted over our heads and closed down on the top of the craft in a hermetic seal. Tesla pushed another button, and a door at the stern of the airship rolled down into the floor, revealing blue sky beyond the opening.

Tesla flipped a switch and pressed the craft's accelerator pedal and we shot forward out of the airship like a rocket. Suddenly we were surrounded by bright, blue sky.

Tesla brought our escape craft around in an arc. We circled the airship which was rocketing through the sky at a tremendous speed. Black smoke poured out of the opening we had just come through at the ship's stern.

Suddenly, without warning, Tesla's airship exploded in a terrific blast of electric fire—it was a ball of spiked yellow-white lightning—[ker-*BLAM*!] And then the fire was instantly replaced with a cloud of gray smoke that rose up and spread itself out in a long swath. Out of the cloud I could see black particles come raining down—the particles were all that was left of the airship.

"Well," I said, "that's it."

"That's all," Tesla said. "The work of half a lifetime."

We watched the pieces of the airship rain down as its ruined mass continued forward above the surface of the Earth. Then the black rain stopped, and Tesla piloted the airship away from the explosion and turned us toward the south.

We had come into the Earth's atmosphere somewhere over the general vicinity of the North Pole. Below lay a white, frozen wasteland. Then, in a minute or two, we saw a timberline in the distance. At our height it was only a black line. We approached that black line and it became a forest, glittering with lakes. We were in the northern reaches of Canada, rapidly moving south.

Then, unmistakably, a familiar shape came into view way down below through the clouds. I had seen that shape all my life on maps, but I had never really seen it before in all its true detail, color, and life.

"Well-a-well," I said. "There she is—Lake Michigan! I can't believe it! We all made it home—and not a scratch on any of us!"

Czito held up his finger, streaked with bright crimson, and said, "I have a scratch!"

"Did everybody hear that?" I asked. "Mr. Czito has a scratch! Mr. Czito, when we get back to Chicago, I'm going to buy you and your scratch all the whiskey the two of you can drink!"

"Mr. Clemens!" Czito said with severity, but then his face broke into a big grin. "Me and my scratch—would like that very much!"

Well, that was the end of it. Tesla's great airship was no more, and he never rebuilt it—at least as far as I know. But since that day who can say with any certainty what Tesla has accomplished? He has revealed some of his secrets to a few such as me, but I do not believe Tesla will ever reveal all his secrets—to his enemies or to his friends.

We approached Chicago, and the place seemed changed since we had left it. Where there had been a clear and dry and windy sky, there were now clouds closing in over the city—and high above those clouds a thin haze was spread out diffusing the rays of the sun.

Tesla brought us down low over the lake, skimmed its surface, and then submerged our escape craft down into the waters below. A few moments later he brought us up out of the lake in a sudden splash. The doors of Tesla's warehouse were about a hundred yards ahead. Tesla pushed a button on the board in front of us and the warehouse doors slid open and we flew up and through them and then landed inside on the floor.

Tesla opened the glass dome of the escape craft and we were immediately encircled by armed sailors. A naval captain came forward, and said:

"We were about to give up on all of you, Mr. Tesla, you've been gone so long."

"Only a few hours," Tesla said.

"Certainly not, sir!" the captain said. "You have all been missing for over a week—eight days to be exact!"

"It has only seemed like eight days," I said.

"No," the captain said. "It has been eight days."

"What is the date?" Tesla asked.

"It is Sunday, April twenty-third, eighteen ninety-three," the captain said.

"That can't be," I said. "We left on April fifteenth, and we've only been gone several hours, certainly less than a day! You must mean its Sunday, April sixteenth."

"No sir," the captain said. "It's the twenty-third."

We all got out of the escape craft, all of us a little shaky on our feet. Two doctors came into the warehouse with their medical bags; one was young and looked to be about thirty years of age, but the other was old and looked to be about a hundred, at least.

"The President wants all of you quarantined," the captain said.

"That will not be necessary," Tesla said. "Our foreign enemies have mingled with our population for a number of years with no ill effect. I propose that the doctors take cultures from all of us, and, if nothing unusual is found, we be released."

"I haven't the authority to make that decision," the captain said.

"Let me telephone the President," Tesla said. "Is he still in Chicago?"

"I do not know his whereabouts," the captain said. "I assume he is in Washington. However, the Secretary of War is here in the city."

Tesla nodded. "Let me speak with Lamont."

The captain led Tesla away to the telephone at the front of the warehouse, and the rest of us stood by the escape craft. The two doctors eyed us with apprehension.

I asked the doctors, "Where did they tell you we have been?"

"In the Far East," the old doctor answered. "They said you had traveled in an airship to the Far East."

"I see," I said. "Well, yes, we were in the Far East you might say, about as far East as a body can get."

Tesla was gone less than five minutes and when he returned he said very briskly, "All of us are to submit to an examination by the doctors here. They will take cultures from us. If they find nothing unusual, we will be taken to see Secretary Lamont."

The doctors and two nurses led us to a little makeshift examination area closed off with screens and curtains. They sent me behind a curtain and told me to take off all my clothes. I peeled off my coat and vest and kept on peeling until I had removed everything but the ornaments of nature, and then the old doctor came in and probed every inch of me from my head to my toe.

"Do you smoke?" he asked.

"Yes," I replied.

"How long?"

"Oh, two or three hours at a time, if I get the chance."

"No, no. How long since you started the habit?"

"That is hard to say, very hard to say."

"Approximate."

"I must've been nine when I started, but I am not sure. I think I experimented a few years earlier, but it was not a habit until nine."

"And how old are you now?"

"I will be fifty-eight in November."

"You must break the habit. It is slowly killing you."

"Yes, that's what the doctor told me when I was nine, and he was right!"

The old doctor nodded self-righteously a moment, and then stopped and glared at me.

"Are you trying to be funny?" the old doctor asked.

"No, sir," I said. "I wouldn't know how."

"I see," he said, seeming to be satisfied with my reply. "Well, you quit that smoking young man. If you don't, you will never reach a mature age."

I did not ask the doctor what he thought a mature age was, but I estimated that he believed it to be somewhere around a hundred and ninety-five or thereabouts.

"Aren't you supposed to take a sample of my microbes?" I asked.

"I am getting to that, young man. I am getting to that. Are you proposing to tell me my profession?"

"No sir, doctor. I should be mad to do such a thing."

"Who is your personal physician?"

"Dr. Clarence Rice of New York City."

"Umm hmm. Know of him. Know of him. Young society doctor, isn't he?"

"Yes, I believe he has been practicing medicine only about fifty years."

"I'm sure he's competent. But if I were you, I'd see another doctor with a little more experience. Now open your mouth."

The old doctor stuck a stick into my mouth with a ball of cotton tied to its end, wiped it around my teeth and gums and then drew it out. He went over to a table and wiped the stick on a glass slide, then put the slide under a microscope, and bent down and looked through the eyepiece of the instrument.

"Um hum," the doctor said. He kept looking through the eyepiece, and then added, "Bad, bad. Um hum. Very bad."

"What?" I asked. "What are you seeing there? It is a strange thing?"

"What?" the doctor asked looking up. "Oh, you mean this here? Oh no, your fluids are all normal. No, what I was thinking of was that smoking."

"Doctor," I asked, "what exactly did they tell you—those Navy boys?"

"They said you people had traveled to the Far East in an airship, that is all. Bah! I know it is a lie! An airship! What nonsense! Let the government keep its secrets, but they are not fooling me, not for an instant."

Well, we were all given a clean bill of health, more or less. At least it was determined that we had not carried any unknown microbes back home with us. We were all whisked in closed carriages to the Great Northern and there we were brought before President Cleveland and Dan Lamont, Secretary of War. Robert O'Brien, the President's private secretary, wrote down our interview. First, Tesla made a statement recounting precisely the events that had transpired since we last saw Cleveland. When he finished, Lamont began to question each of us, starting with Tesla, then me, and then all the others. This interview went on for several hours, and then Lamont announced that we would all be required to sign secrecy oaths. The oaths were brought out, and we all read through them. Houdini was the first to sign his oath, and Lillie West was the last, but sign she did. An interesting thing here: each oath was especially written for each of us individually. None of us fully knew what the others had signed. Such is the nature of governmental secrecy.

Lamont then proceeded to give each of us what he called our "cover stories"—the fictions which would hide what had really happened to us over the past week.

Tesla's fiction was that he and Czito had been called away by George Westinghouse on business, and Westinghouse had been informed to vouch for this claim.

Houdini had been given a fictional week by Lamont, but it was not to Houdini's liking, as it required Houdini to claim that he had been incarcerated in the jailhouse. It was finally agreed that Houdini would claim that during the last week he had started north to Appleton, Wisconsin to visit his old home place, but had instead reached no further than the town of Beaver Dam, where he stopped and spent several days fishing in the lake.

Lillie West and George Ade were a more difficult case. What was to be done with them? Lamont revealed to us that as soon as Lillie's story about the airships appeared on the front page of that *Daily* Record extra, the machinery of government secrecy went into operation. Cleveland had Lamont to call Charles Dennis and order him to confiscate all existing copies of the extra from the streets of downtown Chicago. At that same time, Lamont sent out Pinkerton agents to follow Lillie West and George Ade. If it had not been for Houdini's evasion at the dime museum, Lillie and Ade would have been stopped by the Pinkerton men when they approached anywhere near Tesla's warehouse. As it was, Houdini, Lillie, and Ade had given the Pinkerton agents "the slip." But when Lillie and Ade turned up missing, and the Pinkerton men found the skylight window removed from the top of Tesla's warehouse, Lamont and Cleveland guessed rightly that Lillie West, George Ade, and Houdini had somehow become involved with the conflict between Tesla and the Martians. Lamont called Charles Dennis and explained that Lillie West and George Ade were involved in some work for the U.S. Treasury, something involving tracking down a ring of counterfeiters, and that it was important that their absence remain a secret. Thus it was that Charles Dennis assigned John T. McCutcheon the task of writing all of George Ade's articles until he returned—or at least until he and the rest of us were reckoned as dead. For Lillie West, Eugene Field and McCutcheon continued her column under her by-line "Amy Leslie." McCutcheon knew both Lillie and Ade's styles of writing, and was able to imitate them well enough to fool even the most avid readers of their columns. Sometime during the week, Field complained of the extra work load and McCutcheon was able to locate some of Lillie's unpublished writings, including some material on Edwin Booth, which he was able to adapt into a eulogy. Thus, the absence of Lillie West and George West was seamlessly covered over. Only McCutcheon had an inkling of what the two reporters had really been doing during that week of April 14th to April 23rd, 1893.

As for me, something more than a story had to be told. It was decided by Cleveland that Fred Hall, Paige, and even my family could have no knowledge of my absence. Yet, how could they be kept from knowing? This problem was solved by Dan Lamont who went into immediate action the moment it was clear that we might not be coming back. Lamont took O'Brien with him across town to the slums. There, along Halstad Street, they went through all the saloons searching among the drunkards and tramps for a man who was my exact double in appearance.

"It must've been a seemingly impossible task," I said to Lamont when he told me what he had tried to do.

"Not at all," he replied. "In the first saloon we came to we found half a dozen men who bore a striking resemblance to you. We chose the one who was the drunkest and brought him back to your room at the Great Northern."

There in the room they got that poor old drunk liquored up to the point of petrified sleep. Then they dressed him in my night shirt, rolled him into my bed, and kept him lolling about there for the next week. Whenever he would wake up, they would give him a little food and a lot of whiskey, and he would soon fall into heavenly petrification again. Every once in a while Fred Hall or Paige would come by to look in, and a nurse employed by Lamont would always say my condition was guarded, but steadily improving, and there was no need for alarm. All I needed was rest. "I knew it," Hall would say, "I saw this coming."

When I got back to my room at the Great Northern, my imposter was gone, the room had been aired, and my bed had been freshly made. Still, I felt like one of the Three Bears coming back after Goldilocks had rifled through their belongings, but the one who had been sleeping in my bed was no Goldilocks. I inspected the sheets for vermin, and then got into one of my nightshirts and slipped down between the covers of the bed.

"No cigars!" I said. "What kind of hospital is this? Nurse!"

The nurse poked her head through the door.

"Nurse," I said, "bring me a cigar from that box in there on the table."

"Oh, you shouldn't be smoking in your condition," she said.

"Nurse, if I don't get a cigar and a match in one minute, I'm going to have a condition, all right. I'm going to have a conniption! Now, bring me my cigar!"

She removed her head and closed the door. I waited with great patience for several minutes, but no nurse appeared. Then I got up, and opened the door.

The nurse was sitting at the desk writing something.

I went to the table and opened the cigar box.

"Mr. Clemens!" the nurse said, turning to look at me. "You should not be up, not in your condition!"

"No," I said, "I should not be up! But I am up! I cannot get tended to in this here hospital so I must tend to myself!"

I struck a match and lit the cigar I had put in my mouth.

"Smoking those awful things is not tending to yourself!"

"These are not awful things, madam. They are the staff of life, at least for me. Now, I'm going back to my bedroom to smoke. You stay here and continue with your literary career. Remember, not to dangle participles, if you can help not to, and don't use no double negatives."

I went to my bedroom, closed the door, and got back in bed with my cigar. This was more like it! I sat up in bed with a cloud of smoke hovering over me and drifted into a reverie of sorts. Then I heard voices in the other room.

"He is being very disagreeable today," I heard the nurse say.

"That means he is getting better."

That was Fred Hall's voice. The door opened and Fred Hall and James Paige came through it with grave looks that suddenly brightened when they saw me.

"Mr. Clemens!" Hall cried out. "You look so—so—so much better! Doesn't he, Mr. Paige?"

"Yes," Paige said. "Why, yesterday, you looked so—so—so much worse! Didn't he, Mr. Hall?"

"Yes, indeed," Hall said. "Today you look alive."

"Frankly, Mr. Clemens," Paige said, "you looked so leathery and wrinkled! You looked like you had been living out of doors on nothing but strong whiskey for the last fifty years! Your eyes were so red—and you didn't even seem to recognize us!

"Yes," I said, "I've been out of my head for several days. Deliriously sick! Fever will do that. But I feel much better now. Now, Paige, does your conscience trouble you for the way you have treated me with all your delays?"

"Delays?" Paige asked. "I could almost forgive you for that word. Mr. Clemens, I must confess, it broke my heart when you left me and the machine to fight along the best way we could. But now, all is right. Yes, all is right, and our fight continues—unabated!"

Hall, Paige, and I talked awhile longer. They had managed to make another demonstration of the typesetting machine, but as yet had received no firm commitments from any of the potential investors. But the interest was still there, and several of the men who had seen the machine operate were now only considering just how much of an investment they wished to make.

Paige set on the edge of my bed, describing in detail how he planned to produce ten thousand machines in rapid succession. Then he began to tell me how he was negotiating with the New York investors to amend our contract with them so as to produce some ready cash for the machine. He was making them the offer of accepting no stock and instead asking for half a million dollars in cash. He was not sure if he could get that, but he promised that if they offered less, he would take the cash and send me half of it. Then Paige informed me that all the European patents on the machine had been settled, and that he was going to put me in for a handsome royalty on every European machine that would be sold over there. Paige said this in a magnanimous tone, but, later, after he left, I recalled that my contract with the Connecticut Company already gave me those rights. Paige made some very large and indefinite gilt-edged promises, so cloudy and formless that I could not make out what or how or if there were any substance or meaning to any of them. There I lay in that bed, having sunk more than one hundred thousand dollars into the machine, and I still could not see my way clear to getting any definite return from it. The more Paige talked, the more my head got muddled. He was the smoothest talker I ever heard, and, when he got up to leave, we parted immensely good friends.

Hall left with Paige, and I called for the nurse to bring me a pen and some writing paper. I scribbled a note to my sister-in-law Susan Crane explaining to her my delay in Chicago. It had been my original plan to spend only two or three days in Chicago, and then go to see her in Elmira, but my "sick spell" had interfered with all of that. I now wrote her that I did not want anybody to know that I was sick, for I feared that the very winds might blow the tale around the world to Livy.

I finished my letter to Susy Crane and then called the nurse in to give it to a bellman to put in the mail. With that chore accomplished, I lay back to rest for just a little while. Then there was a knock at my door.

I said, "Come in!"

It was Orion. He had not been back to see me all week, thank God! Otherwise, Livy would certainly have received from him a frightening letter! As it was, I was able to steer Orion away from knowing anything about my "serious illness." I admitted to only having a slight cold. It was not strange for Orion to see me in bed, for he knew I did some of my best writing and thinking while luxuriating on my back. Since I had seen him last, Orion had taken up and abandoned several schemes. His idea of being a correspondent for the World's Fair had long been discarded and forgotten, and I made no mention of it. Orion was now planning on returning home and taking up the raising of chickens. I gave him my blessing, and he went away fired with zeal for his chicken ranch plan. I knew when he reached home he would have forgotten the chickens and be off pursuing another grand scheme.

I lit another cigar and sat contemplating all that had happened to us aboard Tesla's airship. Then I got to pondering the conundrum presented to us by the naval captain when we came back. What had happened to the last week? We had completely lost it and would never find it again—not in all eternity!

Tesla has given a great deal of thought to our missing week and has concluded that it was the result of the explosion of the Master Crystal. As our airship moved rapidly away from the explosion, a part of our motion was caused by the explosion itself. Being pushed along from behind like that, it threw our electrical resonance out of whack with the surrounding ether and this caused the atoms composing our bodies and the airship to slow down their rate of vibrations. What seemed like mere seconds to us was a week of time here on earth and in the surrounding universe. Tesla says this was all the result of an increase of etheric pressure from the exploding Master Crystal and it caused what Tesla has described as a wrinkle in space and time. Tesla has named this freak of science and nature "The Rip Van Winkle Wrinkle" in honor of our friend, Joseph Jefferson.

The scientist Lorentz was informed of what had happened to us on board the airship and has tried to explain it by claiming that the space around our airship was flattened. I did not feel flattened then or now. I cannot hold with Lorentz, although a lot of people are trying to accommodate him lately, most notably a patent clerk in Europe by the name of Einstein. Tesla has looked at Einstein's ideas and has pronounced the young patent clerk to be the "new Ptolemy." In the Ptolemaic theory, epicycles were brought in to explain all the discrepancies. Whenever a planet seemed to move in a direction that the theory could not explain, it was said to be going through an "epicycle"; the planet had decided to take a holiday and go on a little orbit all its own. Now Tesla says Einstein's theory is similar to Ptolemy's, but with this exception: while Ptolemy introduced his epicycles only here and there when a holiday arose, Einstein's theory is *all* epicycle; it takes so many exceptions to Newtonian laws that just about every day is a holiday, and so no real work can get done, at least not beyond the speed of light. Now, on moral grounds I approve and commend Einstein's theory, for I always have felt and believed that work is sin, and I have always tried not to sin. But intellectually, and from practical experience, I cannot stand on the side of Einstein. Yes, his intentions are noble, his expressions are elegant and refined; the elimination of work from the universe is no small goal, and is worthy of our consideration. It is a goal I have attempted to achieve many times myself. So far, I have only eliminated my own work, but who knows what more patient thought may accomplish? No, I must reject Einstein. It is sad, it is tragic, but such is the way of the world.

As I lay there in my bed at the Great Northern smoking my cigar I did not yet have a firm grasp on all these ideas. I only knew that we had lost a week, and it troubled me. Losing a week is not like losing your pocketbook. The latter you might find again, but the former you will not, at least not without the assistance of a time machine. And who do you know that has a time machine? Tesla? Yes, come to think of it, perhaps Tesla.

I snuffed out the stub of my cigar in the ashtray next to my bed. I was feeling a little tired and thought that I would take a short nap. I lay back and fell into a light doze. When I awoke again, the whole night had passed and it was the next morning!

Chapter Twelve

The Superintendent of Dreams

> It's a curious thing, that the more you hear about
> a grand and big and bully thing or person, the more
> it kind of dreamies out, as you may say, and gets to
> be a big and dim wavery figger made out of moonshine
> and nothing solid to it. It's just so with George
> Washington, and the same with the pyramids.
>
> — Huck, *Tom Sawyer Abroad*

We had started out on our quest for the Master Crystal as unrelated individuals and had become knit into a group, a unit, perhaps even a family of sorts. And now circumstances were forcing us to break apart again, and to pretend that some of us were strangers to the others. Those of us who had known each other before the "incident" would continue knowing each other. But those of us who had become acquainted on board the airship would have to deny that acquaintance and even take pains to avoid associating with each other in the future.

We had all said quick goodbyes to each other at our meeting with Cleveland and Lamont. Lillie West and George Ade went off together to return to their jobs on the Chicago papers. Houdini went back to the theatrical boarding house where he had been staying to search for Joe Hyman, his replacement partner for his magic act. I went back to my hotel room, and Tesla and Kolman Czito remained with Cleveland and Lamont for many more hours of talks.

Since Lillie West and George Ade knew each other before our "incident," they would go on as they had before, but they could not write about Houdini or speak to him. And Houdini had to pretend that he didn't know them or me and that we had never met at all. Since Houdini had once been a messenger for Tesla, he was allowed to publicly contact Tesla, if circumstances required it. And I had to pretend that I didn't know Houdini either, or George Ade, or Lillie West. It was a dreary pretense, for these people had become my friends, and I knew I would miss them, and I have.

Fortunately, since I had known Tesla for several years, my friendship with him continued. And, through Tesla, I was told about how the lives of our other crew mates were progressing, for Tesla did not only continue to be in contact with Houdini, but he remained secretly in contact with George Ade and Lillie West as well. Later, some of my friends became acquainted with Lillie West and George Ade and so I managed to hear fragments of News about the two of them. W.D. Howells, in particular, admired Ade's writing and urged me to read the work of this new author whom he had discovered. I never told Howells that I had already read Ade's *Artie* and *Pink Marsh* in the *Chicago Record* installments before they had been published as novels. I had been subscribing to the *Record* and the *Daily* News specifically for the purpose of keeping up on Lillie and Ade.

If this story were a work of fiction, along here I would contrive a marriage for Lillie West and George Ade. But since this is my attempt to tell the truth—the truth with a small t—I must report that Lillie West and George Ade never married. Why, I do not know, nor does anyone else know as far as I can find out. Perhaps, in the end, they were too much alike. Both of them were driven, ambitious people. And in a marriage there can be only one boss, and usually, if it is to be a happy marriage, the boss is the wife. George Ade probably was not the kind of man to be put in harness. To this day he has never married, although his name has been linked with a number of ladies, several of them actresses. What I do know is that George Ade and Lillie West have remained friends through all these years.

Lillie never got the big story about the airship that she had gone after, but she got something else that was much bigger than a Newspaper story: she and Ade came to work for Tesla in some secret capacity. I'm not sure exactly what this work involved, but I know it had something to do with the Martians. John T. McCutcheon and Houdini were involved with this as well. Each of them had some kind of specific task assigned to them by Tesla.

Some of this work was connected with what has come to be known in certain Washington circles as "The San Francisco Incident of 1896." This was where an airship was sighted flying over San Francisco. It was later seen over the city of Sacramento, and flew directly over the dome of the state capitol as it passed low over that city. This time, so many people saw the airship flying through the skies that the story could not be kept out of the California Newspapers. The *Call*, my old San Francisco paper, carried a front page story about the airship complete with illustrations, as did the *Bee* in Sacramento. Tesla has told me that this was a newly built Martian airship and that he and

"Who am I?"

Kolman Czito destroyed it with a portable electric ray cannon somewhere in the vicinity of Pyramid Lake, Nevada.

After the Martian airship incidents of 1896-97, the astronomers Asaph Hall and Percival Lowell kept watching the skies for signs of the Martians, but, as far as they could tell, the Martians had not returned. However, there were signs that the Martians were still among us, and Tesla and the President believed that they were coming here in yet another anti-gravity airship.

When George Ade came to New York, Tesla gave him an assignment over in the Philippines and the surrounding islands. I believe that was around 1900. Tesla told me that when Ade left New York Harbor, he was carrying with him three cases of weapons and machinery that Tesla had designed. McCutcheon had already been sent over there to the Philippines during the Spanish-American War under the authority of the Treasury Department. I believe Ade and McCutcheon were also trying to find out if the Martians had re-activated some ancient tunnels over there. Also McCutcheon was involved in finding the source of counterfeit money being printed by the Martians. At this writing I believe that George Ade, "Amy Leslie," John T. McCutcheon, and Houdini are still involved with Tesla in this work. Tesla has told me that Houdini did some particularly important work for him over in Europe after the assassination of President McKinley.

Lillie West came to be known so widely by her pen name "Amy Leslie" that she finally dropped "Lillie" and had even her closest friends to call her "Amy." In the mid-1890s "Amy Leslie" would come to New York to see Tesla, usually staying with her married sister, Mrs. O'Brien on West 25th Street. It was during one of those visits that she became acquainted with Stephen Crane, author of *The Red Badge of Courage*.

She eventually had a bitter parting with Crane, who left for Florida owing her $800.00. She had to sue him in court to get about $500.00 of this money back, and, of course, this sad tale made its way to all the papers.

Crane's friends claimed that "Amy" was "mentally unbalanced," had the delusion that Crane had promised to marry her, and when he left her behind in New York to go to Florida, she sued him for the money out of spite. Even W.D. Howells, who knew Crane and admired his work, was taken in by this version of events for a time.

However, from Tesla I received another version of the story which I believed to be much closer to the truth. It went like this: Crane had misrepresented his intentions to "Amy," speaking of marriage even as he was involved with other women, some of them with very bad reputations. "Amy" believed Crane as he represented himself to be, and in the course of their romance revealed to him the work she was doing for Tesla, as well as what had happened to all of us back there in Chicago and on Mars in 1893. When some of Crane's royalties were slower in coming in than his spending was going out,

"Amy" loaned him $800.00 with the understanding that it would be paid back very shortly as soon as his latest royalties came in. But instead of the royalties coming in, something else happened. A woman Crane had been spending time with was arrested on a charge of prostitution. Crane went to court and testified that the woman was with him the night of her arrest and so could not have been guilty of the charge. The magistrate was so impressed with Crane's literary renown that he credited Crane's testimony and released the woman. But that was not the end of it. A departmental hearing followed. The arresting detective's attorney, the detective's superiors, and Crane's own Newspaper colleagues all denounced Crane. Well, here was an awkward situation, and anyone else would have had their ship sunk. But Crane was sailing high on his newfound literary reputation, and, taking the tide at its flood, he used that reputation to sail right on out of New York and down to Florida. Now, do you think "Amy" who had just loaned Crane $800.00 might be a little upset by all these developments? Who in all this was the "mentally unbalanced" party—"Amy Leslie" or Stephen Crane? I will only add here that "Amy Leslie's" suit was settled out of court. In 1898, Crane returned to New York and repaid the rest of the loan.

In 1901, "Amy Leslie" finally re-married. Her husband was not a famous author or a captain of industry, but an unknown young man from Texas by the name of Frank Buck. At the time Buck married "Amy Leslie" he was a bellboy at the hotel where "Amy" lived in Chicago. The last I heard, they are still happily married; Frank Buck works for Sol Bloom in his theatrical enterprises and "Amy Leslie"—Lillie West—continues her work as drama critic for the *Chicago Daily News*. I hear that "Amy," Buck, Ade, and McCutcheon all still remain friends.

All of us who made that voyage to Mars aboard Tesla's airship have kept our story a fairly strict secret. But no matter how hard one may try, something of the truth always eventually comes out. There were several "information leaks." The source of some of these leaks could be traced to specific individuals; the source of others will probably never be known.

One leak came from Lillie West. She had told Stephen Crane about what had happened to us, and, later in England, Crane told H.G. Wells, and this gave Wells the idea for his story "War of the Worlds."

George Ade kept his secrets well, but even he was tempted to put his experiences with all of us into his writing. However, he wrote in such a veiled and cryptic way that most people never realized what he was writing about. Ade's revelation came in the form of three short stories. These stories were quite unlike his usual writing, which was invariably realistic in tone, setting, characters, and plot. These three stories were burlesques of the "Incident of '93." Each was written as a story for children, and each told about the "Incident of '93" from the viewpoint of one of us who was involved with it.

The first story was entitled "Handsome Cyril; or, The Messenger Boy with the Warm Feet." In this story, Houdini, who was once a messenger boy, is burlesqued as the character "Cyril" and Tesla is "Alexander." Ade has the villain's henchmen in the story bind and gag "Cyril" with ropes and throw him in the river. "Cyril" escapes and thwarts the villain. I might also note here that the day for the St. *Cyril* who was archbishop of *Alexandria* is February 9th, the same as George Ade's birthday. This was the same St. Cyril who made no effort to stop the murder of the Neo-Platonic philosopher Hypatia who was clubbed to death by a mob of Christian fanatics in the year 415 A.D. I believe that George Ade, in giving Houdini the fictitious name of "Cyril," was making a statement about not only Houdini and himself, but all the rest of us who traveled to Mars on Tesla's airship. I think he was saying that just like St. Cyril, we, too, have stood by and allowed the ancient knowledge to be suppressed.

The next story Ade wrote was: "Clarence Allen, the Hypnotic Boy Journalist." "Clarence" is a burlesque of Ade himself, with elements of Tesla thrown in. "Clarence" pursues a thief who has stolen $37,000 worth of government bonds. He uses "bloodhounds" to track the thief.

The final story of the series was entitled: "Rollo Johnson, the Boy Inventor." "Johnson" was a code name for Tesla in that Mr. and Mrs. Robert Underwood Johnson are Tesla's closest friends. Of the three stories written by Ade, "Rollo Johnson" was the most transparent reference to the "Incident of '93". In the story, "Rollo" is the inventor of a "Demon Bicycle," the fictional counterpart of Tesla's airship. "Rollo" explains the secret of how his "Demon Bicycle" works to "Paul Jefferson" ("Pool-Cue" or "Pool" was Tesla's nickname for Joseph Jefferson, thus, "Pool" = "Paul"). "Paul Jefferson" says to "Rollo" upon the completion of the bicycle, "After four years of incessant toil, you are to be rewarded." Tesla's airship was built in four years, 1889-1893. "Rollo" uses electricity to run his bicycle and as the power for a gun which shoots lightning bolts. The secret plans for "Rollo's" electric bicycle are stolen by a villain. "Rollo" escapes the villain and his cohorts by riding his bicycle through the air and eventually retrieves his secret plans. The villain escapes, but "is never again seen in Chicago."

Thus, George Ade did write about Tesla's airship, but in the form of a literary cipher. A few of us recognized the meaning of his stories.

As I said, we who had become acquainted aboard Tesla's airship were supposed to pretend we never met, but on three different occasions I did cross paths with some of my fellow airship crew mates.

I saw George Ade again on two different occasions. The first time was in 1902. After President McKinley was assassinated, I was contacted by a secret government commission. They wanted me to tell them the whole story of what had happened to me in 1893, just as I had experienced it.

Well, nine years had passed, a very hard nine years. I felt that I could not supply all the detail they were looking for and tried to direct them to Tesla and the others. They said they were contacting all of us, but they wanted my version as best as I could recall. I suggested that if I were given notes from Tesla and all the others concerning their remembrances of our journey and battle, it might help my own recollections. As it turned out, everyone was agreeable to this plan with the exception of George Ade, who, for reasons of his own, distrusted releasing anything to any messenger. He would only agree to deliver his notes to me in person. The committee did not like this idea at all. Then it occurred to me that my personal physician, Dr. Clarence Rice, was also acquainted with George Ade. I suggested to the committee that I could arrange a meeting with Ade through Dr. Rice, a meeting that would seem quite simple and natural and ordinary—just two authors meeting for an informal chat. Thus it was that George Ade and Dr. Rice came up to visit me at Riverdale, New York.

Ade and Dr. Rice came up to the house one afternoon and we sat on the veranda and talked for several hours, Ade talking about his books and his plays being produced on Broadway, and I talking about the Mississippi River Valley and the future of the American Midwest. As Ade and Dr. Rice were leaving, Ade passed to me a package bound in paper and said, "I thought you might find this of interest." Later, when I opened the package, I found it contained not only George Ade's secret notes, but those of Nikola Tesla, Kolman Czito, Lillie West, and Harry Houdini. At present, I still have these notes in my possession and have referred to them to refresh my memory while relating this account.

I only saw George Ade one other time. When my seventieth birthday party was being planned, it was decided that all the literary luminaries should attend, and I made it known that I wanted George Ade and John T. McCutcheon to be invited. I wasn't able to speak to Ade that evening, but while I was delivering my after-dinner speech, I saw Ade sitting at a table across the room. At that moment I was saying that I would be satisfied if my fame reached to Neptune. As everyone else laughed, Ade and I nodded slightly to each other. I doubt any of the others noticed, but even if they did, they could not have understood that Ade and I knew that it was possible that somebody may have read one of my books on Mars.

I happened to see Harry Houdini again just one time. One Sunday in 1905, while I was walking down Fifth Avenue, I had just passed the Waldorf Astoria and crossed over 34th Street when I spied Houdini coming toward me from out of the throng. He was accompanied by two ladies whom I assumed were his wife and mother. He said nothing to me, and I said nothing to him, but I am certain that he recognized me and that he knew that I recognized him. He was no longer a boy, but a very broad-shouldered man. I nodded to him slightly, just as I had done with Ade, and he nodded back, just as Ade had done with me. He did not turn his head, but just kept looking at me out of the corner of his eyes as we passed. His wife and mother were talking to each other and passed by without seeing me.

After Hall and I left Chicago on April 24th, 1893, I managed to finally get up to Elmira, New York, to see my sister-in-law, Susan Crane, and then set off for Europe.

When I reached Villa Viviani in the hills above Florence, my daughters Susy and Jean came bounding out of the old mausoleum to greet me. My wife, Livy, appeared in the doorway, pale and smiling. They all threw their arms around me and into the house we went. I was home.

Did I say a word to any of them about what happened to me in Chicago? No, I kept my mouth shut. Nobody would have believed me anyway. *I* would not have believed me.

I'd like to say that from there on out all was well and we all lived happily ever after. That is the way it goes in fiction; in fact, "happily ever after" is the ultimate fiction, for nothing in life is "happily ever after."

That fall I had to return to America. The creditors for my publishing company were circling us like wolves that had been put on a strict diet. I now thought of Cleveland's words to me about the money powers throwing me out a safety net. I decided to make a quick trip down to Washington to see Cleveland.

When I got to the President's mansion, Cleveland's wife showed me into his bedroom. I stopped in the doorway and took a sharp breath. The man who had been so big to me now lay before me reduced to a ghostly scarecrow. The left side of Cleveland's face had sunken inward forming a horrific cavern beneath his cheek. He reached over to a table next to his bed, removed a rubber plug from a jar of water, and shoved it into his mouth. Gagging and coughing, he adjusted the plug, and his caved-in left cheek ballooned back out to its normal appearance.

Cleveland said, "They operated on me. Twice. They damn near killed me."

The President described what had happened to him in detail, the discovery of his cancer, the secret operation on board the yacht *Oneida* while she stood out at anchor in New York Harbor, and the second operation in which he had almost died. Since then, he had conducted business from his bed, while the actor who was his double moved about the country on fishing trips with Newspaper reporters tagging along at a distance.

"Did they get it all out?" I asked.

"Yes," Cleveland said, "finally. The doctors have told me that I will live. I'll be able to finish out my term. But from now on—for the rest of my life—I will have to wear this damn rubber plug in the roof of my mouth. What brings you here, Clemens? Something happening with the Martians?"

"No, Your Excellency, nothing like that. Just my own troubles. I feel ashamed to bother you with them after what you've gone through."

"It's your finances."

"My creditors want payment. I have nothing to pay them with. I am, in fact, hours away from financial ruin. In Chicago last spring you said something. Something about the big money men throwing me out a safety net if I ever needed it. Did you really mean that?"

"I did."

"Well, I need that net now. Badly."

"I'll wire Henry Rogers about your situation. You know Rogers, don't you?"

"I met him once about two years ago. He seemed to me a likable fellow."

"He and his family adore your books. I'll wire him that you'll be coming to see him."

"If you could, please wire him that my lawyer will see him tomorrow in New York. I believe my lawyer is fairly well acquainted with Rogers. And if it ever comes up with anyone, I'll tell them my physician, Dr. Rice, introduced me to Rogers, for Dr. Rice knows Rogers too."

Everything happened as Cleveland said it would. Through my lawyer, I was introduced to Rogers. The three of us sat down and my lawyer painted the bleak picture of my finances, and when he finished, Rogers said:

"You are in a serious situation. It is good that you turned to me. We must act swiftly. I'll immediately issue the Mount Morris Bank a check. That will set things aright for the moment. But we must begin developing a strategy for the future. You and I, Clemens, will depart for Chicago immediately to see Paige."

Rogers and I became fast friends. He seemed to be familiar with all my books and he knew a good deal about me, my wife, and my family. After a short while, I began to feel as if I had known him all my life. We took Roger's private car to Chicago. There we met with Paige and the Chicago investors.

Paige was his usual self, which is to say, a louse. He refused to release any more of his stock for sale to investors. Rogers told me this would make it difficult for us to attract the right kind of investors in New York. It was finally agreed that Paige and the mechanics would build an entirely new model of the typesetter. If this model passed all its test runs, we would pursue further investors. With these things decided, I returned to my family in Florence, Italy.

In the spring of 1894 my publishing house, Webster & Co., declared bankruptcy. As troubling as this was to me, it was a cause for deep shame in my wife who considered bankruptcy to be a moral failure. I was determined to set things right, and put all my hope and faith in Henry Rogers. By fall the new typesetter was completed, and through that fall and early winter I received letters from Rogers, informing me of how the machine was doing on its test runs. Things would seem promising, then not so good. Finally, during the Christmas season of 1894, I received a letter from Rogers. The typesetter had failed its test runs. The News hit me like a thunderclap. I wandered about that Italian villa in a stupor, trying to make sense of what had just happened. The typesetter had failed! Our last hope out of financial ruin was gone—nothing was left but the thin air of my own delusions.

In March of 1895 I sailed for New York again. As soon as I got off the ship, I went straight to Rogers' office in the Standard Oil Building at 26 Broadway. I went up to the 11th floor and Rogers' secretary took me into Roger's office and left me there to wait. I stood at the window, looking out across New York Harbor to the Colossus of Liberty Enlightening the World. Then Rogers entered the room, and I said:

"Rogers, just before I left Italy, I received this letter from Paige. I want to read it to you."

"All right," Rogers said, gesturing for me to sit down. I sat beside his desk and Roger's sat down in his chair to listen.

I began:

> Dear Mr. Clemens,
>
> It has just come to my attention that Mr. Henry Rogers of Standard Oil has been sending you adverse reports about the performance of the typesetter. I must protest and state emphatically that these reports are, at the least, gross distortions of the facts.
>
> While it is true, two or three changes have had to be made in the new machine, it has, during its test runs at the *Chicago* Herald, delivered more corrected live matter, per operator employed, than any one of the 32 Linotype machines operated by that Newspaper.
>
> If you do not choose to believe my word, then ask Charles Davis, our mechanical engineer. He will give you the facts, for I know Rogers' and Morgan's agents have not been able to bribe or threaten him into submission.
>
> Yours,
> James W. Paige

Rogers sat for a moment, and then rose and went to the window and looked out at the city and the harbor beyond. He said nothing for a long while, but I could tell he was thinking carefully. Finally he said:

"What Paige writes is true—as far as it goes. It is part of the truth, but only part. And often part of the truth is no better than a lie. The machine has performed just as he writes. What he leaves out is the number of repairs that had to be made during those tests, repairs effected by Paige and Davis, expert mechanics and engineers who have spent years working with the machine, who know it backwards and forwards, inside and out. With such men standing by to make any repair at a moment's notice, the Paige typesetter will operate and produce more than the Linotype. But where shall we find such men in sufficient numbers to run the Paige typesetter on an industrial scale? Can we find ten thousand such men in America? No. But we would need more than that to industrialize printing with the Paige typesetter. As long as it requires constant, expert attention and repair, the Paige typesetter is not a commercial proposition."

"But," I said feebly, "Paige says he has corrected the flaws."

"Yes," Rogers said, "and how many times has he made that claim to you in the past?"

"More times than I can count," I said.

Rogers said, "Let's say he has corrected all the flaws, which I don't believe for a moment, I should add. Let's say the machine will work indefinitely without an expert repairman standing by its side. The Paige typesetter still is not a commercial proposition."

"But why?" I asked. "You have seen it operate! It sets type like it was done by the hand of an artist—by the hand of an angel!"

"Yes," Rogers said, "I don't deny that it produces beautiful work, exquisite work. But industrial printing does not need beautiful, exquisite work. Most printed matter is for people who only need legibility. A man reading a Newspaper does not care whether the letters in a word are spaced properly or are all jammed together on one line and all spread out in gaps on another. The man just wants to read his paper. The average man could not appreciate—or even notice—the difference between quality printing and rough work, and, in industrial production, it is the needs of the average man multiplied in great numbers that determines whether a thing is a commercial concern or a money pit. So for this reason alone, the Paige typesetter's elegant work is no edge in its competition with the Linotype."

Rogers sat down in a chair directly in front of me and leaned forward with his elbows on his knees and the fingertips of his right and left hands touching together, and said in a low tone:

"Then there is the matter of Paige refusing to release his stock. Unless he does so, J.P. Morgan and his associates will not invest in the typesetter. Morgan isn't interested in merely making a profit, but gaining control. Without a majority of shares in a company, the direction of its development cannot be controlled. And this is Morgan's only aim: control of industrial, political, and social development. What he cannot control, he destroys."

"That is quite clear," I said. "He has nearly destroyed the American economy. And now I see that Cleveland has surrendered to him and sold him sixty-two million dollars worth of government bonds."

"I wouldn't characterize the President's action as surrender," Rogers said. "Morgan orchestrated Cleveland's second term in office precisely for the purpose of executing this bond deal. Cleveland was working with Lamont on purchasing the gold before he even took office. The President has served Morgan's interests and Paige must now serve Morgan's interests, if he is to survive in business."

Rogers stood up and went to the window and looked out again. He said:

"Paige faces the same choice that I had to make some years ago when Rockefeller consumed my oil business. I knew I could not fight them; they were too powerful. Instead, I made myself useful to them, made myself a necessary part of their organization. And so I have survived and even flourished. Paige might be able to do the same. I say 'might' because Morgan has already invested heavily in the Mergenthaler-Linotype Company. Morgan would be willing to absorb Paige into his organization, if Paige would release his stock, and if the Paige typesetter could be commercially merged with the Linotype into a single system. But Morgan does not deal in 'ifs'."

Rogers turned to face me, and said, "Finally, and most importantly, the Paige typesetter does not serve the plan of the money powers."

"How so?" I asked warily.

"You're a Freemason," Rogers said. "As such, you know that history is too important a matter to be left to chance. For the Great Work to be accomplished there must be a Plan."

"And you think Paige's machine doesn't serve the Plan?"

Rogers said, "Paige speaks of ushering in an Age of Information with his typesetter. Well, that Age will come some day, but not for decades, perhaps not for another century, and certainly not with Paige's machine. You see, the Paige typesetter is *mechanical*; it is a thing of cogwheels and levers. Such a thing, no matter how cleverly arranged, can ever operate fast enough to be a true *thinking* machine. Oh yes, Paige can make some improvements, but the speed of the cogwheel, screw, and inclined plane will shortly bring his developments to a deadlock. Mere mechanism cannot work. Has it ever occurred to you why Tesla has remained silent about the Paige typesetter? He has for a very good reason. He knows it cannot be developed into a thinking machine, and he knows why. The secret to making a true thinking machine is the problem of a rapid switching system. The human brain is an extremely complex switching system, and it is electrical in nature. Tesla has invented precisely the kind of switches that could be used in an artificial brain, a thinking machine, and we believe he is trying to create just such a thing. But the time is not right for such a development. The Age of Information can only be allowed to dawn when other factors—social and political—are in place. But when that age comes, it will not come from the spin of a cogwheel, but from the flash of an electrical impulse."

I held Paige's letter in the tips of my fingers, looking at it.

"So," Rogers asked, "what are you going to do with that?"

I looked at Rogers, then back to Paige's letter. I brought out a Lucifer match from my vest pocket and struck it on the heel of my shoe. The match flared up and I touched its tongue of flame to the edge of Paige's letter. The paper blackened and curled away. I held out the burning scrap until it was consumed, and then dropped the remaining corner into an ashtray on Rogers' desk.

Since that day I have had no contact with James W. Paige. He later sold his interest in the typesetter to the Mergenthaler-Linotype Company for a pittance, and I heard that he tried to promote a pneumatic tire invention, but had no success with it. After that, Paige seemed to drop off the face of the earth. There were rumors that he had been seen walking in the slums of Chicago, somewhere along Halstad Street. At this time I do not know if he is alive or dead.

I was a guest in Henry Roger's home at 26 E. 57th St. for the next several days. Rogers untangled my finances and planned a way for me to earn back all that I had lost.

I would have to work harder than I ever had before in my life. I would have to write another book and it was clear that I would have to return to the lecture platform, but where and how often was uncertain. We sat down with pencil and paper and figured the numbers. It soon became apparent that no usual lecture tour would answer; I would have to lecture at home and abroad to even begin to pay off all my debts. It was finally decided that I would have to circumnavigate the globe.

My wife and I had been prepared to turn over everything we had to the creditors, everything from the copyrights on my books to our house in Hartford. But now Rogers said, "No," and he stood firm. He pointed out that my wife was the preferred creditor, for she was owed sixty-five thousand dollars by the Webster firm. Therefore, as Rogers reasoned it, the Hartford house and the copyrights would go to her. Rogers was even more intractable about the copyrights than he was the house. My books were not selling well at that time and I could find no publisher interested in continuing their publication. I thought it would be a smart thing to shove all those (to me) useless copyrights into the hands of the creditors. But no, Rogers insisted that would be a gigantic blunder. Wait a couple of years, he said, and the popularity of Mark Twain would rebound with the rest of the American economy. Rogers' insights were amazing; they proved to be true and saved my family and me from a life of poverty. Rogers not only saved us sound, but showed the way for me to repay all the creditors one hundred cents on the dollar, which I did by 1898.

One morning while I was staying with the Rogers family that spring of 1895, I came down to breakfast later than usual. Rogers had already left for the office, and the rest of the family was out of the house as well. The Rogers' butler served me breakfast, and then brought me the Newspaper. I opened it up, and there on the front page was the following headline:

"TESLA LABORATORY BURNS TO GROUND"

My eyes raced over the text of the article. It said that Tesla's laboratory caught fire about two a.m. in the morning. Before firemen could reach it to put it out, the entire five-story building collapsed floor upon floor in a heap of rubble.

I lay down the paper, pushed my breakfast plate aside, and rose from the table.

"Something wrong, Mr. Clemens?" the butler asked.

"Yes," I said. "Very wrong. I'm going out. Please call me a cab."

I went to the foyer while the butler rung up the cab company on the telephone. I got my coat and hat out of the closet, put them on, lit up a cigar, and began pacing the hall.

The butler came around the corner and said, "They said they're sending a driver straight over."

"Good," I said. "Thank you."

"Anything else I can do for you?" the butler asked.

"No," I said. "I'll just wait here for the cab."

"Yes, sir," the butler said, and he turned and went back to the dining room.

I kept pacing back and forth until the front bell rang.

"That's the cab," I called to the butler, and opened the door. The driver stood there with his hat in hand.

"Do you have any baggage, sir?" the driver asked.

"No baggage," I said. "I want you to take me to 35 South Fifth Avenue."

"Down around there where the fire was this morning?" the driver asked.

"That's right. You get me down there fast and you'll get a tip that you won't be able to spend in one place."

We ran down the steps, I jumped into the cab, and the driver lit upon his perch on top of the hansom. I saw the reins shake and the horses broke into a gallop, turned onto Fifth Avenue and headed south through the city.

When we got down there to the site of Tesla's laboratory my heart went into my throat. Where a big five-story building once stood was now nothing but a smoky expanse of sky! Down at ground level was a great heap of twisted iron beams and broken and blackened timber and brick. A grayish band of smoke rose from the heap and stretched itself out over lower Manhattan and the East River. A crowd had gathered about on the street and firemen kept them at a distance with a cordon of rope. I approached the crowd and spied Kolman Czito standing by the rope, staring helplessly at the smoking ruin.

"Czito!" I cried.

Czito turned and blinked.

"Mr. Clemens!" he said. "He's gone and no one can find him."

"Who? Tesla?"

Czito nodded, "He was here this morning, but he left about an hour ago with a man in a carriage."

"Well," I said, "I wouldn't be concerned about Tesla. He'll turn up. How did this happen? Somebody left the gas pipe open?"

"No," Czito said. "No one left the gas open. Mr. Tesla closes the laboratory every night. And you know he doesn't make mistakes of that kind."

"Yes," I said, "I know. But—you fellows weren't working on anything that could explode in there, were you?"

"That's what the fire marshal asked. No, nothing. This was not a result of our work. It was not an accident."

"Who did it?"

"I believe my speculations are no better than yours."

"Here's a telephone number where I can be reached. I'm staying at Henry Rogers' residence up on 57th Street."

I wrote out the number on a card and handed it to Czito, and said, "When Mr. Tesla shows up, have him call me."

Czito nodded and took the card.

"Here is my telephone number," Czito said, handing me his card.

I took it, and said, "You say he left in a carriage."

"Yes, it was strange."

"Strange? How?"

Czito shook his head. "I know most of Mr. Tesla's friends. I never saw the man that Mr. Tesla left with."

"What did he look like?"

"I didn't get a good look at him. He was just a man, just an ordinary fellow. Only—"

"What?"

"He was wearing an opera hat. That was a little strange. Most people don't wear opera hats in the morning nowadays."

"An opera hat? You mean, a tall, silk hat?"

"Yes. Yes, I believe it was silk. Why?"

"No reason. But... Say, did you notice anything about the carriage they left in?"

"The carriage? No. Not really. It was just a carriage, I suppose."

"Did it have a brass plate on its door?"

"I didn't notice. Why?"

"It's not important. You have Tesla telephone me, soon as he can, all right?"

Czito nodded, and I turned and got back into the cab that had been waiting for me at the curb.

The next day I received a telephone call from Czito. Tesla still had not shown up. I told Czito not to worry, that I had to go up to Hartford on business, but would be back in a few days, and, by then, Tesla would surely have shown up. I just wished I had believed what I was saying. I had a bad feeling about Tesla, a very bad feeling, but what was there for me to do? I had no idea where to begin to start looking for him.

When I returned from Hartford a few days later, there were no messages waiting for me at Rogers' residence. I immediately called Kolman Czito at his home, and he told me that Tesla was still missing. It was now two weeks since he disappeared. Czito and the police were beginning to believe that Tesla had been murdered, but this belief had been kept out of the Newspapers.

I next called the Chief of Police for New York City. He insisted that he had absolutely no information concerning the whereabouts of Tesla. The report from the fire department determined that the fire which had destroyed Tesla's laboratory had been accidental, cause unknown.

"Cause *unknown!*" I shouted over the telephone. "If the cause is unknown, how in the hell can they know it was accidental?"

"I'm just reading the report they gave me," the Chief of Police said.

"Damn it! What's going on here? Do you think I am a fool? Who the hell is behind all this?"

There was a silence over the telephone and then I heard the Chief of Police let out a long sigh. He said, "I don't think you really want to know who the hell is behind all this."

"What the hell is that supposed to mean?"

"Why don't you ask your friend, Henry Rogers, if you're so curious."

"Don't you try your insinuations on me, goddamn it! If you're saying Rogers had something to do with this, say it, or keep your mouth shut!"

"Guess I'll keep my mouth shut," the Chief of Police sneered, and then loudly clicked the telephone down on his end.

I pulled the receiver away from my ear and hung it up on the pedestal. I then picked up the receiver again, intending to call the mayor, but stopped. I decided I would speak to no one further until I talked to Rogers.

I got my hat and coat and went out for a walk through the city going straight down Fifth Avenue. When I reached the Waldorf Astoria, I hailed a cab and took it south, heading for the Standard Oil Building on lower Broadway. Before we got down there, I called up to the driver and told him to let me out.

I got out of the cab somewhere on lower Broadway, paid the driver, and headed on down the sidewalk, walking toward the Standard Oil Building. As I walked, I tried to form in my mind the words I would say to Rogers. How would I begin the conversation? Could I begin?

As I walked along pondering these things, a light mist of rain began to fall. I looked down at the sidewalk, noticing how the cement was turning dark from the mist. Then I heard footsteps behind me, and they seemed to be echoes of my own footsteps. I walked a little faster. The footsteps behind me kept pace with mine. I walked a little slower. The footsteps behind me fell upon the pavement a little slower. I could stand it no longer. I looked around. The echo-like footsteps were those of a man walking behind me. He wore a "slicker," an India-rubber rain-cape with a hood over his head. In the rainy gloom I could see only a beard inside the hood, but no face.

I turned forward and quickened my pace.

"Mark!"

I stopped, and then turned around slowly. The hooded man approached and looked down at me. It was Tesla!

"Keep walking," Tesla said quietly. "Ahead of me a few steps."

I turned around and started walking slowly. After a moment, I said, "Everyone thinks you're dead."

"Not everyone."

"Why did you disappear?"

"Turn left and go into the restaurant. Get a table in the back."

I did as Tesla said and went into the little restaurant. I took off my hat and asked the waiter for a table in the back. He led me to a little room partitioned from the front of the restaurant by a screen, handed me a menu, and went away.

Shortly Tesla appeared from around the side of the screen and removed his hood and cloak. He had a growth of beard, but other than that he looked to be his usual self. He sat across the table from me.

"It is not necessary to order anything," Tesla said. "The proprietor will let us talk here."

"You look all right," I said.

"I am intolerably filthy. But that will come to an end tomorrow. I haven't returned to my hotel room since the fire."

"You had Czito worried. You had me worried."

"I regret that. But my disappearance was necessary."

"Why? Why was it necessary?"

"I had to disappear for one reason only: to keep from getting killed."

With that disturbing statement, Tesla began to recount how he learned that his laboratory had been destroyed and all that had followed.

Breaking his usual routine, Tesla had knocked off work early on the evening preceding the fire, had dined at Delmonicos, and then had retired to his rooms at the Hotel Gerlach. Around 10:00 A.M. the next morning, Tesla arrived in the neighborhood of his laboratory and found it a smoking ruin. His other employees, some fifteen in number, had arrived earlier, but none of them, including Kolman Czito, could bear to call Tesla to tell him the awful News.

Tesla staggered around the edges of the rubble with tears in his eyes trying to see if anything could be salvaged. A Newspaper reporter from *The New York Times* followed behind Tesla, trying to interview him. Tesla climbed into the smoking ruins of the building and the reporter decided at that point that he had gathered enough facts to write his story. Two firemen went in after Tesla to drag him back out of the collapsed building. The firemen got him back out on to the street and Tesla sat down on the curb and stared down at the pavement. Everything he had was gone, all his equipment and everything from his World's Fair exhibit. None of it was insured.

While Tesla sat there on the curb trying to absorb this disaster, he gradually took notice of a shadow which fell upon the pavement only a few inches from his feet. At first he ignored it. The shadow did not move. In another minute or so Tesla realized that it was the shadow of someone's hat. Another minute passed and Tesla noted that the shadow had not moved, not by so much as one-quarter of one inch, no, not so much as by one sixteenth of one inch. Tesla looked up.

It was the man in the silk hat—the man whom Tesla had encountered in Paris years ago. He was standing perfectly still looking down upon Tesla as if he had been standing there waiting since the beginning of time and could go on standing there waiting patiently and serenely until that day far into the future when time itself decided to end. Tesla's eyes slowly took in the whole height and breadth of the man in the silk hat. The man was dressed exactly as he had been in Paris years ago. In fact, the man appeared to be exactly the same as he was when Tesla had last seen him. Not only was his apparel unchanged, but his face had not aged one instant. It seemed to Tesla that the man in the silk hat was not a part of time as Tesla understood it.

"May I offer my condolences," the man in the silk hat said.

Tesla inclined his head.

The man in the silk hat looked at the smoking ruins, and said, "'And they said, Go to, let us build a city and a tower. And the Lord said, Behold, the people is one, and this they begin to do: and now nothing will be restrained from them, which they have imagined to do.' Would you care to accompany me, Mr. Tesla?"

Tesla looked up beyond the ropes and the barricades set up by the fire department and saw a carriage waiting across the street. It was the same carriage that had carried the man in the silk hat away into the streets of Paris. Like the man, the carriage, too, remained unchanged. The brass plate with the number "44" was still mounted upon its door.

"I. . ." Tesla found he could not speak. He shook his head.

"Come," the man in the silk hat said, extending his hand. "Come with me."

Tesla rose to his feet and looked at the man in the silk hat.

"Is all this your doing?" Tesla asked.

"Yes, Mr. Tesla," the man in the silk hat said, "you know it is."

Tesla stood looking at the man in the silk hat, feeling a mounting, suddenly uncontrollable rage.

"Your heart lies in one of the pans of the balance, Mr. Tesla," the man in the silk hat said, "and what may we find to fill the wants of the other? My own destruction? And that would accomplish—what? Ah, you see the point. My destruction would weigh more than your heart. You would have to place something in the pan along with your heart if you would tip and level the balance. And what could be of such a weight that it would level the pans and leave neither wanting? Perhaps your soul? Are you prepared to place your soul beside your heart in the pan of the balance? Come, Mr. Tesla. Come with me. Come let us see if you and I can level the pans of the balance."

The man in the silk hat held his right hand out to Tesla and swept his left hand up and back toward the waiting carriage.

Tesla looked back at his ruined laboratory, and then turned and walked with the man in the silk hat across the street.

The man in the silk hat opened the door of the carriage, put his foot upon its step, and went up through the door. Tesla remained standing outside on the street.

"Please, Mr. Tesla," the man in the silk hat said from inside, "we have much to discuss."

Tesla got into the carriage and sat across from the man in the silk hat who closed the door. The carriage started off up the street.

"There has been much discussion concerning you of late," the man in the silk hat said. "Much discussion here in the city—and elsewhere. Some of us in the Order believe that you have failed us and that your time has passed. And some of our operatives here in New York and in London believe that the best way to bring your time to an end is with your death. And some of those now seek to act upon their belief before the Order has made its final determination. While there would be consequences to such unauthorized advances, it is possible that your life could be in real danger, hence my warning to you now. It is best that you go into hiding until passions cool in certain quarters."

Tesla sat looking at the man in the silk hat who seemed so quiet and serene. Finally Tesla asked, "Why? Why have you destroyed my laboratory?"

"Why?" the man in the silk hat asked in return. "You know the answer to that, Mr. Tesla, only you are afraid to face it. We have destroyed your laboratory because the things you were doing in it overstepped the bounds established by the Order of the Flaming Sword, the Order which has monitored your work, supported your work, secretly protected and promoted your work at every turn, the Order which nurtured your growth and development from your infancy until now, the Order which arranged for your birth, the Order which gave you your very life—the Order which has the power to take your life away from you now."

"You are a monstrous liar," Tesla said. "You and your people have had nothing to do with my work. I have done it all myself."

"Did you create yourself, Mr. Tesla? Did you create yourself? No, it is we of the Order who prepared the ground, tilled the soil, and planted the seed. And the seed called out to the ether for your soul, and your soul was compelled to answer the call, for the call was your destiny. Yes, you have worked; for the seed puts forth its shoots, and it branches, and buds, and blooms, and bears fruit. And we of the Order have pronounced that fruit good—until now. Mr. Tesla, do you believe your birth was an accident—a mere chance collision of mindless particles in a dead universe? Or could there be a plan and purpose in your coming to this world? We of the Order are the Keepers of Human Destiny. To us has been granted the power over Life and Death and Knowledge. Who determines the course of human events? The average man who gropes weakly in the darkness of his own ignorance for his food and shelter? No, such average men look to their leaders to guide their way. Most men here in America take vain pride in their ability to choose their leaders. But in reality their leaders are chosen for them. A few believe that the great financial powers choose the ones who shall be presidents and kings. But who determines which ones shall wield the golden scepter of Money? We do, Mr. Tesla. It is we of the Order of the Flaming Sword who place men such as J.P. Morgan upon the Money Throne. And it is through them that we create the presidents and kings, the philosophers and artists, the generals and, yes, the inventors. Have you climbed to the top of the Statue of Liberty? You have. And you have noticed that through the windows cut in her crown that you can look out upon—what? You look out upon nothing, Mr. Tesla, or as close to nothing as one can get in New York Harbor—the dreary rooftops of Brooklyn. Have you ever wondered why the Statue faces Brooklyn and not southward to the mouth of the harbor—southward as it should if it is to function as a symbol of welcome as it has been claimed to do? You have wondered. And you know. You know it has been positioned so that the central axis of its body and face lies at a right angle to a line of compression stress that passes north to south through the land upon which its foundations are set. And you know why the builders oriented the statue this way. But you have not considered the surrounding landscape: to the north, the so-called 'Cleopatra's Needle' in Central Park, and, to the west in New Jersey, Edison's laboratory, and, a little further to the north, the birthplace of Grover Cleveland, the United States president who dedicated the Statue of Liberty. I ask you, Mr. Tesla, to study these three sites upon the landscape and search out their relationship to the Statue of Liberty. Study the shapes of the land masses and the surrounding bodies of water. You will find these three sites all lie on lines of land stress which converge upon the Statue of Liberty. When you study these things out, you will begin to see the work of the Order of the Flaming Sword. It is we who planned the Industrial Age and brought it magically to fruition with the talisman of the Statue of Liberty Enlightening the World—the great goddess of knowledge, life, and literacy known in all ages by different names: Persephone, Semiramis, Shekinah, Sufkhit-Abut. And you, Mr. Tesla, have been an important part of our work; you have been essential to the Industrial Age. It was through you that we would introduce the system of alternating electrical current transmission—the one system that would allow the universal parceling and distribution of electrical power. Oh yes, there are many who say that if you hadn't invented AC, someone else soon would have. Not in a thousand years, not in ten thousand years would such a system have been developed, unless some extraordinary individual came forth to illuminate the dark world. And from whence comes such extraordinary individuals? From we of the Order, the viticulturists of human destiny. But now, Mr. Tesla, now you have taken upon yourself further developments. You are seeking to develop electrical systems in which power can be distributed but in which it cannot be metered or parceled—electrical systems that operate not upon the limited material resources of this planet, but which draw their power directly from the ether. This we cannot allow. In this you have overstepped your bounds. In this you will be stopped."

"I will fight you," Tesla said. "I will fight you as I fought the Martian King."

"Kel of *Khahera*?" the man in the silk hat asked, smiling in amusement. "He was a petty tyrant which we created. Yes, you fought him, as we knew you would. And you prevailed, as we knew you would. Kel's methods were clumsy and overt. Ours are neither. Think twice, Mr. Tesla, think thrice. Think long and hard before you decide to oppose us. We cannot be vanquished. But we can allow negotiations. It is possible that we may allow you to continue your work on etheric energies—on our terms. We may allow you to continue your developments in secret to ultimately serve our purposes, but we cannot allow the commercialization of the ether. There, the Order draws its Flaming Sword and commands: 'No further shalt thou go!'"

"I will fight you," Tesla said. "I will fight you, I will fight you."

"Of course you will fight us, Mr. Tesla. There can be no other way. Don't you recall what I told you in Paris? Without conflict nothing can manifest, nothing can stand? Without conflict, what would come of our relationship? Conflict is the bond which holds us together. You shall remain in conflict with us, just as all your predecessors did: Hept-Supht of Atlantis, Parmenides of Greece, Galileo of Italy, Sir Isaac Newton of England, and you, Mr. Tesla, you of the world, you whom we have created, a wonder of both Earth and Mars—a wonder of the worlds!"

Tesla had noticed that all the while as the man in the silk hat had been speaking, a faint, grayish-white nimbus of light had emanated from his person. That light now seemed to be coming from a point on the man's head, directly above the man's eyebrows in the center of his forehead. The rays of grayish light began to turn in a circle very slowly, and then gather speed to turn rapidly clockwise, and then reverse and spin counterclockwise. Back and forth the light spun, as if a ghostly Fourth of July fireworks were pinned to the forehead of the man in the silk hat. The rays of the pinwheel extended outward and penetrated Tesla's forehead and entered through Tesla's skull and into his brain, and Tesla could feel the pinwheel of light passing through to his inner ear like a rotating gravitational field upsetting his balance.

"I know, Mr. Tesla. You have questions. Questions you will not ask—questions that I cannot now fully answer. But I have something that can lead you to the answers you now need to know."

The man in the silk hat once again brought out a book. At first glance Tesla thought it was a Bible, for it was bound in black leather. But it was not a Bible.

"The black book," the man in the silk hat said. "Take it. Go ahead, Mr. Tesla, it has been prepared just for you."

Tesla took the book, but did not open it.

"Yes," the man in the silk hat said, "you will read it later. You will read it. And you will then understand all that you face. You have read the green book. You know its contents. You know it deals with what has been. The black book deals with what will be—the next two centuries of this world—the coming age of blackening, of *Nigredo*, the Black Crow which announces the coming of Rain—as in the days of Noah. But this time it shall rain fire. Three wars shall be fought—three wars so great that they shall engulf the world in fire and blood and death, and then shall come the Great Horror: the powers of the heavens shall be shaken. What shall be your part in all this, Mr. Tesla? That is a question you must decide. Someday you will know the truth to that question, and when you do, you will receive the final book—the red book, the book of fulfillment. But that day is far off for you now. Take the black book and read it. And when we of the Order take the black book away from you, you will know that you are safe and that the following day you can come out of hiding."

Tesla looked down at the black book. The moment he did, the spinning, crawling sensation inside his head ceased. He looked back up to the man in the silk hat, and the grayish rays of light still spun around the man and reached into Tesla's head making him dizzy.

"I will fight you with everything I have in me," Tesla said.

"I cannot ask anything more of you than that," the man in the silk hat said. "Fight us as you would fight a dream, a nightmare; for we are your dreams and your nightmares; we are your loftiest ideals and your basest sins; we are your good and we are your evil. We of the Order of the Flaming Sword are the makers of destinies, Mr. Tesla, the makers of worlds without end! Are you beginning to glimpse the truth now? Are you beginning to understand? Life itself is only a dream—a vision of Mind. All is dream—all the people you have ever known—all men and women and children everywhere, those who have lived before you, those who live now, those yet unborn. All is a dream, God, man, the world, the sun and moon and the wilderness of planets and stars—a dream, all a dream. Nothing exists but you! And you are not you—you have no body, no blood, no bones, you are not material atoms, but a thought! What you call your 'self' is but a mask through which your real self peers. I myself have no existence. I am just another mask through which you gaze. I—and everyone you have ever known—we are all masks, personalities and places, moments called 'time.' All masks, all dreams of your imagination!"

The spinning arms of white light surrounding the man in the silk hat had become a funnel of light. Tesla now witnessed a thing that almost defies description and belief: the man in the silk hat began to change shape, and began to turn into someone else. He became the midwife who had assisted the doctor at Tesla's birth. The midwife then shifted in shape to become the doctor that had delivered Tesla. The doctor shifted his shape to then become Tesla's mother, and then, in succession, his father, his brother, his sister. Tesla's sister then proceeded to transform into other people, each transformation occurring at an increasingly rapid rate so that the people appearing before him could be seen only in elusive flashes. Tesla realized that he was seeing every single person he had ever encountered in his life and in the exact order in which he had encountered them. Before him flashed the faces of Thomas Edison, George Westinghouse, Kolman Czito, Grover Cleveland—and, yes, even me! Everyone Tesla had ever met or seen in the world during his whole life now flashed before him. And as all these people flashed by, Tesla heard the voice of the man in the silk hat saying:

"Already I am passing away, to be replaced with more masks! More veils! More darkened glass!"

Then the flashing, which had become almost unbearable, ceased and Tesla was confronted with an exact double of himself sitting in the carriage where a moment before the man in the silk hat had been sitting. Then an even more curious, almost indescribable experience came upon Tesla: he was, at the same instant, looking out of both his own pair of eyes and the eyes of his double! No, not just looking out—Tesla *was* his own double, existing in two places at the same time—and he was looking back and forth simultaneously at himself as he occupied these two different places. Tesla heard the voice of the man in the silk hat speak again:

"In this flashing, illusory moment, while slumbering Mind wakes ever so slightly, remember! Remember! Who am I? I am *you*! And you are me! And all is one! One Thought! One Existence! One Dream! Dream other dreams—and better!"

Suddenly Tesla found himself standing alone at the foot of the Brooklyn Bridge. The man in the silk hat and his carriage had instantly disappeared. Tesla looked down and saw that he was still holding the black book that the man in the silk hat had given him. He looked around. A few people approached, but paid no attention to him; they behaved as if he had been standing there all along. Tesla looked up and down the street. There was no sign anywhere of the man in the silk hat or the carriage in which they had been riding, but Tesla could see the plume of smoke from his ruined laboratory still rising up above the rooftops of lower Manhattan.

Then from out of nowhere Tesla heard the voice of the man in the silk hat saying:

"A city afire. Thus begins the age of the blackening. This moment is both fact and prophetic symbol. When lower Manhattan burns again in this way, it shall be changed as in the twinkling of an eye, and then shall the age of blackening begin its final culmination."

Tesla turned and looked at the Brooklyn Bridge; only a few people were crossing it on foot. He felt as if he were suspended in a crossroads of time, as if he existed simultaneously in the past, present, and future. He felt at once as if the Brooklyn Bridge had not yet been built, that it stood before him now, and that it continued to exist in a future time when its steel cables were rusted with age. He could see only two or three people up ahead on the bridge, but at the same time he felt as if a great crowd of people were passing by him, trying to escape from lower Manhattan; he could feel these people, but not see them.

Tesla looked up to the sky and saw the plume of smoke drifting high overhead, an ominous gray smoke, the dragon breath of calamity and chaos.

Tesla walked forward on to the bridge, with the black book in his hand, and left the city and the smoke behind.

I had sat there at the table in the back of that little restaurant listening to Tesla. He had finished speaking and just sat there, not so much waiting for my reply, but just thinking to himself about what he had just said. It seemed that it was hard for him to absorb it all and he had been the one who had just described it as he had experienced it.

"Who do you think the man in the silk hat is?" I asked. "Is he an angel or a devil or just a devil of a mesmerist?"

"I don't know," Tesla said. "I don't know what he is. I can't believe he is what he says he is—and yet. . . I don't know. Who do you think he is?"

"Maybe he's Satan, himself," I said. "Or maybe he is what he said he is. Maybe this world is nothing but a big dream. I've often wondered if it is. Maybe we're all living in some kind of big dream factory, and the man in the silk hat is its superintendent."

Tesla nodded, and then shook his head, disbelieving.

I asked, "Did you read that book he gave you?"

"I did," Tesla said. "It was a book of horrors."

"Can I see it?"

"The book disappeared this morning."

"Does that mean that tomorrow you'll be safe?"

"That is what the man in the silk hat claimed."

"Do you believe what he said about that—that now you'll be safe?"

"It is not a question of believing, but of now doing what I must. Tomorrow I meet with J.P. Morgan's representative."

"Why?"

"I shall ask Mr. Morgan to finance my new laboratory."

"And will you be working along the same lines as you had before the fire?"

"I will."

"Are you going to tell Morgan that?"

"Eventually. Not immediately. Until then I will continue my experiments with the ether in secret. But someday I will give free energy to the world, and on that day all war will come to an end, for no nation will ever be more powerful than another—for the reason that no man will ever be more powerful than another."

"You're playing a dangerous game."

"It is the only game worth playing."

"Yes, well, I'm not worried about you. I think you're going to take care of yourself—man in the silk hat or not. I just wish I could say the same for myself."

"I heard about the bankruptcy."

"Henry Rogers of Standard Oil is helping me out. You know Rogers, don't you?"

"Yes."

"He's a pirate, but he admits he's a pirate. That's what I like about him. You think I've sold my soul to the devil?"

Tesla said nothing for a moment, and then said, "Mark, we all fight the devil each in our own way, as best we can."

"How are you fixed for money?" I asked.

"I spent just about everything I had on me two days ago," Tesla replied. "I now only have a few pennies in my pocket, and it is all that I have in the world. My finances are exactly the same as when I first came to this country."

I took out my pocketbook, opened it, and counted out all the money I had. It amounted to twenty-five dollars, all in one dollar bank notes.

"Here," I said, "Take all of it."

"I can't take it," Tesla said.

"Yes, you can," I said. "I'll show you how."

I brought out an envelope I had in my coat pocket, put the money in it and handed the fat envelope to Tesla.

"Go on," I said, "take it. There's more where that came from. For both of us."

Tesla smiled faintly, took the envelope, and said, "Thank you. I'll repay you."

"I know you'll be able to. But if you don't, it doesn't matter. What matters is that you get yourself a decent meal."

"I will," Tesla said. "But not at this restaurant. It has very bad food, but don't tell the proprietor I said so."

We both laughed, and I said, "Well, it must be bad if a starving man won't eat it."

We got up and went out of the restaurant. Tesla nodded to me, and said, "Take care, Mark," and then he turned, pulled the hood of his "slicker" over his head, and walked north up Broadway.

I watched Tesla walk away in the drizzling rain for a moment, and then I turned and went south down Broadway toward the Standard Oil Building.

I no longer wondered what I would say to Henry Rogers. I would say nothing, at least nothing about Tesla. I did not know what Tesla planned to do, but I felt that somehow he would fight through and survive. But would he win? That I could not answer, that I still cannot answer. If he was any other man, I would say he hasn't a chance. But Tesla? Who can say what he may yet do? I cannot. To this day I cannot say with certainty whether Tesla has surrendered or not. Perhaps someday Tesla will know who the man in the silk hat is, perhaps someday I will know, perhaps someday you who read this will know.

The Standard Oil Building loomed ahead of me. I quickened my pace and thought about all that had happened to Tesla and me. I thought about Chicago and the World's Fair, about Tesla's airship and his crystal of infinite power and its theft by the Martians; I thought about Lillie West and George Ade and Houdini who came to pry into our secrets but who finally risked their lives to save our own; I thought about the people rushing by on the sidewalk in front of me—and all the people in New York—and all the people in the world—and on Mars—and on all the worlds that existed everywhere to the farthest, deepest, infinite reaches of space and time. Were we all One as the man in the silk hat had claimed? I did not know that either. I only knew that I had to go on and keep my secrets and play the hand I had been dealt, for nobody I knew save Tesla and a few others would ever believe me if I tried to tell them the truth of what I had witnessed and experienced.

Do you who are reading this in your time now believe my story—my small t version of the truth?

So, you see, I knew beyond any doubt as I walked toward the Standard Oil Building and went up to its doors that nobody in my time would believe a single incident of my story—a single sentence—a single word—

Nobody.

Epilogue

> Now there's the facts just as they happened: let everybody explain it their own way.
>
> — Huck, *Tom Sawyer Abroad*

A University Somewhere in the United States
January 16, 1943

The professor sat behind his desk bent over the manuscript which was laid out in two neat stacks across his ink blotter. A wry smile played upon his lips and his eyes twinkled.

The blank-faced man and his associate sat in the same chairs in which they had sat the day before.

"Well?" the blank-faced man asked. "Did you reach a conclusion? Did Mark Twain write that?"

The professor looked up at the blank-faced man and grinned. "Possibly," the professor said, "Have you read this?"

The blank-faced man nodded.

The professor placed one stack of the manuscript pages on top of the other, picked up the combined stack, squared their edges against the top of his desk, and then held up the entire manuscript and placed it in the hands of the blank-faced man.

"Quite a yarn, isn't it?" the professor asked.

"Can't say," the blank-faced man replied.

"Well," the professor said, "it might be Twain's writing. It's an obvious burlesque of Jules Verne, at least the parts I read thoroughly. Mark Twain did write that kind of thing. In *Tom Sawyer Abroad* he had Tom and Huck travel around the world in a balloon. In this, the writer seems to be using real people who actually existed. Twain sometimes did that sort of thing as well. He wrote a novel about Joan of Arc, and once wrote a piece about Queen Elizabeth I.

Rather ribald, I might say. Then there's this character of 'the man in the silk hat,' clearly another version of Twain's 'Mysterious Stranger.' If I were certain that Twain wrote this, I'd be tempted to say that the original source for Twain's idea of the 'Mysterious Stranger' comes from this story. On the other hand, some of the passages just don't strike me as Twain's style of writing; they sound more like someone trying to imitate Twain but doing it rather poorly. Unfortunately, that critique is not compelling. You see, sometimes the worst imitator of Twain was Twain himself. But then, sometimes Twain wrote very good imitations of himself. And, then, sometimes, Twain just wrote, and that, of course, was when he was writing at his best—parts of *Roughing It* and the first half of *Huck Finn*, for example. So in terms of style, it is very hard to say. I can think immediately of one other person besides Twain who could've written this: George Ade. I was briefly acquainted with Ade at one time through his Mark Twain literary club. Ade was a big admirer of Mark Twain's writings. This is the kind of thing Ade just might have written as a literary hoax, perhaps as a gag on one of his pals such as Peter Finley Dunne. I believe George Ade is still alive. In fact, though I'm not sure, I think he's the only person mentioned in the manuscript who is still alive. You ought to contact him. If he didn't write it, perhaps he might give you an idea who might have. I certainly have no idea who else might have written it. However, there are some curious things about that manuscript."

"What things?" the blank-faced man asked.

"Well," the professor said, "some of the passages are inaccurate about commonly known historical events—inaccurate to the point of absurdity, while other passages accurately describe historical events of the greatest obscurity."

"Such as?"

"Well," the professor said, "most obviously all the stuff about Tesla is so far from the truth that it's hardly worth discussing. Everyone knows Edison invented the light bulb, not Tesla. I think this Tesla fellow invented some kind of electrical coil, as I remember, and that he worked for Westinghouse, but it was Westinghouse who invented alternating current, not Tesla, any history book will tell you that. Mark Twain met Tesla once or twice I think, but then, Mark Twain met just about everyone who was anyone in his lifetime, so there's nothing in that. Twain and Tesla were not friends. I think there is only one letter in existence written by Twain to Tesla, and it is very brief. I find this whole story about Tesla to be rather silly. I think he died years ago and accomplished very little. All his ideas have been disproved by scientists like Einstein and Bohr. On the other hand, I happen to know that the passages about President Cleveland's cancer are very accurate. Even today, very few people know about that. Sometime around the end of the First World War I recall reading a Newspaper article about Cleveland's cancer. I think it was an interview of one of the doctors who had operated on him. I know that the President's

They were still walking away with that military precision.

cancer operation was kept a secret during his lifetime. So this manuscript couldn't have been written before 1918."

"Unless the writer had secret knowledge of the President's operation," the blank-faced man said.

"Yes," the professor said. "If someone had secret knowledge, but. . . who could that be—unless it was Mark Twain himself—or someone like him who knew Cleveland?"

"So what are you saying?" the blank-faced man asked. "Are you saying Mark Twain didn't write this?"

The professor stared down at his desk, and then looked up at the blank-faced man.

The professor said, "If Mark Twain wrote it, I'd say it is one of his lesser efforts at fiction."

"What if it isn't fiction?" the blank-faced man asked.

"Absurd," the professor said. "Impossible. That stuff's pure Buck Rogers. Please! The King of Mars? You've got to be kidding! It'll take hundreds of years to fly ships to other worlds—if ever. No, I assure you, *that* is definitely *fiction*."

The blank-faced man slipped the manuscript into a steel suitcase, and closed its lid.

"Oh," the professor said, "here's something," and he brought out a small watch fob attached to a gold chain.

"I was given this by Mark Twain's daughter," the professor said, handing the fob and chain to the blank-faced man who took the fob and held it up to the light.

"Notice the crystal in it," the professor said with a chuckle. "Imagine if that could have been what gave Mark Twain the idea for the story there—that is, if he wrote the story."

"Can I take this with me?" the blank-faced man asked.

"Why?" the professor asked, his smile fading. "What for?"

"We'll return it to you," the blank-faced man said. "When we're finished with it."

The professor took a deep breath, then exhaled and nodded his head. "Very well," he said.

The blank-faced man placed the watch fob into the suitcase, and snapped its lid shut again. He and his associate rose from their chairs.

"Thank you, professor," the blank-faced man said. "Oh, and about yesterday—if I was a little short with you, I apologize."

"That's all right, young man," the professor said.

"You know how it is with the war and all," the blank-faced man said. "My boss is pushing me all the time. Results, results, results."

"I understand."

"Good day, professor."

"Good day."

The blank-faced man and his associate turned and went out the door. The professor watched them go with a smile on his lips, part bemusement, part wariness, and he listened to their footsteps die away down the hall. Then he looked back down at his desk at another stack of papers: his neglected work from the day before. He picked up one of the papers, studied it a moment, and then began making notations in its margin.

Outside the professor's window, the sky was a steel winter blue. If he had turned around to look, the professor would have seen the two men who had been in his office walk away across the campus. They were still walking with that strange military precision; it was almost a march.

A pigeon lit upon the sill of the professor's window and put its beak close to the glass pane.

The professor continued writing.

The two men who had been in his office continued to walk away; they reached a wooded park and disappeared down one of those secluded pathways where anything seems possible.

About the Author

Sesh Heri has always lived in fantastic worlds. His first conscious memory goes back to the age of one when, while crawling along the ground, he realized he was unable to walk as he knew he normally could. Looking down, he saw that he had the legs of a baby! The shock and confusion of this sight triggered the realization that he had been reborn in the body of a baby and would have to live life all over again.

At the age of two Sesh Heri began drawing detailed pictures, as if by instinct.

At the age of four Sesh Heri sighted his first UFO: a slow-moving, matte black cylinder with rectangular flapping wings. After this first UFO sighting, there followed a lifetime of strange experiences: alien abductions, synchronicities, and psychic phenomena.

Although Sesh Heri has spent many years researching UFOs, leys, geomorphology, alchemy, synchronicity, and other unusual phenomena, the archaic term *jongleur* best denotes Sesh Heri's calling as storyteller, entertainer, and artist.

Also Available From

LOST CONTINENT LIBRARY

WWW.LOSTCONTINENTLIBRARY.COM

THE SUNKEN WORLD

by
STANTON COBLENTZ

ATLANTIS ADVENTURE

by
ANTOINE GAGNE

THE HIDDEN TRAIL

by
THOMAS A. JANVIER

Available at bookstores and Amazon.com

Adventures Unlimited Press

PRESENTS

JOSEPH P. FARRELL

THE GIZA DEATH STAR

THE GIZA DEATH STAR DEPLOYED

THE GIZA DEATH STAR DESTROYED

REICH OF THE BLACK SUN

AVAILABLE NOW AT

WEXCLUB.COM